Darkest Fear

ALSO BY CATE TIERNAN

THE SWEEP SERIES
THE BALEFIRE SERIES
THE IMMORTAL BELOVED TRILOGY

CATE TIERNAN

BIRTHRIGHT

Darkest
Fear

SIMON PULSE
An imprint of Simon & Schuster Children's Publishing Division
1230 Avenue of the Americas, New York, NY 10020
First Simon Pulse edition January 2014
Text copyright © 2014 by Gabrielle Charbonnet
Cover photograph copyright © 2014 by Michael Frost
All rights reserved, including the right of reproduction in whole or in part in any form.
SIMON PULSE and colophon are registered trademarks of Simon & Schuster, Inc.
For information about special discounts for bulk purchases, please contact Simon & Schuster Special Sales at 1-866-506-1949 or business@simonandschuster.com.
The Simon & Schuster Speakers Bureau can bring authors to your live event. For more information or to book an event contact the Simon & Schuster Speakers Bureau at 1-866-248-3049 or visit our website at www.simonspeakers.com.
Cover designed by Jessica Handelman
Interior designed by Bob Steimle
The text of this book was set in Bembo Std.
Manufactured in the United States of America
10 9 8 7 6 5 4 3 2 1
Library of Congress Cataloging-in-Publication Data
Tiernan, Cate.
Darkest fear / Cate Tiernan. — First Simon Pulse edition.
p. cm. — (Birthright)
Summary: "After the death of her parents, Vivi reunites with her long-lost family and learns more about her heritage as a haguara—a person who can shapeshift into a jaguar."— Provided by publisher.
[1. Supernatural—Fiction. 2. Shapeshifting—Fiction. 3. Jaguar—Fiction. 4. Families—Fiction.
5. Orphans—Fiction.] I. Title.
PZ7.T437Darm 2014
[Fic]—dc23
2013025046
ISBN 978-1-4424-8246-3 (hc)
ISBN 978-1-4424-8245-6 (pbk)
ISBN 978-1-4424-8247-0 (eBook)

As always, with love to my children, and to Paul,
the bearer of unconditional things

CHAPTER ONE

"HD," I said, greeting my best friend, Jennifer. I slid into the desk-chair combo in front of her, feeling the backs of my legs stick to the plastic seat. May in Florida.

"HD," she said back, and we gave the lackluster grins appropriate for fifth-period AP US History. Fifth period = the dead zone. It was right after lunch, incredibly hot, and too bright outside, and despite the air-conditioned classroom almost every student in here was about to nod off. I felt like I was moving through muggy air so thick that I had to go slowly and with purpose or I would subside into place, coming to a slow halt, maybe by my locker or something. I bet Ms. Harlow was hating it.

"You did the homework?" I asked, unwilling to lean against my seat because my damp shirt would stick to it. Florida. The state that antiperspirants—and deodorants, if we're being honest—were created for.

Jennifer nodded and offered me a piece of gum. I took it, crunching through the outer shell to taste the burst of icy mint on my tongue, so bright and sharp it was almost painful. Maybe chewing would help me stay awake.

So—HD is not short for Jennifer, obviously, or for my name, Vivi. It is short for Heartbreaking Disappointment, and we'd been calling each other that since eighth grade, which was when it became so horribly clear that was what we were to our parents.

"Everyone take out your notebooks," Ms. Harlow said. "I know you're all excited about finals next week, so let's start reviewing topics that will be on your exam."

Last high school finals, I told myself. *Next week is the last time you'll ever have to take a high school test, ever. Soon you'll be free, free, free . . .*

"Ready for tonight?" Jennifer whispered as we opened notebooks and fished in our backpacks for pens. In the seat in front of me, Annamaria Hernandez flipped her long cheerleader hair, and it almost hit my forehead. Even today, even during fifth period, Annamaria looked pert. Her skin was smooth and dry, her hair was unfazed by the 100 percent humidity—even her clothes seemed crisp and clean. My Piggly Wiggly T-shirt had, let's face it, never, ever been crisp, even before it had been washed so many times it was starting to shred. My skin was shiny and damp, and I didn't know what my hair was like because I'd gathered it into a big lump on the back of my head and stuck a pencil through it to keep it there.

Answering Jennifer, I nodded briefly. She had already wished me happy birthday first thing this morning, and she and some of my other friends had decorated my locker. I wished they hadn't duct-taped condoms to the locker door, but those had all been stolen by second period, so it was okay.

"What's on the menu?" she asked, pitching her voice below teacher-hearing range. Ms. Harlow was on the other side of the classroom, answering Bud Baldwin's question about how long the exam would be. (His name really was Bud. He was Buddy all through lower and middle school, but had finally drawn the line in high school.)

I glanced over—now he was asking exactly what material would be covered. *Probably everything we've been taught in this class, Buddy; that's why they call it a final.*

Keeping my voice low, I said, "Shrimp empanadas, egg rolls, fish tacos, coleslaw, and corn bread." Every year my parents took me on a picnic for my birthday. It was kind of corny, but it was a tradition, and they were very big on tradition. To use almost criminal understatement. Lately we'd been fighting almost constantly, and I wouldn't have been surprised if they'd ditched any birthday festivities at all. But my mom had asked what I wanted like nothing was wrong, and I'd told her. Like nothing was wrong.

"Yeah, that won't make you sick," Jennifer murmured, and I smiled.

"Girls?" said Ms. Harlow. "Pay attention here."

I sat up straighter and tried for at least the illusion of alertness. Next week was the last week. Just one more week.

Some kids were embarrassed to be seen in public with their parents and tried to walk ten feet behind them, or ignored them when they talked. I didn't do that. In public my parents were fine—not really old like Chris Gater's folks, who'd both been almost fifty when he was born. Or oddly young like Tara Hanson's mom, who was now literally thirty-four. Which was just bizarre.

No, on the surface my parents were super nice, friendly, attractive, had okay jobs. Yes, they were Brazilian, which could have been weird except this was Florida and there were tons of various ethnicities here. Their accents didn't stick out like they might somewhere else. In public, on paper, Mami and Papi were great. It was all the hidden, underneath stuff that made my head explode.

After school Jennifer gave me a ride home, as usual, in the Volkswagen bug she'd inherited when her older sister had gone to college. She pulled into my driveway, and for a minute I just sat there, trying to feel eighteen.

"Hey, you can get married now, right?" Jennifer asked brightly.

No. Not ever. Never. "Yep. Course, I need a fiancé first. Or a boyfriend. Or more than three dates in the last two years."

"That's your own fault," Jennifer said. "Guys ask you out but you never go."

And I could never tell her why. I sighed and rolled down the window—the car was instantly stifling without the AC on. It wasn't like we had to slog through three or four months of summer but then in September we would have a real autumn. There was no autumn in Florida. There were nine months of summer and three months of yucky chill.

"You can sign up for the armed forces," Jennifer went on. "And vote."

"Yep." I looked out the window at my house.

"You don't want to go in. It's been bad?"

I let out a breath. "Yeah. I mean, it's not like they're evil. Just determined. Last night they actually said they'd move back to Brazil in order to fully immerse me . . . in their culture. I was like, I'm going to college in three months."

"Crap," Jennifer said, frowning. "I've never understood exactly what the issue is. Like, how do they want you to conform? Be more Brazilian? Speak Portuguese at home? Or be more girly?"

I rolled my eyes. My clothes choices did make my stylish mother crazy, but it was such a tiny chunk of the glacier that it hardly mattered. It was another thing I couldn't explain to Jennifer. I couldn't explain it to anyone. With any luck I would go to my grave without anyone knowing.

Jennifer patted my knee, her short blue nails glittering in the sun. "It'll be okay, you li'l Heartbreakin', Disappointin' thing. You'll have a nice picnic, and then it's the weekend. And three months from now you'll be headed to Seattle."

I nodded, trying to let that make me happy, like it usually did. "True. Three months. Then it'll be cool, gray weather all the time. Mountains. Three thousand miles from here." Of course I would still be me, which was a problem, but there I'd have better luck pretending I wasn't.

Jennifer made a sad face. "You should come with me to New York."

"You should come with me to Seattle." Jennifer and I had been best friends since third grade, and I'd thought we'd stay that way our whole lives. As I got older, though, I realized that I'd be forced to leave Jennifer behind at some point. Because best friends knew each other deep down, shared almost everything with each other. And I was already keeping an enormous secret from her. And always would.

I had to get as far away from here as possible. And she had to go to Columbia in New York City because it was the only school her parents would pay for. The reality of not seeing each other almost every day was starting to sink in, one gray inch at a time. Most of me was already dreading the end of the summer, when we would split up, but a tiny part was relieved, also. Because then I would be free—free to keep my secret. Right now that carried so much weight that it made even losing Jennifer almost seem like a reasonable price.

The front door opened and my mom came out.

Jennifer sighed. "Your mom is so gorgeous. Despite the crazy-making." She said this every couple of months, in case I had forgotten. And it was true. My mom's shiny black hair swung in loose waves below her shoulders; her skin was smooth, tan, and clear, with some laugh lines at the corners of her eyes. Her unusual golden eyes were large and almond-shaped, making her look exotic and foreign. Ha ha. Today she was wearing tailored black shorts and a fuchsia sleeveless polo top. Gold bracelets jingled on her toned arms, and black Tory Burch thongs showed off her pedicure.

Smiling, my mom came to the car. "Zhennifer!"

"Hi, Ms. Neves," Jennifer said. While totally loyal to me, she couldn't help adoring my mom. "Vivi was telling me about this year's menu, the Pepto-Bismol special."

My mom smiled, her teeth white against her tan skin. She was forty-six but looked much younger without working at it. Strangers turned to look at her almost everywhere we went—partly because she was beautiful and partly because she was intensely alive, incredibly charismatic, open, genuine, generous. I'd never seen anyone more feminine, but it was a strong, womanly thing unrelated to pink ruffles or being dainty. Everyone loved her. And I did too, I did. But it was all so much harder than anyone realized.

"I know, can you imagine?" my mom said. "And then coconut cake. Tomorrow you come to bring us chicken soup, okay?"

Jennifer laughed. "I will. You guys'll need it." Turning to me, she said, "Did you make the cake or did you let your mom attempt it?"

"I made it," I said, getting out of the car and taking my backpack from the backseat. I'd made all of our birthday cakes for years, trying more ambitious recipes and decorations each time. My mom was definitely a good cook and could make a perfectly decent cake, but I made great cakes.

"She didn't trust me to make it," said my mom, pretending to look exasperated.

"It was complicated," I said. "Thanks for the ride, H. See you tomorrow."

Jennifer started the car and nodded. "Pick you up at four. Then movie at seven." As she pulled out of the driveway, my mom came over and kissed my forehead, then lightly put her fingers where she had kissed, like she always did, as though to make it stick. She had to go up on her toes these days—at five foot ten, I was a good six inches taller than her. I stood there stiffly, though my deepest core longed to melt into her arms, to just be able to love her. But how could I? It would be the last wall breaking down, the last wall that kept me being myself and not just a clone of her and my dad. That would be terrible. Terrifying. Literally my worst fear.

"My darling," she said, her eyes shining with love but shaded by caution and crushed hope. "My darling. Eighteen." Her hands were on my shoulders; the sun glittered on the diamonds in her wedding ring.

I nodded. We'd done this already this morning. "Yep," I said. "You're home early." My mom taught French and Spanish at a high school in the next county. Her students loved her.

"I had to get home and make your picnic, right?" she said, putting an arm around me as we walked toward the house. "Papi should be home any minute. Where's the big beach blanket? I couldn't find it."

"I think it's in the luggage closet," I said, and entered the cool, dry air of our house.

An hour later my dad was home, the car was loaded, and I climbed in the backseat of his black Escalade next to the laundry basket filled with food. The whole car smelled so good that my mouth tingled with anticipation. But even this, even making my picnic, felt like a bribe. Like, if we do all these nice things for you, then you should do what we want. It made me beyond furious. Ironically, besides this one huge thing, they were fine—didn't hassle me about homework or grades, liked all my friends, let me borrow the car, didn't micromanage my life. We could be happy. I tried to be a good daughter, in every way except the one they wanted. Our house could just be calm and happy. Instead of a minefield.

Sudden anger ignited in me, and I wanted to refuse to go, refuse all the fabulous food my mom had made. Stay home alone with my cake. It would devastate her. Both of them. But then I had already devastated them lots of times.

I was quiet on the way to Everglades National Park. My parents tried to chat, tried to be cheerful, but I could swear that my mom seemed disappointed every time she looked at me—my thick dark hair pulled back into a plain ponytail, my ratty Piggly Wiggly T-shirt, my faded cutoff sweatpants that were the most comfortable shorts I owned.

When I was in ninth grade, she had quit telling me how pretty I could be if only I made an effort. Now it was more like subtext every morning when she saw how I had dressed for school that day.

Sometimes I saw cute clothes at the mall or somewhere and was almost drawn to them, but I always stopped myself. I wasn't trying to make myself as unattractive as possible—that was sort of a by-product. But not caring about how I looked was another way to not be her.

The Everglades are in a park, but they're more like a state all by themselves. We'd been coming here to picnic all year round for as long as I could remember. Years ago we came with family friends, but now it was almost always just the three of us. For a while I had lobbied for someplace air-conditioned, but though I could choose the menu, I could not, apparently, choose the venue.

"Has Jennifer found a dress for the prom?" my mom asked, searching for a relatively safe topic.

I shook my head. "We're going to the mall tomorrow to look again, and then to a movie."

"I saw my friend Marielena the other day," Mami said casually. "She said Aldo was doing well . . ."

The hints about finding a nice boy—almost always some son of one of their friends—were so mild compared to the other stuff that it was easy to let them slide. I kept my voice deliberately casual as well. "Oh, good." I looked out the window as we drove through the familiar park gates. My stomach was starting to knot up. I just wanted to get through this. Later I could go home and lock myself in my room as usual.

Mami was silent, and I saw her and Papi exchange a quick glance.

"Gosh, I'm hungry," I said, sounding artificial even to myself. "It all smells good."

Mami forced a smile. "I hope so. I just can't believe my baby is eighteen. You were the most perfect baby . . ."

Only to become a Heartbreaking Disappointment when I turned thirteen.

"Okay," Papi said, parking the Escalade. "I guess you women want me to carry the basket, eh?"

"Yes," my mother said, and they smiled at each other, genuine smiles. Jennifer thought their relationship was so romantic—they were still really nice to each other and truly liked to be together. Her parents hardly talked—her dad practically lived in the little workshop behind their garage, and didn't even come in for meals for days sometimes. The main things her parents still agreed on were that Jennifer had to follow her older sister, Helen, to Columbia; both girls had to spend part of every summer with their family in Israel; and they had already started saving money for their daughters' weddings, so Helen and Jennifer had better come through and the guys must be Jewish.

Helen might be able to accommodate that, but Jennifer was gay, as she'd announced at her bat mitzvah. Mrs. Hirsch had actually fainted, right in front of everyone. I'd never seen anyone faint before.

So on Jennifer's thirteenth birthday, she'd had her bat mitzvah and made her mother faint in public. On my thirteenth birthday, I'd found out that I was a freak, a monster, an abomination. Of course, I hadn't told Jennifer the truth—I'd mumbled something about how my parents wanted me to be less American and more Brazilian, and that they wanted me to promise to follow their weird Brazilian religion. In that context, I was using "Brazilian" as a euphemism, but Jennifer didn't know that. Anyway, it had been a rough year for everyone. And Jennifer and I had started calling each other HD.

"Viv, grab the blanket, *querida*," said my dad, pulling the basket out. "Aracita, can you bring the cooler?"

"Of course," my mother said, taking the small cooler from the back of the car.

My dad, Victor, was fifty-one but looked at least ten years younger, as if he were a well-preserved movie star instead of a regional manager for a huge office-supply chain. Without being prejudiced, I could say that he was the handsomest dad out of all my friends' dads. He had thick black hair, just starting to be tinged with a few silver threads, green eyes with long lashes, and a strong, straight nose. When I was little I'd thought he was the most hand-some man ever. I mean, objectively, he still was, but now I knew that nothing was that simple.

Mami led the way, I followed, and Papi lugged the basket behind me. We trudged along the hiking path for a good fifteen minutes, trying to avoid the occasional buzzing clouds of gnats and no-see-ums. It was almost six in the evening but still eighty-eight degrees and sweltering, becoming only more sweltering as we got far-ther into the pine trees. My skin was sticky and damp, sweat ran down my temples, and all I wanted to do was take a cool shower. I mean, what was wrong with a nice dinner at Ruby Tuesday? It was air-conditioned. Was it that they wouldn't be able to harangue me if we were surrounded by other people? Even better.

Five minutes more on this trail and we would run into a cypress swamp; if we turned east for a mile, we would come to one of the mangrove stands.

We ignored the clearing with the picnic benches and went instead to a small glade, only about fifteen feet across. It was our special and secret picnic spot, remarkable because it was flat and root-free, shaded by pines and a few knobby cypresses. All around it trees grew so thickly that the light was dim even at midday. I spread the blanket and hoped to get through most of dinner before everything started.

Fiendishly, they waited till I had my fork poised over a slab of my rich, moist coconut cake, its scent swirling up to my face. I'd been thinking about it all day, fantasizing about just planting my face in it and scarfing it up. Now I was much too full, of course, but by the gods I was going to get this down somehow.

"Dearest," said Mami, looking strained, "eighteen years ago today, you came into our lives."

I tried to smile through a mouthful of cake.

The most perfect baby.

"The most perfect baby," my mom said.

Every time she said this, I wondered if she was comparing the perfect baby me to the current me, which seemed by any standard to be considerably less perfect.

Mami hesitated, then went on. "When you were thirteen, we shared with you the wonder, the beautiful mystery of our kind."

My throat closed up, the coconut cake turning to a lump of florist's foam in my mouth.

Papi looked serious. He put down his fork and rubbed the back of my neck, which he always did when he wanted to talk seriously to me. "*Querida,* now you are eighteen. You know we've tried so hard to show you the joy in being who you are. What you are."

The cake moved very slowly down my esophagus, as if I'd swallowed a whole hard-boiled egg. I breathed through my nose, hoping I wouldn't gag.

"I don't want any part of this," I mumbled, my mouth bone-dry. How many times had I said that? Like a million? "This isn't me."

Sounding near tears, my mom said, "Of course it's you, Viviana. Of course—"

Papi went on quickly, "But now you are eighteen, and when a haguari child turns eighteen, she or he is given the family book."

My brain rang with the most awful word I knew: "haguari." My parents pronounced it "ha-HWA-ree," but I'd heard friends of theirs say the *g*: "ha-GWA-ree." It meant "jaguar people." A bit hysterically, I wished that it meant people who totally, totally loved their British sports cars.

"The family book?" I asked faintly. It was the first I'd heard of it. Could they read the dismay on my face? Of course they could.

As we'd sat there, the sun had gradually sunk below the line of trees, and our little glade was now even more private, deeply in shadow. I wanted to jump up and run into the pine-scented darkness and just keep running. I wanted to leave them forever, and knowing this made me want to die. Do you know how hard it is to feel that the people you love the most can't help destroying you?

"Yes," said Mami. "It has the history of our people and the history of our family. When you marry, you will continue the book for your children." She spoke firmly, as if there were no question I would marry and have children—children like me. Like them. Oh, gods. If only I could hold on until I could go to Seattle. It couldn't come soon enough.

I shook my head. "I've told you every way I know how," I said tightly. "I understand what you are, but I don't want to be like that. I want to be regular. You can yell at me every day for the rest of my life, but it won't change my mind. I want to be like me." My face was hard. "I don't want to be like you—I mean . . . the other part. The . . . people part of you is fine. But I'm rejecting the other part."

"How can you say that?" my mother cried, as if this were a brand-new argument, as if I hadn't already said those exact same words a hundred times. "You haven't even tried—" She stopped abruptly as my dad put a hand on her knee.

"Whatever you decide, our book is in—" Papi began firmly, but his words were drowned out by a sudden, startlingly loud growl that made us all jump. An animal growl, coming from . . . behind the trees? In the darkness there? Instantly my parents were on their feet, and my mother grabbed my arm and hauled me to mine.

"What's that?" I asked, peering tensely through trees. A wild dog? Something big. Maybe even a Florida panther? They weren't supposed to be in this area. My blood had turned icy with the sound, and the little hairs on my arms were standing up. There was another growl from the woods, sounding like the snarl of a circus cat when the trainer pokes it with a stick.

And then . . .

"Oh, my gods," I muttered, appalled, wanting to look away. My father had started to change, right there in front of me. It was amazingly fast, like a sped-up film. I'd seen it happen only once before, on my thirteenth birthday, and it had been horrifying. Since then I'd seen him in his other form just a couple of times, and never on purpose.

His other form. His jaguar form.

He was already on all fours, his clothes slipping off, one shirt-sleeve ripping. His face had broadened, his jaw jutting forward, and thick dark fur was covering his tan skin. Bones shifted and moved; muscles swelled; limbs elongated; his spine bent and lengthened. It was repulsive, disgusting. Grotesque.

From deep in his throat an answering snarl—raw, angry, full of menace—made me suck in my breath. His teeth were long and knifelike and—

"Vivi!" My mother's voice was harsh, her grip on my arm painful. "Go! Run!" She pushed me away, toward the edge of the clearing.

I stared at her. "What?"

"Run! Get out of here!" Now her face too was broadening, starting to transform, her shoulders hunching, her spine curving down sharply. I didn't want to see this. What was happening?

"Run!" she said again, but it came out as a half roar. I burst into tears, turned, and ran.

I'd been coming to this park my whole life, had spent countless sweaty hours on the hiking trails, canoeing through the swamps, watching baby alligators from viewing decks above the waterlogged, sun-soaked fields of sedge grass.

Now I ran blindly, my panicked brain barely registering that I had left the trail and was crashing through the woods. Broken twigs jabbed my feet, scratched my arms and face, and still I plunged forward. What was happening, what was going on, should I call for help—?

Another furious, high-pitched roar wove its way through the trees to my ears, making my heart pump harder and my stomach twist in fear. Was it coming after me? I refused to look behind me. Didn't want to know.

And then, with no warning, it began to happen, the way I'd always feared it would: The world shifted in my eyes, details becoming more precise, some colors fading, some enhanced. My running feet sounded like bricks crushing the leaves on the forest floor, the snap of twigs like rifle shots echoing in my ears.

My running became awkward, unbalanced as my legs got tangled in my shorts. I fell, my hands outstretched, and then I was racked with sudden pain that made me crumple up and cry out. My joints were bending unnaturally, dislocating, the bones lengthening horribly. My face was splitting, my jaw unhinging; my skull was in a vise. Every muscle screamed, its fibers being split and stretched. My clothes, annoyingly in the way, fell off or ripped.

Curl up pant pant pain

Curl up small

Muscles hurt close eyes smell dirt smell pine smell me animal me my fur

Pain breathe in slow shallow

Smell dirt smell fear

Open my eyes the pain is fading

Sun down dark but shapes outlines see quite well see everything

Trees and leaves I see lines depth land picked out so sharp

Strong scents fill my nose my mouth pine cypress stagnant water thick and green

Rabbit and insects pungent like roly-poly bugs I smell saw grass and pine needles and birds

Can't hear my parents where am I how far away am I

Where are my parents I get to my feet I am on all fours

I am solid I have strong muscles I am powerful I am jaguar me I am a jaguar

Before it hurt so much took so long was a birth

This is still awful

These eyes can't cry tears

There is no movement it has stopped

Every creature senses me and has gone silent becoming still like a tree a rock a root

Because I am a predator I am at the top of the food chain

Where did I come from which way did I come my new eyes see everything my new eyes see weird but so well

Should I go back to find my parents

The snarls were so scary from the purple shadows maybe I should wait here

Mami said run get out of here now

I sit down it is odd my haunches sit but my shoulders stay up I have haunches it is funny

Mami Papi where are you will you come get me

Ground is not safe want to be up

Cypress tree here I coil muscles and jump like a spring like a jumping bean

I float I land on a branch my claws are steel hooks on the branch they are talons

I am up high these branches can hold me I climb high and high I cannot see any clearing

I cannot see our car

I cannot hear anything but birds and insects and leaves twitching like my ears

There is a breeze up here waves of scents honeysuckle wild blackberry palm bark bird

I don't want to be here I am scared I have no idea what to do

I have never felt so alone

Stars in the sky arc as night comes the darkness grows deeper covers me like a blanket

Nighttime insects begin their scratchy evensong

A big black beetle scuttles past me it smells just like itself

I smell like myself I smell like a jaguar

There is life all around me the night is full of hot little beating hearts

Jaguar me stays very very still for long time but fear is a sparkler in my stomach

I have to see Mami and Papi have to see them have to see them I don't care

I climb down tail first I don't know how finally I jump I land silently on pine needles

I scan for danger nothing here can hurt me nothing is worthy of notice

I am not lost I smell my path the fear scent from my paws as I ran I brushed against trees I tripped on roots I left scent everywhere everything I touched smells like fear my foot bled I smell the drop of blood it is a beacon from fifteen feet away

I move quickly and quietly along the trail I find a pile of cloth it smells familiar it smells so familiar this is what I wore this is mine I can't carry them what to do cannot carry them leave them there

Please let my parents be looking for me be waiting for me calling my name worried about me let everything be okay

This is a prayer this prayer drowns out the sounds of night

I head back to our glade and then a hundred yards away the scents come to me

I smell fear like dark vinegar like sweat and I smell blood cold not hot not fresh sick

I smell death

Blood breaking down meat flesh

I will wait jaguar me will wait I will hide beneath this bush my ears catch every sound every heartbeat my eyes snap into focus on every leaf bobbing on the wind

I wait my stomach is sick my heart is thudding my lungs will explode I wait

There is no threat to me I crawl out from the bush the moon is bright the glade is bright with moonlight I see everything clearly I see everything

I don't understand I don't understand

There is a body a human body

The chest is cut open I go closer sniffing it smells familiar it is family

It is covered with blood my nose wrinkles wet copper scent of blood

My paws are silent there is a jaguar nearby it is alive it is warm but growing cooler

It smells like family it has golden fur splotched with black and dark red roses of blood warm blood dark maroon in the moonlight

I smell fear I smell death there is a human body why is this jaguar dying why

I sniff the jaguar its eyes open they are golden

And beautiful

I know these eyes

The jaguar is Mami she is dying the human is my papi he is dead

There is blood everywhere

My mouth opens my pupils flare my gut churns this is Mami this is Papi

My veins flood with shock with white-lightning adrenaline

Suddenly I drop to the ground

I am in knots

And with no warning I was changing back, diminishing, becoming flimsy and stiff, weak and pale and naked. My lovely muscled strength ebbed away as if I myself were dying. The world became brighter but also less vibrant. Sounds were muted, scents muffled or nonexistent. I was shaking with cold, my skin clammy and damp. I was no longer the top predator in this area; I could be hurt by any number of things. So many things.

The jaguar next to me made a rough sound as I grabbed the edge of the rumpled picnic blanket and pulled it around me.

I crawled closer to her. "Mami?" I said softly, reaching out and stroking dense fur I had never touched before.

She groaned, her beautiful golden eyes meeting mine.

"What happened?" I cried, so far away from understanding any of this that it was like I'd been dropped into another world. Shaking from shock, I got closer and pulled Mami's head onto my lap. It was heavy and warm. Her mouth opened, and I saw her long white teeth were stained with blood.

"Mami, come on," I pleaded. "I'll call for help. I'll get the car." I was babbling, unable to think, forcing my eyes to stay on her, not looking over to where my once-handsome father lay, a cooling body in the moonlight.

As I held her, my tears falling into her fur, she began to change, shrinking and losing her beautiful coat, her coiled-rope muscles.

"Mami, who did this?" Now I could touch her human face, spattered with blood, her long dark hair falling over my knee. I was crying, unable to take in what had happened, how suddenly and irrevocably my life had changed.

Mami managed a wan smile. The ground under my knees was

soaked; several deep cuts in her side were still bleeding heavily. I put my hand over them, trying to keep her blood in.

"My beautiful . . ." Her eyes unfocused, seeming to look past my face at the night sky. I gripped her shoulder.

"Mami! Hold on! I'll get help! I'll find my phone!" But I was too terrified to move even an inch away from her.

She blinked slowly and looked at me again, frowning slightly as if confused. "Donella? I've missed you . . ." I could barely hear her voice.

"Donella?"

Mami smiled slightly, and her eyes focused on me again. "My perfect . . . baby . . ." Then the frown between her eyes smoothed, and her face went lax. Her golden eyes gazed sightlessly at the stars above me.

My parents were dead.

CHAPTER TWO

ON TV SHOWS WHEN PEOPLE CALL 911, EVEN IF
they're hysterical, they can get words out. I couldn't.

I found my phone, covered with dirt and blood, beneath the
blanket I'd pulled around me. I called 911, but my brain had dis-
connected and I didn't seem to know any words. I wanted to be
away from here. The dispatcher asked increasingly urgent questions
that I couldn't answer. Finally he said, "Does your phone have a
GPS?" I nodded, as if that would help. "Turn on the phone's GPS,"
he ordered.

I did. Then I dropped the phone, crawled a few feet away, and
threw up. Then, oh my gods—I realized we were all naked. Not
only was this the worst thing that could possibly happen to us, but
it was also . . . shameful. Like the cops would think we were out
here being freaks. And we were! But not that way.

I had no idea where my clothes were—didn't think I could ever
find them, back in the dark woods. My eyes flew wildly about the
horrific scene, our picnic scattered, my cake smashed and bloodied,

the bodies. My parents were bodies now. Everything they had been, every facet of their personalities, had ended forever. My brain could not begin to comprehend that.

My mom had brought my birthday presents. I grabbed a flat one and ripped it open. It was a cute patterned halter top and a pair of trendy booty shorts that I wouldn't have worn in a million years. I scrambled into them. In the distance, sirens started wailing.

My parents were naked. No child ever wants to see that. I was sobbing now, blubbering without thinking what I looked like, what I sounded like. My face was wet with tears, my nose was running. I wiped it on my arm. I got my dad's shorts on him, and then I threw up again.

I got my mom's top and underpants and shorts on. Then I collapsed in the blood-soaked grass and cried so hard I heaved again, except my stomach was empty so it was just bile. I wished I were dead. I wished I had stayed and been killed too. I wished whoever had done it would come back right now and finish me off, because I simply could not live through this.

The sirens were closer, but they couldn't bring cars right here. I lay there and cried and retched and finally I heard voices and running feet.

They asked me questions. I understood the words but didn't know why they were talking to me. I couldn't sit up. Someone said, "She's in shock. Get her on a board." I started screaming when they put me on a stretcher. I needed to stay with Mami and Papi, because they were all I had. I was strapped down, struggling and shouting, and then someone stuck a needle in the back of my hand. About ten seconds after that I fell asleep.

When I woke up, I was in a hospital room. I looked around grog-gily and saw Jennifer and her parents. I felt thick-headed and unnaturally calm.

"Babe," said Jennifer, and took my hand, squeezing tight. Her face was pale. Her eyes were huge and dark.

"What happened?" I asked, my words slurring.

Jennifer put her hand over her mouth and started crying. I just looked at her.

Mrs. Hirsch came closer. "Hi, sweetie," she said, looking very serious. "I've contacted your aunt Juliana, in Brazil. She's on her way."

"Why?"

Behind her the wooden door wide enough for hospital beds opened. A tall woman with sand-colored hair came in.

"Hello, Viviana," she said gently. "I'm Detective Virginia Parnes. I need to talk to you about your parents."

I tried to sit up. "My parents! Where are they? Are they okay? Can I see them?"

Jennifer choked a little and looked at her mom. Mrs. Hirsch pressed her lips together.

Here's what was weird: I knew they were dead. I remembered what happened. But it was like if I refused to admit it, it wouldn't be true. Like I would pass some kind of test, maybe for loyalty, and

I would be rewarded by having my parents back again.

"Where are they?" I asked again. "Where's my mom?" Just like that I was hysterical all over again. I started yelling for my mom, for someone to get me out of here. A nurse came running, and I felt something cold going into the IV drip. I fell back onto my bed and floated into blessed, empty darkness.

I didn't take final exams or go to prom or show up on Senior Party Day. I didn't go to graduation, but two days after the ceremony I got my high school diploma in the mail. They gave me a pass because of my family tragedy.

My tia Juliana, my mom's sister, came and stayed with me for ten days. She took over and dealt with everything. There was no funeral—our kind didn't have funerals. You know why? Because one didn't call attention to the weakness of the dead. One left them behind and moved on, so they could be scavenged by other animals in a harsher, less Disney version of the circle of life. Of course, in modern society one can't just leave human bodies lying around. But there was no public funeral or sitting shiva or visitation or anything.

However, my dad's office sent a huge fruit basket, and my mom's students brought a sympathy card that everyone had signed to our house. That was all before I got home from the hospital. After I got home, Tia Juliana clucked over me. She was deeply sad but functioning better than I was. Basically I was a total wreck, on tranquilizers, crying, having nightmares. One night she and I were sitting at the kitchen table with a neighbor's casserole in front of us. We looked at each other and suddenly we were both crying. She reached out and took my hand.

I was so glad she was here, especially to deal with the various authorities—the police had ruled my parents' deaths suspicious, but had no leads. There had been the paw prints of a large cat, but some injuries had been caused by a knife blade. No weapon had been found; there were no fingerprints. At the time, I had seen that my father's chest had been cut open. Now I knew that someone had taken his heart. Who would do something like that?

"It was like the Talofomé," I said to my tia, not really meaning it.

"The Talofomé?" Her face was beautiful and sad. "No, *cara*. I'm afraid it was a real haguaro, not a legend. Maybe a haguaro and pelado together." I hadn't heard the word *pelado* in ages—my parents had thought it was tacky to have a separate word to mean regular people, people who weren't haguari. Especially since *pelado* basically meant "naked."

I knew it wasn't the Talofomé, the devil jaguar that parents used to tell their children about, to make them behave. The fairy tale went that the Talofomé was so unhappy at being an ugly devil that he would search the world for haguari and eat their hearts, to try to feel better. Naughty children were especially appealing to him. My parents were old-fashioned in some ways, but they had never pulled the threat of the Talofomé on me.

But someone—something—had taken my father's heart.

A few nights after I got home, we were sitting on the green

living room couch not watching some stupid show on Papi's flat-screen TV, and Tia Juliana quietly asked me what had happened.

Hesitantly, flinching from the pain, I told her. About the growl from the woods, how I ran, how I changed. How I'd come back to find Papi dead and Mami dying. Mami had been her older sister—now Juliana was an only child. Her parents, my grandparents, had died years ago.

Tia Juliana gasped once or twice as I haltingly told my story.

"I'm so sorry I ran away," I said, crying in shame. "I should have stayed."

"And die along with them?" Tia Juliana said, tears in her voice. "You obeyed your mother. She would have been furious if you'd disobeyed her, stayed, and gotten killed." She patted my hand. "I would have been furious too."

That was when I fell apart for the hundredth time. Leaning against her, I cried with huge, racking sobs, feeling like my ribs were splitting open.

"I was a bad daughter!" I cried without meaning to, as Tia Juliana put her arm around me and stroked my hair. There. I'd said it, admitted it out loud. The world might as well know.

"Why do you say such a thing?" she asked, handing me a tissue.

"I didn't want to be . . ." I was crying so hard I could hardly breathe. "Haguari. I don't want to be one! I just want to be normal!"

The hand stroking my hair stilled. Tia Juliana held me without saying anything for a long time. I wondered if she'd get up in disgust.

But now that I was confessing, I kept going. "They wanted me to change with them, do stuff together. I always said no. I didn't come to Brazil these last couple of years because I know all you guys change, and I didn't want to! I don't want any part of it. And now something about being haguari killed my parents!" I was almost howling, curled up so tightly it felt like my bones would snap from tension. "My parents died thinking I was a disappointment! Thinking I didn't love them!" This was the worst, and I shrieked in an agony so much more acute than when the dentist had accidentally let the Novocain wear off while he was drilling my tooth.

"But I did!" I sobbed, hiding my face in the velour of the couch. "I did love them! And now they're gone! I can't stand it, I can't stand it!" *Please let a nurse come in here now and knock me out.* I couldn't take this pain. I couldn't live with it ripping holes in my heart this way. How could I possibly live through this?

Tia Juliana didn't get up. She kept her arm around me and let me cry it out. Finally I slowed to hiccupping, gasping breaths. My eyes were burning and almost swollen shut. I was exhausted and wanted to go to sleep and never wake up.

"You want to be normal?" she said at last. I nodded wearily. "But darling, this is normal. You are normal. You're just a haguara."

"Being a haguara is not normal, compared to the whole rest of the world."

"Everyone is different," Tia Juliana said calmly in her accented English. Her hand stroked my hair again. "There are people with six fingers on each hand. People who have super, innate abilities.

Savants. There are people who have no conscience, who can kill others without caring." Her voice trailed off, but she took another breath. "People with injuries or illnesses that make them different. People who can't have children. People who are extra brave, people who are extra smart or extra pretty or extra something else. What is normal? What does that look like?"

I couldn't think straight, couldn't come up with an argument.

"Your mami and papi knew that you loved them," Tia Juliana said softly. "And they loved you, more than anything. They wanted you to be happy, and thought you would be happiest if you experienced the joy of being haguari. It's our way, the way of our people. We're beautiful and special, and haguari have existed since the earliest times. To deny that is . . . diminishing. And somewhat pointless, *cara*. But I know that your parents loved you so much, as is."

Tears leaked out of my eyes. I'd made a big wet spot on the velour, and I traced through it with my finger, flattening the tiny fibers.

"I talked to your mami almost every week," Tia Juliana said. "Never once did she say you were a disappointment. Never once did she say that she wished you were different."

Amazingly, I had some sobs left, and I started crying again.

"She was proud of you. She wanted you to be happy. You were her dream child, her treasure. And she knew you loved her."

"I hardly ever said it!" I said, bawling again.

"She knew." My aunt sounded quite definite, and I desperately wanted to believe her. Then I felt like such a loser for wanting it to be that easy, that good. I didn't deserve to believe her, didn't deserve to be the daughter of someone who knew I loved her even though I had rejected who I was, who she wanted me to be.

"She knew," my aunt repeated. "And so did your papi. It's okay, *querida*. The three of you loved each other. Love isn't always easy or smooth. But it's okay. You're okay. They're okay too."

I wanted to believe that so much.

Almost a week later, Tia Juliana needed to finally go back to her own family, my tio Marc and my two cousins, who were younger than me.

"Please come with me," she said as I watched her pack.

"I don't want to leave here." I was no longer taking tranquilizers, and my grief felt raw and rough-edged. Being awake was almost unbearably painful, and days went by where all I managed to do was eat a bowl of cereal.

"You shouldn't be alone."

"Jennifer comes over every day," I said, which was true, especially now that school was out. I didn't tell my aunt that Jennifer was due to leave soon for her annual trip to Israel.

"If you change your mind, will you call me?" Tia Juliana asked. She looked at me seriously, her blond hair pulled back in a no-nonsense yet somehow chic bun, her dark eyes so like mine.

I nodded. "Yes. If I change my mind, I'll call you. I'll come."

"You won't have to change, if you come," she said, surprising me. "No one will force you to feel beautiful, or have fun or excitement." A tiny smile played around her lips, the first one since she'd arrived.

"That's a relief," I said. "The gods know I don't want that." We shared a look then, and I knew I'd be grateful to my aunt forever. I had one last question. "Tia, do you know about the family book?" The one Papi had mentioned right before the attack.

Tia Juliana looked surprised. "Of course. Every family has one. The oldest child in each family inherits it." She looked confused, but then her face cleared. "Oh, you turned eighteen! Did you get the family book?"

I shook my head. "I'd never heard of it. Papi was starting to tell me about it, but he . . . didn't finish."

"Oh. Well, it's bound to be around here, *cara*. After I go, you can search for it. It will be like a big scrapbook, but maybe bound in leather."

"Okay." I had no idea whether I wanted to find it or not. It sounded like it would be full of my family tree and haguari history, and I didn't want to delve into that right now. Maybe in a little while.

Then Tia Juliana was gone and the house was extremely empty and quiet. Before this had happened, I'd always loved it when I had the house to myself. I would turn my music up loud, belt out songs, and dance with ambitious, no doubt goofy moves I'd never let anyone see. Now I wandered silently through a house that seemed foreign and cold. In the living room I stopped in front of the altar my parents had made to our gods, Tzechuro and Tzechura.

The altar sat in a small, red-painted alcove cut into the living room wall. Papi had told me the altar had belonged to his parents, and to their parents before them, for generations. It did look really old, the carved wood smooth from time and touch, the symbols almost worn away in places.

The main shelf held statues of the Tzechuri, who had created our people at the dawn of time, as the legends went. Tzechura was reclining, resting on one elbow, looking calmly forward. Her body was dark, very old ivory, inlaid with ebony rosettes and spots. Her eyes were yellow sapphires. Tzechuro was rearing back on his haunches, his face in a snarl, one paw raised with claws outstretched. His eyes were emeralds, and his fangs were mother-of-pearl.

When I was little, my parents would show me the altar and tell the stories of how Tzechuro had been made from the sun and Tzechura had been born of the moon. The sun had seen jaguars and admired their strength and beauty, and the moon had seen humans and recognized that they were the smartest of all the creatures. So the sun and the moon together created a new race that combined the best qualities of jaguar and human, and thus were born haguari.

Apparently all haguari today were the direct descendants of Tzechuro and Tzechura, in the way that many people believe that all humans came from Adam and Eve. When I was little, I'd accepted these stories the way that children accept Bible stories, and when I was ten I realized that this was my parents' religion, and they intended it to be mine, too. I was old enough to know that none of my friends worshipped these gods; none of them had jaguar altars in their houses. At first it seemed quirky, almost amusing, as if my parents were Hare Krishnas or something, but by the time I was thirteen and really being immersed in haguari culture it began to seem freakish and even disturbing. One more thing for me to reject.

But privately, I'd never been able to shake the idea of the Tzechuri as being our gods, my gods. I wanted to be an atheist, but something deep down couldn't accept that haguari had just happened, that we were a weird genetic mishmash. Having gods born of the sun and the moon who combined us on purpose actually seemed to make more sense. As much as I denied it publicly, my inner self always felt embraced by the jaguar gods.

In the quiet house I dusted the altar, which I had refused to do for my parents. On Friday night I lit the altar candles, which I used to sneer at them doing. I couldn't bring myself to sing the prayers I knew. That would be going too far.

About fifty times a day some small sound made me look up, as if Mami or Papi had just come home and was unlocking the door, turning on a light. The continual realization and disappointment that they would never come home again left me wrung out and exhausted.

Jennifer came over every day after school, and then stayed all day for the first days of summer. Much too soon, it was time for her to go to Israel.

"I told my mom I couldn't leave you," Jennifer said.

After I had gotten home from the hospital, she'd held me while I cried. Many times. She'd cried too. Sometimes Tia Juliana had held both of us, and all three of us had cried.

"How long will you be gone?" I asked, like I did every summer. I examined my choices for dinner: chicken noodle or split pea soup. I was still having trouble eating—food got stuck in my throat. My clothes were getting loose.

"Until the first week of August," she said. "Then I have to pack to go to New York. I've been assigned a roommate and everything. Listen, Viv—Mom says she'll pay for you to go to Israel, and my aunt said she'd love to have you spend the summer. Please come. Don't make me go by myself."

Right then I realized she hadn't called me HD since my parents had died. I guessed I was no longer a Heartbreaking Disappointment. Because there was no one left to disappoint.

I got out the can opener and thought about going to Israel. It was tempting. I'd never been. As much as Jennifer complained about it, I knew she actually had a great time there. I'd seen the pictures on Facebook. She had six cousins; they all had friends; they did lots of fun stuff. I could be surrounded by loud, busy people. I could have that in Brazil, too, with my family.

But mostly I wanted to lie in my bed under the covers and never move again.

"That sounds great," I said. "Tell your mom thanks so much. But . . . I guess I'll just stay put." I dumped the chicken noodle soup into a plastic mixing bowl and stuck it in the microwave. My mom had hated the microwave. I punched buttons and the turntable started going around.

"Are you sure?" Jennifer looked worried.

"I think so," I said, and shrugged. The microwave dinged. I took out the bowl and got a spoon and managed a few bites before it felt like if I ate any more I would hurl. I looked over at Jennifer and gave a smile that even I could tell was sickly and unconvincing. "I'll be okay."

Jennifer left for Tel Aviv. We both cried. She hugged me like she'd never see me again.

Then I was really on my own. Other friends from school came by, of course, but I was even more awkward than usual and a couple of times burst into tears. Embarrassing for everyone. So I quit letting them visit. After Jennifer left, my days were endless and silent, as if I were enveloped by a slow, still fog of pain. As if moving too quickly would rip the caul, and the sudden, horrifying brightness of my nightmarish reality would shine on me.

I closed the door to my parents' room and caught myself tiptoeing past it as if they were in there, asleep. Every once in a while, if I was really falling apart, I went in and threw myself on their bed, clutching the pillows, burying my face in the maroon silk quilt, breathing in the faint scents of my dad's shaving cream, my mom's favorite perfume.

It was hard to go to sleep. Sometimes right before I dozed off I was dropped into a memory of running through the woods, sharp scents making my nose twitch. I'd bounded fifteen feet in the air with no effort. I'd heard the quick, faint heartbeats of birds, had smelled a rabbit that knew I was nearby. The memory was clear as a mountain lake, as sharp as a blade of sedge grass, and sometimes it seemed more real than my waking days.

My tia Juliana had dealt with the bank stuff—arranging to have all the bills paid automatically. I had not the slightest concept of how to do any of that, so it was a blessing. Then one day toward the end of June the lawyer called me and asked about some papers: my parents' green cards, their marriage certificate, my birth certificate. I said I would find them and bring them to her. Tia Juliana had already worked with the lawyer, but I guessed there were a few loose ends.

My dad's office had once been a small bedroom. We'd only needed two of our four bedrooms, so we had a guest room and his office. The room was cool and dark, with the wood paneling that was in almost every room in the house. Most of the rooms had been painted, but this one was still woody. It smelled like his aftershave. It felt like he was in the kitchen and would walk in here any second.

His files were organized and labeled neatly in English, and under the IMPORTANT PAPERS tab I found a small silver key. I remembered that he kept really crucial stuff in the fireproof safe on the floor of the closet. Though it was small, it weighed a ton. I dragged it out, pulling and pushing it along the textured olive-green carpet, and fitted the silver key into its lock.

Inside were files, again labeled in my father's handwriting, and it took only a minute to find the documents the lawyer wanted. I set them aside in a little pile, then flipped through the rest of the important files. There were photographs of my parents at their wedding, which had been on a beach in Brazil. My mom looked young and impossibly beautiful, and was gazing adoringly up at my dad, who grinned as if he had just won the jackpot. There were pictures of me as a baby and toddler, laughing, dark-eyed, my hair in two cute braids. Here I was, being held by the hand as I walked on that same beach during a family visit. A photo of my eighth birthday party showed Tia Juliana pregnant with my cousin, and my mother's parents looking elegant and silver-haired. They had died not long after that.

Now I leaned against the wood-paneled wall and watched dust motes floating and swirling in the shaft of sunlight coming through the high window, a montage of childhood memories scrolling through my head. I'd been happy until I was thirteen, had felt secure and loved, smart and pretty. Now my parents were gone forever. When I thought about how much I had pushed back, how I'd thrown their traditions in their faces for the last five years, I felt terrible.

From the time I was fourteen, I'd refused to go to Brazil each summer and for holidays. Instead I'd stayed with Jennifer, my parents planning their trips around the trips to Israel. I'm sure not only my parents but also my aunt and uncle had been hurt by that. In ninth grade I'd tried to join the Christian church down the block, even though it had felt like a betrayal larger than my parents—a betrayal of the Tzechuri. But I'd needed parental consent, and they did not consent. I didn't speak to them for three days over that. My defiant, anticarnivore vegetarianism had lasted two months, brought to its knees by Jennifer eating a warm pita stuffed with shawarma and tahini.

I dressed like a slob and wore no makeup. That wasn't about being haguari; it was about being the opposite of my mom, who was stylish and beautiful and loved being female. My schleppiness had driven her nuts, though she'd tried not to show it. Looking back, it must have crushed her, my ratty T-shirts and sloppy shorts. I bet she'd been looking forward to having a beautiful, girly daughter who would enjoy shopping and ask her for eyeliner tips. Until the terrible day that they'd revealed the family legacy, I had been that girl. Early pictures showed me in adorable outfits, hair held back in matching barrettes. I'd looked forward to growing up and wearing fashionable clothes like my mom. Had practiced walking in her high heels. At the beginning of seventh grade, she let me wear mascara and lip gloss to school. I'd worked on tossing my hair just so all summer. I'd felt grown-up in the new bras we'd gotten to deal with the sudden boobs.

And then I'd found out, at the end of seventh grade. Found out why I hardly ever got sick, why I was graceful and strong and good at any sport, why I was so pretty even as a twelve-year-old that strangers would stare at me. You don't see an ugly jaguar, right? It had seemed like a nightmare, a bad movie that just did not end. I was completely freaked out, horrified, appalled . . .

My reaction had totally taken my parents by surprise. They'd never known anyone who wasn't thrilled and honored to be one of such a magical species. But I found the change revolting and scary. It was grotesque to me, and even ending up a gorgeous jaguar did not make it better. My parents couldn't believe I felt that way, and the more they'd tried to cajole me out of it, the more I'd dug my heels in.

For the next five years, my parents had been angry, or sad, or frustrated. The one time they'd been truly furious was during one of our arguments: Pushed too far, I'd made fun of the Tzechuri. I no longer thought our uniqueness was cool or interesting—it was embarrassing. If my friends asked, I said we were Protestant. The day I'd told my parents that, and said the altar was awful, was the day my dad drew the line I couldn't cross.

"How dare you!" my father had actually shouted, his handsome face flushed. I'd jumped, wide-eyed. "You can refuse to do this or that, you can cling to whatever belief you need to, but one thing you will not do is mock the gods of our people!"

I wasn't nearly brave enough to challenge him on that, and I never criticized the Tzechuri again.

Now, as I sat in his office, I would have given anything for him to be back, even if he was yelling at me.

While I'd been musing, the sun had disappeared. Dark clouds tumbled past the window like a giant shaking a fuzzy gray blanket. A bolt of lightning lit the office paneling brightly, and seconds later there was a rolling boom of thunder in the distance. I shook myself, turned on a lamp, and went back to the files.

All this stuff was mine now. It was a horrible, overwhelming thought.

Time for an ice-cream sandwich. I'd found that I could eat

most of one without feeling sick, and they'd become a staple. That, soup, and pudding. Pudding was a big favorite now. In the past, whenever I'd felt especially down or didn't know what to do with myself, I'd bake something. Me and refined carbs were *likethis*. Maybe I could try that. Maybe I could make . . . a lemon cake or something. I didn't feel like it—just the idea of doing it made me feel tired. But maybe I should force myself. For medicinal purposes.

I made a space at the back of the fireproof box to put the files back in. As I tapped them down, my fingers brushed against something smooth right at the very back of the safe. Fishing it out, I saw that it was a large plastic bag with folded red silk inside it. Some sort of special memento or something.

I opened the bag and took out the red silk. It was wrapped around . . . more photos. I hoped they weren't . . . too personal or anything. Looking at them, I saw to my relief that I'd already seen ones similar to these in my mom's photo albums. My mom had grown up in São Paulo. My dad's family had owned a cattle ranch in central Brazil. These exact pictures weren't in her albums for some reason, but I recognized most of the places and the people. Some of the photos had been cut—maybe to fit a space in an album that never got made? Or to cut someone out, like an old boyfriend? It was sad seeing pictures of the beautiful little girl my mom had been, knowing that she had grown up to be even more beautiful, and now she was gone. All the memories in these photos, every experience she'd had that had helped her become who she was—they had all been for nothing.

My breath was coming shakily, and I'd resigned myself to another bout of crying when I stopped at the last photograph. I'd never seen it before. It was of three teenagers: the blond one was my tia Juliana, young and vivacious; the middle one was my mom, laughing at the camera; and my breath caught on the last one— because she looked weirdly, eerily like me. If I'd had big eighties hair and a tiny bathing suit. Like my face had been photoshopped into an old picture.

There was writing on the back: *Juliana, Aracita, Donella. Irmãs. Irmãs.* Sisters.

Donella. The name my mom had said right before she died. She'd looked at me and said, *Donella? I've missed you.*

My heart was beating wildly—I really did look a lot like the girl in the picture. Had my mom confused me for her? Who was she?

Was this a third sister? Neither my mom nor my aunt had ever mentioned having another sister. Or . . . maybe this was just a good friend of the family, and they were really close, so they jokingly called themselves sisters?

After a moment I decided no. I looked a lot like my mom, except my eyes were dark brown and hers had been golden. Donella and Juliana had eyes like mine. Juliana, as the only blonde, was the most different. But all our faces were very similar.

Had Donella died young? It still seemed odd that no one would ever mention her, even sadly or in passing. It was like she'd been wiped off the face of the earth.

My stomach rumbled—it had been ages since I'd eaten anything. I put the lawyer's papers on my dad's desk and took the photos to my room.

The next day, I realized I could go through everything in the house and no one would stop me. I cringed at the idea—if I found weird stuff, I would freak out. Some things you just don't want to know, especially about your parents.

But . . . there was the family book. Papi hadn't had a chance to tell me where it was, only that I would continue it for my kids. My nonexistent kids. Was I ready to see it? Would I at least find out who Donella was?

Our living room was lined with bookcases, full of books in English, Spanish, French, and Portuguese. After I took the papers to the lawyer's office, I would go through them. Maybe.

That afternoon Ms. Carsons, the lawyer, gazed at me with concern. I'd felt shaky and trembly driving there. The sun had seemed too bright, noises too loud. I had to start getting out more. But as soon as I had that thought, another thought followed it: *Why?*

I sat on the dark green leather chair in Ms. Carsons' office as she went over a bunch of legal stuff, wills and probate and whatever, and I gave her the documents. A lot I didn't understand—it was hard to concentrate. Basically she said I had enough money and that she would take care of everything. I nodded and agreed to whatever she said. I was getting up to leave when she put a gentle hand on my arm.

"Viviana, are you . . . are you talking to anyone? Like a counselor? Or a grief therapist?"

It hadn't occurred to me. "I have my friends," I said. The best of whom was in Tel Aviv. I hadn't been returning texts from the rest.

"You've gone through an unimaginable tragedy," Ms. Carsons said softly, concern in her light blue eyes. "You need to talk to someone. You need to not be alone."

"Hm," I said. People kept telling me that. "Okay. Thanks."

Chapter Three

IT WAS A RELIEF TO COME BACK TO THE FAMILIAR air-conditioned scents of our house. Actually, there were no scents of either cooking or laundry because I was doing neither one, so in that way the house smelled different. But all of the rest of it was . . . home.

Taking my time, I looked at every book in every bookcase in the house: the ones in the living room, the ones in the hallway, the ones in my dad's office. I didn't find anything that seemed like it could be our family book. I pictured it as being like a scrapbook, like Tia Juliana had said, or a Christian Bible. My parents had told me that our religion didn't have written documents—everything had always been passed down orally. For aeons, apparently.

The books in my dad's office were all for his job. My mom had a desk in the corner of the living room that she had hardly ever used. She'd graded papers at the big kitchen table, and used my dad's computer. But I went over to her desk and saw Post-its on her bulletin board, notices of dentist appointments and a shop that repaired furniture and a loyalty card to our local ice cream shop. One more visit and she would have gotten a free cone.

It was strange sitting in the chair, looking at the desk. Even her desk was feminine—whitewashed and stenciled, with scaled-down lines and a delicate frame. Timidly I opened a drawer, saw extra pens and pushpins and a staple remover. The middle drawer had a tube of lip balm, rubber bands, a tiny vial of her favorite perfume, a picture of my dad, and a Valentine's card I'd made her in fourth grade. When I'd made that card, I'd thought my mom would live forever.

Tears ran down my face, but I was used to it and just wiped my eyes with the hem of my T-shirt. I pulled the drawer out more and heard paper crumple in the back. Feeling with my hands, I found an envelope stuck between the drawer and the desktop, and gradually eased it out without ripping it.

It was a regular letter envelope, addressed by hand to my mom. It was empty, no letter inside. I looked at the return address and my breath caught in my throat. Donella Garrison. Quickly I scanned the post office stamp—it was dated more than ten years ago, but long after that photo of the three sisters.

Donella Garrison. The actual address was smudged, as if the ink had gotten wet, but I could still read it. Esplanade Avenue, New Orleans, Louisiana. My aunt Donella had lived in New Orleans. Maybe lived there still.

The Internet gave me the same address, a husband's name—Patrick—and a phone number. I called the number with a shaking hand. I would have to tell her that her sister was dead. Maybe she'd hated my mom. Maybe she would hang up on me. Maybe she would tell Tia Juliana that I'd contacted her, and then Tia Juliana would be mad at me for discovering the family secret.

There was no answer. No answering machine.

It was even harder to call the second time, hours later. Still no answer.

The next morning, when I woke up, I knew what I wanted to do for the first time since my parents had died.

I wanted to go to New Orleans.

"Oh no, not by yourself," Jennifer said, when we Skyped that afternoon. "By the way, you look like crap. Have you looked in a mirror lately?"

"Why not by myself?"

"Viv, seriously, how much do you weigh? I'm worried. I'm going to call my mom and have her go over there."

"I'm fine. I'm going to drive there. I have a GPS."

Jennifer was silent. In the background I heard people talking and laughing loudly.

"To find this mystery aunt. Who is probably a mystery for a good reason."

"Yeah?" I cleared my throat and sounded more definite. "Yes."

Someone came up behind Jennifer, and she waved them away.

"I don't like it. It seems like too far to drive by yourself. I wish I could go with you."

"Thank you, H."

"I know you're going to do what you want," Jennifer said, resigned. "But promise me you'll eat. If you lose any more weight, I'm telling my mother. Take your cell phone. Do you have Triple A?"

I smiled, and I was so unused to it that it felt odd, like my face was wrinkling.

"Okay, okay, and yes," I said, loving Jennifer so much.

"Call me when you get there. Let me know what happens with the mystery aunt."

"I will. Later, HD."

"Bye, babe." Jennifer made a kissing sound at the camera and hung up.

Now that I'd had this idea, I couldn't let go of it. I tried to think of all the grown-up things I should do before I left town, like stopping mail and telling the neighbors. After asking Mrs. Peachtree next door for advice, I sold Papi's Escalade at CarMax, because I was eighteen and could do stuff like that.

My tia Juliana called as I was finally doing laundry so I could pack. At first she had called every day, then every couple of days, and now about once a week. I didn't want to tell her about going to New Orleans to find Donella. She'd never mentioned Donella to me, and until I knew why, I didn't want to upset her or, worse, have her try to stop me. Instead I told her that I was turning off the house phone to save money, and she should call my cell phone from now on. I didn't mention New Orleans, didn't mention I was leaving town, and hoped she wouldn't plan a surprise visit.

It was even harder than usual to sleep that night. My brain

churned with ideas of what I might find in New Orleans, and over and over I went through my mental checklist of things I needed to do before I left. Finally I gave up, exhausted. I was only going to be gone a couple of days, after all. It wasn't like I was leaving forever.

In the middle of one of my nightmares I bolted up in bed, my hand over my mouth. Cold sweat stuck my T-shirt to my skin, my heart was pounding, and my breath came in fast pants. I'd dreamed I was back in the Everglades, in the clearing. I'd heard the first growl, the one that had made the hairs on the back of my neck rise.

There was a can of warm, flat soda on my bedside table, and I took a gulp. This was the first nightmare in several days—I'd thought I was getting better.

Then . . . I heard something. My very first thought was that Mami or Papi was getting home late and unlocking the kitchen door. My second thought crushed that one. But . . . someone or something was trying to get in.

Get into my house.

In my dream, in the clearing, all three of us had heard the growl. The attacker was in the deep shadow of the woods but obviously knew we were there, had followed us or something. The attacker must have seen me run away. Knew I had escaped. They hadn't waited around—otherwise they could have killed me while I was waiting for the cops. The gods knew I'd been an easy target right then.

Scritch. Scritch. Something was definitely messing with the kitchen door.

They were coming to get me. They knew where I was, knew I was alone, and were coming to finish the job. Suddenly the legend of the Talofomé came into my mind, but I dismissed it. Like Tia Juliana had said, this was just an evil haguaro, with maybe a pelado partner.

I couldn't breathe. When I was little—actually, until last month—whenever I'd heard a scary sound at night, all I'd had to do was remember that my parents were there. As soon as I'd realized that, I would quit worrying and go back to sleep. This was the first time I couldn't take comfort from that thought. The first time I had no one to protect me. No one except myself.

Terror made me shiver with cold as I scrambled into sweatpants and grabbed my aluminum baseball bat. Holding the bat tightly with one hand, I dialed 911 on my cell phone with the other. This time I could speak, and in an urgent whisper I begged them to send a patrol car to my address. As I hung up, I heard glass breaking in the kitchen and had to bite my lip so I wouldn't scream.

Should I lock myself in my bedroom? Climb out my bedroom window? Horrible images of my parents flashed through my mind—I wouldn't be able to defend myself against this. If this person had killed my parents, then I had no chance.

Or . . . maybe it was just a random break-in? Someone who thought the house was empty because of the uncut lawn and the pile of newspapers by the front door?

I swung the bat onto my shoulder and started silently down the hall, praying to hear sirens. At the kitchen doorway I leaned against the wall, listening. After the glass breaking it had gone quiet, as if they were making sure that the noise hadn't alerted anyone.

Very slowly I poked my head around the corner. I saw well in the dark, of course, and so I could clearly make out the gloved hand snaking through the broken pane on the door, reaching for the deadbolt.

Sudden fury lit my blood with adrenaline. How dare they? How dare someone come here to hurt me or to rob this house? I sprang forward on bare feet, the bat raised high, then slammed it against the hand as hard as I could. Shockingly, I heard their bones breaking, followed by a horrified scream of pain, then the welcome sounds of police sirens. I raised the bat again as the hand was dragged out of the broken pane, and then footsteps ran through the garage and out the side door.

Quickly I punched the garage door opener, and it started to rise just as patrol cars swung into the driveway. Running out to meet them, I shouted, "He got out through the back! He's in the backyard!"

Two officers ran toward the back, and another one pulled out a clipboard to take my statement. I showed her the broken glass, and saw that it was dripping with blood.

"I hit their hand with my bat," I explained. "I guess it got shoved down on the broken glass."

The officer looked at the blood running down the door and said, "They'll be lucky if it didn't almost cut their hand off. Can you describe the intruder?"

"Well, it was a person," I said without thinking. It had been a hand and not a paw that I'd smashed.

"Yes, honey," said the policewoman. "I figured it probably wasn't a bear. Do you need to sit down?"

An hour later, the cops hadn't caught the guy, I'd given them as much information as I could ("black glove"), and the curious and alarmed neighbors had all made sure I was okay and then gone home.

Before they left, the police made sure the kitchen door could still lock, and even found a small piece of wood to cover the broken pane in the door.

"Will you be all right here?" one of them asked. "Do you want a ride to a friend's house?"

Jennifer's parents would take me in with no question, I knew, but I shook my head. "I'm okay. Thanks for coming so fast."

There was no way I could sleep after that. I stayed alert, bat in hand, and listened to every sound from every corner of the house. Why hadn't I thought of that before, that of course my parents' attacker had seen me? Maybe because I'd been a complete raving basket case. Like it or not, I was a haguara, and the attacker knew it. And had come to kill me tonight.

Good thing I was leaving town.

When the sun came up, I felt gritty-eyed and wrung out, but still determined to head to New Orleans. I waited till a semidecent hour, then talked to my neighbors on both sides, asking them to call the cops if they saw anyone at my house, telling them I'd be home in just a few days, and giving them my cell-phone number.

Finally, feeling as if I were about to drive off the edge of the earth, I grabbed the suitcases I'd packed, put everything else I might need into a couple of laundry baskets, and loaded the car up. With my baseball bat on the front seat beside me, I started the engine, then turned it off again. Back in the house, I ran down the hallway to my parents' room, where I yanked off the bedspread and grabbed the top sheet from their bed. I bundled the sheet up, carried it to the car, and threw it in the backseat. Then, very carefully, as if I had just started driving, I backed Mami's green Honda out of the driveway.

I'd totally underestimated how not eating solid food for a month could deplete my energy and ability to think clearly. Not to mention the break-in last night, and staying awake till dawn. It was a twelve-hour drive from Sugar Beach on the western coast of Florida, to New Orleans, but by four o'clock in the afternoon I could barely see straight. I checked into a Holiday Inn and cried until I fell asleep. Crying was still a normal state for me, like breathing.

Once again my brain kept me awake most of the night—I would sleep, dream, wake up, cry, then repeat the pattern. The next morning I finally woke, feeling more tired than when I had gone to bed. I showered to clear my head and get the crying grit out of my eyes, and filled the car with gas. Then I headed west again to New Orleans and, I hoped, the answers to some questions.

The drive up through Florida, then quickly through Alabama and Mississippi and into Louisiana, was not the most interesting drive in the world. It wasn't ugly, but the land was flat. The trees were mostly pines. No hills, no mountains in the distance, no Blue Ridge Parkway vistas. And the farther away from home I got, the more twitchy I became. I was really tempted to turn around, drive back home, and curl up in my bed. Except the house was violated now, my safety there compromised. Maybe it had been a random break-in. After all, why would my parents' attacker wait a month to come after me? Unless it had taken that long to figure out where I lived. Which meant they had known that my parents were haguari, but nothing more, like their names or address. I was so sick of thinking about it.

This trip to New Orleans was the best thing I could do right now. Before last night, I'd felt my parents' presence in our house, smelled their scents, felt the dimming reverberations of their voices. When I was at home I could picture them in every room, in every lighting, doing all the things that had made up the hammock-cocoon of my life.

But everything at home that reminded me of them also reminded me of my searing grief. The more I wallowed in my grief, the worse I felt. I needed to take a break from it. Plus, last night's break-in had shattered that cocoon and taken away my memories' almost magical power to keep me connected to my parents. Now I was out here on the road and so much more alone. Not only was my anchor up, but it had run out on its chain and was lost in the sea forever.

I pressed down on the gas and kept going.

In the afternoon I crossed the Mississippi River. It was wide, greenish-brown, and had tankers docked along both banks. Getting off the bridge was confusing, and I got a little rattled, especially when someone honked at me, but I found the right exit, and my GPS program took me to the address I'd gotten from the envelope. I'd tried calling again this morning, with no better luck than before.

Esplanade Avenue bordered the French Quarter. I drove along the French Market to Esplanade, which was wide, with huge live oak trees that met overhead. The median was planted with big, familiar shrubs: azaleas, oleanders, camellias. Parked cars lined both sides of the street, and I drove slowly, looking for a place to stop.

Then I was there. A wrought-iron fence lined with tall, thick shrubs enclosed the yard, broken by a clear space behind an ornate iron gate. I parked and peered through my car window, able to catch only a glimpse of the house. *What am I doing here?* I wondered even as I got out of my car. An old, uneven brick walkway, splotched with moss, led to the house, which I now saw was enormous. Hesitantly I pushed the gate open and stood looking at where my aunt might live.

Both the covered front porch and a second-floor balcony ran right across the whole width of the house. French windows nine feet high stood in pairs on either side of the double front door, which was wooden and pointed in the middle like a church window. A thick mass of confederate jasmine covered half the porch railing and climbed to the second floor. It had rained this morning, and between the heat and the humidity, the air was scented so heavily it was almost cloying.

Slowly, unable to imagine how this was going to play out, I climbed the wide marble steps and rang the doorbell. I had rehearsed my speech all the way from Florida. *Hi, my name is Vivi Neves. I think I'm your niece. . . . I have bad news. . . .*

There was no answer. I was both relieved and disappointed. Well, I could wait. After coming this far, I couldn't stand to leave, even for a while. The thought of getting in my car again made me feel desolate, and I had absolutely no plan B. At the bottom of the porch steps I paused, seeing the narrow brick path that ran around the house. It felt nosy and presumptuous, but I followed it into the side yard. The fence and tall shrubs separated this yard from the side street, and I walked past the overgrown garden beds and across the grass so I could see the entire house at once.

The architecture was so typical that it looked like it belonged in a movie set in New Orleans. Tall, beautiful, a bit ramshackle, the house had once been painted lavender, but bare stucco now dotted the walls like a disease, and the dark green shutters were peeling. Lacy black wrought iron defined balconies and porches, but some of it was rusty, and I saw places where pieces had broken off.

The yard showed the same signs of neglect—bushes were overgrown and shapeless; the raggedy lawn was sprinkled with weeds and dead tree branches. More weeds choked the formal garden beds, as if they were trying to strangle the old roses and hydrangeas, the plumbagos and daylilies.

My gods, it was hot. The air was thick and damp. Lush, oversized plants were everywhere, as if nature were determined to reclaim what had once been swamp. It was so similar to home.

What was I doing here? I was stalking a stranger who I thought might be my mother's long-lost sister. There was no reason to think she would want to see me. Or that she still lived here. Or that she was even still alive.

All of a sudden I felt awash in despair, and I sat down abruptly beneath an enormous magnolia tree. I thought of the long, long drive back home, and how home reminded me only of anguish, nightmarish pain, and now fear and vulnerability. Once again I started to cry. I was so tired. I was hot and uncertain and lost. I didn't know what to do with myself.

Physical and emotional exhaustion overcame me, and I must have fallen asleep, siting there on the bony roots of the tree. Waking from scary, disjointed dreams that left me heavy-limbed and upset, I found myself on the ground, in the darkness, in a strange yard. For a second it was like being in the woods, in the Everglades, and my muscles instantly tensed.

What time was it? I started to get up, and then I heard it: a very low growl that turned my blood to ice in my veins. It was soft, like a motorboat engine seconds before it explodes with power. Just like that day with Mami and Papi.

I froze, my breath snagging in my throat. Lit with instant adrenaline, I stayed very still and scanned the yard. Was this it? Had last night's attacker followed me? Was it my turn to die?

The growling continued, and with horror I realized it was above me. Cold sweat beaded on my forehead and my back where my shirt was already sticking to me. I couldn't breathe, couldn't swallow. Slowly I looked up into the magnolia branches, and there it was: a jaguar. Its golden coat, broken by black rosettes, stood out against the dark brown bark. Its eyes were yellow, cold, and fixed on me in a predator's hungry gaze. Did it have a smashed paw? A deep slice in its palm?

My hands curled in the dirt as I edged up to a sitting position. I didn't know how to change into my jaguar form on purpose—I had refused to learn. I couldn't put two thoughts together. I'd come all this way just to die, and without understanding why. Like my parents.

I tried to say, "What do you want?" but my words were soundless puffs of air.

The jaguar gave a louder growl, showing long, knifelike fangs. I was lightheaded, about to faint. Unable to move, hopeless at defending myself—for me, fainting would be a blessing. My eyes were drawn to the powerful tail that lashed back and forth, thunking against the tree trunk.

And then . . . it gave a fierce, sickening roar, and leaped at me.

Chapter Four

MY EYES SHUT AS I WAITED TO FEEL VISELIKE jaws closing around my skull. Seconds passed. Finally I slit one eye to see the jaguar crouched in front of me, snarling, its tail whipping left and right. It was going to toy with me, play with me before I died. All four of its paws seemed fine, not broken or cut, I noticed a bit hysterically. Was it a jaguar jaguar or a haguari? Was there a way to tell? I knew so little about it. Surely it was a haguari.

I felt lost in its yellow eyes and couldn't pull my gaze away, even as my brain registered the quiet opening of a door and then a shadowy figure moving toward us. I tried to shriek "Run!" but it came out as a near-silent squeak. The figure came closer. Surely the jaguar would pounce on me the instant I looked away, but I held my breath and slid my glance past it to see a young, dark-haired woman walking closer. I stared at her, hoping she knew this animal, hoping I wasn't luring her to her death.

The jaguar thumped its tail against her legs as she strode past it. "Stop it," she said firmly, shooting it a disapproving look. It snarled at her, opening its jaws and displaying deadly fangs that glowed in the darkness. She pulled back her foot and kicked its flank, her colorful striped espadrille barely making a sound against the heavy muscle. "Stop it! Go inside!"

Yellow eyes narrowed. She sighed and shook her head, then looked at me, her face kind. "Are you lost?"

I slowly pointed one finger at the huge cat.

"Don't mind him," she said, crouching down to my level. "He's being a butt."

The jaguar's mouth opened, and a slow, deep rumble came from its chest. If the young woman hadn't been there, so unconcerned, I would have peed myself.

I swallowed, trying to lubricate a throat gone dry with fear. Finally I managed, "I'm looking for Donella Garrison. Or Donella Féliznundo." Which had been my mother's name before she got married.

The young woman blinked at me, and oddly, the jaguar did too. They exchanged a look like people do, and then the jaguar turned abruptly and loped through the shadows back to the house. I saw its large form slink up some concrete stairs and through an open doorway.

I let out a deep breath, not aware I'd been holding it. The amber light of a streetlamp cast patched shadows on the woman's face, which was now regarding me more coldly.

"What do you want with her?" Her voice was unfriendly.

Swallowing again, I sat up a little straighter. I was really hungry, really thirsty, and really tired. If she left me, I would probably just lie down again and sleep under this tree for a week. "I think's she my aunt. My mother's sister."

Someone else came out of the house: a guy, wearing beat-up jeans low on his hips and a plaid short-sleeved shirt, unbuttoned. His hair was dark red, long, and messy. He came and stood silently next to the girl, his arms crossed over his chest.

"I'm Vivi Neves," I told them. "My mother was Aracita Féliznundo before she got married, and she had, I think, two sisters: Juliana and Donella. I'm looking for Donella. I think her married name was Garrison. Do you know her? Does she live here? Did she used to live here, maybe?"

"Your mother is Aracita? Donella's sister?" the guy asked, looking at me intently.

"Yes," I said. "Do you know her? Donella?"

"Huh. Maybe you should come inside," said the young woman, standing up.

I didn't even feel like I could stand, but I managed to get to my feet without toppling over.

"Donella was my mother," the guy said slowly, looking at me. "I'm Matéo Garrison. But my mother's sisters are dead."

"No," I said, shaking my head. Donella was his mother? *Was* his mother. Was she dead also? "Juliana is alive. My mother was alive . . . till May."

This guy would be my . . . cousin. A cousin I never knew I had, never spent summers with, never saw in family albums. What had happened between my mother and her sister?

The guy frowned. "Aly's right—you should probably come in."

I didn't know what else to do. I hadn't planned for anything after this. Steadying myself, I followed Matéo and Aly through the over-grown grass to four cement steps leading to the side door, which had once been painted white. A large piece of glass barely held in place with chipped putty made up the top half of the door, and the bottom half had decorative molding.

I heard voices as I climbed the steps; the door led into an enormous kitchen that seemed to be full of people. Smells of cooking food made my nose twitch, and I couldn't remember the last time I had eaten. Some cold cereal at the Holiday Inn this morning?

The room quieted as people registered that I was there. A quick glance showed that everyone seemed around the same age—early twenties. No one was old enough to be my aunt or uncle.

Matéo said, "Come on this way," and walked through the kitchen to a hallway beyond. The girl, Aly, and I followed him. I was wiped out, strung out, and still freaked about the jaguar . . . who must have been my haguaro cousin. Walking through a crowd of strangers, all of whom were looking at me, didn't calm me down.

The three of us went down a dark, wide hallway toward the front of the house. Right before we got to the beautiful gothic front doors, Matéo took a left into a lovely formal parlor with old-fashioned furniture.

"You want to sit down?" he said, gesturing to a deep blue velvet couch with an ornate wooden back. I sat down on it, hardly able to believe that I was here, that I had found an aunt I had never known about. "What was your name again?"

"Vivi Neves. Viviana."

"You said your mother is my mother's sister?"

"Yeah."

Matéo turned and went to a wall covered with all sorts of framed photographs. He took one down and brought it to me.

It was a copy of the photo I'd seen in the bag in my dad's safe.

"Who are these people?" he asked, setting the frame on the table and sitting down.

"This is my tia Juliana, my mother, Aracita, and then Donella. This was taken in Brazil."

Matéo nodded as if I'd passed a test. And he'd just passed my test too—if he had this photo, he truly must be part of my family.

"I never knew Donella existed," I said again. "Is she . . ."

"My parents died a year and a half ago," said Matéo.

"Oh, no," I said, feeling myself deflate even further. I'd never known that Donella existed, but finding out that I'd come all this way for nothing was almost unbearably disappointing. "I'm really sorry." Matéo and I simply looked at each other. I began to see a family resemblance in the line of his jaw, the slant of his dark eyes. Despite his tan, unfreckled skin, his hair was a very dark red, and I guessed that was the Garrison part.

"Why are you looking for my mother?" Matéo asked.

Here we were—the crux of the matter. My throat tightened. "I wanted to tell your mom . . . that her sister is . . . dead." My voice trailed off. "My parents died . . . a month ago, at the end of May. Juliana knows. I wanted to tell Donella myself." A month ago. In some ways it felt like just last week, and in some ways it felt like two years. A lifetime.

"I'm so sorry," Aly said, and put her hand on mine briefly. I gave her a thin smile and saw that she was younger than I'd first thought—maybe twenty or twenty-one. Matéo looked about the same age.

It was all so surreal—the truth that my parents were actually dead, that I had driven all this way by myself, that I was now sitting talking to a cousin I'd never known I'd had. I thought of my other cousins, Juliana's son and daughter, who were eight and ten years younger than me. They lived in Brazil, but I still knew them better, had seen them more, than this cousin just a few states away from Florida.

"I'm sorry too," Matéo said. "I thought—the way my mom talked, I thought your mom had died a long time ago. But it was recent?"

"Uh-huh." My voice was tiny. "So you were . . . that jaguar outside."

Matéo looked at me as if I were an idiot. "Yeah, of course. I found a stranger sleeping in my yard." His eyes narrowed as he regarded me. "Did you say both your parents died? Was it an accident? A car wreck?"

"No," I said. "They were . . . attacked. Someone killed them." My eyes felt hot and started stinging.

Matéo frowned. "Oh, no."

I nodded, a minuscule movement. "My dad's heart." I let out a deep breath. "His heart was cut out. Someone took it. They tried to take my mom's. But I came back and saw her, and she was alive. For a minute. She looked at me—she looked at me and said, 'Donella? I've missed you.' Then she died. So I wanted to know who Donella was."

"Oh, how awful," Aly said softly. "You do look like her, you know. Donella. How did you find out who she was?"

My face was wet with tears, which I barely noticed. "I found this same picture in my dad's safe. Later, in my mom's desk, I found an empty envelope—a letter your mom had sent to my mom. It had this return address on it."

"How did you get here? Where do you live?" Matéo asked.

"I drove. My mom's . . . my car is out front. We live—I live—in Sugar Beach, Florida. A little town by the Everglades, on the west coast."

"Hm," said Matéo. He and Aly exchanged a look. Leaning forward, he traced around the picture frame with one finger. He seemed to be thinking about something, and I didn't interrupt him. All I wanted to do was lie down somewhere and cry.

Aly put her hand on Matéo's shoulder and rubbed it gently. "It's weird that your parents were killed, and your dad's heart was taken," she said to me, watching Matéo. His face didn't change. I wondered if Aly was a haguara—if not, she was incredibly accepting of our affliction. "Donella and Patrick—Téo's dad—were killed too.

At first it looked like a car wreck, but there was an explosion and a fire, so the police investigated it. Téo's parents were inside."

"Oh, no," I said again. "I'm so sorry." Was our family cursed?

"They did autopsies," Matéo broke in. "Because it was a suspicious death. Their hearts were missing. We figured it must have been some psycho. If there was any evidence, it was burned up."

"Wait—their hearts were missing?" I asked. I took a deep breath. "You know what? Two nights ago, someone tried to break into my house, my parents' house. I hit his hand with a baseball bat, and the cops chased him but didn't catch him. But I couldn't help wondering if it was the same person who killed my parents. I mean, I don't know why they were killed. I don't know why someone would be coming after me. I guess I thought it was something about us, my family. But now, with your parents—I don't see how their deaths, their missing hearts, could be a coincidence. It's too weird. But what's going on? Is our family in particular being targeted?" My shoulders drooped. I'd come here hoping for answers—not more questions. My brain was barely stringing sentences together—I didn't want to think about it anymore. Tomorrow. I could think about it tomorrow.

"I don't know," Matéo said. "But it's definitely suspicious."

"Yeah," I said. My thoughts were coming in fits and starts. I wanted to talk to Matéo for a whole month, nonstop, but another wave of fatigue came over me and I realized I was going to collapse. Reluctantly I stood up. "It's been so great meeting you," I said. "Both of you. But I'm more tired than I realized—I can hardly think straight. I just got to town—can you point me toward a hotel? Not too expensive. But safe?"

Aly patted my arm. "Did you see all the weirdos in the kitchen?"

"Yeah. I mean . . . I didn't think they were weird," I said awkwardly.

Aly laughed. "They are. Basically, most of them live here."

I must have had my doglike head-cocked-to-one-side look, because Matéo explained. "This was my parents' house. Now it's mine. It's really big and expensive to keep up. So we rent out rooms. Right now we have . . ." He paused and counted silently. "Five people, plus us. One of our friends just moved out last week, so you could have her room."

I was embarrassed. "I wasn't hinting—I really am fine with a hotel." I didn't know how I felt about suddenly staying with a bunch of strangers, even if one of them was my cousin.

Matéo stood. "No—it's settled. You're family. You should definitely stay here."

I hesitated, thinking about how my parents always welcomed people into our house. Friends of friends, children of friends— they were glad to host them. Sometimes our guest room was occupied for weeks. Once, the daughter of someone my mother went to school with stayed for three months, while she worked to save money for college.

Despite the whole boarding-house thing, this felt familiar. Matéo looked like my family, was my family. And I was truly running on my last bit of adrenaline. The idea of getting in my car to drive to a hotel was more than I could face. I could stay one night. If things seemed weird tomorrow, I would have more energy and could find a new place to stay.

"Okay. Thanks," I said.

Aly got to her feet. "Let's move your car into the yard."

Walking back out through the large, old-fashioned kitchen was a little easier because only three people were still there. Aly introduced me to two girls and a guy, all of whose names and faces went right out of my head a second later. Matéo showed me how to drive around the corner and pull in through a side gate. This led to a larger area covered with crushed oyster shells where four other cars were parked. I left my mom's Honda next to a pickup truck, and Matéo shut the gate behind me.

I only needed my smallest case, just for one night. Matéo grabbed it. Too weary to feel self-conscious, I fished my parents' sheet out of the backseat, and then we crunched over the shells to the side door. This time the kitchen was empty.

Inside, Matéo said, "I'll give you the full tour tomorrow. Right now we'll just go upstairs—you look wiped."

I gave him a wan smile and wondered if I could make it up a flight of stairs. I'd noticed the staircase when we'd walked past it before—it was wide and beautiful, rising upward in a graceful curve. Faint music drifted down from above. I felt vibrations as people walked on the floor overhead.

"There are five bedrooms on the second floor," Aly said as I followed the worn places on the wooden stair treads. The handrail was as smooth as marble, worn down by a hundred and fifty years of hands stroking it, gripping its sides. "And then six more on the third floor—they used to be servants' quarters."

Matéo had snapped off lights as we'd left the downstairs and didn't bother turning any on as we reached the second floor. Moonlight and light from the streetlamp shone through tall windows, casting pale, slanted rectangles across the wooden floors and patched plaster walls. As with the downstairs, everything looked run-down, in need of paint. I heard a toilet flush, heard hushed conversation and low laughter. Maybe I shouldn't stay here. But as soon as I had that thought, I knew that I couldn't possibly make it anywhere else. I felt barely conscious, swaying on my feet.

"That's our room," Aly said, pointing toward the back of the house. "This one in front is where Coco sleeps. You'll stay in this other front one—it's nice and big and has its own bathroom." She smiled at me, and I tried to smile back. "There's a hall bathroom," she went on. "Three people share it: Coco, James, and Suzanne. James and Suzanne are in the room next to yours. Then Dana and Tink live upstairs."

Matéo, walking ahead, opened a tall door leading to the right-hand front bedroom. He set my case on the floor. "Here you go. The bathroom is tiny—it used to be a closet—but it's all yours."

I stopped in the doorway. Our house in Florida was a typical seventies one-story ranch, with eight-foot ceilings, plain doors, small windows, and a peaked roof in the family room. This house was enormous, with fourteen-foot ceilings on both floors, nine-foot-tall

French windows everywhere, and ornate plaster and wide, fancy molding on the baseboards and around the ceilings.

It was one of the grandest rooms I'd ever been in. The tall double bed with a half tester was draped in coral-colored watered silk. The mattress came up almost to my waist. In one corner of the room, an oval full-length mirror on a stand reflected our shadowy selves. Between the two French windows that led to the second-story porch was an enormous armoire, maybe seven feet tall and six feet wide. Its wood was dark and shiny and its fittings were brass. Heavy silk curtains that matched the bed hangings gave off little puffs of dust as Aly closed them, and she sneezed.

"Sorry," she said. "I don't think Miranda ever cleaned in here. We'll hit it tomorrow. I'll get some fresh sheets."

"It's fine. Beautiful," I said, but Aly had already gone.

When Matéo clicked the bedside light on, we blinked—it seemed almost too bright, after the darkness. "There's the bathroom," he said, pointing to a door on the other side of the bed. "There should be towels and stuff in there."

"Thank you so much," I said, overwhelmed. "This is gorgeous. I really appreciate it." My eyes started burning, and I blinked several times. I'd felt very alone since Tia Juliana had left, and that last night in my parents' house I'd felt the most alone ever, waiting in the darkness with my baseball bat. Which I now remembered was down in my car. Damn it. I was sure I didn't need it, but still.

Anyway, to be here now with family was comforting.

Aly came back, her arms full of folded linens. "Do you want me to help you put them on?" she asked.

I shook my head. "No, thanks, I can do it."

"Okay, well, we'll talk tomorrow," said Matéo.

"If you need anything else, there's a cupboard in the hallway where we keep spares and extras," said Aly, and I nodded. "Sleep well."

"Thank you," I said inadequately, and they left, closing the door behind them.

I peeked in at the bathroom. It was small and narrow, with a shower, sink, and toilet—no bathtub, which was fine. Overhead, someone walked almost silently in an attic room. The tall windows showed the darkness outside, and I went over to them, wondering how sturdy the locks were. We were on the second floor, but I remembered how easily I'd jumped fifteen feet up into a tree, and shivered. Surely the attacker hadn't followed me here. Guiltily I wondered if I was exposing my cousin—and everyone else here— to danger. But Matéo's parents had been killed a year and a half ago, and he hadn't mentioned any ensuing attacks on himself. So maybe I was being paranoid. Maybe trouble hadn't followed me.

I kicked off my shoes, pulled back the covers on the tall bed, and climbed in. Flopping down onto the pillows felt like dropping into a bowl of marshmallow fluff. Holding my parents' sheet like a stuffed animal, I breathed in their scents until I fell asleep.

Chapter Five

I PULL MY MOTHER'S HEAD ONTO MY LAP. HER blood runs red and unexpectedly warm down the skin of my legs. I stroke her fur, look into the golden eyes. Beneath my fingers she begins to change, shrinking, fur disappearing, hair growing long and black. The change continues as I watch in horror—her skin melts away; her muscles wither and curl back from her shining white skull like drying apple peels. Her golden eyes stare at me from fleshless sockets, unable to blink. Screaming, I drop her skull, kicking to get away from it. Then I'm staring at a skeleton, lying on blood-soaked grass. A skeleton with my mother's eyes and hair.

I jolted awake, skin clammy with sweat, heart pounding. Yet another nightmare, though this was a new one. Would I ever not have nightmares?

It took a minute before I remembered where I was, why I was sleeping in this tall, fancy bed. The room was dim, and I clicked my cell phone to see what time it was. Two thirty. Narrow blades of hot sunlight sliced through where the curtains met: It was light outside, so it was two thirty in the afternoon? When I'd collapsed last night, it had been barely ten. I'd slept for . . . sixteen hours? I hadn't slept that much since—

Frowning, I went to the windows and pulled open the curtains. Bright light streamed in, making me blink and step back, warming my skin even through the glass. Summer in New Orleans.

I looked around the room, seeing what I hadn't noticed last night. The walls were a pale green, faded and uneven in color. Some of the plaster had cracked and been crudely repaired. The ceiling had cracks in it too. But the furniture was beautiful—I assumed real antiques. My small case sat on the floor, but I didn't feel up to opening it and finding something to wear. Or taking a shower. Or brushing my hair. Instead, I realized I was hungry.

Before I opened my door, I listened, hoping to not hear voices. Facing a bunch of strangers would be a challenge. Maybe everyone was at work. I opened the door and found myself in a hallway that was wider than my room at home. Double French doors lit the hallway at each end, front and back. Through the window panes I saw porches; the one in the back of the house looked screened in. All the doors that opened off the hallway were shut, and I pulled mine shut too. Barefoot, I padded downstairs, the wooden steps cool and satiny. My eyes were again drawn to all the beautiful architectural details of the house. The woodwork was detailed in a way you don't see in modern houses, and even the doors were well made and beautiful. Crystal chandeliers hung from flowery plaster medallions in the centers of the ceilings; the long panes of glass in the windows were wavy and old.

The house was quiet, but I felt weird about exploring without Matéo or Aly. I wondered where they were, then heard the sound of . . . maybe a drill? It was coming from the double parlors on the right-hand side of the house. I poked my head in the door. What had once been a formal dining room was now a . . . workshop? Rows of small hand tools hung neatly on one wall, and two large worktables were covered with table saws and drill presses and miter boxes. A fine layer of sawdust coated everything. Matéo was bent over a table, placing something carefully in a small vise. I must have made a sound, because he suddenly looked up.

"Sorry," I said. "Didn't mean to disturb you."

"Hey," Matéo said. "I'm glad you finally woke up. I was starting to think you'd fallen into a coma."

I laughed awkwardly.

"Come on, get some breakfast," he said, putting his work down.

"This house is so beautiful," I said. "Is it really old?"

"Nah, not really," Matéo said, shrugging. Together we headed to the kitchen at the back of the house. "Maybe 1860 or so. There are much older buildings in the Quarter. You want an egg?"

My stomach recoiled. "Maybe just some toast?"

"You got it. First some coffee."

I started to say I didn't drink coffee, then thought it might be rude to reject everything he offered. When he placed the handleless bowl of coffee with milk in front of me, it smelled really good. I took a tentative sip.

"This is great," I said, deciding my mom hadn't known how to make coffee.

"It's hard to make bad coffee in New Orleans," my cousin said. "But it has to be CDM. Café du Monde. Makes all the difference." When toast popped out of a toaster, he spread it with butter, then put it in front of me. The warm bread melted the butter, and it was an explosion of flavor in my mouth. Not wanting to overwhelm my system with solid food, I forced myself to take small bites, waiting in between each one.

"Um, where is everyone?" I said.

"Most of them are at work or school," said Matéo, sitting down with his own bowl of coffee. "Some are still asleep." Leaning his elbows on the table, he closed his eyes and drank his coffee as if it were a ritual.

"It's . . . fun that they all live here."

"Yeah, I guess," he said, opening his eyes. "It sort of happened without me planning it. I was at school in Colorado, and then I got the phone call from the cops." Sadness shadowed his face. "There was a lot of stuff to deal with, you know."

"Yeah. My tia—our tia Juliana did a lot of that for me." What would Tia Juliana think if she knew I was here? Would she be angry? Shocked?

"I ended up just staying, moving back here," said Matéo. "Aly was still here, going to Tulane. We've been going out since we were sixteen."

"Wow."

Matéo grinned a little bit. "So Aly moved in, and that was great.

And gradually, friends started crashing here. There's so much room. Finally I was like, I'm charging your asses."

"How many people live here now?" I asked. "I know you told me."

"Five, plus us. And now you. So eight."

I wasn't at all sure I was going to stay, but I didn't need to decide right this second. So here we were, two cousins getting to know each other over coffee. Except that we were both members of a hidden, ancient race, for lack of a better word. A race that was neither human nor animal, but both. After years of not wanting to know, I now wanted information about our kind. Maybe I would get comfortable enough with Matéo to ask him about it. Someday.

"What does Aly do?"

"Customs," he said, as if that explained anything. "Alyna Cortez, official U. S. Customs and Border Protection agent. New Orleans is a huge port, close to South and Central America. There's a lot of drugs, a lot of smuggling. She can explain it better than I can."

"Oh. What were you doing in your workshop?" Stupid, mundane questions, instead of *Who do you think killed your parents? Who do you think killed my parents? Why in the world would someone steal people's hearts, for gods' sake?*

"I'm a luthier," Matéo said. "I repair stringed instruments, like guitars, violins, basses. Then some nights I'm a bartender at the Fortress, in the Quarter." He smiled and drank the last of his coffee. "You should come with Aly—it's a cool place, and a lot of our people hang out there."

"Our people?"

"Haguari," he said, smiling.

I blinked. "Are there more of us here? You know more haguari?"

Matéo grinned. "Yeah, of course. We're everywhere."

This was astonishing—I'd never met more than maybe eight haguari in my whole life, besides the ones I was related to.

"Last night when you changed, I wondered if you worried that your friends would see you," I said.

"The friends here? Nah. Everyone who lives here is one of us."

"All the people here? All of them are haguari?"

"Yeah, sure," said Matéo. "Couldn't you tell? Were there many of us in—where? Sugar Beach?"

"Yeah—I mean, no, I couldn't tell, last night. But in Sugar Beach—I mean, my parents had a few friends. There are others in Florida, I think. It doesn't seem like a lot, though. I guess I thought that we were rare. I knew there were some in other countries. But not many anywhere."

"No, cousin," said Matéo with a smile. "There's tens of thousands of us, all over the world. Maybe even a hundred thousand. Maybe more. It's not like we have conventions. There're a lot here in New Orleans—you'll be meeting them."

While my brain tried to absorb this amazing fact, Matéo went on: "Did the police ever come up with anything, about who killed your folks?"

"No. I think they're still looking. I guess. What about you? Did the police discover what happened? How much did they investigate?"

"They got nowhere," Matéo said. "When the cops first told me that their hearts had been taken, I wondered if it had been an organ harvester, someone who killed people and harvested their organs and sold them on the black market."

"I hadn't thought of that," I said.

"I asked the cops to check hospitals everywhere, anywhere they do heart transplants. But they found nothing—no hearts suddenly becoming available. It didn't occur to me that someone was collecting haguari hearts in particular."

"No, of course not." I hesitated, then went on. "You know, I was there, when my parents were killed."

Matéo looked dismayed. "You mentioned that you saw your mom—she said my mom's name."

I shuddered. I hadn't talked about the actual event since Tia Juliana had left. "Right. I told you that. Yeah. We were picnicking for my birthday. Then we heard a snarl, a big cat snarl, coming from the woods." I could tell Matéo things I hadn't even told Jennifer.

Matéo leaned forward, his eyes intent. "Wait—you heard a snarl? It was a haguaro who attacked your parents?"

"Yes, it had to have been," I said. "Or a haguara. Some of their injuries were definitely caused by claws. Some by a knife. You mean . . . did you think a regular person killed your parents?"

"Yeah," Matéo said, looking stunned. "I mean, there was no evidence except ash. I guess starting a fire seemed pelado, as opposed to having your skull bitten. But if it was a haguaro . . ." He shook his head. "Okay, tell me everything."

"Um, so we heard this ugly snarl, and my parents jumped up." Would it ever not be searingly painful to remember that day? "Mom told me to run; she pushed me. My dad was already changing, turning into a jaguar. I just ran. Later, I don't know how much later, I went back. My dad was dead. His heart was gone. My mom was still . . . a jaguar. I held her, and she changed back. I asked who did this, and she just looked at me and said, 'Donella? I've missed you.' Then she died." I didn't need to share the "perfect baby" part. It was enough that I'd gotten through the telling of it.

"My gods, how awful," Matéo murmured. "What a nightmare."

I nodded and drank some coffee, wondering if I was going to fall to pieces, as usual.

"If it was a haguari who killed your parents, then maybe it was a haguari who killed mine," said Matéo. "I hadn't even considered that. This is New Orleans—if it wasn't an organ thief, then I figured it was some bizarre voodoo weirdness."

"Do people really do voodoo like that here?" I asked.

"Well, you hear about stuff," Matéo said. "I didn't know what to think."

We sat there in silence for a couple of minutes, drinking our coffee, both of us lost in thought. I gave Matéo some time to absorb the probability that haguari were attacking their own kind. Or at least one haguari.

After a while, Matéo said, "Aly was right—you do look like my mom, at least when she was younger. She had gained weight, gotten older. But pictures of her when she was your age . . . I can see how your mom mistook you for her."

"It's just . . . I never knew about her at all," I said. "Only Tia Juliana. I'd never heard her name—not once. What about you? Did you know about my mom and Tia Juliana?"

"Yes—my mom told me about them. When I asked where they were, she said, 'Gone.' But she never explained. I saw how sad it made her, so I quit asking. I thought they'd died, so it didn't occur to me to look for them. I guess I figured someday I'd go to Brazil and research them or something."

"I wish we knew what happened between them," I said.

"I wish we knew who killed them," Matéo said. "They have to be linked, right? Don't you think? But how? Why?" He pushed back his chair and went to the sink, his back rigid with frustration.

"Your folks died here, in New Orleans?" I asked gently.

He shook his head. "They were on a road trip. They were barely out of the city, just a bit north of the lake."

I let out a breath. It was such a relief to have someone to talk to about this. When Tia Juliana had been with me, I'd been too much of a mess to even think about the hows and whys. I was still a mess, but functioning on a basic level.

"I can't believe everyone who lives here is haguari," I said. "That's more than I've ever met, practically. And they're all young." This seemed amazing.

Footsteps in the hallway made me look up, and a second later a solidly built black girl came into the kitchen. She looked sleepy and was wearing running shorts and an old T-shirt. Her arms and legs were toned and muscled like an athlete's, and her hair was cut quite short and dyed bright maroon. Her face was lovely, heart-shaped, with very full lips and slightly tipped light brown eyes.

"Coffeeeeee," she moaned, her eyes half open, her hands sort of clawing at the air.

"Sit down," Matéo said, fixing her a bowl. "Vivi, this is Dana LeFevre. She lives on the third floor. Dana, this is my cousin Vivi Neves, from Florida."

Dana squinted at me. "Hi, Cousin Vivi. Welcome to Big Cats R Us."

My face felt frozen as I managed a "Hi." For the last five years, practically all my waking moments had been filled with keeping secrets and denying what I was—not only to the world, but to my parents and myself. To have someone be this open—actually make a joke about it—was shocking.

That was the irony. I'd completely and consistently rejected everything about the haguari side of my parents' lives. Then I'd found this surprise aunt, had come here, was thrilled to meet a new cousin—only to find that I was immersed in much more haguari culture than I'd left at home.

How did I feel about that? I liked Matéo and Aly so far. The idea of this—living in a big house in New Orleans with a bunch of cool people—sounded like fun, almost like the dorm I would have been living in, if things were different.

But they were all haguari. My cousin had changed into a jaguar and back last night, so he was obviously really comfortable with it. They probably all were.

I wasn't. The night I'd changed, when my parents . . . it had been weird and scary. I hadn't been myself, hadn't thought like myself, hadn't experienced things as myself. I'd felt not human, and it had been disturbing. How could I make actual decisions in that state? I was afraid that I could forget what being human was and just be . . . lost, forever. I never wanted to do it again.

If I stayed here, it would be like living in a nudist colony but insisting on staying dressed.

If I didn't stay here, where would I go? Back home? Where people were breaking into my house to kill me? Somewhere else? Brazil? What were my options?

"You made it there alive?" Jennifer's face took up my whole laptop screen. She looked tanned, healthy, and concerned.

"Yeah. It was a hard drive, though." I hadn't told Jennifer about the break-in yet. She would only worry, and there wasn't anything she could do. And what was one more secret piled on top of all the secrets I kept from her? "But I'm here at my cousin's house. He seems nice. And his girlfriend is nice too." I wished I could mull over all the haguari pros and cons with Jennifer, but that was never going to happen.

"Hm." Jennifer didn't sound convinced. "Hold up the computer so I can see your room."

I pointed the laptop camera and did a slow three-sixty of the room I was staying in.

"Wow, it's gorgeous," said Jennifer. "One of those old New Orleans houses, huh?"

"Yeah."

"But your aunt and uncle are dead? That's awful," she said. A big straw loomed on the screen, and she drank some kind of Israeli soda.

"Yeah." There was so much I couldn't tell her. I wanted to talk with her about the similarities between my aunt and uncle's deaths and my parents'. It had been so comforting to talk about it with Matéo, to feel not so alone and freakish. And this was my best, best friend.

"So what are your plans?" Jennifer asked briskly. "I expect you to be home by August twelfth, which is when I get back. You can help me pack for college." She made her usual wrinkled-nose face at the mention of college.

"Oh, I'll be back long before then," I assured her. "I don't know how long I'll stay here—probably just another day or two. Then I'll go back home."

"Good," said Jennifer. "Can't wait to see you."

"You too, HD."

CHAPTER SIX

I WASN'T BACK HOME BY AUGUST 12.

I didn't deliberately decide to stay in New Orleans—it was more like I just never left. It was such a relief to be somewhere new, doing new things, talking to people who didn't know me or my life in Florida. It was a relief to be away from that silent, empty house that would never feel safe again. Back home I had neighbors, friends, teachers, friends of my parents—all of whom knew about my parents, all of whom wanted to sympathize with me and help. Here, I was just Matéo's cousin who was visiting.

Did I feel like a hypocrite, living with seven haguari and not fighting with them about it? Yes. In this house, with these people, it was natural and unremarkable, and every one of them reveled in their dual natures. For them it didn't seem bad. Myself—I still had no interest at all in changing. I was 100 percent happy being 100 percent human. None of my housemates pressured me—none of them seemed that interested. It wasn't a big deal. It was casual.

All of them changed frequently, sometimes in the house. A

couple of times I was woken by growling or snarling—above me, or down the hall. I'd been scared, the first time; then I had realized they weren't, ahem, fighting. One time I was heading for the stairs, and the hall bathroom door was open. Someone—I couldn't tell jaguars apart—was on his or her hind legs, drinking from the sink. That was my life.

I was in a different universe: At home, being haguari had been the one single huge source of conflict, anger, and strife in my life. It had damaged, even destroyed, my two most important relationships. I would have rather died than acquiesce. Here, it was . . . no big deal.

The inconsistency made my head spin, made my guilt about my parents even more crushing. I didn't know my own mind, my own feelings or beliefs. I was seriously adrift, with nothing tying my feet to the ground.

Which meant anything could happen.

After a week I started buying groceries for the house, and after two weeks I started paying rent. Matéo didn't want to accept it, but I made him. I hated feeling like I was sponging, though he didn't see it that way and neither did Aly. He insisted I accept a family discount, though.

The household became more familiar to me as we shared meals, hung out, watched TV together. Dana was from Mississippi and had lived here five months. She was a sixth-degree black belt in tae kwon do and often traveled to meets and demonstrations around the country and even overseas. The house joke was, "Don't piss Dana off—she's a black belt." Because, ha ha, of course it was *Don't piss Dana off—she's a haguara*. Much more dangerous than a black belt.

"Girl. You do not do that to eggs."

That was Coco, frowning at Suzanne. Coco Peréz Falto was a sous-chef at a fancy restaurant uptown, and Aly had told me that Coco's girlfriend, Charlotte, was a waiter at the same restaurant. Charlotte didn't live here, but apparently was often around—I hadn't met her yet. Coco had been the first person to move in, more than a year ago, and was Aly's best friend. Like the rest of us, she was unusually pretty, and had fair skin, blue eyes, and wavy, medium-brown hair that she kept above her collar. Like me, she never wore makeup and didn't pay much attention to her clothes, unless she was wearing her white, crisply starched chef's coat.

Suzanne made a face and whisked the eggs harder, which ensured that they would be tough and rubbery when she cooked them. Coco looked over at me, and I mouthed, *I know*. We shared mutual good-cook shrugs of pain. One morning a few weeks ago, I'd actually felt like baking and had made orange-cranberry scones, with homemade lemon curd to go with. Coco had loved them, and the next thing I knew, I was teaching her some of my baking specialties and she was showing me how to make a remoulade sauce.

The only couple who lived here besides Matéo and Aly was Suzanne and James, who slept in the room next to mine. Thank heavens we had closets in between us and thick, old-fashioned walls. Suzanne Edmunds was tall with black hair, very pale skin, and light blue eyes. She'd come here from Connecticut to go to law school at Tulane University, and she had what I secretly felt was a Northern chilliness, a sort of stuck-upedness. Her boyfriend, James Fortunato, was black, very tall and very slender. As a third-year med student, he was hardly ever here. His clean-cut good looks and preppy clothes made him look like someone in a J.Crew ad. He was sweet and laid-back, and often visited his parents uptown. Suzanne and James had lived here for almost a year.

With so much going on, I had minutes at a time when I forgot to be crushed by life and devastated by grief. One afternoon I noticed that I had smiled twice already that day. Another morning I realized that my clothes weren't swimming on me as much. July melded into August, and life in general took on an easy, hushed quality, as if the heat and humidity muffled sounds, muffled thoughts, muffled fear.

"Why are you still there?" Jennifer cried. "I'm coming home tomorrow!"

"I . . ." My voice trailed off. I really wanted to see her. Jennifer coming home from Israel was always the highlight of any summer. Usually I would be waiting in her driveway with a helium balloon or flowers from the grocery store. She would be exhausted from the trip but so happy to see me, and we would go lie on her bed, telling each other everything that we had already Skyped about the whole time she was gone. Then she would crash because of the time difference and I would sneak out.

"I've just . . . sort of settled here. I keep thinking about going home, and the thought of walking into my house—"

"You could stay with me," said Jennifer.

"You're leaving for college in two weeks."

"Yes," she said pointedly. "I'm leaving for New York in two weeks, and then I won't see you till winter break. Therefore you should come home tomorrow so we can see each other."

I hesitated.

"You don't have to drive. You could fly. It would take an hour and a half," she pointed out.

"I know." I paused, finding the thought of going home frightening and oppressive. "I just . . . don't want to be there," I said lamely. "I didn't tell you this before because I didn't want you to worry, but someone tried to break into my house the night before I left. I was terrified, wondering if it was the same person who'd killed my parents."

"You're kidding!" Jennifer's face was worried and too close to the screen camera. "Why didn't you tell me? What happened?"

"I was sleeping and woke up when someone broke the glass in the kitchen door. I called 911 and then waited with my baseball bat."

"Oh my god, sweetie. That must have been so scary!"

"It was awful," I said honestly. "I totally freaked out. I was so glad to leave the next day, and every time I think of going back, I get scared all over again."

"Of course you do," Jennifer said. "That's why you should stay with me."

"It isn't just that," I said, sighing. "It's like, when I'm here I can—"

"Pretend?" she said, but not meanly.

"I guess. I do want to see you . . . would love to see you. If we could meet in a bubble somewhere, where I wouldn't have to see anything else."

Her brow furrowed. "I wonder . . . maybe Mom would let me come to New Orleans to see you?"

"That would be awesome. You could stay here. I would love that." Of course, as soon as the words left my mouth, I wanted to smack myself: I was living in a house of . . . aberrations. "Freaks" seemed too mean a word for the people I was enjoying living with, even Suzanne. But we were not normal.

As it turned out, I didn't have to worry. Mrs. Hirsch was sympathetic, but she didn't want Jennifer to come to New Orleans and stay with people she didn't know. I was hugely, hugely relieved.

It was obvious that Jennifer was really hurt I wasn't coming back to see her, but every time I tried to psych myself up for it, I felt panicky. I did not want to go home. She tried to be understanding, but she couldn't believe she had to get ready for college without me. We'd always planned to do it together, had talked about it a million times. Even two years ago she'd been planning her college wardrobe, pulling things out of her closet and examining them with an eye toward being a college freshman. I would lie on her bed, reading a magazine while she held up one outfit after another and asked my opinion.

"Yeah, that seems okay," I would say, or "No, that doesn't seem New York-y, you know?" But more often than not I just had no idea, and she'd finally gotten exasperated.

"Vivi, it's not a good sign that your dyke best friend has more fashion sense than you do," she'd pointed out, and I'd laughed.

"I promise to let you go through my clothes," I'd said. "Make sure they're college-worthy."

Back when I was planning to go to college.

I still planned to go. Someday. I wasn't up for it now. Probably next year. Tia Juliana had tried to talk me into sticking with my plan, but in the end I'd convinced her that there was no way, and she'd notified Seattle University.

Conversations between me and Jennifer became more strained the closer she got to leaving for school. I knew part of it was me and part of it was her going to a school that she didn't want to go to.

"So, they're putting me on a plane in a couple hours," she told me toward the end of August.

"You and Helen?" I asked.

"Yeah. We took all my boxes to UPS yesterday. They should get there soon." She tried to look positive.

"It might surprise you," I said. "You might like it more than you think." Our eyes met, and we both knew I was saying lame stuff a parent might say, because it was better to say that than something like, *I know it's going to suck. Wish I could help.*

In Sugar Beach, my days had been all melty and surreal as I wandered through our house. I hadn't begun to process what had happened—Mrs. Peachtree next door had offered to help me clean out my parents' clothes, to take them to her church's yard sale, but I'd just looked at her blankly.

Now that I'd been here almost two months, my days had acquired a somewhat amorphous form: I woke up, had a cup of coffee with Matéo if he was around, and puttered around the house. Sometimes I'd clean the kitchen or vacuum or something, since no one else really seemed to. Twice a week Matéo made pickups and deliveries of the instruments he repaired, and I often went with him.

One day we were eating fast food in the car, in between a delivery uptown and a pickup from a school in the Lakeview area, when he asked a question out of the blue:

"Will we ever know?"

I knew what he meant. "I don't know," I said. "It's not like we can go back to the Everglades and look for clues."

"Let's go over what we know," he said, and I stifled my impatience. We'd done that so many times already.

"Your parents were killed a year and a half ago," I said. "There was nothing special about the date: It wasn't a holiday. It wasn't your birthday."

"Right." Matéo bit into his hamburger fiercely.

"It looked like an accident. But because they weren't positive, the police did an autopsy." Keeping my voice gentle didn't make these harsh facts any more bearable.

"Right."

"They found that both of your parents' hearts were missing. When they reexamined the car, they found that there was nothing wrong with it—no reason for it to catch on fire or explode."

"So the cops thought maybe my folks were killed somewhere else, then put in their car, and then the car was burned to hide the evidence." Matéo stuffed his burger wrapper back into the bag and started the engine. "But they never found any other clues." He let out a heavy sigh and headed down Carollton Avenue toward the lake. "Okay, now your parents."

"We've been over this a bunch." And it still wasn't easier to talk about.

"I know, but what gets me is, you were gone for a while, maybe an hour, maybe more," Matéo said.

"Probably a couple of hours. The sun went down," I remembered.

"Then you came back and waited to see if there was any danger."

There had been a large azalea bush, I remembered. Despite the smell of blood and death and fear, I'd remained there silently for minutes, my animal instinct taking over.

"Yeah."

"But your mom was still alive," Matéo went on. "She still had her heart. So the guy must have stopped long before you came back. It wasn't you coming back that made him run away, right? Because by the time you got there, he was gone. You didn't see anything while you waited."

"Right," I said slowly, thinking.

"So what stopped him? Or her, or them," Matéo amended.

"Maybe my mom fought back too hard? Maybe my dad had really injured him, before . . ."

We sat there silently for a minute; then Matéo said, "I think you should ask Tia Juliana. See if there are any other instances in our family or in a haguari community where someone's heart got stolen."

The idea was reasonable but not appealing. I still hadn't told her I was in New Orleans. Basically, I was lying to her every time we talked.

"Okay," I said slowly. "And what about all the people you know? You said there were a million haguari here. Can't you ask around?"

"I've thought of that," said Matéo. "But is it safe for me to do that? What if the murderer is connected to us somehow, or is here in New Orleans? If I start asking around, will it be dangerous?"

"I don't know. But yeah, it might be."

"We gotta think of something," he said. "We just need to . . . think of something."

CHAPTER SEVEN

BUT WE DIDN'T GET VERY FAR. I TRIED TO CALL
Tia Juliana, but her housekeeper told me the family was at the
beach and wouldn't be home for a few days. Sometimes I was sure
that if I thought hard enough, the answer would come to me, and
sometimes I just wanted to never think about it again. We didn't
want to give up, but right now we seemed to see nothing but blank
walls in front of us.

About a week after Jennifer left for Columbia, Aly came home
from work and tossed a flyer onto the kitchen table.

"TGIF! And ooh, it smells good in here," she said, giving Matéo
a kiss. He was making pork chops for dinner, and I was about to
faint from the delicious aroma. Dana was peeling sweet potatoes,
and I was shelling fresh lima beans, which I'd never known existed.
My mom had always made the frozen kind.

"What's this?" I asked, wiping my hands on my shorts.

"It was on the bulletin board at the dry cleaner," Aly said. "I
don't know, I thought you might be interested. Okay, let me get out

of my work clothes and I'll set the table." She breezed out of the kitchen, her heels clicking on the wooden floor.

I looked at the flyer. It was a HELP WANTED sign for a coffee shop. Tink leaned back in his chair and read it over my shoulder. Tink Owens was the last live-in member of the household, and was a total sweetheart. He worked for the Department of Wildlife and Fisheries, patrolling the millions of Louisiana's bayous and lakes for people hunting or fishing illegally, or polluting, etc. He was an enormous blond offensive-lineman kind of guy, really nice but really big and loud. When he was home, the energy in the house totally changed. Matéo had told me Tink had lived here last year for several months, then with his boyfriend for a couple months; then the boyfriend had kicked Tink out, and now he'd been back for about six months.

"I've gone past that coffee shop," Tink said. "It's uptown, in the Garden District."

"Okay," I said. "But why did Aly give this to me?" I already paid rent, and I didn't actually need more money. The insurance company had tried to suggest my parents had done a murder-suicide situation, but in the end, faced with a lawsuit by a lawyer Ms. Carsons had hired, had been forced to pay up. It still amazed me how people could put a dollar amount on a life. I would give all the money back, and a million times as much, to have one more day with my parents.

"It was just an idea," Aly said, coming into the kitchen. Her ponytail, tank top, and cutoff shorts made her look more like herself. The first time I'd seen her work persona, all polished and in grown-up clothes, I'd barely recognized her. "I thought you might be tired of watching Téo sand things. You could get out into the world, meet some people."

Now I was mortified. Of course I was here too much. I was here all the time. Everyone else came and went because they had actual lives, but I was just . . . always here. I opened my mouth, starting to stammer, and Aly smiled and put her fingers against my mouth.

"Don't even go there. We love having you here. I hope you stay here as long as you want, for years and years." She brightened, hit by a sudden thought. "You could be our live-in nanny."

Matéo nodded in approval and leaned over to kiss Aly's dark hair. "Thinking ahead. Smart woman."

"But working in a coffee shop would be a relatively low-pressure way of dipping your toes back into society." Aly pulled open a drawer and grabbed some silverware. "Anyone know who's home right now and wants dinner?"

"I'll go bang on doors," Tink said, and lumbered out of the kitchen.

"Get out into the world?" I asked.

Aly nodded, and Matéo went back to the stove. "You don't leave the house much, sweetie. New Orleans is such a neat place; there's so much to explore. Seems like it might be good for you."

Well, that was putting a fine point on it.

"I go running sometimes," I said. "I've run all the way to Bayou Saint John. That's miles."

"Did you interact with anyone?" she asked kindly.

"Um."

"Uh-huh." She gave me a knowing look. I considered mentioning going to the grocery store with Matéo, or going out to dinner with them, but the look on her face stopped me.

I thought about it all through dinner. Tonight it was six of us sitting around the long wooden kitchen table: Matéo, Aly, me, Dana, Suzanne, and Tink. My whole life, dinnertime had been the three of us: Mami, Papi, and me. We had always eaten at the dining room table with a tablecloth and candles and wine for the grown-ups, except for movie night, when we ate on trays in the living room. Papi and Mami both cooked, and in the last couple of years I cooked sometimes too. Jennifer loved eating at our house, with the table set and the candles lit. At her house people ate when they wanted, wherever they wanted, and Mrs. Hirsch hardly ever made an actual dinner. They had a lot of takeout. So mealtime at Jennifer's house was fun for me.

Now dinner was different almost every day—sometimes just me, sometimes all of us, sometimes just a few. Sometimes we would go out—there were so many great, not too expensive restaurants. But nights like this were my favorite: people sharing in the cooking, a bunch of us here. Mostly I ate quietly while my roommates took turns talking about school or work. At twenty-four James was the oldest, and though he was kind of shy, he told amazing stories about the weird stuff he encountered during his various medical rotations. I loved hearing about his hospital shifts, but he was rarely here for meals. Suzanne was twenty-three, and had stories of her own about law school. She was in her second year, but had already decided to focus on business law, which I thought sounded intensely boring. But after hearing about some of her international cases, I decided that even business law could be fascinating.

Coco was twenty-two and had been working in restaurants since she was fifteen. She was already saving money to open her own café someday, and we'd had a lot of fun conversations where we planned the seasonal menus.

Then there were Aly and Tink, whose jobs had the most potential for drama. Aly's office had just raided a Mardi Gras krewe for undeclared taxes, but it had turned into much more when they'd found drugs hidden inside some Mardi Gras floats. Aly had actually had to pull her gun, and my mouth dropped open as she described slamming a guy against a wall, kicking his feet apart, and cuffing him.

And just last week Tink had busted some Vietnamese fisherman netting undersized alligators. It was legal to take alligators of a certain size, but apparently some Vietnamese restaurants thought younger gator meat was more tender.

Aly, Tink, and Matéo were only three years older than me, but next to any of my roommates I felt like a lost kid, not knowing what I wanted to do or be. I had no direction, as if the death of my parents had permanently derailed my future and made all my plans pointless. Now I realized that living in a house of interesting people had made it less necessary for me to be interesting myself. Not that working in a coffee shop would make me interesting. But being here all the time felt like hiding, and was definitely not putting me on the path to having a life. And I needed to make a life—re-create it. My life had gotten stripped away. I didn't have any choice—I needed to create a new one.

The next day was Saturday. Bravely I plugged the address of the coffee shop into my GPS and headed uptown. I'd driven around with Matéo, but uptown was still new to me. New Orleans reminded me of the Roman two-headed Janus, the god of beginnings and transitions, past and future. So much of this city seemed to look to the past: the beautiful Victorian houses, cute streetcars, Southern graciousness, and old-world charm. But there was also a modern sensibility and an acceptance of differences that helped me understand why so many haguari would want to settle here.

Like Matéo's neighborhood, uptown was a collection of grand streets with large, beautiful houses next to streets with small, sometimes run-down houses. They were stitched together block by block, all kinds of people living literally next door to one another. In Sugar Beach, neighborhoods had been more all of one thing or all of another. New Orleans was less homogenous.

The coffee shop, Ro's, was on the corner of Magazine and Leevey Streets, about six blocks from the Mississippi River. It was much bigger than I expected and had its own parking lot in the back. It looked like it had once been a store, a grocery store maybe, with large plate-glass windows and weather-beaten doors with glass insets. Two bow windows in front had tables nestled in them, complete with comfy-looking padded chairs.

My chest started to feel fluttery as I circled the block and parked in the parking lot. "Quit being such a weenie," I told myself. "You're eighteen and this is a coffee shop, not NASA."

Before I had time to chicken out, I got out of the car and headed purposefully for the sidewalk. The low idling of an engine made me pause, and I looked back to realize with amazement that I hadn't turned the car off. I grabbed the door handle and found that I had hit the lock switch on the door without thinking. For a moment I stood there, stunned at my stupidity, and then I remembered that unless I clicked the lock thing on the key fob, not all the doors would be locked. Sure enough, the back passenger side door opened, and I climbed in, reached to the front, and turned the engine off.

I locked the car and put my keys in my purse. Once more into the fray. My first big step forward was marred by the long strap of my purse getting caught on the side mirror and yanking me back.

Vivi, please, I thought. I stood quietly for a minute, getting a grip on myself. I'd never applied for a job before. The only summer jobs I'd had were for my parents, working in their offices or helping them around the house for minimum wage. Once Jennifer and I had tried to open our own snowcone stand with her dinky toy snowcone machine. We tallied up how many snowcones we'd have to sell before we'd be rich enough to retire forever. It was five hundred. At ten dollars a snowcone. We were nine.

Our business was ill-fated.

There was a back door leading off the parking lot, but I didn't know if it was for customers or just employees. Probably safer to go around to the front. The sidewalk leading to Magazine Street was narrow and broken, disrupted by thick tree roots that made the concrete buckle dangerously. A thin strip of neglected grass separated the sidewalk from the street, and I thought how pretty it could be if someone planted something there.

At the front doors at last, I took a deep breath and stepped inside. The scent of coffee tickled my nose, along with the smells of cinnamon, floor cleaner, and sugar. There was one main room, filled with small, square, dark tables, each with two or three chairs. Most of the tables were filled. Some people had pushed two tables together to sit in a group.

The back wall was divided in half by a hallway that I guessed led to the parking lot. It was painted with warm ocher tones, stippled and overlaid with darker colors to make it look old. On the left-hand side was a long counter framed by glass-fronted display cases of baked goods: muffins, cakes, pies, scones. The wall behind the counter was mirrored, and *What We Got* was written on the mirror in colored markers. Beneath that was a list of drinks and food items and their prices. A heavyset girl with short, dyed black hair and a nose ring smiled at me as she wiped the counter. Several tattoos showed from beneath her striped T-shirt. "Hi. What can I get you?"

I held up the flyer. "I'm here about the job?" My cheeks burned, and I felt awkward and inexperienced.

But she just nodded. "Cool. I'll get the manager." She lifted a hinged part of the counter and went down the hallway toward the back of the building. A minute later she returned and smiled again. "Manager's office is the second door on the left."

"Thanks." I should have asked if the manager was nice. I should have asked if she liked working here. I should have asked—

The hallway was dimly lit. Two bathrooms were on the right. The first doorway on the left was open and seemed to lead into an unused kitchen. The second door was closed, and I knocked on it, feeling like I had a small apple lodged in my throat.

Someone said, "Come in."

Slowly I opened the door, intrigued by the voice. I didn't know what I was expecting, but somehow I was surprised to see that the manager was a young guy, maybe in his early twenties. Twenty-one? The instant impression he made was that I was looking at the devil—that this coffee shop was managed by a beautiful, angry, seductive dark angel. Seeing his perfect, sculpted profile, I blinked: I hadn't known that guys came in this format. In the few seconds before he looked up at me, I devoured him with my eyes, picking up on heat, tension, a faint scent of spices, and a complete lack of friendliness. The desk he sat at was old, metal, and covered with papers. Finally he looked up at me, but didn't smile.

Had I brushed my hair today? Or even yesterday? I didn't know.

"Hi," he said, his glance flicking over me. "Hayley said you're here about the job."

"Yes," I said, sounding weirdly breathless. If he smiled, would I see fangs? How did he do on a full moon? "I saw your flyer." Now what?

"Okay, why don't you sit down and fill in this application?" He pushed a clipboard toward me, and I sat in the metal chair next to his desk, trying not to gape at this stunningly attractive person. He looked back at his papers and started entering figures on a large, old-fashioned adding machine that spit out tape. He was a devil consigned to accounting hell. Or something.

I bent over the clipboard, taking the opportunity to examine him through my eyelashes. He really was unusually good-looking. Almost too good-looking for a normal person. Everyone has a little something wrong with their looks or their hair or their bodies—I have good hair and skin, but my mouth is freakishly wide, so when I laugh it looks like my head is hinged, like a Muppet. And my shoulders are broad, which fits with the whole girl-athlete thing I have going, but my wide hips and too-big chest do not. I'd always envied Jennifer's slim, narrow frame, and she'd always wanted what she called "the Féliznundo booty."

This guy actually seemed to have nothing wrong with him, though he was sitting down and I couldn't tell if his body was as perfect as his face. I would bet money that it was.

Busily I wrote my name, Viviana Neves (Vivi), and my birth date, May 28. Matéo had said I could use his address, and I put down my cell-phone number.

I had no experience. Should I be honest and hope he would give me a chance? Should I lie and then maybe get caught?

I was tapping the pen against my lip, pondering my integrity, when the manager shifted in his chair and my nose caught an intoxicating scent of . . . coffee? Sandalwood? Cypress? What was his name? Had he said it? Had I already spaced it? Glancing up quickly and, I hoped, surreptitiously, I saw that his hair was a deep, lightless black, straight and quite short on the sides, a little longer on top. Suddenly he met my eyes, and, embarrassed, I went back to work on the application—but not before noticing that his were a fascinating light, clear green with a thin rim of gold around the iris.

Heat rose in my cheeks, and I pushed the clipboard back to him. This was dumb. I couldn't do this. I wasn't ready to be around regular people. Being out in the world was making me feel horribly and unexpectedly vulnerable. Matéo's house was a cocoon that kept me from dwelling on myself. But here I was, applying for a job, and I don't know why, but it all came roaring back to me right then: My parents were still actually gone, dead, and weren't ever coming back. My life from here on out would be me applying for jobs, without them, forever. My eyes filled with tears.

He glanced at my information, his beautifully angled black eyebrows framing those icy green eyes and long black lashes. "You didn't fill in the 'experience' part."

"I'm not experienced. I mean, I don't have any waitressing experience," I amended lamely, and gave a little *hmph* to clear my throat. Since he wasn't looking, I quickly brushed my hand over my eyes to get rid of the tears. *Come on, keep it together, Viv.*

"How come you're applying here?" His nose was thin and straight and arrow-shaped, the nostrils flaring to the sides, and his sharply angled jaw balanced his strong chin. What had he asked me? Oh—why I'm applying for the job.

Because my cousin's girlfriend told me to.

"I can do it," I said, surprising myself. "This is a nice place. I can do the work, and it will be good for me." I hadn't meant to say that. Now that I was facing him, I saw that he had beautiful, symmetrical bone structure. High cheekbones like blades, a chiseled mouth. Clear skin, paler than I would have expected for summertime. Maybe he was a vampire. Ha ha ha—that would be crazy, right? Things like that don't exist! Next we'll believe that some people can turn into jaguars! I focused on a tiny scar right at the corner of his mouth, a paler curving line like the outline of a nickel. In summary, I was tearing up and gazing at him like he was a hamburger and I was starving. I'd blown this.

"Are you okay?" he asked.

I nodded. He hesitated as if he wanted to contradict me, but just said, "What do you mean, good for you?"

"Good for me to get out," I said, and sniffled. "Instead of sitting around." Could I sound stupider? No. I did not think so. I never should have come.

He flicked his gaze back at the application. "You're eighteen. Are you going to college here in New Orleans?"

"No."

I was confounding him. I needed this to be over.

"Have you ever had a job of any kind?"

"No. Well, babysitting. Working for my parents." My voice was small. I was trying to control my breathing.

"Do you live with your parents?"

"No." Shuddering breath that I tried to disguise by clearing my throat again. "I . . . live with my cousin."

The guy looked at me without blinking, then turned back to his desk. Was I dismissed?

Swallowing, I wondered if I should stand up and get out. How humiliating, to start crying in the middle of an interview. I hadn't cried in almost a week. I'd thought I was doing so much better. This gorgeous guy must think I'm nuts. I thought of how my mom had always seemed in control of every situation, was always so gracious and charming, able to talk to anyone, able to do anything. She would have looked stunning, breezed in here, made this guy adore her without even trying, and waltzed out with whatever job she'd come in for.

I truly was not very much like her.

"Here's the schedule," the guy said, turning back to me. He handed me a sheet of paper while I gaped at him. "I need someone here from five to about one a.m. We close at midnight but there's cleanup. Does that time work for you?"

"Really?" I said.

"Do you want this job?" Perfect eyebrows arching even more perfectly.

"Yes."

"Can you work those hours?"

"Sure."

"Can you start today?"

"Yes." My heart was pounding.

"Okay. Come in at four thirty. I'll tell Hayley you'll be in, and either she or Talia will show you the ropes."

"Okay."

"Okay. I'll see you later, then."

"Okay. Bye. Thanks."

I grabbed my purse and almost raced out of the office and down the hall. I waved good-bye to Hayley and said, "I'll see you later."

She smiled and gave me a thumbs-up.

Once I was in my car, rolling down the windows to let hot air escape and cranking up the AC, I realized I didn't know his name, how much the job paid, if I was hired or if this was a trial, how many hours I would be working each week. In short, I knew nothing useful about the job except where the building was, when to show up, and that the beautiful devil manager would hire weird, inexperienced girls who cried during the interview.

This should be great.

Chapter Eight

When I got home, Matéo and Aly gave me high fives about my job.

"That's awesome!" said Aly. "Good for you! I'm so glad you checked it out. But I can't believe you're starting today! We're going to a concert in Covington tonight and were hoping you would come. A bunch of us are taking Coco's van. But if you're starting your shift at five o'clock, that won't work." Covington was the town directly across Lake Pontchartrain from New Orleans, about thirty miles away.

"Oh, no," I said, trying to look disappointed. There was no way I was ready for loud music and dancing with people I still didn't know all that well.

"Okay, we'll be home by midnight or one or so," said Matéo. "So we'll just see you back here later. Congratulations on your job. Glad it worked out for you."

"Thanks," I said, then noticed that Aly was looking at me, her head cocked to one side. "What?"

"Did you wear that to the interview?" she asked.

I looked down at the boxy blue T-shirt I'd gotten in the men's department at Target and my favorite cutoff sweatpant shorts. "Yeah?"

She shook her head. "No. An employee needs to look tidy and put together. Also, we need to put your hair into a braid or something, so it doesn't get all over the place."

I felt like a kid again, sitting on a chair so that Aly could brush my hair and put it into a French braid that started at the top of my head and ended halfway down my back. Since the most I ever did was scrape it back into a ponytail, the effect was quite striking.

"Wow, look at your face," said Aly, meeting my eyes in the mirror.

"What?"

She shook her head, a little smile on her lips. "You're beautiful. It's just usually your hair is drowning out your face, and you dress . . . extremely casually. But look at you—you're gorgeous. Your skin and eyes. Do you ever wear makeup?"

My mom used to beg me to wear at least lip gloss. She was one of the most beautiful women I've ever seen, and wore mascara every day of her life. When I thought about how hard I had pushed back, how obnoxiously I had refused to do the slightest thing that she wanted, and not just with makeup, my chest hurt.

Mutely I shook my head.

Aly shrugged. "You don't have to. You're beautiful."

I looked in the mirror, really seeing myself for the first time in ages, and saw barely a trace of the pretty little girl I had once been.

I'd lost more weight than I'd realized, and my cheekbones were visible, changing the shape of my face. When I was little, I'd wanted to grow up to look like my mom, and I did mostly look like her and my aunts. But now I saw a bit of my dad in my face—stronger bones, straighter eyebrows. I was also six inches taller than my mom had been, and even in this too-skinny state still outweighed her. She'd been petite, finely boned, feminine. After I'd rejected being haguari, I'd spent a lot of energy trying to be the opposite of my mom. Looked like I got my wish.

"I don't see what you see," I said finally.

Leaning over, Aly gave me a little hug. "Someday you will, *hermana.*"

Hermana. "Sister," in Spanish. Matéo had told me Aly's family had originally been from Colombia, but now lived in Ohio. I managed a watery smile.

Next, Aly rejected every article of clothing I had brought, just as Jennifer had often done, refusing to go out in public with me unless I changed my shirt or wore different shorts. I'd thought it was funny, but it was less funny now. Finally Aly chose a shirt from her own closet, a black tank top that had FEAR BUILDS WALLS on it in huge white letters. It was much smaller than my regular shirts, and fitted me closely. I looked at myself in the mirror uncomfortably—the tank top emphasized my boobs, distorting the letters of "fear." *Feeeeaaaaaarrrrr.*

"Gosh," Aly said, looking at me. Feeling uncomfortably that she must mean my chest, I picked up a white short-sleeved button-down shirt of mine and put it on, leaving it unbuttoned and tying the ends at my waist. Better.

"You have no skirts or dresses?"

"No," I said.

"No pants except jeans? No shorts except running shorts and jorts?"

I really had nothing to say to that.

"I have a skirt," said Aly firmly.

"I'm not really a skirt kind of girl," I said, almost wincing as I remembered saying that to my mom so many times.

"Trust me," said Aly, handing me a flouncy black skirt with an elastic waistband. I held it up to myself. It came several inches above my knees. "In heat like this, skirts and dresses are the only way to go. You should know that, being from Florida. Put that on." I did. In the mirror I was practically unrecognizable: tidy and girl-like.

My makeover was interrupted by Jennifer calling, so Aly was thwarted from doing anything else to me. I popped open my computer and clicked Skype, and there was Jen. I knew this had been her first week of classes, and was bummed to see she looked stressed.

"HD!" I said. "I'm so glad you called. How's it going? Have you had a class yet?"

Jennifer nodded. "Intro to pysch. It was okay."

"You love psych. How's your roommate? Lucy, right?" I'd heard about her during Jennifer's orientation week.

"She's fine." Jennifer seemed distracted.

"Oh. Well, how's everything? You look tired."

"Yeah—still getting settled." She pushed her wavy, shoulder-length brown hair behind one ear. "I don't know, Viv. I just don't think I'm going to like it here."

"Maybe it'll be better than you think," I said. "Your courses should be good. Maybe you'll meet some hot chick who'll make it all worthwhile."

She didn't even smile—just nodded, looking off to the side. Then she looked back into the camera and bit her lip. "I wish you had come home to see me," she said, sounding like she was about to cry.

Oh, no. I let out a deep breath. "I know. I'm sorry. I was dying to see you. Just . . . leaving here, going back home—I couldn't face it."

"I know. I just miss you." She gave me a trembly smile.

"I miss you too."

"I like your hair like that," she said.

"Get this—it's for work! I actually got a job. In a coffee shop. I'll probably last about two hours, if I'm lucky."

"You got a job?"

I gave a rueful laugh. "Yeah—can you believe it? It just seemed like it was ti—"

"Vivi! You're not staying there!" Jennifer said, staring into the camera. "What do you need a job for? You're going home any day now, right?"

"Well, no, I'm not staying here for good, of course," I said quickly. "This is just temporary. But there's no reason for me to go back home, especially if you're not there. I might . . . I might stay here a couple more weeks. I thought a job would help keep me busy, you know. Keep my mind off things."

Jennifer bit her lip. "Vivi—promise me you're not staying there. Promise me you'll be home at Christmas when I come back. I have to do Thanksgiving up here with my aunt, but I'll be home in mid-December."

That was easy. No way would I still be here at Christmas. "Absolutely," I assured her. "I'll be home long before then. I'll be so happy to see you at Christmas. It'll be great."

She didn't say anything, just looked at me through the computer screen. "Okay, I have to go. I have a weird bio lab. On a Saturday."

"Ew," I said sympathetically. "Okay. Have a good lab. Talk to you soon."

"'Kay." She shut her computer, leaving me feeling unsettled. But it was time to head to Ro's, and I couldn't dwell on it right now.

As I drove, I wondered if I was a wuss for agreeing to wear what Aly had picked out. Why had I let her dictate my clothes but not my mom? Maybe . . . Aly was trying to change the way I looked. With my mom I'd felt that she was trying to change *me*. Had I been wrong? I would never know. I sniffled and turned left on Jackson Avenue.

I arrived fifteen minutes early. Hayley, the girl with the nose ring, was really friendly, and started showing me everything right away. It felt weird, wearing a skirt. I was very aware of it swishing around my legs, but Aly was right—it was a lot cooler than shorts.

It was comfortable and I didn't feel vulnerable, which was what I usually feared from skirts and dresses.

"Okay, got it, I think," I said, after Hayley showed me where all the teas were kept and how to use the hot-water urn. I realized I hadn't seen the guy, the manager, and said, "You know, I don't even know the manager's name."

Hayley laughed, showing her tongue stud. That had to hurt. "His name is Rafe—Rafael Marquez."

Rafael. Rafael Marquez. I said it silently a couple times, trying it out.

"He's getting his degree at Tulane, studying art," Hayley said. "Look—those portraits were part of his junior-year portfolio." She pointed to the right-hand wall, past the hallway, and I saw a drawing of Hayley and more drawings of people I didn't know. We walked over to them.

"Aren't they amazing?" Hayley asked proudly, and they were.

"Yes," I said, hardly able to believe that the guy who had hired me had done this. The portrait of Hayley was a charcoal drawing, or at least mostly black pencil, but small parts were colored in, like her eyes and her lips. In real life Hayley was cute but not gorgeous, and she was heavier than modern standards of beauty, the way I was when I wasn't carved out by grief. But this drawing, unmistakably Hayley, somehow drew out the best parts of her—her small, perfect nose, the smile in her eyes, the pretty bow of her upper lip—and made her look beautiful.

"These are all people who work here or used to work here,"

Hayley said, waving at the other drawings. "But let me show you how to work the espresso machine."

I watched carefully as Hayley measured finely ground coffee into the little handled thingy, and saw how she tamped it down firmly.

"This is the portafilter," she said. "Where the coffee goes in. You use this little tamper and pack it firmly but not too tightly. Then you lock it into place on the group head. This is the group head." She pointed.

"Okay," I said, trying to remember everything.

"So, Rafael is the grandson of the woman who owns this place—Carlotta Fontenot," Hayley said, lowering her voice as she clamped the espresso arm into place. "He manages it for her. She is nuts, I'm telling you, hates everything in here. When she comes in, we hunker down and weather the storm. So don't let her get to you."

I gave Hayley an alarmed look, but she just smiled and shrugged, leading me through a doorway behind the counter to a large room. "This is the old kitchen, from when it was a restaurant. No one uses anything except this back fridge. At night we wrap everything up and put it in here."

"Where do y'all get the food from?"

"We get everything from a wholesale bakery," said Hayley. "Sometimes someone wants their croissant heated up, so you just zap it in the microwave for fifteen seconds, okay?"

"Yep." A regular oven would be so much better and wouldn't make the croissant soggy. Even a little toaster oven would do. But people probably wouldn't want to wait while it warmed up properly.

A few minutes before five, Talia, my evening coworker, came in, and Hayley introduced us. Talia was a very short, very round black woman, maybe in her late fifties. She seemed nice and no-nonsense at the same time.

"Okay, I'll let you guys get to it," Hayley said, taking off her apron.

"Thanks for everything," I told her, and she smiled again. "I'll see you tomorrow." After Hayley left, I asked Talia, "How long have you worked here?"

"Here, three years, just part-time," Talia said, bustling around behind the counter, arranging things just so. "Mostly I work downtown at a law firm as a personal assistant." Talia moved more quickly than I would have thought, organizing supplies for the after-work rush: ice, syrups, plenty of ground coffee beans; whole milk, two percent, skim milk in the fridge on the right; soy milk on the left. "Personal assistant," Talia repeated dismissively. "That means secretary, honey. I been working there thirty-five years for the old man. I know what a secretary is. They wanted to make me office manager and whatnot, and I said, 'No, sir! I don't want to be managing this and that. I want to do my job and go home!'"

"Yeah," I said. "I know what you mean."

Besides showing me a million things I couldn't possibly remember, Talia was happy to dish on our coworkers. While it was still a bit quiet, we walked around, straightening tables, lining them up properly, moving chairs to be evenly distributed.

"Hayley's a sweet girl, but she keeps going for the wrong kind of guy," said Talia, grabbing a chair. "She deserves better, but she doesn't listen to me, no. Her current beau is too old for her, and rides a motorcycle!"

"Gosh," I said, clearing off tables and putting everything in the busing bin Talia had given me.

"I don't know what Hayley's mother is thinking, letting her go with him," Talia went on. "Hayley lives with her mother and sister in a double on Camp Street."

I wondered what a double was.

"You still live with your parents, honey?"

"Ah, no. I'm living with my cousin right now."

Thankfully, Talia didn't pursue that. She headed toward the back kitchen, and I followed her, lugging the busing bin. "This here is the fancy dishwasher Rafael put in," Talia said, showing me a big metal square up on a counter. A stack of heavy plastic trays sat next to it, and Talia picked up one filled with plastic tines. "Stack the dishes in this."

She showed me how to arrange the special tray, and then I did one by myself while Talia popped her head out front to make sure no one needed anything. She was back in a minute and said, "I also don't know why Hayley keeps punching holes in herself, why she keeps getting the tattoos. That doesn't improve any girl's looks, in my opinion." She squinted at me. "You got any of them tattoos?"

"Oh, no," I said, and she nodded in approval.

"And Rafael," she went on, and my ears pricked up. "Rafael is one good-looking boy."

He sure is, I thought, but I said, "Oh?"

"But he isn't dating anyone that I know about," Talia said, lowering her voice. "He doesn't seem to have much free time, with his art and his school and whatnot. Did you see his drawings over there?"

"I did. They're amazing."

"Well, he lives in the carriage house behind old Mrs. Fontenot's mansion, a few blocks away from here."

Did she really mean an actual carriage house, like for carriages?

"His parents live in Mexico," Talia said. "But he's lived with the old woman as long as I've worked here, and the old woman is bats for sure. And mean as a snake."

"Gosh." I didn't need to add much to the conversation; Talia seemed happy to have someone new to talk to.

"I feel sorry for him, but he seems to deal with the old lady okay."

"Oh, good," I said, watching as she showed me where all the clean plates and cups went on shelves under the front counter.

"But he ain't gay, I'll tell you that," Talia whispered. "I'd be able to tell for sure. A person's business is a person's business, but I would know. And he is not."

I bit back the word "gaydar."

Throughout the evening Talia showed me the things Hayley hadn't had time to, like how to mix up the chocolate syrup from a package, and how to make cute foam hearts on top of cappuccinos. Following her example, I learned how to wait on people, but I had to keep asking her how to make certain drinks. There was a printed guide, but there were so many different kinds. I had to take the guide home and try to memorize it.

Whenever there was downtime, Talia chatted. And chatted. I wondered if Rafael was in the office, but decided Talia wouldn't be talking about him so openly if he were.

He was too serious for a young guy, in Talia's opinion. He was only twenty-one, and would graduate college next summer. He'd worked here longer than Talia had, though he'd just become manager last year. All the workers liked him, but he wasn't a glad-hander and he didn't suffer fools. He needed to lighten up, Talia thought. He was too old for a young man.

"Glad-hander"? All these new words I would have to look up.

My biggest fear about being a waitress was that as soon as some stranger was mean to me, I would cry, in addition to my normal crying jags. But I managed to get through my shift without making any huge mistakes and without any customers making shark chum out of me. Besides the drink making, I sometimes needed Talia's help with the cash register, but on the whole I didn't do too badly. Maybe people could tell it was my first day and gave me a break. Maybe I had just gotten lucky. At any rate, by the time Talia locked the door at midnight and we did the cleanup, I was wiped out and felt like I could sleep for sixteen hours all over again.

After Talia set the alarm and relocked the front doors, we walked together to the parking lot, Talia with a mace sprayer in one hand. "They say mace is illegal; you gotta use that pepper spray nowadays," she said, shaking her head. "I don't think so. Some fool be coming at me, I want to stop them dead, you know?"

"Yeah, definitely," I agreed. "Thank you so much for showing me everything today. You were really patient."

Talia's wide smile seemed to glow in the night. "It was my pleasure, honey. You're a sweet girl. I'll see you tomorrow, you hear?"

"Yes, thanks. I'll see you tomorrow."

As I headed back to Matéo's house, I thought of the times I'd driven home late in Sugar Beach. I had loved it because I had the roads to myself and felt like I was the only person awake. Here there were cars, lights, action, even at this hour. Lots of people going places. The city was alive around the clock. I pictured New York being like that, and hoped Jennifer could enjoy it.

It was silly, but driving this late made me feel older. It was almost one a.m., I had done a full day's work without disgracing myself, and somehow I felt like I'd turned a page in a horrible book. I was living in a new place, doing new things, being with new people. My old life had been destroyed, but my new life was not all that bad.

Chapter Nine

WHEN I GOT TO MATÉO'S HOUSE, THERE WASN'T
a single car in the back parking area. I knew most of my roommates
had gone across the lake, but surely someone had to be home. A few
lights were on, but it was creepy that there were no cars. I wished
Matéo had bright outdoor lights—where I parked on the crushed
shells under the trees, it was dark and felt oddly removed from the
other houses and the life of the city.

"Don't be such a big baby," I told myself sternly. "Get out, lock
the car, and go inside."

Peering through my windshield, I thought about how prevalent
crime was in New Orleans. I told myself I was a big bad cat with
big bad claws. Top of the food chain. But I didn't know how to
change on purpose—that was something that came with practice
and experience. Experience that I had steadfastly refused to get.
And I still didn't want to.

Breathing shallowly, I got out of the car and forced myself to
walk, not run, across the yard to the side door. The hairs on the

back of my neck stood up, and I felt like the tall dark bushes held hundreds of eyes staring at me. It took several seconds to turn the key in the lock and jiggle it just so. Then I quickly stepped inside and locked the door again. When a big form came in from the hall, I almost screamed, but let out my breath in relief as I saw it was Tink.

"Hey, Vivi," he said, surprised. "Where is everyone? I got home a couple hours ago and the place was dark."

"I think just about everyone went to a concert over in Covington," I told him. "Where's your truck?"

"Shop. I'll pick it up tomorrow morning."

"Ah." Setting down my purse, I went and stood in front of the fridge, wondering what I felt like eating. I should have gotten a muffin at work. Every bit of energy had drained out of me, but I also felt weirdly hyped up, like I wouldn't be able to sleep for a while.

"There's some ribs in there," said Tink, putting his glass in the sink.

"Hmm. Maybe I'll just fix some cereal or something."

Tink and I both made ourselves bowls of cereal and decided to eat upstairs on the balcony. I was so, so glad someone was home and I wasn't here by myself, and glad it was Tink, who was friendly and funny, instead of, say, Suzanne. It wasn't that Suzanne was mean or anything, but apparently it took her a while to warm up to new people.

Tink and I went through my room and I raised one of the tall

French windows that led out to the wide balcony across the front of the house.

"You want the porch light on?" I asked.

"Nah," said Tink. "It'll just draw bugs to us."

"'Kay." I lowered the window gently into place, and we sat in beat-up wicker chairs, eating our cereal in the warm, jasmine-scented darkness. It was comfortable, cozy. Gradually I started to unwind. Maybe I would even be able to sleep.

Sitting together on the dark balcony made it easy to talk, and I found myself telling him about Jennifer, and how I had planned to go to college. Wryly Tink told me how his parents still hoped he would meet a nice girl and get over the whole gay thing, and I said that my parents had wanted me to be different too.

"Different how?" he said.

I shrugged, tipping my bowl up and drinking the milk. "More like them. I . . . wasn't really happy about being haguari."

Tink's eyes widened. "What do you mean, not happy?"

"I was shocked," I mumbled, putting down my bowl. "I felt like a freak. I thought it was horrible. And then they changed in front of me, and I was terrified. It was a nightmare." I'd never told anyone that, not Tia Juliana, not Matéo or Aly, no one. Somehow, sitting here in the darkness with the heavy night air all around us, it was easier to spill my guts.

In the distance a sudden flash caught my eye: a crisp, forking bolt of lightning. A few seconds later thunder rumbled toward us, sounding like giants bowling in the heavens. The verdant, electric scent of rain came to me, and a moment later drops began to pelt the leaves of the trees. Another burst of lightning, sharply angled and branched like arteries, lit our faces, and the following thunder was so loud I felt it vibrate in my chest.

"Wow," Tink said at last. "That must have been so hard, for all of you."

"Yeah." I laughed drily. "Understatement."

The rain pattered down, bouncing on the lacy iron railing, hitting the balcony floor. A fine mist brushed my face in a sibilant, cooling kiss. It was past one thirty, according to the glow-in-the-dark hands on my watch. Why weren't Matéo and the others home yet?

"When my parents told me—me and my twin brother—we thought we'd won the lottery," Tink said, sounding dreamy. "It was like finding out we were superheroes. To this day, it's the one purely beautiful thing in my life." He looked out at the rain, perhaps looking back far enough in his memory to where he wasn't a disappointment to his parents. Maybe we could let him into the Heartbreaking Disappointment club. I thought back to my last conversation with Jennifer and felt bad about how it had ended. I would have to call her tomorrow. Or rather, later today.

"So what did your parents think about your reaction?" Tink asked, pulling me back to the present.

"They were stunned," I said. "They couldn't believe I wasn't happy about it. But to me it felt like they were asking me to be happy I was Frankenstein or some—" Lightning whitened the porch like a mortar exploding; a simultaneous *boom!* of thunder drowned out my voice. And the power went off.

For a second we sat there, staring at each other. We'd already been sitting in the dark, but now my room lights were out, and the streetlights. Tink smiled, and I smiled back. "This happens," he said.

I nodded. "It happens at home, too."

Standing up, I went to the balcony railing and looked down the street. Everything was as dark as the inside of a cave. A huge, sheeting wave of rain made me step back. It sounded like someone was standing in the yard spraying a fire hose against the house.

Struck by a sudden thought, I turned back to Tink. "Did your parents ever tell you about the Talofomé?"

He nodded and grinned. "My mom said that her grandmother used it to scare the daylights out of her. She was afraid to go outside at night, scared that the Talofomé would sneak up on her and rip out her—" He stopped, looking at me.

I made my voice light. "But we all know it isn't real, right?"

"No, of course not. It's a dumb legend. I have friends at work, and their grandparents told them about the loup-garou, the local werewolf. The Talofomé is just our version of that. I guess every culture has its own evil creature."

"Yeah, I guess," I said, feeling unsettled. "Maybe we should go in."

Tink shrugged. "With no power, there's no AC. It's going to be pretty stuffy inside soon."

"Oh. Right." More mist blew across my skin as I watched the rain come down with such force that it was almost sideways. With no streetlights, no house lights, no moon or stars, the only thing glowing in the night was the French Quarter in the distance. It was so important for the tourism industry that it had its own dedicated power grid.

Something—some movement—caught the corner of my eye. Moving closer to the balcony railing, I looked down into the side yard. All I saw was rain, the trees blowing in the strong wind, the long grass getting whipped and flattened.

And . . . a big shadow. Blinking, I wiped the mist out of my eyes and peered down. Saw nothing.

Then—

The shadow moved along the fence inside the yard. A big dark shape. A jaguar shape. My eyes wide, I turned and looked at Tink. He was on his feet in a moment, moving silently and gracefully for such a big guy. Slowly I pointed down into the yard. When Tink spotted the shadow, his brows furrowed as if he was trying to figure out who it was.

Despite the comfort of having Tink next to me, I felt like I'd swallowed a hard plastic ball, and my heart thudded heavily in my chest. Down in the yard, the shadow stopped, and even through the intense darkness it seemed like it was looking up at us.

"Do you recognize him?" I whispered, assuming it was a him.

Tink's blue eyes narrowed. "Don't think so. Not sure. The rain. But no one I know would be doing this without identifying themselves."

There was an enormous magnolia tree in the yard—the one

I'd fallen asleep under when I'd first arrived. The one Matéo had jumped down at me from. Tink and I now saw the big jaguar coil and spring, disappearing up into the thick branches.

One of the tree's limbs ended about twelve feet from the corner of the porch. We couldn't see the haguaro, but the shaking of various leaves told us he was climbing. He reached the branch closest to this porch. He was coming to get us.

Like with my parents. Like the person who had tried to break into my house. Like the person who had killed Matéo's parents.

Get inside, I told myself, just as I had earlier in my car. *Get inside and lock the window.* Grabbing the hem of Tink's shirt, I edged sideways toward my room. Tink didn't budge, forcing me to let him go. Then I heard it: the low, rumbling, blood-chilling growl of a predator. The closest branch shook and bent under the big jaguar's weight.

"Tink! Get inside!" I hissed, quickly raising my window.

He didn't respond, just stood at the edge of the balcony staring at the tree. What should I do now? My knees were about to give out from fear. I had to get inside and slam the wooden shutters closed and lock the window, but I couldn't leave Tink out here alone.

The next deep-throated growl was much closer, and I realized that it was Tink, and he was changing. His wide shoulders hunched, arms bent at the elbows. Standing in the window frame of my dark room I felt frozen. My legs were trembling and I could hardly breathe. What should I do? What?

It all happened so fast that most of it was a blur. Tink completely changed in about twenty seconds. The tree branch dipped, and the enormous jaguar jumped twelve feet onto my balcony. With an ugly roar, Tink reared up on his hind legs, and I saw that the two cats were matched in size, wide paws spread, crushing jaws opened. A huge crack of lightning illuminated the porch, making Tink and the stranger look like giant shadow puppets, frozen for a split-second snapshot. Somehow my legs moved, and with stupefied animal instinct I backed through my window and dove beneath my high bed, although I knew that would be no protection at all.

Covering my ears against the horrible sounds outside, I squeezed my face up tightly as if that would block out the knowledge of what was happening. Would someone hear them over the lashing violence of the thunderstorm? Surely someone would call the police. Would that be good or bad? Beneath my bed, I pressed my back against my wall, my hands curled so tightly over my ears that my nails hurt my skin. My breaths came fast and shallow—the last time I'd heard sounds like this had been the worst day of my life.

Porch furniture crashed. Heavy thumps landed against the outside wall, making me wince. My heart beat so fast it felt like beetle wings in my throat. That haguaro was going to kill Tink, and I wasn't helping. I had run, just like with my parents. Lightning made crisp, fleeting shadows in my room; thunder rolled through me, vibrating in the floor and wall. I curled up tighter, feeling like such a coward, wishing I would just pass out.

Screams of rage and attack shook a whimpering sound from

me. Despite my covered ears, I could hear them loudly, and I knew which snarls were Tink's and which were the unknown jaguar's. If this had been a normal house break-in, I'd have run downstairs and called for help. But who could help in this situation? Only another haguari. Like me.

When they crashed into my room, roaring and howling, it was like having a car drive through my window. My eyes flew open, but I stayed huddled under the bed as they rolled together on the floor, falling against my armoire, sending my long mirror crashing to the ground.

Stop it, stop it, stop it, I whispered, but what came out . . . was a soft growl.

My eyes open wider I smell dust

Look I have a paw a wide paw with long deadly claws

I am jaguar again why

Furniture is breaking

I am under a bed I begin to crawl out

I yell *Tink I'm coming* it is a roar

I feel my strong muscles I smell jaguar me I smell Tink jaguar I smell a stranger

I roar the strange jaguar stares at me it has death in its golden eyes

My chest feels hollow I roar so loudly I shake the windows

I go closer and raise a paw with sharp claws out

The floor vibrates lightly someone is coming human footsteps

I will fight I roar again and swipe at the stranger talons out like a steel rake

He swings back at me I duck my anger is overcoming my fear

"What's going on here?" Matéo is here I am so glad

"Vivi!" That is Aly she will help she is strong "Where's Vivi?"

I'm here! I growl

The strange jaguar breaks free away from Tink's fierce strength

He runs outside he jumps off the balcony

He jumps into the tree

After a long time of fear and ugly sounds now it's quiet

Except for the rain

And Tink's heavy panting he is breathing hard

Lightning makes sharp dark shadows on the walls

Thunder rumbles like my growl through my belly

Matéo and Aly are here they smell like not jaguars

They smell like family

My room is broken

I go to Tink I make no sound we push our heads against each other

Rubbing our scent on each other

Tink lies down it is still raining the smell of rain is in my nose the wetness the damp breeze in my room

I smell blood Tink is bloody there is blood on the wooden floor

Tink has long slashes on his side more footsteps Dana

"What the hell happened?" Dana runs in

Matéo kneels by Tink

I want to change back I want hands what is wrong with Tink

How do I get back I want to cry but these eyes can't

How do I change I am stuck I am stuck

I drop to the ground by Tink and put my head on my paws

I do not want to be a jaguar I can't do anything I have no thumbs

"Tink, man, you okay?" Matéo says "Change back so I can check your injuries, okay?"

"Vivi?" Aly kneels next to me she rubs my back her hand on my fur is electric

I want to cry but I can't I look at Aly I can smell a hundred Aly scents

How do I change back? Sort of a weird growl-yodel–quiet roar

Tink is changing he is smaller he smells not jaguar he has no fur

Matéo brings his clothes Tink groans he puts on his shorts he smells like Tink he is not family

Dana has a box she sits by him

"Okay, hold still." Matéo dabs at blood on Tink

"She doesn't know how to change back." Tink points at me

"Yeah—I heard." Aly "I'm trying to figure out how to explain it. Though you're very beautiful, like this." She pats my shoulder "There aren't that many of us who are all black."

I look down at my paws I look at my flank she is right I am black like night shadows

A black jaguar my rosettes show only under bright lightning

"Okay." Aly "You feel both jaguar and human, right? You can understand me, but you could understand Tink as a jaguar. Right?"

I look at her

"There's a place between my eyes, on my forehead. When I need to become human again, I focus on it. Aly is there, in my brain right there, and I latch on to the idea of being a person, being the person named Aly, and I clutch it."

Words just words I have an itch I lick my arm my rough tongue feels good

"Yeah." Matéo is putting something on Tink's side the smell stings my nose my nose wrinkles "You sort of latch on to your human part. It's like a third eye, in your forehead. Didn't your parents tell you this?"

I don't know I don't remember where is my forehead

Aly laughs "You should see your face! Your eyes practically crossed!"

I raise one lip I show Aly my long, long fang she stops laughing I feel laughter in her

I want to change back where is Vivi I don't know how to change I am lost forever I am trapped

"You can't do it, can you?" Dana is talking at me "Weird." She looks at Matéo "I have some cuva rojo."

Matéo looks at me he shrugs he pats human Tink "I guess that would be okay. I don't know what else we can do."

"She's gotta learn." Aly

Dana leaves I hear her feet

"Maybe we should start with her as a human." Aly

Dana is back she has a box she opens it she has a small thing

"I'll do her nose." Dana sits in front of me she shows me something I don't know what it is

"This is a drug that will forcibly change you back into your human form. It comes from a plant in the rain forest. Our people have used it for thousands of years. I'm going to blow the liquid up your nose. It will feel weird, and the change is kind of abrupt, but it will change you back. Do you want to do it?"

Words words words I don't know

"Do you want to try again yourself?"

I am so tired what a long day I close my eyes I rest my head on my arms I get comfortable

"Okay, I guess you better. It's okay, Vivi. Everything's okay, you hear me?" Aly rubs my shoulder it feels good

Something cold touches my nose my eyes pop open

Dana's face is right there her lips puff liquid in my nose in my nose

It is icky it smells very strong it is somehow familiar it is cold it is uncomfortable

I leap to my feet snorting

I sneeze three times

A cold wave comes over me I crumple in on myself

In rapid succession I lost fur, muscle mass, and the vision, hearing, and taste of a big cat. Less than a minute later I was shaking, feeling the smooth hardness of the wooden floor against my naked, clammy skin. Aly was ready with the cotton blanket from my bed, and she covered me up even before I was completely human.

"Holy shit," I managed, my voice trembling.

"I know, it's kind of harsh," said Aly, patting my shoulder under the blanket.

"Oh, my gods," I moaned, struggling to sit up. My muscles felt like I'd just gotten off the rack. I was sure I'd feel a hundred times worse tomorrow.

"Did you know that guy, Vivi?" Tink asked, carefully easing back into his polo shirt.

"No," I said. What had happened?

"I didn't either," said Tink. "He just came out of the blue and attacked. Man, that was some fight. The weird thing is that he wasn't trying to kill me. There were a couple times when he could have tried to get his jaws around my head. But he went for my side instead."

The thought came to me clearly. "He was trying to get your heart." The slashes along Tink's left side said as much. Had he been after me, but Tink had been in the way? My spine tensed and went cold.

"Why not just kill me, then, and take it?" Tink asked.

We were all silent for a moment; then it dawned on me, the horrible truth. "He wanted you alive," I said slowly. "He wanted the heart still beating." The devastating memories of my parents flooded back to me—the deep cuts in my mom's side, my dad's chest split open. Oh gods, Papi had been alive . . .

Jumping up, I staggered into my lightless bathroom and barely made it to the toilet before I threw up convulsively, tears finally streaming down my cheeks. Papi had been alive when his heart was taken. I couldn't bear that knowledge.

When I was done, I didn't have enough energy to stand up. The whole day had been too much. Finally Aly tapped on the bathroom door and came in.

"We'll talk more about all this tomorrow," she said, helping me stand up, tucking the blanket more tightly around me. "Rinse out your mouth."

I nodded and went to the sink.

"You okay, Viv?" Matéo asked, back in the room, and I nodded wearily.

"I mean, not really," I amended. "Matéo—was that the person who killed my parents? He was here. I feel like he came here for me, or maybe for you, and Tink got in the way."

Matéo and Aly stopped and looked at me, concern on both their faces.

"Remember how that guy tried to break into my house, two nights before I came here?" I reminded them. "Has a strange haguaro ever attacked anyone here before? Is it just since I've come here?" My voice was rising and becoming tenser.

"I don't know," Matéo said solemnly. "It would be weird for him to come after me now, after a year and a half."

"Maybe he came for me," I said, slumping against my tall bed. I pulled the cotton blanket around me more tightly.

"Why would he be after you?" Aly asked. "Were your parents— did they know something? Does he think you know it too? I can't figure out why your family would be targeted."

"I can't either," I said tiredly, and then a thought drifted into my brain. "You know, that was my birthday, my eighteenth birthday.

My dad started to say something about a family book that I would get now that I was eighteen. But he never finished telling me what it was. Could it have had some sort of dangerous information in it?"

"Well, the oldest kid in every family gets the family book when they turn eighteen," Matéo said. "I have mine."

"My brother has ours," Aly added. "It's partly haguari history, and partly my family's history. Like a practical jaguar handbook."

"I looked everywhere for mine, but didn't find it," I said.

Matéo rubbed his forehead. "You know, I can't even think straight right now. It's almost three o'clock. Let's talk about it tomorrow."

"Okay," I said. "I'm totally wiped out."

"We'll lock everything up tight. I'm sure that guy won't be back tonight, especially with most of us here." Moving to my window, he pulled the outside wooden shutters closed and slid their metal bar through the hasp. The window itself, miraculously, hadn't been broken, so now he pulled it down and latched it.

With the power still out it made the room seem extra dark, and I thought about how clearly I had seen in the darkness as a jaguar. The room felt hot and stuffy, and the smell of blood seemed to overpower everything else. As I stood there, trembling and vulnerably human, the electricity came back on, flooding the room with unwelcome light. I saw the broken mirror, the furniture shoved aside, the gouges in the wood, Tink's blood . . .

"Oh, jeez," I said in dismay. The AC hummed on, and cool, dry air flowed over us.

Dana reappeared in my doorway, holding a broom and dustpan.

"We'll clean this up better tomorrow," she said, throwing a towel over Tink's blood. Quickly she swept the mirror glass up, clearing a path between my bed and the bathroom. "There. That'll get you through the night."

"Thank you," I croaked. With the blanket still wrapped around me, I climbed into my tall bed. Matéo tugged the bedspread over me. Aly gave my foot a last pat through the covers. My head felt like it weighed a hundred pounds, and it sank deeply into the pillow. I heard them leave my room as I pulled my parents' sheet to me and inhaled its scent.

Exhaustion came over me like a wave of ether, and I plunged into a dreamless sleep.

Chapter Ten

I'D LIVED ALONE IN MY HOUSE IN SUGAR BEACH for a month before I came to New Orleans. In that time, I'd been hysterical with grief, furious at fate, kind of nuts, numb, sad, depressed . . . I'd been a bunch of different emotions, but I'd never been scared until that very last night. It had felt strange being alone, but strange and scared are two different things, and I hadn't felt scared, hadn't even realized that maybe I should, until I'd heard glass breaking in the kitchen. Until then, I hadn't once thought that whoever had killed my parents was going to come kill me. Their deaths had seemed . . . random, though I saw now how stupid that was. One haguaro killing other haguari? Not random.

Coming to New Orleans, putting so many miles between me and Sugar Beach, had felt safer. Finding Matéo and hearing that his parents' hearts had been taken also—it had been creepy, though we weren't 100 percent sure that their deaths had been caused by a haguari, as my parents' had been. It could have been something about the older generation, or even something related to whatever falling-out my mother and her sister had had.

But now the net was wider and seemed to include all of us. The jaguar had climbed the tree to get to me and/or Tink. The nightmare wasn't over.

I slept heavily, as if my dreams had fled in fright, and woke the next afternoon feeling like I'd been flattened by a steamroller. A shower and four ibuprofen helped, and once I was in clean clothes I felt better. The towel had sopped up all of Tink's blood on my floor, and I tossed it into my laundry hamper with a grimace, then swept up the rest of the broken mirror. When I bent down to scoop it into the dustpan, I saw my face, fractured and splintered among the shards.

"Very poetic," I muttered, and threw it all into the trash.

Aly was in the kitchen, reading the newspaper. "Hey, how are you feeling?"

"Okay. Sore." I glanced at the clock. It was almost two. I poured my own coffee. I'd become addicted to it and looked forward to it every morning. Maybe Ro's needed to use CDM coffee for the regular-Joe cup of coffee instead of the fancy Italian stuff they had. Perhaps I should bring this topic up with my boss, Mr. Stunning. Because after only one day, I had worthwhile ideas about how he could better his business.

"How's Tink?" I asked, holding my bowl in both hands and inhaling the scent.

Aly wrinkled her nose. "His side was pretty messed up. But we heal quickly. He'll be okay in a few days."

Of course, I'd been pondering every second of what had happened the night before, including the surprising ending. Since our polite conversation had been taken care of, I opened my mouth to ask about the stuff Dana had shot up my nose—but just then a slender girl with bright red hair came into the kitchen, wearing nothing but a large New Orleans Jazz Festival T-shirt.

"Hey, Charlotte," Aly said. "Haven't seen you in a while. This is Téo's cousin, Vivi."

At last, the elusive Charlotte!

The red-haired girl smiled at me. "Hi. I'm Charlotte, Coco's girlfriend. Is there coffee, by any chance?"

Aly pointed. Charlotte got two mugs, added sugar and milk, and filled them up. "Nice to meet you," she said, heading back upstairs.

"You too."

Matéo passed her on his way into the kitchen. "Hey, Charlotte." In the kitchen, he opened the fridge, then looked at me. "You doing okay?"

I nodded, thinking that "okay" had been radically redefined in the last three months.

"Have you had any ideas about who that could have been last night?"

"No," I said. "I wouldn't recognize any of my parents' friends in their other forms. But that guy just wanted to attack anyone he got to, starting with Tink. Tink isn't in our family, so this guy is collecting haguari hearts. But is it just one person? Or a human-haguari partnership?"

"I don't know," Matéo said. "I can't figure out the why, you know? It's not like we have buried treasure or know valuable secrets. He seems to just . . . want hearts."

I shivered, my own heart feeling heavy.

"Should we start asking around?" Aly asked Matéo. "I mean, more than we did when your parents . . ."

"I don't know." Matéo looked frustrated and rubbed the bridge of his nose. Tia Juliana did the same thing sometimes. "I'm not sure what to do. If we ask people, will that alert whoever's doing it and make us even more of a target? I mean, the whole thing is crazy."

For a few minutes we were all quiet, weighing our thoughts. Like Matéo, I didn't know what to do, or what we should do. I decided to ask a question they could actually answer.

"So what was that drug Dana gave me?"

"Cuva rojo," said Aly. "That's one name for it. It's from a plant usually found in the Amazon rain forest."

I vaguely remembered Dana saying that.

"How does it work?"

Matéo shook his head. "No one knows. For obvious reasons, it hasn't been tested in science labs. But our people using it is depicted in the earliest Olmec records. Pretty much everyone in our culture knows the plant, knows how to make the serum. It's considered a bit of a crutch, so we do want you to learn to change by yourself without it."

I started to say that I didn't want to learn, and then realized that even if I didn't plan on changing on purpose—and I didn't—it had been scary last night when I hadn't been able to control changing, and then didn't know how to become human again. "I'll think about it. In the meantime, do you think we should look through your families' books? See if there's any clue to what's going on?"

"Yeah," said Matéo. "Good idea. Right now I have to make a delivery—I'll be back around five."

"I'll be heading to work then," I said.

"I'll ask my brother to bring ours, the next time he comes," said Aly. "And we can compare notes later. What's neat is that when Téo and I get married, it will show up in both of our families' books, in the family tree section."

It was almost shocking to hear her speak about marriage so easily—she was only three years older than me.

"When do you think you'll get married?"

"We haven't set a date—we're not even officially engaged yet!" She laughed. "But we've talked about having kids sooner rather than later, like when we're twenty-five or so. So I guess we'll get married sometime before then."

It was hard to wrap my mind around—I still felt like such a kid in some ways. But my parents' deaths had aged me a lot too.

Later, heading off to my normal job at a normal coffee shop was a bizarre juxtaposition: Last night we'd been attacked by a strange haguari and I'd ended up in my jaguar form, unable to change back. I'd gotten some ancient rain-forest drug shot up my nose, which had somehow managed to transform my entire physical being. It was the stuff of a science-fiction movie. Now I was a barista. I remembered Tink saying it had been like finding out he was a superhero, and I gave a wry smile.

"Hey," said Hayley, when I came in the front door of Ro's. Today she had on a short black skirt, black-and-purple-striped stockings, and a shredded white T-shirt that said MY OTHER CAR IS A BROOM. Her hair was spiked all over her head in purple and black, and her eyes were outlined in heavy black Egyptian lines.

"Hi," I said. I was wearing my own clothes and felt boring and frumpy next to her. "How's your day been going?"

"Busy this morning, bit of a lull, then busy, now lulling. Weekend mornings are always crowded, but weekend afternoons and evenings are usually lighter. How did your night go? Exciting?"

I almost startled, wondering how in the world she knew what I'd gone through, then realized that of course she was talking about my first night at work. That had been yesterday. I let out a breath and tied on an apron.

"It was fine. Talia's great. Both of you have been great at explaining things and being patient with me."

"No prob," said Hayley. "You want to catch up on the dishes first?"

"Sure," I said. I grabbed the full busing bin and carried it through to the kitchen to the professional dishwasher, hoping I remembered how it worked. The kitchen had the big fridge and storage shelves, boxes of supplies, and this great dishwasher that could do a load every two minutes. I studied the controls again, started the first load, and looked around.

There was a really cool Wolf range and a set of professional double ovens. They were both dusty. I wished I could have them for Matéo's house. I could be a baking fool.

Aly had been right about the job. It had only been one day, but it was fun to have something to look forward to, a place I needed to go. Structure. Now, seeing these great ovens, I thought maybe it was time to start baking more. It always cheered me up. My tons of baking supplies were back at home, but I could use what Matéo's mom had had. My aunt. It was still an odd thought—my mystery aunt.

Ten minutes later I brought a heavy bin full of washed and dried china out front and started filling up the shelves beneath the counter. Glancing out into the room I saw that there were maybe eight customers, and again it seemed peaceful and wonderfully ordinary after the awful scare of last night. I'd just straightened up to get more milk from the back when I saw the side wall.

"Whoa." The front of the coffee shop and the right-hand wall were large glass windows. The left-hand wall was solid and plain, separating this shop from the antique store next door. Hayley had told me that in addition to whatever Rafael was working on, they often showcased local artists' work. Yesterday there had been a row of moody black-and-white photographs of flowers. Today the wall was covered with large sketches from the floor to the twelve-foot ceiling. I'd walked right by them without noticing. They were just rough images lightly done in charcoal, but I could make out tropical flowers two feet across, twining vines, a bird of paradise, several tiny animals peeping out from leaves near the floor.

"Awesome, right?" Hayley said, untying her apron.

"Did Rafael do this?" I asked, walking out from behind the counter so I could look at the sketches more closely.

Hayley nodded. "Yep. Fabulous, huh?"

"Yeah, it's awesome," I said, trying to imagine the details.

"It'll be better once it's all painted in," Rafael said from behind me, and I almost jumped. I'd only seen him sitting down yesterday; now I saw that he was taller than I'd expected, maybe three whole inches taller than me, and more heavily built than I'd thought. Stubble the color of coal made a precise mask over the bottom of his face, and he looked even more dangerous, even more fallen, even more attractive than he had yesterday.

"It's going to be amazing," I told him, trying not to fall into his arms. He nodded almost absently, not smiling. He was not a smiley guy. "How long do you think it will take you?"

"I don't know. I have to do it in my spare time." Again I noticed his straight-arrow nose and large, icy-green eyes. He was tough-looking, really guy-looking—not at all feminine, despite the almost sculptural fineness of his features.

"I guess you don't have much of that," I said. I was unusually aware of him, even aware of his scent, which reminded me of sandalwood and cypress. If only I could follow him around, inhaling deeply. Yes, that wouldn't be at all weird.

Feeling fidgety, I went back behind the counter and began fixing a refill iced latte for a customer. Hayley was getting ready to leave, putting on more black lipstick, pursing her lips at the mirrored wall behind the shelves. Trying to ignore Rafael, I busied myself with straightening the counter, wiping things down, cleaning the glass case fronts. Hayley took off and then I was busier, and soon I noticed that Rafael was gone. I relaxed a tiny bit.

During work last night, whenever I'd had a spare minute, I'd examined the drawings Rafael had made of people who worked here. Of course I only recognized Talia and Hayley out of the eight drawings, but they were all incredible, vividly alive though not photographic. In Talia's drawing he had caught her fire, her spirit, shining out of her brown eyes. She looked proud and strong, and I imagined she'd be like that if she weren't a personal assistant to some old lawyer.

When Talia herself came in ten minutes after five, she exclaimed, "So sorry I'm late, honey! My car stalled out and—oh my gawd in heaven!"

I grinned at her as I washed the milk frother thingy. The steam wand, it was called. "Rafael did that. It's going to be cool, huh?"

"That boy is wasted here, and I'm not lying." Talia bustled down the hallway and went into the ladies' room, coming out a few minutes later in turquoise leggings stretched to their limit and a colorful African-print tunic. Her short hair was cornrowed in a complicated pattern that swirled around her skull, and I was reminded of a Zen garden with the pebbles raked into perfect lines.

My second day was less of a breeze than my first. We had fewer customers, but I had my first run-in with a crazy person, a woman swathed in several layers of clothes and carrying several big shopping bags. She kept trying to order things we didn't have, and I was starting to get seriously rattled when Talia muttered, "Just say yes and make her a café au lait with four sugars."

I did just that. The customer sipped it suspiciously; then her face split into a smile and she became very gracious.

"Thanks," I told Talia, when the customer was gone.

"She always wants that. You'll get used to 'em," Talia said.

By eight o'clock the only people in the place were four students, each sitting at a different table, each with a laptop. I tried to imagine last night's attacker bursting into Ro's, startling everyone, and I couldn't really see it. Right now Ro's was my safe haven.

To my fevered delight, Rafael had been in the main room most of the evening, working on his mural. He was using a metal ladder to get the high parts, and I have to say I enjoyed watching him climb up and down. At one point a student close to him dropped a sheaf of papers and they went everywhere; Rafael stopped what he was doing and helped the guy pick them all up. Such a nice guy, for a fallen angel.

During a quiet moment I bought myself a mini ham and cheese quiche and an iced coffee and leaned against the counter, watching Rafael sketch in some more details. At twenty-one, he was three years older than me, and the same age as Matéo and Aly. Somehow he seemed older, less lighthearted. I remembered what Talia had said about his parents, how they lived in Mexico, and wondered what his story was.

The guy who'd dropped his papers came up and got a refill on his coffee, counting out a few singles and the exact change. I put down my quiche and fixed it for him, smiling as he took it and shuffled back to his table. The students made me think of Jennifer, and I hoped she'd liked her weird bio lab yesterday. I would try calling her tonight after I got off, but of course I wouldn't tell her about last night's freak show.

Just two months ago I had planned to be a college student—had made lists of what to bring, researched plane fares. Of course, my parents had been disappointed that I wanted to go so far away— they'd been pushing for something much closer to home, like Eckerd, or U of Miami. In the end I'd applied to exactly one college, had been accepted, and they had caved.

Now I would give anything to go to a Florida school, be able to go home on weekends, see my parents. My quiche turned to sludge in my mouth and I threw the rest of it away.

Around nine o'clock I was on the floor cleaning out the ice machine, and Talia asked out of the blue, "You got a boyfriend?"

"Oh. No," I said, pouring a mild bleach solution through the machine as Talia had shown me. You wouldn't think an ice machine could grow mold, but it could. So incredibly gross.

"Oh, a girlfriend?" Talia grinned.

"No, I'm not gay. I just don't have a boyfriend," I said.

"Well, you are one pretty girl," said Talia. "You might meet someone nice in here. You never know."

It wouldn't matter if I met someone nice or not.

Chapter Eleven

Talia had unknowingly hit on one of my sore spots: my lack of dating experience. I smiled, knowing she was trying to be friendly, but inside I felt the familiar cringes of embarrassment. I'd been on exactly three dates in my whole life, and none of them had been a success. The first one, when I was fifteen, had been with the son of one of my parents' friends. He'd been good-looking and pompous, and tried to act like he was much older than we were. His dad had driven us to the movie in their fancy car, and Gerry had held my hand and stroked my arm and my thigh. With his dad in the front seat. By the time we got to the theater I was hissing at him to cut it out.

It had ended badly with him asking me out again even though I was frigid, and me turning him down because he was a schmuck. His parents had been offended I didn't want to jump all over their little prince. The whole thing had been a disaster.

My second foray into dating was for the junior-senior prom at school. Ian Banks had asked me to go, and I'd said yes. I barely knew him—he was in my physics I class and we'd never spoken. My mom had been thrilled and bought me a much too expensive dress and insisted I wear flats so I wouldn't tower over Ian too much. I'd been furious. It wasn't my fault I was gigantic. Ian had been nice enough, but not very interesting. Mostly he seemed to want all of his friends to see us together—whenever one of them came near, Ian put his arm around my shoulder or leaned in as if we were talking. Once he kissed my hand. By eleven o'clock I was more than fed up.

My mom had been disappointed I was home so early.

Then there had been Carlos. He was a new student at our school and I'd been assigned to be his buddy for the first few days, until he knew his way around. Even Jennifer had noticed how hot he was, and we'd shared a bunch of suggestive eyebrow-raising. When Carlos asked me out that weekend, I was glad to go—he'd been super nice all week. I even told my mom that it was an actual date.

He arrived at seven as promised: a plus. My mom peeked at him through the front curtains and gave me a thumbs-up, mouthing *He's so cute!* at me before thoughtfully disappearing into the kitchen.

I answered the door with a big smile, but when he saw me, his smile faded.

"I'm not too early, am I?" he asked.

"No, you're right on time."

"Oh. Well, I can wait while you get ready."

"Uh . . . I am ready." I was wearing jeans and a tank top with a Guero's Taco Bar logo. There were no rips or stains anywhere. I had brushed my hair.

"Oh."

"Is there a problem?" I asked a bit tartly.

"Oh, no," he said, but his enthusiasm was MIA.

"What's the matter?" I crossed my arms over my chest.

"Nothing," he said. "Just—I know you don't dress up for school, and that's okay, I guess, but I thought you'd take more trouble to go out. Like, makeup. A nice dress."

I'd been so, so, so, so disappointed.

"I don't wear makeup," I said. "I don't wear dresses. This is me."

"But you're so pretty," Carlos said, continuing to wade into the La Brea Tar Pits of my dismay. "You'd be a knockout if you fixed up a little. You'd look like a model. Except not skinny."

"Good night, Carlos," I said, and shut the door. He'd waited there for a minute, I guess to see if I'd change my mind, but by then I was already in the kitchen wolfing down Oreos.

So actually I don't think that even counts as a date.

Now here I was at work, wanting to inhale the intoxicating scent of the devil man, as if I was ready to take off the training wheels of amour and leap right into the major leagues.

"Honey?"

My head snapped up as I saw Talia standing over me, smiling. She untied her apron and straightened out her tunic. "Tonight's my early night," she said. "I gotta pick my mama up from bingo." She leaned down and took my face between firm, warm hands that smelled like apricots. "Vivi. The Lord has blessed you with beauty. And you're a sweet girl, too. But you are throwing the Lord's gift away, with the hair and the ratty shirt and the sloppy shorts. Yesterday you looked so cute."

After my depressing Carlos memory, this was awful, and not even my mother had ever spoken to me so bluntly. I was shocked.

Talia gave my cheek a little pat, then got her purse and headed out.

My face was burning. Had Rafael heard her say that? Had anyone heard her? Seething, I bent over and worked on the ice machine. At first I was really mad—how dare she! It was none of her business! Then I admitted that she wasn't a mean person and probably thought she was being helpful and motherly. And I had already come to terms with the fact that I needed some new clothes.

It had just been galling for her to say it so plainly when she hardly knew me. Was I actually still pretty? Did I even care about that nonsense?

When the ice machine was churning out perfectly clean ice, I scanned the room to make sure no one needed anything. Two students were left, typing away on their computers, empty coffee cups on their table. I went to clear the empties, passing close to Rafael on his ladder, his comfortably worn-looking green T-shirt stretching across his broad shoulders as he worked.

I was not ready for the major leagues. Clearly. I wasn't even ready for T-ball. How depressing.

Over the next two hours, only a few people came in. Most of them were easy, but a gorgeous blond woman wearing skintight yoga clothes came in and asked for some weird complicated thing.

"Yes, no problem," I said, and quickly consulted the guide, which I had tried to memorize earlier, and thought I had. I didn't find what she wanted.

"I'm sorry—I'm new here," I told her. "What's the name of your drink again?"

Large blue eyes blinked at me. "I don't know the name," she said with a touch of impatience. "I don't work here, do I? I just want the—" and the rest of her words sounded like "blah blah almond blah caramel blah blah fat-free something something."

I looked at her helplessly.

"Look, if you don't know how to make it, find someone who can," she said, annoyed.

Swallowing, I went over to Rafael, who had already started to climb down the ladder.

"I don't know how to make her drink," I said, flustered. "I'm sorry. I can't find it in the guide."

"It's not in the guide," he said, and followed me behind the counter.

The blond woman's eyes widened as she focused on Rafael. She was probably ten years older than him but clearly thought he was worthy of her notice.

"Thank you so much," she said, her voice much softer. "This girl just can't get a simple order right."

I decided it would be a good time to wash dishes, so I wouldn't, I don't know, punch her in the nose. Leaning down, I stacked the dirty crockery better so it wouldn't tip as I carried it back.

"Vivi can do simple orders," Rafael said, surprising me. "And medium orders. And even complicated orders. But your order is on another level entirely."

Standing up with the bin, I saw her smiling at him, and I recognized the fake girly bashfulness that Cammie Nederflander had used on Harry Donner right before the homecoming game. Almost snarling with disgust, I edged past Rafael and went into the back kitchen.

As I loaded the waist-high dishwasher rack, I heard him asking her to walk him through it, step by step. He wasn't being flirty, exactly, but his manner was definitely calming her right down. Finally, the world's most asinine drink was completed, and I actually heard the woman giggle.

Giggle.

I pulled the handle on the dishwasher viciously so the strong jets would drown her out. After that load was done, I heard the metal ladder move against the concrete floor out front, so I knew Rafael had gone back to his mural. Which meant I had to go be the counter person. I just prayed that the ridiculous-drink person was going to limit herself to one.

She did, but she took ages to finish it. She chose a table close to where Rafael was working and sat so she could watch him. I groaned to myself, though I probably watched him just as much for the next two hours.

Finally the woman seemed to get tired of Rafael actually

working, so she went up to him and I saw her slip a piece of paper into his pants pocket. Gritting my teeth, I started to put the lids on all the metal containers of cream cheese and butter. *I don't care,* I assured myself. *It's not like I want him.* No, I was objecting to her stupid feminine wiles because they seemed so fake to me.

Yeah, that was it. I objected to her on philosophical grounds.

It was a relief to lock the front door at midnight. This time last night, Talia had locked the door, we'd cleaned up, and then I'd gone home and a jaguar had attacked my friend. Twenty-four hours ago. It was unbelievable, and I was glad I wasn't here by myself. Not that Rafael could protect anyone from a murderous haguaro. If anything, I'd have to protect him. This thought made me grin, and I indulged in further fantasies as I washed everything and put food away into the big fridge.

In the meantime, I saw shadows and underpainting appear, outlining flowers and plants and animals. I'd never had a shred of artistic talent, so seeing Rafael draw and paint so beautifully and easily was fascinating to watch. Plus, he was, of course, much higher on the "hot" scale than any guy I'd ever seen in real life. And didn't seem to realize it, which made him that much more compelling. It was almost as if meeting Rafael, knowing someone like him existed, had flipped some kind of awareness switch in me, so I could now actually feel attraction. Now I knew what it felt like to want someone.

Not that I would ever act on it. For one thing, I was a total awkward newbie with a gift for choosing the wrong people and then realizing I couldn't stand them. For another thing, even if Rafael was somehow not another wrong choice, I had no wiles. Zero wiles. This girl had no game at all. To even try would be to court disaster. Finally, if I could possibly surmount obstacles one and two, I still couldn't ignore the big white jaguar in the room—my nature, which had been thrown in my face just last night. How could I ever get serious about anyone, especially now that I knew I might accidentally change under extreme circumstances? It left me only one choice—to go out with fellow haguari. Which, no thank you.

But he certainly was fun to watch, and his painting was magical. As I finished sweeping, an enormous white morning glory bloomed on the wall right below the ceiling.

"That's beautiful," I said. "I love morning glories."

"These big white ones are called moonflowers because they bloom at night."

"Oh."

"They glow in a dark garden," he said, outlining a vine in deep gray paint. He sounded dreamy, as if he wasn't aware I was there. "Their scent is sweet, but not cloying like jasmine. Just . . . light." He looked up and saw me standing there, and seemed to come back to himself. "Oh—is today Sunday?"

"Uh-huh. I've locked up and everything's done."

"Great. You got the bathrooms?"

"Oh, no—I didn't realize. I'll do them now."

"Okay. And I need to close out the till for the week." Rafael got down and started putting lids on paint cans.

I got the bucket of cleaning supplies and started on the women's room, already dreading what I might find in the men's room. Feeling a lot like Cinderella, but with no prince anywhere in my future, I started scrubbing the sink.

"I've got the till, and I'm taking the trash out back," Rafael said, walking past the open door.

"'Kay. Thanks."

I finished that bathroom, cleaning the floor by dropping paper towels on it and swishing them around with my feet. Then I faced the men's room, which to my relief was not as heinous as I'd feared. I was halfway through that one when it occurred to me that I hadn't heard Rafael come back in. He'd been gone for several minutes, but he wouldn't have left without telling me. He needed to lock up, anyway.

Leaving the bathroom half done, I headed down the hall to the back door that led to the parking lot and the alley where the trash Dumpster was. The door was ajar, and I pushed through it.

"Rafael!" He was sprawled on the gravel, out cold. Blood trickled from a gash over one eye. The big trash bag had split open and trash was everywhere. Then my ears picked up the sounds of sneakered feet running in the distance, at least a block away.

Rafael had been mugged—the weekly bank bag stolen.

Seeing his beautiful dark angel's face with a lump on his temple and blood running down into his ear lit a fire inside me, and suddenly I was enraged. Without thinking, I raced out of the parking lot through the gap in the bushes, then paused and listened. The feet, two pairs of them, were moving fast, still running and headed toward the river. On the other side of Magazine Street, Leevey became narrow and unlit, leading into a less than great neighborhood. That didn't even make me pause as I shot across Magazine and plunged into the tree-lined darkness.

Naturally, I'd always been speedy and all athletic stuff came easily to me, so I could run flat-out without even breathing hard. It took less than a minute to pace the thieves.

I am fast I am upon them

I jump out in front of them

They are like roadrunners their feet peddling trying to stop

Their eyes are wide and scared their mouths are open

Give it back! My words are not words they are a roar it is startling

It is deep and threatening

My head is as high as the tops of their legs they are staring down at me

Down because I am on all fours I am a jaguar all of a sudden again

I am a jaguar how why

It was so fast it was easy it didn't hurt

This is the fourth time and yuck hot stink of urine yuck wrinkle my nose the pants are wet their fear is in their skin their sweat their hair

The white guy holds a bag I want the bag of Ro's

I swipe at it my claws in don't shred the bag

The guy falls over sideways in a crumply heap he has fainted

I am surprised I didn't even claw him the black guy the one who stinks spins and turns

He runs away

He is my prey

I can catch him I am strong I am fast I can bring him down

My jaws can crush his skull

I don't want to crush someone's skull

I don't want to think that

Down the street a light comes on lights up a porch I hear people speaking

I can't change back can't change back can't change back

I pick up the bag in my mouth it smells like money like old money like hands like sweat like Rafael it has old smells

I can retrace my steps I leave the guy on the sidewalk

Stick to darkness stick to shadows I am black I absorb light I am dark and silent

I slip through the inky darkness

I stay out of headlights the cars are loud they smell bad like burning

I need Dana I need cuva rojo Dana is not here

What can I do I have to run back home run all the way to home I will be seen I will be seen

This cloth these are clothes they smell like me they are mine

Where is Vivi what can I do I close my eyes

I think about Vivi standing on two feet Vivi so tall

I can't change

There is a sound it's Rafael he's moaning Rafael is waking up

I need to help him he can't see me like this

I have his money he is waking up I need to help him I don't have hands

I need to help him with hands oh my Tzechuri help me

That's it my bones are crunching down I am shrinking I am lessened

And with startling rapidity I was a naked freak in an alley. Jesus.

Feeling shaky I grabbed my clothes and wriggled back into them as fast as I could. My ponytail elastic was gone, so my long dark hair hung in a thick curtain around my shoulders. Picking up the bank bag, I tried to rub away the teeth imprints that had dented the thick rubber. I headed back through the bushes in time to see Rafael get unsteadily to his feet, one hand on the knot on his head. His black hair was stained with blood, and a few spots had dripped onto the shoulder of his green shirt. He still looked like a devil, and I couldn't believe any muggers had dared to attack him.

"What happened?" Rafael said a bit groggily. "What are you doing?" He looked around the trash area as if to orient himself. Then he inhaled, and his eyes snapped into focus on me, suddenly sharp.

"You got mugged," I told him. "They must have knocked you out."

He looked at me intently, his head slightly to one side.

"You got mugged," I said again, wondering how hard he'd been hit.

"You," he said slowly, his chest rising and falling.

"No, not me," I said. "You got mugged. By two guys." Jeez, did

I need to get him to a hospital? "Remember? You were out here?"

For a few moments he looked at me as if I were speaking gibberish, as if he were seeing me for the first time. Finally he said, "I remember . . . I hit them with the trash bag. Goddamn it! A week's worth of money."

"No—I chased them," I said, holding out the bank bag. "I . . . took it back." At that late moment I realized how bizarre that would seem. And in fact Rafael was staring at me, his dark brows angling down sharply.

"You chased them?" he said; then he shook his head and gave a little laugh.

"I guess I didn't think it through," I said honestly. "I was just so mad. You had a big lump on your head and were bleeding. . . . Anyway. At least they didn't get the money."

His mouth was open slightly; he was still breathing hard. "You're . . . you're—"

"I'm fine," I told him quickly.

He frowned, looking confused again, as if waiting for me to say something else. At last he reached for the bag, unzipped it, and saw the money inside.

"I'll get a new trash bag," I said, and darted through the back door. Rafael was still standing there looking thoughtful when I returned with a trash bag and the broom and dustpan. He was silent as we cleaned up the spilled trash, silent as he carried it to our small Dumpster and heaved it in. From the corner of my eye I saw how his T-shirt hugged his excellent chest, how his jeans outlined his

strong legs. My gods, he was devastating, in a dark, mysterious way.
Except he'd gotten mugged and needed my help. Hey! I had sort of
protected him, like in my fantasy!

"Well, the bathrooms are done," I said briskly, ignoring that I
hadn't quite finished the men's. I had to get out of here. "If you're
okay, I'll go home. I mean, are you okay? You can drive? Or do you
need to go to Urgent Care or something?"

"I'm okay," he said. His eyes were dark gray in the dim streetlight, but they seemed to penetrate my skull as if he could see right
through me. As if he could see that I wasn't normal. "Do you want
to tell me . . . I mean, how you got the bag back from them? Why
would they give it to you?"

*What an excellent question. Maybe because they saw my three-inch
fangs? Just a guess.*

"I just . . . maybe I just surprised them? I said I would scream?"

He narrowed his eyes, perhaps turning on his X-ray vision. "I'm
not a little guy. They whacked me on the head with the butt of a
gun. Why would they give you back a bag they'd just stolen?" It was
like he was waiting for me to pull out my concealed Uzi.

"I don't know," I said inadequately. "I was just so mad and I ran
after them and yelled, 'Give it back!' And they were so surprised,
and I said I would scream bloody murder . . ." *Make a note: Improve
lying skills.*

"They didn't pull their gun on you?"

"Whew, no. I'm glad I didn't know they had one. Jeez."

"Look, just tell me."

"Tell you what? Look, I don't know why they dropped the bag. It was stupid of me to go after them, I get that. But I'm glad I did, and now I'm ready to call it a night. You're welcome!"

Without waiting for him I strode inside. He followed me and locked the back door. I got my purse from the small employees' room, and Rafael turned off the lights as we went: hallway, employees' room, bathrooms, back kitchen, display cases, counter area, front room left and right.

Ro's was in almost total darkness, the only light coming from the green "on" button on the cooler case and the red illuminated exit sign that had its own electricity.

Rafael's blood was dark against his short hair, drying against his skin. His fine-boned face was mostly in shadow but striped by the streetlight outside, and I saw where a swollen goose egg marred his smooth forehead.

"Are you sure you're okay to drive?" I asked. "Do you want to get some ice before we go?"

"No—I'll get some at home. I'm okay," he said, setting the alarm by the front door.

The street seemed well lit and noisy after the empty darkness of the shop. Together we walked around the building to the side entrance of the parking lot. Now I felt unexpectedly vulnerable, as if last night's haguaro might be watching, might be waiting. Having Rafael here would be a liability, if I had to defend myself. What a weird thought.

Part of me was waiting for him to tell me not to bother coming back tomorrow. Or ever. I had cried during the interview, gotten rattled by an order today (was that just today?), forgotten to do the bathrooms, and then, to cap it all off, chased muggers. I mean, thank the gods he didn't know about the whole jaguar thing, because I was guessing that would definitely push it over the edge.

"Vivi. Thanks. Don't chase muggers again, but thanks. I'll see you tomorrow."

"You're welcome," I said again, and let out a breath of relief as I headed to my Honda.

His small truck, with a camper covering the back, was the only other vehicle in the lot. He clicked the keys to make it beep. "Drive carefully."

"You too," I said, feeling the tension in my shoulders. "Put some ice on that bump."

"Will do."

I got into my car, happy that I still had a job.

Chapter Twelve

It was a weird drive home. Once I was in the safety of my car, I began trembling from leftover adrenaline. After five years of never, ever changing even when I was upset, I had suddenly and involuntarily changed twice in two days. It was as if the nightmare with my parents had triggered something in me, something I had no control over.

Last night I'd been scared, had felt threatened. Tonight I had felt fury—and then an unsettling sense of exhilaration as I chased my prey. Laughing grimly, I turned onto Esplanade Avenue. At a red light I looked down at my hands, imagined them as large, powerful paws. I had run so fast. Had felt so powerful.

If there were no other cars at home when I got there, I decided I would go to some public place that was still open. There was no way I'd be in the house by myself, after last night. To my relief, when I pulled in through the side gate, I saw several rooms lit up. Not only that, but the kitchen door opened as I parked, and Aly came out.

"Hey!" she said. "You just get off work? How'd it go?"

"It was okay," I said. "Are you going out? It's past one."

She shrugged. "After last night I just wanted to . . . be around a bunch of people. I'm going to go meet Téo at the Fortress. What about you? You still freaked?"

"My manager got mugged tonight," I blurted, "and I accidentally changed again and chased the muggers and took the money back and one of them peed himself and one fainted and I almost thought I wanted to bite one's head but I didn't. It was awful!"

Aly's dark eyes stared at me for a long minute. "You . . . changed, and chased muggers . . . and got the money . . ." Then, unbelievably, she was laughing, her teeth white in the moonlight. Laughing so hard that she had to sit down on the concrete steps, she put a hand against her purple satin halter top and tugged down a short, swirly skirt that made her tan legs look amazing.

"You chased muggers!" she gasped, then gave more peals of laughter.

A blue hatchback pulled into our yard and cut its headlights. A tall, dark figure wearing green medical scrubs got out, and the car alarm beeped.

"Hey," I said to James as he walked wearily toward us. He was the roommate I knew the least, mostly because he was almost never there. Suzanne had said sometimes he was at the hospital for up to eighty hours at a time. My impression was that he was both too sweet and too shy for Suzanne, but maybe I just didn't know them enough.

"What's so funny?" he asked.

Aly just waved her hand in front of her. "Tell you later. Oh, my gods."

James gave a tired smile and went inside. Still gigging, Aly pulled herself together.

"Oh, my goodness," she wheezed. "I can't believe you! Chasing muggers. Good grief."

"You don't understand," I said stiffly, heading up the steps into the kitchen.

"What don't I understand?" Aly asked, following me inside. James had apparently already gone upstairs, because we had the kitchen to ourselves.

"I changed without meaning to," I said tensely. "Like last night. I can't control when it happens. And I was terrified, because Dana wasn't there with her juice and I thought I'd have to somehow get home without getting shot as an escaped zoo animal."

Aly's brows came down soberly. "I see. That must have been really scary."

"It was terrifying."

"Terrifying," she agreed. "But how did you change back this time?"

"I don't know," I said in frustration. "I heard my manager moaning—he'd been knocked out and was coming to—and I thought, 'I have to help him. I need human hands to help him.' And then I was suddenly changing back."

"Okay." Aly nodded. "Obviously we need to teach you the basics as soon as possible. You can learn how to not change, and you can learn how to change and change back. We can teach you."

I couldn't believe that life itself was forcing me to learn this after I'd resisted it for so long. I didn't say anything.

"Now I'm glad I ran into you," Aly said firmly. "Change your clothes, brush your hair, and come with me to the Fortress."

"Oh, no," I said. "I don't think so. Not tonight. I'm . . . shaken up. Plus, it's a bar. I'm only eighteen."

"The Fortress is connected to a dance club next door where they don't serve drinks," said Aly. "Lots of underage kids go there."

I grabbed a bottle of cranberry juice from the fridge and poured myself a big glass. I needed time to process what was happening to me—what I was becoming. I really just wanted to go upstairs and go to bed. James was here, and I'd seen Tink's SUV, Coco's van, and Charlotte's Mini Cooper. I wouldn't be alone. But Aly had been so nice to me, and really wanted me to do this.

"But of course people bring alcohol from the Fortress into the dance club," I said.

Aly shrugged. "Welcome to New Orleans. Come on, please come."

"Well, okay," I said, and had to smile at Aly's look of happiness.

The Fortress was on Ursulines Avenue in the French Quarter, a bit away from the strip clubs and tourist traps on Bourbon Street. We left the car in a pay-to-park lot and walked down the block. It was early September but still hot and muggy, of course—by the time we'd walked half a block, my clean bowling shirt was sticking to my back.

Despite the fact that it was almost two in the morning, the

streets were far from empty. Groups of gigging college girls, men wearing matching foam team-mascot hats, and even some families with little kids were filling the streets. Little kids in the French Quarter at two a.m.? What were they thinking?

I heard the music when we were still half a block away. The neighbors must have loved that. A line of people was waiting outside behind a velvet rope. Aly confidently walked past them.

"What did this used to be?" I asked her, gazing up at the big stucco building of the Fortress. It looked vaguely governmental.

"An armory, where weapons were stored. Then I think it was an orphanage."

"Huh."

"Hey, Noah," Aly said to the huge, forbidding bouncer at the arched doorway.

His dark face split into a pleased grin. "Hey, Aly. How's life treatin' you?" He immediately unhooked the blue velvet rope, and we sailed through like celebrities. Behind us, the people waiting grumbled.

"Good," she said. "And you? We're going into the Keep."

"Good enough," said Noah. "Okay, you go on in, then." He waved us through the thick, studded wooden door.

"Thank you!" Aly said, and I echoed it, blinking to adjust to the darkness inside. We were in a dimly lit black-painted hallway. Two big arrows were painted on the wall—one said THE FORTRESS and the one opposite said THE KEEP. Really loud music boomed at me from each side. I'd never been to a place like this. There weren't dance clubs in Sugar Beach, which was more of a quiet residential town instead of a hopping spring-break destination. I remembered Jennifer telling me about going to dance clubs in Israel. I wished she were here with me.

The Keep hallway led to a cavernous space, painted black like the hall and crowded with people. Small pendant lights in different colors illuminated circles on the dance floor and tinted anyone who danced beneath them. Along one wall was a long bar with a black top and a shiny front made of corrugated metal. The mirrored wall behind the bar was lined with glass shelves holding all sorts of bottled sodas, and fancy neon signs advertising Coke and Barq's Root Beer. While we waited for the bartender, I looked at the bottles and tried to decide what I wanted. Some had Japanese writing on them; some were from Italy or France or Mexico.

"Aly!" The bartender was a pretty woman with long, wavy caramel-colored hair. She wore dangly earrings and a small diamond stud in her nose, and I was jealous. Haguari didn't get piercings. Picture the effect when one changed.

"Posey! This is Téo's cousin, Vivi!"

"Hi, Vivi," Posey said, smiling. "What can I get you?"

"A limoncello?" I said. I assumed it was non-alcoholic, since we were on the Keep side.

Posey got me one still frosty with ice, and Aly ordered a Tamarind Charritos from Mexico.

"Isn't this great?" Aly said, sipping her drink.

"Yeah," I said, raising my voice to be heard. I watched the crowd for a few moments before I remembered what Aly and Matéo had said. Some of these people could be haguari. Right here in this room.

I leaned closer and spoke into Aly's ear. "Do you think there might be haguari here tonight?"

"Of course. There already are." She made a vague gesture at the whole room.

"Now?" I scanned faces, but unsurprisingly, none of them had whiskers and fuzzy round ears.

"Sure."

"Can you tell just by looking at them?" I asked.

"Hardly ever just by sight from a distance," she said. "I mean, I know a bunch of these people. Often you can tell if you get close to someone. Mostly a scent thing. Sometimes you can pick up on people's energies that feel like yours."

"Really?"

Aly nodded. "The more you know your own nature, the easier it is to see it in others. But a lot of it has to do with frequency, or practice. I'm not explaining this well."

"Frequency?" I drank my limoncello and felt way in over my head. The long day's fatigue had come back with a vengeance, and the music was giving me a headache. My brain kept flashing on Rafael, lying on the ground in the parking lot. I had been so mad. . . .

"Yes," said Aly, speaking right into my ear to be heard. "Someone who changes back and forth a lot seems to be easier to recognize than someone who hardly ever changes. And the more one changes oneself, the easier it gets to recognize it in others."

"Wow." There was so much I didn't know.

"Did you ask any of these people about Matéo's parents?" I asked.

Aly scanned the crowd. "I don't think so. I think we mostly asked older people, and Donella and Patrick's friends. Téo was right—I'm torn between wanting to spread the word as far as possible, and being afraid that that would tip someone off, make them target us."

"They're already targeting us," I reminded her.

Frowning, she nodded.

Just as I was about to suggest that we call it a night, Aly ran into some friends, so I met new people whose names I instantly forgot. Without meaning to, I started having fun, and for the next hour Aly and I hung out, sometimes dancing with each other, sometimes with her friends. Despite being really tired and sweaty, I somehow felt more full of life or whatever you want to call it than I'd felt in . . . a long time. Maybe ever.

"I need to get a skirt," I said breathlessly when we took a break. "These shorts are hot."

"I'm telling you—dresses and skirts are the way to go," said Aly, holding her dark curly hair off her neck. "We'll go shopping."

Jennifer was the only person I went shopping with, usually. My mom and I had always ended up fighting, as I rejected everything she picked out, and she did the same to me. Once, when I'd insisted on shopping in the boys' department, she'd stormed out of the store.

I didn't want to replace Jennifer, even though I liked Aly so much and she'd been great to me. No one could replace Jennifer, but it was just so easy to be around people I didn't have to hide anything from.

Around three a.m. Matéo got off work next door and came to find us.

"Ladies!" he said, grabbing Aly and kissing her, then giving me a hug. He looked more spiffed up than he usually did—his dark red hair was tidy, he had shaved, and he was wearing a deep-blue button-down shirt.

"Hi, baby," said Aly, kissing him back. They kissed a lot. And hugged. They were very physical, just like my parents had been. Was it a haguari thing? A Hispanic thing? A young people's thing? I'd never wanted to be like that with anyone. So among people I was a freak, and among haguari I was a freak. Excellent. I fit in nowhere.

"You look tired, *prima*," said Matéo, using the Portuguese word for "girl first cousin." He took a drink from Aly's soda.

"I am, actually," I said. "Been a long day."

Aly put her hand on Matéo's chest. "Vivi needs to come with us to the river tomorrow. She really needs to learn some skills. She needs to see some haguari in action."

"Oh, no," I said. What an awful idea. "That's okay."

"Perfect." Matéo nodded and pointed the bottle at me. "Let's go home, sleep until noon, and hit the river. We'll be back by four thirty so you can go to work."

"Oh, I don't know," I said, but Matéo and Aly both ignored me and headed for the exit.

Between now and tomorrow morning, I needed to think of a way to get out of it.

CHAPTER THIRTEEN

THEY BULLDOZED ME. WE GOT STARTED EARLIER, well before noon. I got about six hours of sleep and felt like I had packed a whole lot of life into the last week. Not all of it good. A nice quiet day, some of it spent soaking in the tub in the hall bathroom, would have been just the ticket. But Matéo and Aly seemed to not hear me when I made lame excuses, and instead they put a knife in my hand so I could make sandwiches.

I did not have a good feeling about this and glumly put my plain dark-green bikini on under shorts and a tank top. I didn't want to see other haguari change. I definitely did not want to change again myself. All I needed was to learn how to not change, even under extreme circumstances. That didn't seem to require being around a bunch of haguari.

Coco and Charlotte, Dana, Tink, Suzanne, and even James were all going, and there would be others besides. A whole bunch of us freaks of nature, frolicking in the wild. Perfect.

We carpooled, taking Aly's Camry and Coco's van, and drove for a good forty-five minutes—the last fifteen over a rutted dirt road. The thick pine woods around us were reminiscent of the Everglades, and my mouth went dry and my palms started to perspire.

"Where in the world are we?" I asked.

Aly looked back at me and grinned. "Mississippi. The Congala River. We're almost there."

The rutted dirt road gave way to driving through brush. Thin branches noisily scraping the sides of the car made me flinch, and I expected us to plow right into a tree at any second.

Then all of a sudden we were through the trees, the horrible scraping sounds stopped, and we rolled to a stop in a flat clearing. Several other cars were there—the other haguari. My heart went into my throat. I'd worked so hard not to have any part of this whole culture. Now I was surrounded, and they would be changing, possibly right in front of me. What would my parents think if they saw me now? I'd skipped family vacations to Brazil in order to avoid our kind. Now I was immersed. Would they be happy? Would they be frustrated that my cousin had succeeded where they had failed? I thought that they would probably be happy. Certainly more happy than I was, right now.

Then I had another thought: What if I recognized one of these people as the jaguar who attacked Tink a few nights ago? I made a mental plan not to be alone with any person I didn't know. Which left Matéo and Aly and our roommates. I would be the dork cousin sticking to them like glue. Fabulous.

"Everyone grab something," Matéo said, getting out of the car.

I got the large beach blanket, but when I held it in my hands I felt sick. This was such a terrible idea. It was way too similar to the last day with my parents—the beach blanket, the picnic. But Matéo, Aly, Coco, and Charlotte were already heading down a slight hill to a stretch of sandy beach. I wanted to climb back in the car and cry, but was too embarrassed.

So I clenched my teeth and followed my cousin to the water.

There were seven other people there—three guys and four girls, all looking to be in their early twenties or possibly even late teens. To my relief, they were wearing bathing suits or cover-ups. I did not need nudity on top of this.

"Hey, everybody!" Aly yelled. "This is Téo's cousin, Vivi! Make her feel at home!"

Smiles and waves from everyone. I tried to look comfortable and cool.

I'd never been super popular in high school. I had friends and a little circle of people I hung out with and Jennifer, but I'd never cared enough about my appearance and had never bothered with whatever popular thing people were doing, so I was often on the outside, much more than Jennifer. No one hassled her for being gay, and she had a thousand friends and had been our class president in junior year. I'd been her campaign manager.

"Hey, Vivi?"

I looked up to see Matéo smiling at me.

"Spread out the blanket and we'll put our stuff on it," he said. "Then we'll go for a swim."

Trying not to seem like a total loser, I flapped the blanket out flat, then left my shorts and tank top on it and followed everyone down to the water. The river was about a hundred feet across, with thick woods lining the other side. This side had a small sand beach, but the other side was a sharp drop-off of about fifteen feet. If you were in those woods and not watching where you were going, you could step right off and fall into the river.

The chilly water felt incredible compared to the steamy, muggy air, and I sank in it up to my neck. Sugar Beach was about five minutes from the ocean, and I'd always loved the white-sugar sand of Florida beaches. This sand was tan, and the water was reddish and somewhat clear to about four feet. After that you couldn't see the bottom. Stretching out, I swam to the opposite shore and back. In seventh grade I'd been the starter on the swim team, loving the competition, loving beating my own best times. But after that summer I quit being on teams.

"Hi. I'm Mimi." A slender girl with very short light-blond hair had swum up to where I was treading water in the deepest part of the river.

"Hi—I'm Vivi."

"That's a pretty name. Where are you from?"

And so on. I made small talk and tried to be friendly, which I accomplished by pretending I was someone who'd had no tragedy in her life and was not a freak of nature. Then I remembered that everyone here was a freak of nature, and something inside me froze a little.

Several people seemed to be of Brazilian descent, though only one person had any kind of accent. Besides Mimi there was Elaine, who was from New York, and Flor and Estrela, who were twins originally from Minnesota. I recognized their names as being Portuguese—Flor meant "flower" and Estrela meant "star." I didn't know if those were their real names or nicknames. One of the guys was called Tito, which was a typical nickname for a younger brother in a family. The other guys were Miguel and Danny, who was Elaine's brother. I picked up that Miguel was a new member of their gang—their conversations were of the getting-to-know-you type.

I was so glad that at least I knew everyone we had come with. For a while I sat by Charlotte, whose bright orange hair was covered by a white, wide-brimmed hat. She was wearing what she called her "sun burka," which was a pink-and-white long-sleeved sunproof top and long pants. "I don't tan," she told me. "I fry."

Coco smiled at her and said, "I like fries," and they exchanged a look that made me want to move out of the way.

Next to slim, dark Tito, Tink looked extra big, blond, and beefy. His side had almost healed already, I was glad to see. Miguel was a mélange—probably half white and half black. His features were African-American, but his eyes were green and his hair was dark blond. I decided that he should go be a model in New York—they would love him.

Being nice was exhausting, though (along with last night at the dance club) this was the most fun I'd had in months. Even Suzanne seemed to loosen up, splashing water on James and then shrieking when he tried to dunk her. This was the first time I'd seen James when he didn't look dead tired. Usually he and Suzanne seemed like an odd couple, but today I saw how well they fit together when they weren't stressed and overworked.

After lunch I lay down on our blanket and shut my eyes, hoping to not have to talk to anyone for a while. These people were all fine; it was just still hard for me to socialize for more than about half an hour at a time. Matéo and Aly's friends were funny, bright, and interesting—the cream of the haguari crop, I imagined. None of them were stuck-up; none of them seemed odd or off. Obviously Matéo and Aly would have recognized the intruder from the other night. It couldn't be any of these people.

Besides my family in Brazil, I'd never been around so many haguari, especially ones my age. It was hard to believe. I tried to picture Jennifer here. I thought she would like them, would fit in. If she had no idea what they were.

The hot sun was making me drowsy, and I was just dozing off when I heard Mimi say, "The equinox is coming up soon."

"I know," said Aly, next to me. "I can't believe it's September already."

"We should have a party," said Matéo, and voices chorused, "Yes! You should! A party at your house!"

Aly laughed. "That would be fun. We'll do a service inside; then the party can be inside and outside."

I lay very still on the blanket, trying to control my breathing.

I knew what Aly meant by "do a service." My parents had held services in their house on the seven major haguari holy days throughout the year, to worship Tzechura and Tzechuro, the jaguar goddess and god. I had hated, hated, hated it. It had seemed like the final embarrassing symbol of their weirdness, and by the time I was fifteen, I had thrown so many fits about it that they finally let me quit participating. Deep inside I felt so disloyal to the Tzechuri, but I just wanted my parents to be normal, to go to a regular church on Sundays or a regular synagogue on Saturdays.

It kept getting thrown in my face, the haguari thing. It was still shocking to find out how widespread haguari were—I had known it wasn't only my parents and my relatives, but I hadn't experienced the reality of that. Even when we went to an actual temple of the Tzechuri in the little Brazilian town my tia Juliana lived in, it seemed like something only about my family. But there were lots of us—people I wasn't related to and would never know.

Here were all these otherwise normal young people—they were in college or had graduated, they had jobs or were getting grad degrees, they had families and siblings and other friends. It was a whole world of haguari that wasn't about me or my parents. Listening to them talk, it sounded as if their growing up had been so different from mine, with haguari friends, a wider community where everyone shared similar experiences, the same religion, the same genetic mutation. With just me and my family I'd felt so incredibly abnormal. So other.

"I'm about ready," said Dana, standing up and brushing sand off her bottom.

"Me too," Aly said, drinking the last of her diet soda.

I opened my eyes and sat up. "Ready for what?" I asked Aly softly.

"Time to change," Aly said. "You ready for your first lesson?"

My heart sank. The big question: whether peer pressure and a fear of looking like an uncool prude would convince me to do what my parents hadn't been able to convince me to do in five long years.

Feeling like a complete wuss, I shook my head. "I just can't," I whispered.

Aly stopped stowing things in the picnic basket. I was trying not to look at the others, who had gone to the edge of the woods and were slipping out of their bathing suits. As much as I would hate to go skinny-dipping with a bunch of people I'd just met, it would be easy-peasy compared to what they actually wanted me to do with them.

Out of the corner of my eye I saw Miguel start the horribly identifiable hunching over. I shifted on the blanket so my back was to them. Behind me laughter changed to a deep rumble.

"Really?" Aly asked at last.

"You guys coming, babe?" Matéo asked from the top of the little hill.

"One sec," she called back.

"I've never changed on purpose," I reminded her. "It was awful when I did it accidentally, last night and the night before. I have no idea how to change back. Maybe I can, maybe I can't. I hate it. It's scary. I can't control it."

"That's why you need to learn," Aly said.

"I can't. I know I have to, just so I know how to not ever change again, but I don't want to learn in front of all these people."

"It's so weird that your parents didn't teach you," Aly said.

I didn't want to talk about all their useless attempts.

"Look," I said, "you go on with Matéo. I'll stay here and load up the car. Do you think you'll be back by like three thirty?"

"I don't want to leave you," she said.

"I'm fine," I insisted. "I'll load the car and take a nap in the backseat. Just remember that I have to be at work at five."

I didn't watch Aly and Matéo change. Something in me still found it grotesque. I had no idea how I had changed the last two nights. I knew why—big emotion—but not how. It had hurt the very first time, and it had hurt the day my parents died. It had taken a lot longer. These last two times had been fast, and I'd hardly been aware of it. Was that what it was supposed to be like? Before I finished putting the blanket in the car trunk, Aly and Matéo were gone, running through the woods with their friends, a pack of jaguars.

What would happen if they came upon a person? Those kinds of questions freaked me out. I didn't know how they dealt with it.

I rolled down all the windows on Aly's car, grateful it was parked in the shade, at least. Opening the cooler, I took one more icy soda and then lay down on the backseat, the seat indentations making my back arch uncomfortably.

I didn't know what to do. I didn't know who I was. Since I was thirteen, I'd formed my whole persona as opposite to my parents. Opposite to my mom. Somehow cutting out the haguara part of me had seemed okay then. Now, around all these haguari, I was only half a person. Trying to be opposite of Matéo and Aly seemed ludicrous—even scary. Without them, who did I have? Jennifer in New York. Who I couldn't even tell the truth to.

It was really, really hot, even in the shade. The fabric of the car seat smelled hot. The trees overhead were oppressive—stolid witnesses to my fears and uncertainties. I pressed the cold can against my forehead and started to cry.

CHAPTER FOURTEEN

AFTER THE CATACLYSMIC, SCREECHING HALT OF my life in May, I had entered a stasis where I had spent weeks wandering numbly around my parents' house. Then I'd found the picture of Donella, and my life had jolted forward again.

Now, as a sweltering New Orleans September went on, I felt my life stabilize, in a way. Matéo and Aly offered several more times to teach me how to change at will, and though I knew I needed to learn, I chickened out each time. Instead, to ensure that I wouldn't accidentally change, I tried to avoid any upsetting situation, which wasn't that hard. My days acquired a pattern, and it was becoming almost as familiar as the get up, go to school, go home, eat dinner, do homework pattern of my former life. Now it was sleep in, eat breakfast, hang out, go to work, come home, hang out some more, go to bed around two. Repeat. I was getting to know all my roommates more, including my cousin. More important, I felt . . . accepted. Even though I never changed with them. No one ever teased me about that, and I wondered if Matéo or Aly had told them to lay off me. Although there was so much I apparently didn't know, because of my heritage and the little I had absorbed from my parents, I was still one of them.

And it felt really good. After refusing to belong to my own family, not really fitting in at school, not having a boyfriend—now I was one of a group. When they made inside jokes, I got them. When Coco and Aly spoke in Spanish, I understood most of it. Matéo and I found that our families had used a lot of the same idioms—one day he'd planned to make dinner and had food out, pots ready, and then decided he didn't want to bother. Without thinking, I'd said, *"Ajoelhou, tem que rezar,"* like my dad had always said to me. Basically it meant, "You're kneeling, so you're going to pray." Kind of like "Finish what you started." Matéo had laughed because his mom had said the same thing to him. He was my family.

About a week after the river picnic, Mrs. Peachtree called me. Back in August we had talked about things, because it looked like I wouldn't be back for a while. We had agreed that she would take any houseplant still alive from the house, and that once a week she would take any mail, drop it into a big manila envelope, and mail it to me. I kept the water and electricity turned on, but canceled the Internet and cable TV service. It would be easy enough to get it back once I returned home.

In return for all this, plus Mr. Peachtree cutting the lawn and making the house look lived in, I sent them a check every week. At first she hadn't wanted to accept it, but I'd pointed out that she and her husband were essentially acting as management agents. At the start of September we'd gone to monthly checks, because I had no idea when I'd be back. Every so often Mrs. Peachtree and I would call each other to check in, so I wasn't really surprised when I saw her name on the caller ID of my cell phone.

"Hi, Mrs. Peachtree," I said.

"Hi, sweetie," she said. "How are you doing?"

"Fine. Still working in the coffee shop. So everything's okay."

"Good. Listen, did your friend find you?"

"What friend? Jennifer? She knows I'm here."

"No, not Jennifer, I know her. This was a man. He said he was a friend of your parents, and he had something of theirs for you?"

I stopped sorting laundry and sat down hard. "When was this?"

"A couple of days ago," Mrs. Peachtree said. "When Phil saw him looking in the window at your house, we went over there real quick."

"Oh, good," I said faintly, my heart in my throat. "Did he say who he was?"

"Said his name was Felix Winston, and that he worked with your dad. He said he'd found something of your dad's at the office and wanted to return it to you."

"Hm. Yeah, my dad did work with someone named that. I think I met him once. What did he look like?"

"Indian," said Mrs. Peachtree, who was from south Texas. "Like Mexican Indian, you know?"

"Yeah." I remembered Felix Winston as being tall and light-haired. "Did he leave anything with you?"

"No. He said he'd come back later. I said it was hard to know when you'd be here—with work and all. I made it sound like you still lived here but were unpredictable."

"Thank you. This was just a few days ago?"

"Yes. Anyway, I haven't seen him since."

"Did you mention New Orleans?"

"No. Didn't give him your cell number, either. But he seemed to think he could look you up or something. So I was curious if he'd found you."

"No," I said. "But could you do me a favor and let me know if you or Mr. Peachtree ever see him again?"

"Sure, honey. Everything else okay?"

"Yes, I'm still enjoying being here. I'll probably be back before too much longer, though."

"Okay. You let me know if you need anything, okay?"

"I will. Thanks, Mrs. Peachtree."

Of course I told Matéo and Aly about it right away. Since it had been just a few days before, it wasn't the person who had attacked Tink. But it definitely hadn't been Felix Winston.

"We were already on guard," said Matéo. "Now we'll be extra on guard."

"Hey, should we maybe get an alarm system?" I asked. "I know a lot of houses have them."

Matéo looked at me. "We're a bunch of haguari. What's an alarm going to do that's better than anything we can do ourselves?"

He had a point. I pictured the alarm contacting the police and them showing up in time to see a bunch of large jungle animals fighting.

"Oh, you know, I wanted to show you this." Matéo took out a photo album, one of his mother's from before she was married. It was amazing, looking at it. I saw so many familiar pictures, except these had Donella in them. She had been cut out of the pictures we had at home. Other albums showed Matéo as a little kid, in Mardi Gras costumes, school uniforms, with friends. His school photos. It was still hard to believe that both our families had lived in America, not all that far apart, and yet had never met, never gotten together for holidays, never exchanged birthday cards. What could have caused that?

Matéo was closing the album when a picture fell out. I picked it up and looked at it, an odd feeling going down my spine.

"What's this?" I asked.

Matéo gave a sad smile. "That's my mom with one of her old boyfriends. Actually, they were engaged, and then like two days before the wedding, she ran off with my father. It was a big scandal. Her parents had loved her fiancé. But she said she knew my father was the love of her life, and she had to be with him." He shrugged. Then he saw my face and frowned. "What?"

I let out a breath. "Matéo . . . this is my father."

We stared at each other, then at the picture again. It was definitely my dad: young, handsome, smiling, in horrible eighties clothes. He had his arm around Donella's waist and was gazing at her adoringly. She was laughing at the camera, her face so much like mine.

"Are you sure?" I asked Matéo. "Sure that this was who she was engaged to? It wasn't someone else?"

"No," he said slowly. "She told me the story a bunch of times. She thought she was in love with him, but then she met my dad and was crazy for him, even though he wasn't Brazilian. He was American, and his parents are Irish. Mami told me that her parents didn't speak to her for two years, and when they finally met my dad, they couldn't stand him."

"Did she ever tell you her fiancé's name?" I asked in a tiny voice.

"Victor. Victor somebody. I don't remember."

Victor was my dad's name. My dad had been engaged to another woman, and not just any woman. To my mom's sister.

"Maybe this is why the big split happened," I said. "Why there were no pictures of Donella, no mention of her anywhere."

"I can't believe this is your dad," said Matéo. "That he was who Mom was engaged to. This could definitely be why the sisters quit speaking to each other."

My mind was reeling. It was one thing to find out that your parent had once been engaged to, or even married to, someone else. But to find out your dad had been engaged to your mom's sister? A sister you'd never even known existed? It hinted at a much more complicated story. Would Tia Juliana tell me anything, if I asked her? Would she just get mad? Surely she had to know the whole story.

"Is there any way this could be related to the attacks?" I asked.

"How?" Matéo said. "It's bizarre, but who would be upset

about it after all this time, except the four of them? And they didn't kill each other."

"So this could be why the sisters split up, but probably doesn't have anything to do with their murders." I was having trouble taking this all in.

"I guess so," said Matéo.

I pushed the album away. "I better go get ready for work." I still had an hour but wanted some time alone. Matéo nodded and put the albums away—he seemed as freaked out as I was. Upstairs, that picture kept popping into my mind. My dad. He and my mom had seemed so perfect for each other, so happy. Victor and Aracita. I'd seen their wedding pictures a million times. The eighties had a lot to answer for, stylewise, but still. My grandparents had been in those pictures, looking happy. So had Tia Juliana, who'd been barely twenty. I'd always thought my parents had been destined to be together. They were so affectionate. How had Papi ended up with my mom after being dumped by Donella? Obviously my mom had known all about it. How many more secrets was I going to stumble onto?

Aly and I had gone shopping last week, and now I pawed through my clothes trying to find something to wear. I decided on a new vintage bowling shirt, more my size, instead of my usual huge. I'd become a convert of the skirt club, and today's was short and pleated, with an inexplicable printed border of kittens going around the bottom. I was even wearing sandals instead of my black high-tops. Okay, so they were Birkenstocks and not platforms, but they were sandals. And comfy.

My long, thick hair was defeating my attempts to subdue it when I heard my computer ping. I lunged for it and flipped it open.

"Jen! I tried calling you last night."

She sighed. "I was at a dorm party."

"That sounds fun." I leaned over the bed, untangling a knot in my hair. Would I tell Jen about my parents? I tried to think it through.

"What are you doing?"

"I have work in a little bit." Once again I held a hair elastic in my teeth as I swooped up handfuls of hair.

"Still doing okay?"

"Yeah," I said. "I pretty much know how to do everything now, so I don't feel so stupid." I shrugged. "It gives me something to do, a place to go. I like the people there."

What else could I talk about? My parents? About accidentally changing into a monster at the drop of a hat? About somebody snooping around, trying to kill us? I considered for a moment while I managed to braid my hair, pulling it around in front to get the last bit. Then I snapped on an elastic and sat down on the bed.

"How's the hot boss?" she asked.

I made myself grin. It was a relief to have something normalish that I could tell her.

"Still hot. Still apparently completely uninterested in a social misfit with no fashion sense and poor social skills. Go figure. Did you get the latest pictures of the mural?" I'd been sending her progress shots from my phone.

"Yeah. It's incredible, and he's not even finished. A brilliant artist," Jennifer mused, looking at the ceiling. "Misunderstood . . . needing love and understanding . . ."

I howled with laughter and threw my socks at my computer. "Anyway, how about you?" I asked. "How's rooming with Lucy going?"

"She's fine," said Jennifer, but I read between the lines. "She's not awful or anything. I just . . . have nothing in common with her. Not a thing. Not a single thing."

I gave her a sympathetic smile. "That's a bummer. Can you get a different roommate next year?"

"Oh god, I'll still be here next year," Jennifer moaned, dropping her head into her hands.

"How about your classes?" I asked quickly. "You said you were liking your public policy class."

"Yeah." Jennifer raised her head a little bit. "The one I'm finding super interesting, actually, is the social services one—like, social work."

"Yeah?"

"Yeah. So that's my highlight. Out of endless hours of misery."

I smiled at her hyperbole.

"Are you going back home for Thanksgiving?" Jennifer asked.

I hadn't given it a thought. "You're going to be up there, at your aunt's, right? So . . . there's kind of no one at home to have Thanksgiving with. I don't know."

"It's like you're making a whole nother life without me," said Jennifer.

"You're kind of doing the same thing without me," I acknowledged. "It sucks."

"Yeah." Jennifer sighed.

"Have you met any nice girls?" I asked, wiggling my eyebrows.

Jennifer gave a little smile. "There's a girl, Amy, in the Columbia B'nai Brith. There might be something there."

"Oooh," I teased her, and she smiled bigger.

"I have to get to class," she said. "Take care—call me soon, okay?"

"Will do," I said, and blew her a kiss. "Gotta fly."

"Oh, Lord Jesus," Talia muttered, looking at the front door.

"What?" I asked.

"I need to go reorganize every single thing in the kitchen," she said, heading through the doorway behind the counter. "Yell if you need me."

I was still wondering what she was doing when a sharp rap on the glass case made me jump.

"Girl!"

There was no one there. Then I saw a shadow through the glass case and peered over it. A tiny old woman, maybe in her early eighties, dressed all in black, was about to rap her cane against the glass again.

"Please don't do that!" I said quickly. "I'm sorry—what can I get for you?"

"Make me a cup of coffee, and not that fancy bilgewater my grandson serves!" she snapped. "Fix me a cup of coffee and chicory with hot milk! Café au lait! You know how to do that?"

"Yes, ma'am," I said, grabbing a thick ceramic coffee cup and saucer. Gods, this must be Rafael's grandmother, the crazy old woman people kept talking about. *Great. Thank you, Talia. The view from beneath this bus is great.*

Fortunately, just last week, Rafael had given in to my almost daily requests that we get some regular New Orleans–style coffee on hand, since I was now addicted to it. He'd agreed, and already enough people had started requesting it that he'd bought several French presses so I could make it fresh.

"Don't lie to me!" the old woman snapped as I reached for the electric teakettle, and I almost jumped again.

"Excuse me?"

"You can't!" she said, and I expected to see fangs at the corners of her thin, wrinkled mouth.

"Can't make you coffee?"

"Can't make me good coffee!" She was practically howling, and people were turning to watch. My cheeks got hot.

"I can try," I said. Weeks of working here had toughened me up a bit, and I no longer got as rattled when faced with a difficult customer. Now, as the old woman scowled fiercely at me, I took one of our small, three-cup French presses and put it on the counter in front of her. She frowned at it suspiciously. Then I took a can of CDM and carefully measured three and a half scoops of coffee into the glass carafe. The old lady's black-beetle eyes flared when she saw the can, and her lips pressed together tightly.

I poured in boiling water, then took a wooden chopstick and stirred the coffee and water until there was a fine tan foam on top.

I let it steep for a moment while I zapped a small pitcher of whole milk in the microwave. Finally I eased the press down, trapping all the grounds of the coffee at the bottom of the carafe. Inhaling deeply, I couldn't help smiling—it smelled so good.

Now for the *au lait* part. I poured the hot coffee into the cup until it was half full, then filled it up with the steaming hot milk.

"Do you want sugar?" I asked.

"One sugar! Regular sugar from sugar cane!" she barked. "Not that fake rat poison! Not brown sugar! Not sea sugar hand-dried by organic virgins! Regular sugar!"

Dixie Crystals it is. "Yes, ma'am." I added one scant teaspoon of white sugar, then pushed the cup toward her.

Frowning at me so hard that her overgrown and overblack brows almost met, she reached out a slightly trembling skeletal hand. Slowly she took the cup by its handle as I watched her. Talia came in very quietly from the back and waited on another person who had come up.

The old woman took a tentative sip. Her lips pursed as if a frog or snake would slither out. Then, completely unexpectedly, her face rearranged itself into a kind of scary semblance of a smile.

"Why, that's lovely coffee," she said.

Next to me I felt Talia's eyes about to bug out of her head, felt her hand freeze as it reached for a rugelach in the case.

I smiled back at the woman, who was surely Mrs. Fontenot. "I'm so glad. Can I carry that to a table for you? Do you want a scone or something to go with it?"

"Only this. This is good." Almost cackling, the old woman walked surprisingly quickly to a small table and sat down. She was tiny, with thin, light bones like a songbird, and I felt like a giraffe next to her. In case she wanted a refill, I carried the rest of the coffee and the small pitcher of hot milk to her. She sipped again, making a happy humming sound.

Back at the counter I grinned at Talia, who wasn't even pretending to not be shocked. Very subtly I did a small *who's your daddy* dance.

"Girl, I'm going to call you David from now on," Talia murmured. "'Cause you just knocked down Goliath."

"So that's the famous Carlotta Fontenot," I whispered. "The one who owns this place?"

Talia nodded and put a slice of coffee cake on a plate for a customer. "I've never heard her say a nice word to anyone. Except Rafe. She loves that boy."

"Coffee with chicory soothed the savage beast," I murmured. Then the words "savage beast" made me think of, you know, *my family*, and I let out a sigh.

Down the hall, I heard the back door swing shut with a bang and hoped that it was Rafael so he could see my victory. And it was. My skin felt electric with anticipation, and when he appeared, my eyes drank him in. He smelled like heat and sunlight and wore a black T-shirt and an old, soft pair of chino shorts. His legs looked strong and tan, and for me they tipped him into the perfection category.

"Hey," I said, praying that he couldn't see the schoolgirl crush in my eyes.

"Hi," he said. "Everything okay?" He pushed a paper grocery bag onto the counter. Inside were three gallons of milk, and I took them out to put them in the fridge.

"Looka there," Talia said quietly to him, and gestured to his grandmother.

"Grandmère," Rafael said, sounding surprised.

She smiled at him, and he looked even more surprised as he walked over to her. They kissed on both cheeks, and he sat down in the chair across from her.

"That girl makes good coffee," said Mrs. Fontenot, pointing a gnarled finger at me.

Rafael looked over at me, and I smiled. For just a moment our eyes locked, and I realized I didn't usually look directly at him. More like, watched him when he wasn't looking. Finally I tore my eyes away and put the milk into the counter-high front fridge.

"Huh," said Talia, watching me.

Please don't say anything inappropriately personal, I wished silently. Like about my appearance, or her hope that I would meet a nice person to date. After she'd torn apart my looks I'd felt unsure about her, but she'd acted like nothing had happened and was so obviously not a mean person in general that I'd gotten over it. With my new clothes, I'd never be a teen model, but I did look less sloppy.

"Huh what?" I asked.

Talia threw a dish towel over her broad shoulder and looked at me. "You and Rafe."

She saw way too much. My eyebrows rose innocently. "Whaaat?"

Leaning over, Talia grabbed the busing bin. "No one's ever been able to please that old lady," she said, keeping her voice low. "You're the only one. I think he's going to have to marry you."

Okay, teasing was teasing, but I'd known I could never get married since I was thirteen years old. My face fell and I said more shortly than I intended, "Well, he's out of luck."

Talia looked taken aback and opened her mouth to say something else, but I grabbed the window cleaner and some paper towels and went to the front doors, where I vigorously spritzed glass that didn't need cleaning.

I stayed busy for the next hour, and when I looked up again, Mrs. Fontenot was gone and Rafael had gone back to his office. Talia tried to be friendly, chatting with me, but I was preoccupied and not in a good mood.

Still, I was surprised when she called, "Night, honey! See you Tuesday!" at ten o'clock and swished out the back door to the parking lot. I frowned—was it bingo night? I couldn't keep it straight. I hoped Rafael was still here—I hated being anywhere all by myself. There hadn't been any more weird attacks or even an inkling that I was being followed. But it wasn't over, I was sure of it, and I wasn't about to relax.

When Rafael came out from the back with his wooden box of paints, I let out a tense breath.

"You're almost finished," I said, gesturing at the huge wall mural.

Over the past few weeks it had become a vibrant, living thing: a dense, detailed painting of a rain-forest scene, but with New Orleans plants and people and animals woven into it. His grandmother, sitting primly in a straight-backed chair, was painted by the right edge. A vining fuchsia plant made sort of a crown around her delicate white-haired head.

The banana trees and the wild ginger that grew out by the parking lot were painted next to huge ferns and primeval palms that shaded an unlikely assortment of bush babies, birds of paradise, canaries, deer ... Now there were just a couple of smallish spots that were still white, and every day I checked to see if they had been filled in. Maybe tonight was the night.

Because Rafael was there and I was in no hurry to leave, I didn't kick the customers out right at midnight. The more people the better. I took my time cleaning everything, and swept instead of vacuumed so I wouldn't disturb anyone.

Around twelve thirty I looked over and saw Rafael on the ladder, adding details to something near the ceiling. I headed in his direction, wiping down tables as I went, and had to stand almost right next to him to see what he was working on.

My heart almost stopped. He was painting a jaguar.

I mean, of course, right? The whole thing was jungle—anyone would have put in a jaguar or tiger or something. It just took me aback, is all. The jaguar was gracefully stretched out on a wide, rough-barked branch, reminding me uncomfortably of the night I had done just that, and not that long ago. Its eyes looked out of the painting as if considering what to do next. I could practically see the powerful tail lashing back and forth, almost feel the jungle pulsing around it. I moved to the left and the eyes followed me. I moved closer to the ladder and the eyes still followed me.

Rafael looked down at me. "Good kitty," he said, and I stared at him.

Chapter Fifteen

Did he mean—he didn't mean—he pointed at the jaguar with his paintbrush. "Isn't it?"

Oh. "Uh-huh," I said, nodding. "It's beautiful."

Leaning in, Rafael carefully traced a thin black line around one of the jaguar's eyes. That was when I noticed that they were green, with a gold rim around the iris. I thought of my mother's golden eyes. Why did these look familiar?

Then I got it. My breath caught in my throat as I realized that the jaguar's eyes were Rafael's. He'd painted his own eyes into the mural, in a jaguar. Solemnly I looked from the painting to him, and he glanced down at me. I looked back at the painting, and now the large cat actually resembled him quite a bit. Like "Self-Portrait of the Artist as a Large Cat." The cheekbones, the shape of the forehead, the straight nose like an arrow, the eyes . . . It was unmistakably Rafael.

Oh my gods, was he a haguaro? Heading back to the counter, I wondered what on earth it all meant. Why else would he do that?

Except—he couldn't be a haguaro. That would be too much of a coincidence, even in New Orleans. And wouldn't I feel it if he were, the way Aly said I could? I saw him at work at least three times a week. Surely even I would be able to pick up on it? But I mean, he'd painted a jaguar to look like him. That was an awfully big clue. Wasn't it?

The last two customers finally left. I was in the back kitchen putting away the last load of clean crockery when Rafael came in and washed his hands at the sink. I realized that he and I were alone here, which had happened before, of course, but now I wondered if he was a haguaro and if he should be on the suspect list for the attack on Tink.

I watched him wash his hands. He was definitely beautiful enough to be a haguaro. And I knew so little about him . . . Maybe I should get out of here.

"How tired are you?" he asked.

"Um, tired," I said.

"Too tired to sit for me?"

Um . . .

He must have seen the confusion on my face, because he gave a half smile and said, "I always do portraits of the people who work here. If you're not too tired, I could do it tonight."

The idea of Rafael drawing me was tantalizing. Lamely, I told myself that if he intended to attack me, he would have done it before this. He'd had plenty of opportunities. So either he was a haguaro but not the attacking haguaro, or he wasn't a haguaro at all. Plus, the portraits he'd done of the others were amazing, and I'd love to know how he saw me.

I was excellent at rationalizing things. "Okay," I said.

"Great," he said. "I know it's late, but I don't have many chances to grab an hour."

"Okay."

"I was thinking maybe you could sit in one of the armchairs in the window?" he suggested, and I felt a tiny thrill that he had thought about me that much.

I nodded and went to the window closest to the mural. A pair of faded pink old-fashioned armchairs made a cozy nook in the bay window, and I sat in one stiffly.

"I don't know how—" I said. I'd been about to say "how you want me" and then felt a sixth-grader's giggle rising in my chest. Ruthlessly I pushed it down.

Rafael stood there and looked at me, clearly seeing me as shapes and shadows, lines and curves. A still life. When he suddenly looked into my eyes and smiled, I almost fainted. If only. If only he were a haguaro and I wanted to be with a haguaro, which I didn't. But wait—if he wasn't a haguaro, and I didn't want to be with a haguaro, didn't that mean . . . oh. No. Because I myself was still a haguara. Never mind.

"Are you comfortable?" he asked.

"No."

He nodded. "Get comfortable. And make sure you can sit like that for a long time."

Feeling goofy, I tried various positions while he pulled a chair over for himself and set up a small wooden easel. I could not get comfortable. Finally he was ready and he looked at me around his sketch pad.

"Vivi."

I loved the way my name sounded on his lips. He couldn't be a haguaro. I'd be able to tell, right? And he would have defended himself against the muggers. And his grandmother—I couldn't picture that tiny, proper old lady as a fierce jaguar.

"Vivi."

"Yes?"

"If I weren't here, if you weren't posing, if you had to kill an hour, how would you sit?"

That was easy. I leaned over, stretched one arm out on the table, and rested my head on it. I could sleep like this.

"Okay," he said, sounding distracted. "Maybe . . . take your hair down."

This was actually feeling pretty sexy, despite the fact that I smelled like coffee grounds and sugar syrup and cleaning liquid. Reaching up, I pulled out the elastic holding my braid and then combed my fingers through my hair. *If I were more secure and less painfully self-conscious, I would give my head an abandoned shake like in a shampoo commercial, and then he would be overcome and—*

"Okay, now get into whatever pose you want," he said.

I slumped over the table again, pushed my hair out of my face, and got comfortable. Rafael adjusted his sketch pad slightly, looked at me intently for several minutes, and started working.

After a minute and a half, my back started aching. After approximately four minutes, my feet went numb. I wished I had thought to curl them under me or something. How could I possibly do this for an hour? Why had I slumped over on the table? I was going to look like a big shapeless lump, like Quasimodo. If I had sat up, I could have tucked my shirt around my waist.

Just relax. Relax. Relax.

Surprised that my brain came up with something so useful, I paid attention to it and slowly forced myself to let go of all my frantic thoughts. It had been a long day and I'd been on my feet since five o'clock. Breathing in and out, I deliberately relaxed all my muscles, starting with my toes and working my way up. Without realizing it, my eyes slowly closed, my breathing slowed, and I kind of . . . fell asleep.

I knew where I was, could feel the ache in my back, but was sort of dozing off and drifting into fantasies about making out with Rafael, holding hands, smiling at him in the sun, sharing a peach with him and watching the golden juice run down the dark stubble on his chin . . . I leaned over and licked it off, inhaling his scent. He smiled and kissed me, and then my hair fell over my face and his strong fingers brushed it back.

Blinking, I realized that Rafael was standing next to me, and his fingers were brushing my hair back.

"Your hair slipped a little," he said, his fingers leaving a trail of heat on my skin.

"Oh."

"You've been doing a good job of being really still," he said, walking back to his easel.

"Oh, good." I brought my left hand up and shook it so I could read my watch. "Is it really two thirty?"

Rafael looked around his sketch pad at me. "Yep. Time flies, et cetera."

"Are you almost done?"

He looked at me again, those dark slashes of eyebrows angling downward. "Bored?"

"Yep."

It was startling when he grinned—it happened so seldom—and it made his striking, angular face astonishingly more attractive. I blinked dumbly a couple times, then let my mouth curve into a grin also.

"Actually, yes, I'm about done. You can sit up."

I couldn't help groaning as I slowly uncurled my back and arched it in the other direction. Every muscle screamed, and I imagined all the little sinews knitting and unknitting, being stretched. Rafael had gone back to work, looking at the sketch pad so intently he didn't seem to notice me staggering to my feet and stretching again. I was so tired, and I still had to drive home.

"Can I see it?" I asked.

It was a minute before he answered. "Hang on. One more minute . . ."

Well, at least I didn't have to sit here any more. I got my purse from the employees' room and went to the bathroom. My hair was fuzzy and messy-looking, I was of course wearing no makeup, and had dark circles under my eyes and colorless lips. I had let Rafael immortalize this forever. Excellent.

He was standing in front of the easel when I came out, leaning over to finish some small lines in one corner.

"Can I look now?" I asked.

"Yeah, I guess so." He added another small line and smudged something with his pinkie.

Time to see the truth. I had been curious as to how Rafael saw me, but now was scared to find out. If he saw me as ugly, I would feel awful. But it wasn't like I planned my days around making sure I looked fabulous all the time. There was an uncomfortable contradiction here that I needed to figure out.

Turning, he saw me hesitating, walking as slowly as possible. His green eyes were intent as he said, "If you hate it, we won't put it up, okay?"

"Okay," I said, then realized it would have been more polite to insist that I wouldn't hate it, no matter what.

I got very near the easel before I let my eyes focus on the drawing. Then my mouth dropped open and my fingers reached out to touch it. Only Rafael's warm hand, touching mine, reminded me not to smudge it.

Was this me? Was this how he saw me? It looked like me, but an impossibly optimistic version. It was bigger than I expected, maybe eighteen inches by twenty-four, and on the same mustard-colored drawing paper as all the others. He'd used pencil and charcoal, and white pencil for the highlights; with that limited palette he'd created a drawing that was so real-looking that it was almost sculptural.

Instead of slumping gracelessly, I was arched sinuously over the table. Instead of looking tired, I looked thoughtful. My shirt wasn't lumpy—it defined my body without looking skintight. I saw the breadth of my shoulders, the smooth muscles of my arms, the delicate arch of my collarbones. Because of the dumb position I'd chosen, my body was bent and angled in an oddly provocative pose, as if I'd wanted to call attention to my boobs and waist. At the bottom of the drawing you could even see my skirt riding up on my thighs. What had I been thinking, sitting like that?

But it was my face that was so shocking. I'd hoped I hadn't drifted off enough to actually drool, but in this drawing I gazed out at the viewer, my dark, almond-shaped eyes half-closed as if it were a hot day and the heat were making me sleepy. My nose was straight and finely carved, my mouth fuller than I'd thought. My lips were slightly parted as if I were about to say something. And my hair—my thick rat's nest spilled over my shoulders and across the table like dark syrup, flowing and silky, framing my face and trailing halfway down my back.

I looked . . . incredibly feminine and sexy, not in a porn-star way, but with a strong, womanly attitude, as if I knew how beautiful I was, knew that any man who saw me would fall under my spell. It was bizarre and stunning—and yet it really did look like me.

Minutes passed as I stood there staring, and then I saw something that made me inhale sharply. I'd been sitting at the table closest to the mural wall. Rafael had sketched in part of the mural behind me, making it subtle and shadowed but unmistakably there.

The eyes of the jaguar stared out right over my shoulder. My back blocked the branch he lay on so it looked as if he were curling over me, staring at the viewer. If one got fanciful and imagined it at an extreme perspective, it could look as if I were prey, and the jaguar had caught me and was holding me as his.

"Um . . ." Rafael's quiet voice brought me back, and I realized I hadn't said anything in several minutes. My hand felt warm—Rafael was still holding it. Gently I tugged on it and he let me go.

"Wow," I said finally, my throat dry. "Gosh."

"That isn't how you see yourself," he said.

"Noooo," I said slowly. "Not really." Not at all.

"That's how you look." He sounded quite sure.

Oh, what I wouldn't have given for that to be true, for me to truly be strong, confident, and beautiful. Like . . . my mother had been. "Hm."

"Do you hate it?"

"No—of course not. It's beautiful. It's amazing. No. Just . . . not used to it."

"Should I put it on the wall with the others? Or rip it up?"

My eyes flared and I turned to him. "Don't rip it up!"

He didn't say anything—it was almost three in the morning and he looked as tired as I felt. A buzzing from inside my purse made us both jump. I tore my eyes away from him and pulled out my cell phone.

"Hello?"

"Vivi? Are you okay?"

"Hi, Aly—yeah, I'm fine. How come you're awake?"

"Téo just realized your car wasn't here," she said, then yawned. "It's fine if you're out. Just wanted to make sure you're okay."

"I'm on my way home now," I said.

"Okay. Drive safe."

By the time I slipped my phone back in my purse, Rafael had put his drawing things away and was locking the back door. He clicked the lights off one by one, and once again we were in darkness in the big front room. The mural jaguar's eyes glowed at me, and I looked away from it. Something unusual and intimate had happened here between us tonight, and I didn't know how to act, or if I was the only one who'd felt it.

Rafael set the alarm by the front door, punching in numbers on a keypad. "No one's ever made my grandmother coffee she liked." I smiled as we went out through the front door and he locked it. "All these years she's been hysterically angry about the coffee, but I didn't realize it was because she wanted local coffee with chicory. She didn't actually say so."

Maybe I was the only one who had felt it. "You and your high-falutin bilgewater."

He laughed. He actually laughed, putting back his head. It was wonderful to hear, to watch, and I wished I'd had more dating experience, enough to deal with this overwhelming attraction. The three failures I'd experienced had only made me more uptight and anxious. On top of that I was now terrified of accidentally changing in case of strong emotion, or of someone being able to tell that I was Not Normal.

Even now, I realized that Rafael was the only guy I'd met in the last two years who'd even made me question my dating ability, and that made me wonder if I should risk it. Could I kiss him without changing? How far could I go before my whole system short-circuited, turning me into a lethal predator?

My mind was whirling with these thoughts as we headed to the parking lot, and it took me a second to process that Rafael had said something.

"What?" I asked.

"I said, you're eighteen, right?" Under the parking-lot lights his hair was shiny and black. I wondered why he kept it so short, almost militarily short. All the same, he was one gorgeous guy.

"Yeah. How old are you?" Talia had told me, but I asked anyway.

"Twenty-one. Twenty-two next February."

"I'll be nineteen next—" On the first anniversary of my parents' deaths. They had died on my birthday. I would never be able to have a happy birthday again.

"What's the matter?" His voice was soft.

"Nothing," I said unconvincingly, unable to look at his sharp beauty in the warm night air.

He touched my chin, put two fingers beneath my jaw and very, very gently tilted my head so I had to look at him. "You know, sometimes you're right there, and sometimes you're far away. And the faraway place is . . . broken."

My eyes widened at his devastatingly accurate description, and to add to the general awkwardness of my social skills, tears welled up, making my lashes spiky and my vision blur.

"I think . . . I'm broken too." So not what I had meant to say. So not strong and confident and beautiful.

"No." Maybe I imagined him saying that. But I didn't imagine Rafael leaning closer, bending down slightly, and slowly, gently, pressing his lips against mine.

I hadn't kissed a boy in well over two years. I'd only ever kissed three boys, if you counted Jennifer's fourteenth birthday party when we played spin the bottle. Now I was kissing the hottest guy I'd ever seen. Jennifer was going to freak.

I was freaking. Was I even doing this properly? Rafael made a little sound and put his hand on my back, holding me a bit closer. He tilted his head to make our mouths fit together better, and I reached my arms up and looped them around his neck. He was only three inches taller than me, and we fit together very well. Soon I felt his warmth the whole length of my body, and we were kissing and kissing, slanting our mouths this way and that to get as close as possible. I wanted our chests to melt together, my arms to fuse around him, his hands to leave their imprints on my skin as if I were clay.

Rafael broke our kiss first and was quiet for a moment, pressing our foreheads together. "I know you—but why—why are you—" he muttered, then took a deep breath and shook his head. "I'm sorry."

"About what?"

He stepped back, putting distance between us. I looked up into his eyes, allowing myself to get lost in them as surely as I would get lost in a jungle.

"I don't understand you. I don't know why—" His face was tight.

"Why what?"

He shook his head, looking frustrated. "Never mind. I don't know. I'm sorry."

Not what any girl wants to hear, especially after taking an extremely infrequent chance of kissing someone. I took a step back myself, trying to think of a snappy response. Unfortunately, I hadn't been dumped by nearly enough guys to develop a worthy arsenal, and my mind was scrambling.

"It's all so . . . complicated," Rafael said, running a hand through short black hair, making it stand up.

Oh please, how lame is that? I mean, yes, it was horribly complicated on my side, but he didn't know that. He was trying to tell me his life was complicated? I cocked one eyebrow, sighed, and opened my car door. Well, now we knew: He was an incredible artist. Period. That didn't make him an incredible guy.

"It's okay," I said, striving for casual. "It was just a kiss, Rafael. I don't need you to put my face on your home screen."

"No, you don't understand," he began, but I slid into my car and shut the door with a satisfying bang.

Yes, I did. I understood that the kiss I had reveled in was a big mistake in his eyes. I understood that it wouldn't be happening again. I understood that the guy who had drawn me with such exhilarating vision was just a small part of an unworthy total.

I started the engine without looking at him directly, but glanced in the side mirror as I pulled out. He stood there watching me, his haunting, angular face looking more upset than I would have thought. Almost tortured. His jaw muscles clenched; his hands made fists. He really did look upset. What in the world was going on with him?

I drove carefully, my brain bombarded by questions, fears, embarrassment, doubt . . . and fortunately made it home without running into a streetcar or mowing down a tourist. I parked between Coco's van and Tink's SUV and went inside, the warm night air seeming to encase me.

The light was on over the side steps. To my surprise Matéo opened the door for me.

"Hey, *prima*," he said. "Thought I heard your car. You're back late. Everything okay?"

"Yeah, whatever." *I just made out with my boss who then rejected me.* "Listen, Matéo . . ."

"Yeah?" My cousin's hair was wine-colored in the dim light from the lamp on top of the fridge.

"I need you to teach me how to change. And how to not change."

Chapter Sixteen

As they had told me, it took more than five minutes to learn. My parents had tried more than once—the first lesson was on my thirteenth birthday. We all know how that went.

My cousin and I started the next morning. Matéo asked me if Dana could help too, and I'd said yes even though I was going to be embarrassed enough to have Matéo witness my ineptitude. For convenience's sake, we decided not to go out in the woods somewhere but instead practice upstairs in the attic. Besides the six small bedrooms (formerly for servants), there was a larger room on one side where people stored stuff. One small window in the gable let in light, and the ceilings sloped dramatically to end in knee walls.

"This is my heavy bag," Dana said, patting the large punching bag hanging from the ceiling. "Feel free to use it."

Yeah. That wasn't going to happen.

"Are these your weights?" I asked, pointing at a bench and a large set of free weights.

"Uh-uh. Those are Tink's," she said. "But I use them too." She made a fist and curled her arm to show off impressive muscles. I grinned and tapped her bicep—it was rock hard.

"Let me know if you want to go running sometime," I said. "I like running."

"Oh, that would be great," Dana said. "No one around here runs."

"Stuffy up here," Matéo said, and opened the small window. Air moved, but it wasn't any cooler.

The child me had seen no benefit to knowing how to change, had been scared of changing, had emotionally rejected the world that included change. The slightly more grown-up me recognized that there was a benefit to knowing how to not change. Until I could trust myself, control myself, there was no way I'd be able to get close to anyone. If I ever had anyone to get close to. Apparently I still didn't, because dark, lovely Rafael of the Searing Kisses had a "complicated" life. My life wasn't exactly a Happy Meal, you know?

"Okay," said Matéo, rubbing his hands. "Let's get started. First, we have to kill a squirrel."

"What?" I cried, horrified, even as Dana started laughing. "Oh, you butt."

"No, no squirrel," Matéo snickered.

"They're delicious!" Dana said brightly.

I groaned and covered my face. "I can't do this."

"Okay, kidding aside," said Matéo. "Now, how often have you changed?"

"In my whole life? Four times."

"Four!" Dana was even more surprised than Matéo.

I ticked them off on my fingers: "My thirteenth birthday, then the day my parents . . . then that night the jaguar attacked Tink, and then the very next night when I chased the muggers."

"Wait—you chased muggers? In New Orleans?" Dana shook her head at my idiocy.

"It's been pointed out that that was a bad idea," I acknowledged. "Anyway, it seems that ever since my parents . . . died, extreme emotion seems to make me change, whether I want to or not. Like the Hulk. I need to learn how to not do that."

"You can learn that," said Matéo. "Do you remember how you changed, the very first time?"

"No. I have no idea. Is it like a genetic-timer kind of thing, where we're programmed to change when we're thirteen years old? Like thirteen full moons a year, times thirteen years . . ."

"That's an interesting theory," said Matéo seriously. "But no, that's not it. Do you remember what you did right before you changed?"

"Had birthday cake." The last one my mom had made for me.

"What else?"

"What do you mean, what else?"

"Something to drink?"

"Oh, yeah. Punch. Red punch." I stared at him. "Oh jeez, was there some of that stuff in there?"

"Cuvaje rojo," Matéo confirmed. "The same species of plant, but different. Cuvaje rojo causes haguari to become their jaguar selves.

Cuva rojo causes haguari to become their human selves. Almost all parents help their kids change the first time that way. It's easier and faster. Then you learn how to do it on your own."

"So they drugged me."

"Or . . . they shared with you some of our culture's natural and traditional medicine," Dana said pointedly. "Like matzo-ball soup, or boiled willow bark."

"Those don't make people undergo a profound cellular meta-morphosis," I felt compelled to point out.

"Moving on," said Matéo. "The way my parents taught me is to start with meditation."

"Mine too," said Dana. "Basically concentrating intently on everything your body is feeling. When you can isolate certain feel-ings, you can increase them, or call on them at will."

That was all we did that day: meditate, focus on our bodies, isolate muscles, control our breathing. I listened to my heart beat, my lungs fill with air, my stomach gurgle from breakfast. I saw the weird little lights behind my eyelids when I closed my eyes. When it was over, I felt very relaxed and calm, but not any closer to learning what I needed to know.

But it was a start. I had started.

I had the next two days off from work, which I was glad about. It would give me some time to get a grip on my emotions. When I finally had to go back, I dressed with extra care. I didn't know what to expect from Rafael—would he be standoffish? Mean? Ignore me? Lead me on again? In any case, I would feel less vulnerable if I looked okay.

As it turned out, my awesome fifties-housewife dress was wasted: Rafael wasn't standoffish or mean or anything, because he wasn't there—and neither was my portrait. Despite everything, I had looked forward to seeing it join the others on the wall. To know that Rafael didn't want to put it up hurt—like maybe he thought I would read too much into it or something.

Talia and I worked till midnight and the evening passed quietly, with no one kissing me and nothing happening that would cause me to accidentally turn into a jaguar.

Rafael came back the next day, and I was glad I'd made the effort to wear a short, pine-green fluffy skirt and a slim-fitting black T-shirt cut for a girl. I was getting more used to how I looked in clothes that fit me, but I pretended to ignore how Rafael's eyes seemed to linger on my legs and my face. Actually, his eyes lingered on the middle parts too. Since I was at about an eighth-grade level of dating experience, I went with my eighth-grade instinct of acting distant.

When Hayley, Talia, and I were all there, Rafael told us that he'd hired two new people, who would start the next day: Kathy, working on the day shift with Hayley, and a guy named Joey who would pinch-hit for whoever needed a sub.

"Yay!" said Hayley. "I mean, I miss Annie, but I'm so glad to have someone to help me full-time. Annie used to work here," she added for my benefit.

"I think they'll work out," said Rafael. "Vivi, could I see you in the office for a sec?"

Here we go. I followed him stiffly back to the manager's office and was bummed when he shut the door. If he tried to fire me because of that kiss, I was going to break something over his head. And then sue his ass.

In this small room I was even more aware of his scent, the freshness of sandalwood and cypress. Was it maybe his shampoo? Today he was wearing a pale gray linen button-down shirt that had been washed so many times it was about the thickness and strength of Kleenex. I wanted to bury my face against his chest and inhale deeply.

"I wanted to tell you again that I'm sorry," he said.

"I told you, it was no big deal." I tried to look bored.

"It was a big deal to me. I don't go around kissing everyone. Or anyone, really."

Hm. I bit the inside of my cheek so I couldn't blurt, "Me either!"

Rafael let out a breath. "If things were different—I mean—" He stopped, looking frustrated. "Anyway. I didn't want you to think I was playing you, and I wanted to apologize. I wish things were different." He paused, looking at the floor, and muttered, "Really do wish."

"You're not firing me?" I asked meanly.

His head jerked up. "Oh, no. Thanks for the vote of confidence."

"Just making sure." In truth, his apology had been good. It helped to know that it wasn't me. But I was still irritated.

"No. Obviously." Now he looked irritated too. "Unless you don't want to work here anymore, because of me."

"No, I'm okay," I said coolly. "Are we done here?"

"Vivi, don't—" he began, then just nodded. I opened the door and left, feeling a little better somehow.

The new people worked out well. I didn't see much of Kathy—she worked days with Hayley. Joey worked with Talia on my nights off, and then with me on Talia's nights off. He was a couple of inches shorter than me and totally muscle-bound. He was another student at Tulane, studying law with an art history minor, which was how Rafael had met him. His hobby was bodybuilding, and he competed in amateur events all over the U.S. He was dark and intense, with a strong New York accent. He thought the heat in New Orleans was going to kill him. He had been here three years. In his own way he was as gossipy as Talia, so it was fun to work with him. I wondered how well he knew Rafael but didn't want to ask.

And about Rafael: We were both acting like nothing had happened. He was in the coffee shop almost every day, reservedly friendly with everyone. Usually he spent at least an hour working on the huge mural, which was becoming more mesmerizing by the day. I still thought he was one of the most gorgeous guys I'd ever met, but he was making it easy to let go of the crush I'd had on him.

In the afternoons I looked forward to going to work, and in the early morning I looked forward to going home. Matéo's house felt a lot like my home now—not like my house in Florida, but like I was home when I was there. We hadn't had any more weird incidents, and without speaking about it had adjusted our schedules so no one was ever home alone. Around one in the morning I'd turn in off the side street and would breathe a sigh of relief when I saw Tink's SUV, Coco's van, Aly's Camry.

Matéo had finally gotten around to showing me his family's book. It was a lot like a scrapbook. Like a cross between a scrapbook and an illuminated manuscript.

"Jeez, how old is it?" I asked.

"Well, my pages are only three years old," he said. "But this stuff here in the beginning . . . look, there's a date." He pointed at a date written in faded purple ink on the corner of a page that was brown with age.

"Oh, my gods," I said. "Sixteen sixty-seven."

"Everything's in Gaelic until the early nineteen hundreds, of course. My father's father went back and translated it all, writing a modern version of these pages so we'd be able to read them without all the old-fashioned stuff."

"Cool."

"So here's our family tree. Most of it." Matéo unfolded a sheet until it was about two feet by three feet. "This branch is my father's family, my parents, and me. Then you can see my mom's side—all our relatives."

"Yeah," I murmured, scanning names that I remembered. But everything earlier than my great-grandparents was new to me. Matéo had more information about my family than I did.

"And then when Aly and I get married, I'll have to copy her

history onto new pages." Like Aly, Matéo spoke casually about their future, taking it for granted that he'd found his life partner. I was envious, but couldn't begin to imagine settling down with someone this young.

It was fascinating, seeing Matéo's family's book, and it made me more determined to find mine the next time I went back to Florida. Matéo's was thick—it would take hours to go through the whole thing. It had some general haguari history, sections on our religion—even a code of conduct written in 1811. (Basically, don't kill your neighbors or their children or their animals or servants.) What I found really interesting were the very old descriptions of haguari clans: the Far clans, Asians, and the Sun clan, Africans, were seen as fascinatingly foreign, back in the sixteen hundreds. Then there was the North Clan, which encompassed all haguari from North America and the middle countries down to Panama. The South Clan, which Aly and I both belonged to, was all of South America. Patrick Garrison had belonged to what he called the Patch Clan.

"What does that mean?" I asked. "His family was from Ireland, right?"

"Yeah," said Matéo. "So, European. He explained that Europe was seen as a bunch of little patches of clans, compared to the larger clans of North America and South America, China, and Russia. Europe is a bunch of smaller countries all jammed together, but really different from each other. Like a patchwork quilt. So they called it the Patch Clan. But I've also seen really old books that called it something like the Puzzle Clan, because it was like a puzzle, made up of smaller pieces."

"Did each European country have its own clan? How did they get lumped together?" I asked.

"It was more like, in the very beginning, the haguari spread, starting in South America," Matéo explained. "First they were one clan, then two or three, then more and more as we expanded across the globe. I'm sure within the Patch Clan, or South Clan, or any other clan, there are smaller subclans. My dad always thought that the tradition of claiming a larger group was designed to help stop infighting. More to build a sense of community and brotherhood, so that we didn't kill each other off."

"Could it be a rival clan trying to kill us?" I asked.

Matéo looked thoughtful. "It could be. But if it is, why don't they just kill us? Why take our hearts?"

I had no idea. The idea of all of our separate clans was something I needed to explore—my parents hadn't told me about it. Most of their friends had been Brazilian, but I didn't know if that was coincidence or a deliberate choice to associate only with what I now knew were South Clan members. I wished I knew more, but I had only myself to blame. Still, a whole world of knowledge was opening up for me, and it was fascinating, weird, and a little scary.

"You know, look here." Matéo pressed the book open wider. "I never noticed it before, but this should be much more filled in, with my mom's family history. Instead there are just a few lines, and then boom, she married my dad. It was like she didn't even have a family when they got married." Matéo said.

"That's, weird. I'll definitely look for my book, next time I go home," I said. "But I bet there isn't any more information there about your mom and my dad ever being together. The whole thing is so strange—but I remember my friend Jennifer telling me about two of her aunts who didn't speak to each other for over twenty years because one of them kept their dad's prayer shawl and the other one wanted it. That was just a shawl. Not a fiancé. So who knows?"

I had hoped that Matéo and Aly would forget about having an equinox party, but they didn't. One day I found them in the kitchen, making lists of party food and discussing how much ice to get.

"Let me know what I can do to help," I said, trying to sound sincere. My love/revulsion relationship with haguariness was ongoing. I was making so little progress with my changing lessons that Matéo was mystified. I accepted and liked all my housemates, and was growing to truly love my cousin and Aly as family. But the idea of the rest of the haguari world still upset me, and the thought of being surrounded by a bunch of them at a party was stomach-churning. At the same time, I wanted to be a good cousin and a good friend, and I wouldn't walk out on Matéo and Aly when they were looking forward to this.

"Oh, we will," Aly assured me. "You're going to be chopping, decorating, you name it."

I couldn't help grinning. "You got it."

The day before the party, my tia Juliana called to wish me a *Feliz Fécinte*, a happy equinox. She asked if I was going to observe it in any way and was surprised when I said yes. I still hadn't told her that I was living in a completely different state with a cousin I'd never known about, and the more time that passed, the more I had no idea how to tell her. She knew I was working in a coffee shop, but she thought it was in Sugar Beach.

"You sound better, Vivi," she said in her accented English. Thankfully, she wasn't speaking Portuguese to make sure I kept up.

"I do?" Taking stock, I realized I did feel less crushed, my pain not as rawly searing. My days were busy with work, lessons with Matéo, and hanging out with everyone I lived with. I was hardly ever alone, didn't have much time to dwell on anything.

"It's still . . . awful," I said. "I still miss them, still can't believe it happened."

"I know, darling. I feel the same way. My only sister is gone."

That would have been a good opening into asking about her other sister, but I couldn't bring myself to go there. As far as Matéo and I could figure, the split between the sisters probably happened over Donella dumping my dad, and then my dad marrying my mom. But why had Juliana been part of it? I might not ever know.

"But you're eating?" Tia Juliana went on. "Sleeping okay?"

"Yes," I said. "I've gained most of the weight back. I still have nightmares, but not as often." I wanted to tell her that I was trying to learn how to control the change, but she would want to know who was teaching me. I was keeping secrets from even more people in my life—Jennifer, Rafael, my aunt. It was exhausting.

"Tia, have you ever heard of anyone doing the same thing to other haguari? Cutting out their hearts?"

Tia Juliana was quiet for a while, and I wondered if it hurt too much for her to think about.

"You know," she said slowly, "now that you ask, I do remember something about that many years ago, when I was a little girl. Horrified whispers at temple. Let me think about it. Maybe I'll ask one of the temple elders."

"Okay. Thanks. I'm just wondering if there's a bigger picture."

"Have you heard of anyone else?" She sounded surprised.

"No, uh-uh," I lied. "It's just that it was so strange, and it had to have been another haguari. I'm still trying to make sense of it."

"Of course, my dear. Have a good Fécinte—have you thought about coming here for Finados?"

Finados was All Souls' Day—November 2 in Brazil. In America it was the day after Halloween—All Saints' Day—but most places didn't observe it. Traditionally Catholic cities like New Orleans usually did: Kids had school off; many businesses were closed. Among haguari it was one of the more important observances because the boundary between living and dead, between human and jaguar, was the thinnest.

"Um, I think I'm going to stay put," I said.

Tia Juliana sighed. "I won't let you refuse to come for Christmas. You will be here."

"I'll definitely think about it," I promised.

"I won't take no for an answer," she warned.

"I have to see Jennifer, too. She'll be home from college."

My tia went on to ask about Jennifer and her family and quit pestering me about coming to visit. Maybe I would go to Brazil for Christmas. I didn't know. The thought of driving back to Sugar Beach to see Jennifer seemed so strange. I had a whole house there full of my things, full of my parents' things. Of course I would have to go back someday. And I was dying to see Jennifer. I just . . . wasn't sure if I could do it. If I stayed here I could pretend nothing bad had happened in Sugar Beach. Or like Sugar Beach didn't exist.

That was dumb. It would have to change someday. But not today. Today I had to help get ready for a party. Still, time kept passing, and though my life was acquiring patterns again, nothing truly felt solid or sure or predictable.

And, of course, it wasn't.

CHAPTER SEVENTEEN

FÉCINTE FELL ON A SUNDAY THAT I HAD OFF FROM work. Of course I hadn't participated in an equinox ceremony in years; now I was helping Aly and Matéo fix snacks, clean the house, and tidy the yard. It made me feel so disloyal to my parents, but what would be the point in refusing to take part in this now? Which led me to think, what had been the point of refusing to take part with my parents? It had made total sense to me then, had seemed like absolutely the only thing to do. My world was turned sideways. Before, I had thought of myself as the stalwart conscientious objector; I now looked back and saw myself as the tantrum-throwing four-year-old. It felt awful.

To ramp up the contradictions, in some ways I was happier and more, I don't know—comfortable?—than I'd ever been. Surrounded by people who were exactly what I'd hated and feared becoming, living a life that required me to lie to my nearest and dearest—I felt inexplicably more like myself.

I needed a shrink.

"What are you doing?" I asked Matéo. He'd locked up his workshop with its delicate and expensive tools, and had vacuumed the downstairs. Now he was tying a wide red ribbon across the bottom of the stairs.

"The party is downstairs and in the yard," he said firmly. "No couples sneaking upstairs."

"Oh. How many people are coming tonight?" We'd gotten mini pumpkins from the grocery store and cut branches of pyracantha from the tall shrub in the yard. Their red berries looked autumn-y and festive as I arranged them on the side table in the front hall.

"I didn't really keep track," he said. "And people will probably bring friends. Maybe sixty altogether?"

"Haguari or peladi?" It felt daring, using this word, as if I were swearing.

"Haguari. About sixty or so."

"So does everyone keep it all secret all the time?"

Matéo tacked the ribbon to the wooden chair molding on the wall, then stood back to survey his work. When I'd first met him, I'd thought he was kind of odd-looking, with his Johnny Depp face and Rupert Grint red hair, but now he was just Matéo, my cousin.

"I think pretty much everyone keeps it a secret," he said finally. "The few stories you hear about someone trying to live more openly all have a bad ending. End up being an urban myth."

I looked at him somberly. "So we always have to live two lives, pretending to be something we're not." It seemed like an unbearable burden.

"Oh, Vivi!" said Aly, coming downstairs with a cardboard box. "Can you help me decorate the altar?" A few steps from the bottom she picked up on the tension in the air and looked from Matéo to me. "What?"

"I just asked Matéo if everyone always kept being haguari hidden," I told her. "And he said yes, and it just seems overwhelming. Looking ahead to keeping this to myself for the rest of my life. I mean, my best friend Jennifer doesn't know anything about it, and she never will. So what kind of friends are we, really?"

Aly ducked under the ribbon and sat down on the bottom step with the box next to her. "That's a question we all wrestle with, obviously."

Actually, I'd been so preoccupied with me, me, me that it hadn't occurred to me that, yes, duh, every haguari must have to deal with that. It was like I thought I was the only haguara with problems or issues—like it was simple and easy for everyone else.

"How do you deal with it?" I asked.

"Everyone handles it in a different way," Matéo said. "At some point, almost every single haguari wants to live openly, and to hell with people who can't accept them."

Aly smiled wistfully at Matéo. "And almost every single haguari comes to equate our special nature as a liability, making us vulnerable to being persecuted or discriminated against in society."

"That's exactly what it feels like!" I said.

"The five stages of being haguari," Matéo intoned, holding up five fingers. "Denial, anger, bargaining, depression, and acceptance."

Those were the five stages of grief—they'd been explained in a pamphlet I'd gotten at the hospital. I started to argue about it, but then began recognizing almost all of my behavior as being one stage or another. Except for the acceptance part. Hadn't gotten there.

There was room on the step next to Aly and I sat down. My feelings seemed so important, so huge and heavy—it was unsettling to think they were just a typical pattern that everyone felt.

"People I talk to here seem so thrilled to be haguari," I said glumly. "Tink said it was like finding out that he was a superhero. Am I the only one who was horrified?"

"I've wondered if that's why thirteen is the magic age when a kid finds out," Aly said. "Because you're still kid enough to think, oh, awesome, cool! Without being grown-up enough to foresee the not-always-positive consequences of it."

"But just about everyone I've ever talked to about it has run into problems somewhere in their lives," Matéo said. "Like anything else, there are pluses and minuses. Sometimes it seems like all pluses, and sometimes like all minuses."

"But the keeping-the-secret part of it," I said. "That must take such an effort, forever."

Aly shrugged. "It becomes second nature, something you do without thinking. The more you do it, the easier it is. But . . . that's also why most haguari seem to hang out with and have relationships only with other haguari. Because it's easier, and you don't have to hide."

Rafael came to mind: his dark attraction, the feel of his mouth on mine . . .

"Do we ever have relationships with non-haguari?" I asked.

"Of course," said Aly. "My mom knows someone who is married to a pelado. For like thirty-eight years and counting."

"And she's never told him?" I couldn't see how that was possible.

"I don't think so," said Aly, shrugging.

"What about kids?"

"Haguaro plus haguara, cute little haguari," said Matéo. "Haguaro or haguara plus pelado or pelada, cute little peladi."

"So their kids aren't haguari?" I frowned. "They're just regular?"

"They're usually really good athletes," said Matéo. "Good-looking. Charismatic."

Aly laughed and kicked his shin with her bare foot. "Not that you're prejudiced or anything."

Laughing too, he reached over and smoothed her dark hair behind her ear. They planned to get married someday and wanted to have kids. Had they really been set up as a couple when they were teenagers? It seemed too personal to ask.

"So basically the answer is to not be close to any peladi?" I could hear the put-upon childishness in my voice and I hated it.

Aly looked at me, and I felt embarrassed. "I think we each find our own answers," she said mildly.

Biting my lip, I nodded. "I guess I'll go decorate the altar."

Aly handed me the box and I tried to smile, managing only a closed-lip grimace. They didn't say anything as I headed into the front parlor, the one I'd sat in the first night I'd come here. I set the box down and glanced at my watch—I'd offered to make some spice cookies and a pumpkin cake, but I still had plenty of time.

The night I'd come here, the room hadn't been well lit and I'd been so exhausted and discombobulated that I hadn't even noticed the altar on the side wall. I'd seen it since then, of course. This room was where we sometimes had game night or just hung out, and I'd often dusted in here as part of my self-given chore list.

Like my parents' altar, this was made of carved wood and looked quite old. Matéo had told me it had belonged to his parents. It must have been so difficult for Donella, to be cut off from her family. I imagined her setting up this altar in this house, knowing she would probably never share holidays with her first family again. My parents' figures of our gods were finely carved and inlaid with semiprecious stones. This Tzechuro and Tzechura were painted wood, simpler than ours, as if handmade by a primitive artisan.

Beneath the altar was a small bookcase, maybe three feet high. On the top shelf were framed pictures of Donella and Patrick and of Matéo as a small child. Donella of course looked like my family, and Patrick looked about as Irish as you could get: very pale, freckled, green eyes, bright red hair. They were smiling happily, their arms around each other.

On the next shelf were framed pictures of Matéo and Aly. One picture looked quite recent and one looked several years old—Matéo was thinner and they were both obviously younger, younger than I was now. And already life partners.

On the bottom shelf were several red and orange candles and a small brass incense holder. Kneeling, I opened the cardboard box and saw folded red velvet, some dried branches tied in small bundles by brown ribbon, two narrow wine glasses, some gold beads, and several other small brass figurines. Looking at them more closely, I saw that they were like that poster of evolving hominids that starts with apelike creatures and ends with Chris Hemsworth. This set had a plain jaguar and a plain human, and then other figures that were bits of both—a person with a jaguar head, a jaguar with human hands and a human smile, a sphinxlike cat with a woman's face. I'd never seen anything like them and I was still looking at them when Aly came in.

"Aren't those cool? They were my grandmother's. Mom let me have them when I moved in with Téo."

"They're awesome."

"I usually put them on the top shelf, with a candle on either end. I've never known whether to start with the person or start with the jaguar, so I alternate. And then I drape the velvet around the altar shelf. It would be nice to gather colorful leaves to symbolize autumn, but we might have to settle for some acorns or something."

I smiled. "I'll look around outside."

Together we arranged the rest of the things, and for the first time in my life it seemed, well, joyous to celebrate these gods. Aly was clearly so into it, so comfortable with it—she made it seem fun. My folks had also been into it, obviously, and comfortable with it, but my fear and dismay had pretty much sucked the joy right out of our holidays.

"Excellent," Aly said, standing back to look at it. "A lovely Fécinte altar."

"Yep. Works for me," I said. "Thanks for letting me help."

Aly looked at me in surprise, then hugged me. "You're family, sweetie."

That meant so much more than I had realized, and I felt a warm glow in my chest. "I better start making cookies. Is the kitchen free now?"

"The ovens are, or they were a few minutes ago. Dana is in there putting shrimp on skewers."

"I'll get going, then."

It was relaxing to bake again. Whenever I did, I realized how much I missed it. Besides getting good grades, my baking had been the one thing that made my parents happy, that wasn't fraught with tension and disappointment.

The spice cookies I'd made many times and didn't need a recipe for. The dough was really stiff and I really, really missed the big KitchenAid mixer that had been my sixteenth birthday present. When the dough was done, I covered it and put it in the fridge for an hour while I made the pumpkin cake.

While the cake was baking, I quickly scooped out spoonfuls of cookie dough, rolled them into balls, and dipped each ball in a bowl of granulated sugar. When they baked, they spread out, their surfaces cracking, and the sugar made a beautiful pattern over their tops.

The kitchen soon smelled like heaven, and I opened the windows and the door to let some of the heat out. The pumpkin cake came out perfectly, though it would have been prettier in one of my molded bundt pans.

The cake was getting a sprinkling of confectioner's sugar when Suzanne came in, her arms covered with small wreaths made of dried leaves. Like Florida, New Orleans didn't have many trees whose leaves changed colors in autumn. The few deciduous trees' leaves simply turned brown and dropped off, as if they didn't care whether they put on a fall show.

"Those are so pretty," I said. "Where did you get them?"

"I made them," said Suzanne, and she took one off her arm and set it on my head. "I went home to Connecticut last fall and gathered these leaves, then pressed them in all my law books. James helped me sew them onto these frames." She smiled, and I blinked because she was usually so serious or in a hurry or overworked.

"They're beautiful." I looked at myself in the glass door of the oven.

"I have enough for all of us," said Suzanne. "Now I'm going to go upstairs and get ready, unless you guys need me for anything."

"What are you going to wear?" Coco asked, coming in from the hallway.

"I have a fabulous dress," said Suzanne, putting a crown of leaves on Coco's head. "And I'll put my hair up and weave the wreath around it." She looked pleased with the mental image.

Coco and I exchanged glances. Of course neither one of us had even thought about what to wear or how to deal with our hair. The party was supposed to start in an hour, when the sun went down. Maybe I should try to get something together.

"Oh, man," Coco moaned, eating a cookie. "We need to hook you up with a restaurant or bakery or something. You can't keep these from the populace."

Grinning, I bit a cookie too, and nodded my agreement. Yes, I was a rock star when it came to baking. I put the cookies and the cake on top of the fridge, where they would be out of the way, and followed Coco upstairs to get ready.

My "getting ready" consisted of taking a shower, putting on clean clothes, and getting my brush impossibly tangled in my hair. Standing in front of the mirror, I turned the brush this way and that and ended up with a huge hunk of hair on the side of my head with a brush handle sticking out of it. I was near tears, staring at it, when I heard a ping on my computer. I flipped it open and answered the Skype call—Jennifer was the only person in the world I would let see this. But even Jennifer looked startled at my appearance.

"Hi. My brush is stuck," I said glumly. "I'll need to cut it out. It might finally be time for that Mohawk you tried to talk me into in eighth grade."

I could tell when she was trying to smother laughter. "No, don't cut it," she said when she got a grip on herself. "It's still salvageable. Just take little bits of hair at a time and gently pull them away from the brush. Little tiny strands, tugging gently so you don't break the hair."

Sighing, I climbed onto my bed and arranged the computer so she could see me. "So what's up?" I asked, pinching a weensy strand of hair and gently tugging as instructed.

"Amy did not pan out," said Jennifer. "But I have a study date on Tuesday with a girl from my social services class."

"Oh, good," I said. Amazingly, I managed to free a tiny bit of hair. If I could do that a thousand more times, I might be okay. I pinched another strand.

"How's everything with you? Does your aunt Juliana know you're there yet?"

I made a face, tugging another strand free. "No. I mean, I hate it—I want her to know. But I still don't know the whole picture. Juliana was the youngest, so maybe they actually told her Donella was dead. I don't know. In the meantime, my cousin is having a party here tonight. I've been helping them get ready. And as you can see, I've planned a special outfit."

Jennifer nodded agreeably at my white schoolgirl top and weird kitten skirt, no doubt thinking that at least it was better than usual. "Cool. That'll be fun. You like their friends, right?"

I nodded. "Yeah. I haven't met all of them, but I've liked the ones I've met so far."

"There was a sorority party yesterday," Jennifer said. "Lucy is pledging, so I went for a while."

We chatted about nothing in particular until all my hair was miraculously untangled, and then I had to go somehow flatten it out because I now looked like half a dandelion. We blew kisses at each other and I shut my computer, then dunked my head in the bathroom sink to start over from the beginning.

As I carefully combed conditioner through my wet hair, I thought about the hundreds of nights that Jennifer and I had stayed up until dawn, talking about everything, listening to music very quietly so her mom wouldn't come in, watching our favorite music videos over and over. Those days felt like a long time ago, and Jennifer and I both seemed so different. Was this how we would drift apart? Slowly but inevitably? I hated to think that.

With my hair still wet, I put it into one long braid and set my leaf crown on top, then checked myself out in the mirror. Not too bad. A tap on my door made me call, "Yeah?"

"It's me," said Aly. "Can I come in?"

"Sure."

She opened the door and stood there, swirling so I could get the full effect of her dress.

"Oh, awesome," I said. "That is perfect."

"I made it," Aly said, crossing the room to admire herself in the old armoire's mirrors. The long framed mirror had been broken the night of the attack, but the armoire had mirrored insets in its doors. "This sundress used to be all white, but I spilled hot sauce on it and couldn't get it out. So I dip-dyed it."

The straps that tied over her shoulders were still white, but the smocked bodice was a warm golden yellow at the top, shading to a deeper gold and then orange at the waist of the skirt. The orange blended into carnelian, then scarlet, and finally, at the bottom of the skirt, a rich blood red.

My mom had always worn red, orange, or fuchsia on the equinox, formally welcoming autumn, as pointless as that was in Florida. I remembered a beautiful sleeveless orange silk dress, a slim sheath that made her look like a candle flame.

"That is amazing," I said sincerely. "You look like you're on fire."

"Thank you." She looked at my white top and kitten skirt and seemed unsure whether to say anything.

"What? It's a skirt," I said.

"Noooo," she said slowly, looking me up and down. "With that shirt, you look like you just escaped from Sacred Heart. But I have just the thing."

Chapter Eighteen

People began to arrive just as the sun was setting. Matéo and Tink had made a fire pit in a treeless part of the yard and set up lawn chairs. We'd moved a long folding table outside as well, and now it held bowls of spicy nuts and roasted pumpkin and squash seeds. I'd set out my plates of spice cookies and the pumpkin cake and covered them with clean dish towels to keep bugs off. Other traditional Fécinte foods were apples, pumpkins, cider, mulled wine, and pomegranates—foods that symbolized autumn and the harvest. Frankly, it seemed awfully vegetarian to me, but I guess we couldn't exactly have antelope haunches hanging from the trees and rabbits spread to dry on the azalea bushes.

Back in my room, I looked at my image in the mirror doubtfully, wondering if I could really go downstairs like this. Aly had said she'd had the perfect thing, and I believed that this dress was perfect—for her. But I was five inches taller and much curvier than Aly, and I felt like I'd been forcibly poured into it.

The dress itself was gorgeous, a deep crimson silk, heavy but not shiny. The fifties-style bodice was very fitted and left me unable to take a full breath, and the deep scoop neck made my boobs look like they were about to fall out. The small cap sleeves were okay, and a very full skirt swung and rustled with each step I took. The effect was retro and feminine, but not froufrou.

Also, Aly had dealt with the Hair That Could Not Be Contained and given me some kind of magical updo, making a complicated bunlike thing on top of my head, circled gracefully by Suzanne's wreath of leaves.

I didn't look at all like myself. I didn't feel at all like myself either. I looked . . . not exactly like my mom and not exactly like my dad, but like a mixture of both. Which my eighth-grade biology class had totally explained. I looked older, tidier, more feminine. Really pretty.

"I have outdone myself," Aly said, nodding approvingly. "You're going to knock them dead."

"I can't breathe."

"Take little breaths and be glad it's not an actual corset."

"My boobs are going to fall out."

Aly snickered. "So don't lean over. But yes, you're a brick house. You look amazing. Come on." Correctly assuming that I was about to chicken out, she grabbed my hand and pulled me out of my room. Since my feet, like everything else, were also bigger than Aly's, none of her shoes worked. My shoe choices were flip-flops, Birkenstocks, or high-top Converse. So I was barefoot.

At the top of the stairs I hesitated, breathing shallowly. It was darker and quieter up here; downstairs was full of lights and people talking and autumn scents. Maybe I should just hang out in my room, call Jennifer. Watch some TV on my computer.

"Walk down these stairs or I will push you down them," Aly whispered.

"Nice," I whispered back, but obeyed her. The foyer below was crowded. All the doors and French windows were open so people could go in and out easily, but the bar had been set up in the parlor, so it was seeing plenty of action.

I felt horribly self-conscious, like I was wearing a bathing suit, and the heads turning and conversations quieting didn't help any. A slow flush heated my cheeks, and if no one had been watching I would have scuttled back upstairs.

A long, low whistle made Aly chuckle behind me, and Matéo stepped out of the crowd to reach up and give me a hug on the bottom step. He was wearing a light linen shirt of a deep pumpkin color—one would think it would clash with his hair, but it didn't. "You look beautiful, *prima*," he said. "Like a queen."

"Don't hug me too tight," I panted in alarm.

"Come, meet some people. Have some wine," my cousin said.

Once again I started to remind him that I was only eighteen, but then thought, *You know what? I'm eighteen, this is a private party, and I can have a glass of wine if I want.*

"Okay," I said, following him into the parlor.

"Holy frijoles, Vivi," Tink said to me, his blond head towering over the crowd. "Who knew you had that hidden?"

Was he talking about my chest? Oh, gods.

Pushing slowly through the crowd, Tink said, "Vivi, this is my boyfriend, Peter."

The guy holding Tink's hand was a couple of inches shorter than me, with beautifully cut fine dark hair—very good-looking in a nerdy way. He seemed like an odd match for Tink, who was so big and athletic, and with a little jolt I realized that he, like everyone else here, was haguari. This slender, well-groomed guy could turn into a jaguar, and though he wouldn't weigh any more than he did now, ounce for ounce a jaguar's muscles were many times stronger than a person's.

"Hi, Peter," I said, and we shook hands.

"Tink told me about the attack several weeks ago," said Peter. "That must have been awful."

"It was bad," I said in great understatement. "Thank heavens Tink was there."

Putting his arm around Peter, Tink grinned at me. Matéo had told me that they'd lived together for a while, and then Tink had moved back home. I wondered what had happened—they seemed to be getting along well now.

"Here you go," Matéo said, handing me a clear plastic cup of warm wine. A few orange slices floated in it; I smelled cinnamon and pepper and other spices. My parents had given me little tastes of wine sometimes at family dinners or holidays. I'd never liked the puckery, tannic taste. But this—this was delicious. It soothed my throat, and I felt like I could drink a gallon of it, which would not be a good idea.

"Vivi! Is that you?" Suzanne's wide blue eyes were disbelieving to the point of almost being insulting. I knew I usually looked fairly casual, but was it that big of a change? Okay, of course it was. Irritated, I gulped down some wine. Its warmth curled up comfortingly in my belly. I was grateful when Aly took my arm and steered me over to introduce me to some friends.

Of all the people at the party, I knew the ones I already lived with, plus Charlotte and several of the people we had gone to the river with, and now Peter. After meeting the third stranger, I stopped being able to put names with faces and resigned myself to having to fake it through a lot of conversations. Having a cup to hold and sip from gave me something to do during the few awkward silences. But everyone was pretty friendly, most of the guys were openly admiring, and after about half an hour I realized I was having fun.

Someone possibly named Sydney was telling about how she almost changed by accident on a Disney World roller coaster when she was fourteen. It was so funny, and I wondered if I would have felt different about everything if I had grown up around a lot of other young haguari. Why had my parents decided to settle in a place where we were practically the only ones? After months of listening to Matéo and Aly tell stories about growing up, how much fun they'd had, how many haguari their parents had known, it was easy to believe that I might have had a completely different viewpoint on the whole thing if I'd been surrounded by kids like me.

"I was like, I hope this harness can still hold me, and planning how to leap out when we were near the ground. . . ." Sydney was saying, and we were all laughing, picturing it.

"And you could run and go hide in the Animal Kingdom," I suggested, and she said, "Exactly!" and the others wiped tears of laughter from their eyes.

It was fun, fitting in like this, feeling like I was a member of a special club just by existing. These people were interesting, friendly, and bright. I was one of them. Smiling and sipping, I glanced around. Across the room I saw the altar that Aly and I had decorated. As people passed it, they casually touched their fingers to their lips, then to the statues, usually one or the other, not both. My parents had never done that—what was that for?

At some point someone refilled my cup again, and I inhaled the spicy wine scent deeply and swayed a bit on my feet. I needed to eat something. I sidled away from my group and headed outside to the food tables, my bare feet a tiny bit numb on the cool marble front steps. In the yard, all of my cake and cookies were gone, which was a gratifying disappointment. Someone had brought some not-very-Fécinte hamburger sliders, which I was thrilled to see. A couple of sliders, a handful of curried nuts, and a hunk of pomegranate filled my plate, and then I saw Charlotte at the next table cutting an apple pie, and I quickly got in line.

After I had acquired a piece of pie, I headed to an empty spot on the cement garden bench under the crape myrtle tree. I snagged it, balancing my plate on my knees and setting my wine on the ground. The grass was slightly damp, and when I inhaled, I smelled earth and wind. Looking up, I saw dark gray clouds moving quickly across the sky, blotting out the moon and stars. I hoped it wouldn't rain till much later—this many voices inside the house would be overwhelming. There seemed to be much more than sixty people here, all of them like me. It was unbelievable. It was hard to feel like a freak. In fact, surrounded by so many strangers, I felt the most normal I ever had.

I was snarfing my way across my plate when a guy sat next to me, his leg touching mine. He was talking to other people in front of him but turned to say hello. His polite glance became a more focused head-to-toe exam, and then he smiled and held out his hand.

"Hello there. I'm Alex," he said.

I put down my plastic fork and shook his hand. "Vivi."

"I'm very pleased to meet you, Vivi," he said, and his voice took on a silky note. "Why haven't I met you before?"

"I don't know. I've been here almost three months," I said, realizing with surprise that that was true.

"Ah," Alex said. "Well, I've been traveling a lot."

"What do you do?"

"I'm a buyer for restaurants," he said, turning more toward me. Over his shoulder I spotted a girl looking at us with irritation, as if I had distracted him from her. "Basically I travel all over a radius of five hundred miles and find the best seafood, meat, vegetables, and so on. The closer the better. Then I hook them up with restaurants here in town and get a cut of all the purchases the restaurants make.

Lately I've been sourcing more organic stuff—it's more in demand, and people are willing to pay for it."

"That's really interesting," I said admiringly. "I never knew that was a job."

"There are many buyers in every city with a lot of restaurants," Alex said.

I smiled at him, hoping I didn't have anything on my teeth. Just in case, I took a big sip of wine. Alex grinned and drank from his own cup. He was really good-looking and seemed oddly familiar—something about the way the corners of his dark eyes crinkled, and the wave of his thick black hair, sparked recognition in me—but I was sure I hadn't met him before.

"What about you? What do you do?"

"I'm taking a year off between high school and college," I said, trying not to sound defensive. "Right now I'm working at a coffee shop, trying to figure out what I want to do."

"Cool," said Alex politely.

Nervously I drained my cup, and then I realized that the world was tilting very slightly, and my tongue felt a bit thicker.

"Can I refill your glass?" Alex said, holding out his hand.

"Yeah, sure," I said somewhat breathlessly. "Maybe just a soft drink or something?"

"You got it." Alex disappeared into the crowd while I leaned back on my hands on the bench and tried to evaluate these new sensations.

This was being tipsy, I decided, and grinned a little. Very faintly, very far off, I thought I heard a low rumble of thunder. The clouds were poufy like gray wool that hadn't been spun yet, but the festive paper Chinese lanterns lit the yard well enough so people wouldn't trip. Everywhere I looked, people were smiling, talking, leaning close to each other. It was so fun. This was a great party, and I was having a lovely time.

"Here you go," said Alex, handing me a cup. "Actually, they were all out of soda. It was a choice of beer or wine. I went with wine."

"Good choice," I said, and drank. *Dee-lish.*

"Everyone! Can I have your attention!" Aly stood on the front porch, banging a spoon against a metal pot. "Come on, people! Come on inside! Time for the ceremony!"

"Ah, yes, the reason we're all here," said Alex. "May I escort you inside?" He held out his arm, seeming so old-fashioned and gentlemanly that I smiled and said, "Uh-huh."

Standing up was unusual. I normally had a great sense of balance, but my spine had gotten wobbly and was harder to control. Thankful that I was barefoot and not wearing heels, I took Alex's arm, unable to tell if it seemed natural or if I had lunged at him alarmingly. Time to put the wine down.

Alex was tall, at least five inches taller than me, which I didn't see often. We moved toward the house, me leaning on Alex's arm perhaps a bit more than I meant to, and headed up the front steps with a sea of people. As the crowd shuffled through the double front doors, I suddenly felt too hot and kind of claustrophobic. People pressed around me on all sides, the floor lurched beneath my feet, and there was no air. My stomach started to roil, and panic began its slow, cold crawl up my legs to my throat.

We were heading in for the Fécinte ceremony. Aly and Matéo had put it together and it would be really cheerful with all these people. I'd resigned myself to take part in it, realizing I was less willing to hurt my newfound cousin than I had been to hurt my own parents. But now I was thinking I had to get out of here because I might barf. The very thought of more wine made my throat clench, and I deeply regretted the nuts that now sat sourly in my stomach like curried rocks. Plus shrimp and pie and sliders . . . oh no, what had I done?

I disentangled myself from Alex's arm and looked up at him. "Excuse me a second. I'll be right back." Giving him a lopsided smile, I edged cautiously through the crowd, my lips pressed tightly together in a face that was suddenly clammy and tingling. Ducking under the ribbon closing off the stairway made the whole world slide sideways. I swallowed hard and breathed through my nose. *Please do not let me tumble down these stairs,* I thought, and clutched the wooden handrail. The world was tilty and my feet kept misjudging the height of the steps. I was sure people were watching me head upstairs, and I would be so mortified if I looked as stupid or as wasted as I felt.

By the top step I was gulping convulsively. Relief mixed with dread as I quickly wove my way to my room at the front of the house. Thank the gods I lived here and didn't have to worry about getting home.

I felt awful.

The hallway was dark, and already the sounds from below were muted slightly. I practically crashed through my bedroom door, yanking on the ornately carved brass doorknob that sometimes didn't catch properly. Tacking my way toward the bathroom, I reached it not a moment too soon, and for the first—and I promised myself the last—time in my life threw up from drinking too much. My whole system was saying, *I forcefully reject the crap you shoveled into me tonight, and I will now expel it without your consent!*

Afterward I felt drained and trembly but much better. This party was definitely over for me, though I could faintly hear the blessings they were saying for a metaphorical harvest, the acknowledgments of Tzechuro and Tzechura as the god and goddess of our people. They didn't sing the traditional song that I'd learned as a child, I guessed because it was in an obsolete mingling of Spanish, Portuguese, and old Olmec. Not everyone here was from the same background: Our people existed on every continent, in most countries, in every race. We'd been around a long, long time. Vaguely I remembered hearing my parents talking about it—I'd been in the backseat of the car, almost sleeping, and we'd been driving home from a party at their friends'. Papi had been saying that Hassan's mother felt that the Egyptian Tzechuro and Tzechura were much more authentic than our Brazilian ones. Mami had laughed and said that her mother had always felt the same way—that we, the Brazilian haguari, were the real, oldest haguari, the original ones. Other clans were new upstarts. They had both laughed, then quieted their voices so they wouldn't wake me up.

I was pretty glad they couldn't see me now.

Getting to my feet with a groan, I was thankful to see that Aly's gorgeous dress had escaped much damage. I took it off carefully and hung it up, then put on the huge T-shirt I slept in. Being able to breathe in deeply felt wonderful. I don't know how women used to wear actual corsets.

"Yep, definitely a freak of nature," I muttered, looking in the mirror over the sink. My face was a pale green similar to my bedroom walls, with large dark circles under my eyes. Brushing my teeth and splashing cold water on my face helped, but all I wanted was to go to sleep and never, ever drink again.

When I opened the bathroom door, the first thing I saw was my lovely tall bed that was practically calling my name. With any luck, I wouldn't get the spins when I lay down. Then a small, silent movement caught my eye, and a huge jaguar stepped silently through my doorway, nudging the door open with its wide shoulder and heavy head. Its mouth dropped open, and its lips curled up to show me its fangs.

Chapter Nineteen

"Who are you?" I asked sternly. "You need to go back downstairs."

The jaguar's wide nose wrinkled and its eyes narrowed as it took two soundless steps toward me.

"Look, this is a private room. The party is downstairs. Out!" I frowned and pointed at the open door. A low, rumbling growl floated through the room, as if thunder could emanate from the jaguar's deep chest. It took another step closer, enormous muscles moving with grace and unmistakable power.

That was when it occurred to me to be scared.

What if this wasn't a party guest? What if it was the jaguar who had attacked Tink? Or maybe even it was a party guest, but Matéo and Aly didn't know it was a traitor.

I took a step back toward the bathroom. After ten minutes of throwing up, I was shaky and not at the top of my game. I still hadn't mastered changing on command. Unfortunately, I would be able to deal with this threat only as a jaguar myself.

"Who are you?" I tried again. "What do you want?" My voice sounded much less sure. How long would the solid wooden bathroom door last against a grown jaguar? About fifteen seconds. Maybe.

The big cat gave another growl that seemed to shudder right through my gut. My only option was to rush back into the bathroom, try to get the door locked in a split second, then scream for help out of the open window. Which was on the other side of the house from the fairly loud party. By the time I got the window open, the cat would have smashed right through the door.

Then it would cut my heart out. And I would never know why.

The edges of the room got blurry and dark. My fingers felt icy—I was going to faint. That would make things simpler for everyone. I took another step backward, and again it came closer. It was now one leap away. A split second would see its jaws closing around my skull.

Through my increasing haze I didn't hear footsteps in the hall, but then Aly was there, pushing my door wider. "Vivi? I heard that you—"

She saw the big jaguar and frowned. "What are you doing in here?"

"Oh gods, Aly, do you know him?" I asked thinly, weaving on my feet.

"Vivi! Sit down!" Aly hurried over and pressed me down onto the antique slipper chair in front of one window.

Across the room the jaguar roared, but in a small way, not shaking the windows.

"Shut up, you idiot!" Aly snapped. "Don't you see that you've scared her to death?"

The jaguar blinked and immediately sat down, then sank to the floor, changing back into a human before my eyes. The thick pelt disappeared, muscles atrophied, smooth tan skin emerged . . . in less than thirty seconds the familiar, dark-haired, naked human was standing up.

"Alex?" I said weakly.

"I'm so sorry, Vivi," he said sincerely. "I thought you'd think it was funny. I kept waiting for you to laugh."

"Funny?" I repeated.

"It's not funny to be threatened by a stranger," Aly said sharply. "Vivi, I'm so sorry. This oblivious idiot is my brother, Alex."

"I'm really sorry," Alex repeated.

"Hello? Naked guy? Still threatening," I said, keeping my eyes locked on the wall.

"Oh." Alex got a pillow from my bed and held it over his crucial parts. "I think my clothes are in the hall." He turned and hustled out, but of course we got a great view of his bare butt.

Aly shook her head and sighed. "He's older than me by a whole year, but that hasn't sunk in yet. Now, what happened to you? Coco told me she saw you come upstairs, not looking great."

"I drank too much," I admitted. "Got sick as a dog."

"Oh, no!" Aly laughed ruefully. "Yeah, that mulled wine can knock you on your ass. How are you feeling now?"

"I was doing better till I came out and found a strange jaguar in my room," I said.

"Really, so sorry," said Alex, coming back into my room and tossing the pillow back onto my bed. His jeans were zipped but not snapped, and his shirt was unbuttoned and hung open, exposing his great chest. He looked like the cover of a steamy romance novel. "I really thought you'd laugh, maybe throw something at me, maybe change yourself. I didn't realize you weren't feeling well."

"I didn't recognize you," I said, suddenly remembering that I was sitting here in nothing but my underwear and a big T-shirt. I crossed my arms over my chest.

Alex looked surprised.

"Let's go downstairs and leave Vivi alone," Aly said firmly, standing up. "Are you okay? Do you need anything?" She rubbed my shoulder and tucked a loose strand of hair behind my ear.

I shook my head. "I think I'll just try to go to sleep. But thank you again for everything you did to get me ready. I felt like Cinderella. Till I barfed."

Aly smiled. "I was glad to do it—it was fun to show you how beautiful you are. I know you'll feel a lot better in the morning. Now, come on," she said, taking Alex's arm. As I saw them standing next to each other, I realized why Alex had seemed familiar: There was definitely a family resemblance. In a way, Alex was more handsome than Aly was beautiful—I mean, Aly was really pretty, but he was gorgeous. As beautiful in his own way as Rafael was in his way.

Once they closed my bedroom door, I went over quietly and locked it. I was not up for any more surprise visitors tonight.

After the party I was even more determined to learn how to change. If I'd been able to change, I would have felt safer when Alex had come in. Also I had, for once in my life, felt like one of the crowd. All of them, everyone at that party, knew how to change, how to express both sides of themselves. I was the only one there who didn't. I didn't want to be that person. I didn't want to stand out among my own kind.

It was hard to find time to practice together—apparently September was an especially busy time for luthiers. "It's all the kids, going back to school," Matéo had explained. "All their violins suddenly need repair or adjusting or even just tuning. This town is full of school bands and orchestras, and it's crazy until mid-October."

Usually I worked five out of seven days at Ro's, but my schedule was flexible—sometimes I had Sunday and Monday nights off, sometimes a Tuesday and a Friday, or whatever. I didn't have kids or a school schedule to work around, so it was easier for me to change at the last minute. Privately, I allowed myself to pine for Rafael. I found myself thinking that it would have been so awesome if he had come to the Fécinte party, because then I would know for sure that he was haguari and he wouldn't seem off-limits. Then I remembered that I didn't want to date any haguaro at all. But it was all blending and fading, my objections to my species, my outraged rejection of everything I was.

Slowly, little by little, I was seeing examples of how to be haguari, how to live a normalish life, how to have fun. It wasn't that Matéo and Aly and our friends did anything different than my parents had. I think it was just knowing about all the others like us in New Orleans, knowing how many there were of us. I was starting to think that my parents either hadn't known how many haguari there were all over the world, or that they had chosen to live separate from them on purpose. Surely they had to have known. Why wouldn't they have wanted to be part of a bigger community? Why wouldn't they have wanted me to know other kids like me, besides my own cousins who were still too young to change?

One afternoon at the beginning of October, Matéo and I were practicing in my room. I could now meditate quickly and easily, and could isolate each of my muscles and my senses. I'd learned a lot since I'd been practicing with him, but still, for whatever reason, had never once managed to turn into a jaguar. We'd tried using cuvaje rojo and cuva rojo a couple times to jump-start the physical sensations, and they always worked. But on my own I simply could. Not. Change.

I was fed up and discouraged. After weeks of work, I was no closer to being able to control changing than I was before. Suzanne had wondered out loud if it was like a foreign language, easier to learn when you're younger. I'd wanted to smack her.

"Do you still, still maybe . . . not like being a haguara?" Matéo asked. "Could that be why you can't get there? 'Cause something in you just doesn't want to accept this?"

Near tears, I sat on the floor in my room. I was wearing a tank top and yoga pants, my hair hanging hot and heavy down my back. "I don't know. I mean, I want to learn how to do this. I know I need to—just to feel safer. I'm doing this by choice."

"No, I mean, if you could choose to not be a haguara, would you?"

I opened my mouth to say, "Of course," but then thought it through. Thought about the amazing people I'd met, how easily people around me embraced their natures, how many people I'd met who were like me. My attitude had definitely changed. Definitely. So would I still choose to not be this? Would I still choose to have this cut out of me, the way I'd wanted when I was younger?

"I don't know," I said, rubbing my eyes.

"Even apart from the change," Matéo said. "Even without the change. As people we're strong, fast, have lightning reflexes. We make beautiful dancers, incredible athletes, and exceptional soldiers. Our immune systems are amazingly strong. Isn't all that really cool?"

I hunched my shoulders. "Yeah, of course." My folks had tried to tell me all this. Naturally, I had blocked it out.

"Don't you feel beautiful? Don't you like being strong?"

"Yes." Another shrug.

Matéo ran his hand through his dark red hair. "Vivi . . . you should have learned how to do this by now, frankly."

"I've been trying!"

"It's not working. We know you can change, because you have. But it's like you have some internal block against it. If you were thirteen, I could teach you how to change in like three, four days."

That stung. My mouth opened, and feelings I didn't know I still had came pouring out. "Of course I have an internal block against it! I hate everything about it! I always have! Just because you and your friends like to prance around all jungly doesn't mean that I do!"

Matéo's eyebrows rose, and then his eyes narrowed. With no

warning he scooped me up into his arms and carried me out of my room to the hallway. I was only two inches shorter than him but hoped I weighed at least forty pounds less. All the same, he carried me without effort.

"Okay, put me down," I began—

—and then he dumped me over the second-floor railing.

My gurgled scream was cut short, but the next split second seemed to take minutes. It registered that I was falling from a tall height, and that I would soon crunch down hard onto the wooden floor fourteen feet below. Oddly, my brain had time to process all this, to see the chandelier as I fell past it, to gauge how quickly the floor was zooming up to meet me. Without thinking I twisted in the air, and then facedown I landed on my hands and feet, limbs spread to absorb the shock. I didn't go splat, didn't hit my face—my hands and feet spread solidly on the floor and I stuck my landing. Apart from a slight stinging sensation on my palms, I wasn't hurt at all.

I looked up in amazement to see Matéo grinning at me over the banister.

"You lunatic!" I yelled, scrambling to stand up. "You could have killed me!"

"No," he said. "I couldn't. That's the point."

I stood there, breathing hard, clenching my fists. He had shown me my innate nature, the nature that took over when my rational self blanked out.

Then I became aware of it . . . a tingling, almost a clenching at the base of my neck, as if a thick muscle were quivering with electricity. My attention focused on it, I paid attention to it, and then I just . . . grabbed it. I felt that sensation and gripped it, holding it tightly, and wasn't really surprised when my vision changed, I dropped to all fours, and my ears picked up the drip coming from the kitchen sink forty feet away. I didn't let go, didn't back away. For the first time in my life I recognized the jaguar part of me and followed where it led.

It didn't hurt, but it felt weird as hell. It wasn't scary, but it was shocking. Within a minute I was my jaguar self.

Fur scent my scent my black fur

I'm strong fast like an arrow like a cold river that crashes onto sharp knifelike rocks

I am night-colored night-scented with blotches of shadows on my shoulders my head my flanks

The floor smells dry under me I leave my scent with my paw pads

I hear a bird outside I could catch the bird could swallow it

Sound above and ear twitch see heat smell heat

He's there watching me from up high

I put my head back pull in air push out sound feel it rumble out roll through the air like waves

They hit the wall they go up he hears them his eyes go wide

He is my prey

Behind me door flies open hits wall she comes out her blue eyes her dark hair

I tell her stay back he is mine my prey I show her my teeth my strong jaws I tell her stay back she comes no closer

His voice floats down "Beautiful" It sounds odd not like bird not animal but human

He thinks I am beautiful I am

He did this he threw me down I see his teeth he is laughing

I am not laughing we do not laugh I will show him

Stairs one big jump and one big jump and land on high floor claws gouge the wood

Around this turn claws gripping wood fast fast he is smiling

He sees my face sees how fast I come at him his smile disappears

I hit him like a boulder in his chest hit him like a wave knock him down

He falls heavy slamming into the ground the rug there the dust goes up into my nose

His scent is different he is changing

I am standing on his chest his chest is roiling under me like the swell of a wave

He smells male he smells like family like strong jaguar I know him

Pull in air dust woolly rug scent pull in air it coils inside and curls like a fist

It rolls out into his face he is growing strong he is writhing and changing

Now he is golden he is jaguar

My roar shifts his fur sparks light in his eyes the spark is lit in mine

He is bigger and heavier than me the fight is on

He is family I am so mad I am strong I smack him hard

My bones shake my muscles ripple

He snarls he shows his teeth I show mine I bite his shoulder the skin breaks

It splits under my fangs separating like cloth his blood is warm and salty and sweet

He knocks me off and slams my head shaking me loose

My mouth drips blood he roars at me

I am not afraid

We hold on we roll we hit a big thing it scrapes the floor

We hit a little thing it tips something cold and heavy falls on my back and breaks

There is dirt everywhere there is plant in my mouth there is plant in my ear there is dirt in my eyes but I don't let go

We roll and I kick his belly hard and he bites me but not too hard but he knocks me over

He stands on me I kick his belly with my hind claws

My back legs so strong so heavy with muscle he roars at me I snarl and kick again

He hits my head and roars I kick again his fur comes off in my claws

I feel his skin feel the peel of fur and skin in my claws

He drops his head he takes my neck in his teeth he closes his teeth he shakes me hard

Shakes my eyes closed his fangs puncture my skin I feel it my blood is tart and sweet-smelling he is crushing me

I let go I go limp I let go my muscles soften and smooth out

He shakes me pulls my shoulders off the ground the woolly rug stained with blood

He thrashes my head back and forth my teeth click together

I smell my blood I am limp I let go I said I let go I am a puppet

My blood is hot and wet and I am sticky

"What the hell are you doing?" A person yells that is Tink Tink is here the jaguar grunts Tink kicks him hard in the flank

My cousin drops me I lie limp on the rug

Matéo snarls at Tink he paces around me because he won

He shows Tink his fangs red with my blood I have red fangs too

"I will kick your ass," Tink says. "Move back!"

My cousin does not want to he won his tail lashes back and forth

He paces he watches as Tink moves close to me

Tink kneels by my head I smell cloth I smell lotion I smell shampoo I smell him he is a person he is not my family

I growl at him the sound leaking out of my throat

"Stop it." He is in charge and I lie still

"Vivi, you need to change back so I can see your neck."

She is here with blue eyes and scent of lemons

"Matéo! Come on! Help here!"

I smell Matéo the jaguar then I smell person skin and blood and person hair

My cousin sits on the rug I pant and try not to swallow dirt

My head hurts my neck hurts my bones hurt my muscles hurt

"Vivi, let go of the jaguar and reach for your other self, your human self. It's right there. Feel it right there and reach for it."

He rubs my forehead my short fur flattens in all directions

It is distracting my eyes roll to look at him

I feel his finger on my forehead where my mother used to kiss me she used to touch me there I feel my short fur bending under his finger I feel like

Like Vivi is standing there waving at me

I see Vivi I go to her we join together we meld together becoming one . . . and then becoming her.

Suzanne threw a bath towel over me. Soon I felt mostly like myself and sat up, holding the towel. My neck stung and felt sticky. When I put my hand up, it came away wet with blood.

"You bit me!" I stared at Matéo accusingly.

"I had to calm you down. Maybe I bit a little too hard." He didn't look sorry.

"You bit my neck!"

He shrugged. "You bit me first. That's what happens, cub. When you attack someone bigger and stronger than you, you get bit."

"Hold still." Tink had a washcloth and started wiping off blood. "Okay, it's not too deep."

"Well, I didn't want to hurt her," said Matéo.

No one seemed shocked or upset. Tink obviously felt Matéo had gone too far, but just a little.

Tink slapped a couple of Band-Aids on my neck and grinned at me. "People will think you have a hickey."

"Ew."

"Tell 'em a vampire bit you," he suggested cheerfully, and even Suzanne smiled.

"Ha ha," I said darkly, trying to gather my towel and my dignity.

"You're missing the important thing here," said Matéo, "which is that you changed, and changed back, at will. You finally felt what you need to feel when you change form."

That was true. I really had, for the first time in my life. And I'd remembered something important: When I'd changed into a jaguar, I'd felt the muscle at the back of my neck that Matéo had talked about. It was where my father had always rubbed, kneading that muscle. I'd always thought he did it just because it felt good—it had been so casual, as he passed by, as we talked, as we watched TV. Now I saw that he'd been making me aware of what I needed to become a jaguar.

And then when Matéo had been talking to me, as I'd tried to change back ... My eyes filled with tears. My human part was right in my forehead, where Mami had kissed me every day. She would kiss my forehead right there and then press it with her fingers, as if to make the kiss stick. I'd never put it all together. I would need to think about all this more.

Suzanne handed me my watch and the clothes that I'd left downstairs. The ending up naked was obviously a huge drawback, I decided. There had to be a better way. In the meantime I had to get ready for work. Back to reality.

Chapter Twenty

"We're lepers," Jennifer said morosely.

"God, I guess we are," I agreed. I pushed my computer screen farther away on my bed and lay down next to it. My head would be sideways, but Jen could deal.

Jennifer had dated Cammie for almost two months, now that it was mid-November. But they'd recently broken up because Cammie was premed and always crazed with work and homework and they practically never saw each other. So Jennifer was feeling girlfriendless and like a loser.

For myself, I'd told Jennifer about the thing with Rafael back in September. Since then, I'd gotten hit on three times at work by customers. One guy was actually cute and seemed nice, and I'd been tempted, but though I definitely felt a little more in control of myself these days, I still felt "other," compared to regular people. So I'd said no. More than once.

"Too bad Alex didn't work out," Jennifer said. "He sounded hot."

"He was hot. Is hot," I amended. "I possibly would have gone out with him, as my only choice. But Aly forbade him to ask me, and told me he was a huge playboy who loved 'em and left 'em all over Louisiana. So it was a no-go." Plus, he was a haguaro, and I was still unsure about dating a haguaro. Obviously I was setting myself up for eternal spinsterhood.

"Maybe you could have been the one to change his evil ways." Jen sounded wistful.

I sighed. "We always want to think that—that we'll be enough for someone to change. But it never works that way. Besides, an actual relationship with him wouldn't have worked. He's only in town about once a week. But I'm glad we're friends. We went to Fellini Night at the Prytania Theatre last week."

"How was it?"

"A lot like my actual life," I said, and she laughed. I noticed that her face was thinner and she'd lost the deep tan she'd gotten in Israel.

"When do you have to let Seattle U know for sure if you're going next year?" she asked.

"February. They said they'd hold my spot till then."

"And?" She raised her eyebrows.

"No ands about it. I'm definitely going, of course."

Jennifer nodded and then dropped offscreen as she reached for something. "Why don't you switch and come up here? It doesn't have to be Columbia." Her face reappeared and she bit into a Fig Newton. "There's a million other schools here in New York. We could even be roommates, get an apartment."

"That would be so fun," I said. "I don't know. Still have my heart set on Seattle."

"But you were only going there because it was as far away from Florida as possible," she reminded me. "You don't need to do that anymore."

I nodded, feeling a familiar sadness. "Yeah. That's true. I feel like I've lost all my reasons to do anything." I hadn't meant to sound so down, but Jen made a sad face.

"I know, sweetie," she said. "But now instead of just doing stuff to be the opposite of what your parents wanted, you get to find what you yourself actually want."

"That has occurred to me."

Her head turned to look offscreen, then turned back. "Oh my god, Vivi! I totally forgot! Look at this weird thing!"

"What?"

I heard the rustling of paper, and then her face centered on the screen again. She looked serious, but also unsure.

"What is it, H?" I asked again.

"It's something I saw in the paper, the *New York Times*. I don't even know why I saw it—I was skimming the page, and then this caught my eye. I wasn't even sure I should tell you."

"Jeezum, what is it? You're weirding me out."

"It's . . ." She held up a newspaper page, but of course it was totally blurred and I couldn't read any of it. "It's, well, it's someone who . . . died like your parents."

In less than a second my skin turned cold. "What?"

Jennifer read from the newspaper. "'A suspicious death was reported last Tuesday after hikers found a . . . body.'"

I realized I had quit breathing, and I forced myself to inhale.

Jennifer gave a concerned glance at my face, then went on. "This happened a bit upstate, close to Woodstock. It says, 'The body has been identified as twenty-six-year-old Margaret McCauley. The cause of death was trauma to the chest. Upon autopsy, it was discovered that her heart had been removed. Police suspect that it was a ritual killing, but have no leads. Relatives of Ms. McCauley could shed no light on motive or suspect.'"

A minute passed as I digested this. Once again, the ridiculous notion of the Talofomé popped into my mind, and I shook my head.

"That seems weird, doesn't it?" Jennifer's voice was soft.

I nodded, then cleared my throat. "Really weird. What day was that from? I'll look it up online."

"It was from Monday. I've been meaning to call you ever since I saw it."

"Okay. Thanks. I'll look it up, see if I can find out anything else."

"Okay. I'm sorry, babe. Should I have not told you?"

"No, of course you should have told me." I tried to give a reassuring nod. "Of course you should have told me."

"Okay. I better run. I have my Saturday lab."

"Right," I said. "Thanks. I'll talk to you soon. Have a good lab."

After we hung up, I lay on my back on my bed, looking up at the pale coral watered-silk fabric that was gathered under the half tester. When my heart stopped pounding, I sat up and flipped my computer open again. It took only a couple of minutes to search the online archives of the *New York Times*, and I soon found the article. Not really an article, just an inch or two of type. I made a note of the reporter's name. I had to talk to Matéo about this.

My thoughts were interrupted by my bedroom door flinging open so hard that it crashed against the opposite wall. I jumped, my heart lurching all over again.

"Oops," said Alex, standing there and flashing his bad-boy grin.

"How about knocking?" I said. It was true, what I'd told Jen— Alex and I had fallen into an easy friendship. Because we weren't going to date, we didn't have to worry about appearances or seeming cool. I found that beneath his smooth, practiced charm he was actually smart, caring, and funny. And really full of himself. As a boyfriend, he would have broken my heart. As my pseudo-someday-possible cousin-in-law, he was comfortable.

"I was going to. I don't know my own strength."

My nerves were jangled and upset and I didn't want to deal with him right now.

"I'm here to ask you to come with us," he said, casually sitting next to me on my bed. "We're going to the river."

"Oh, I can't, sorry," I said, trying to look bummed. "I have work. Is Matéo here?" I wasn't on duty today, but my schedule changed sometimes. No one would know.

"No, he's going to meet us later. Call in sick," Alex suggested.

"Oh gosh, no. My personal integrity won't let me."

Alex chuckled and leaned back against the headboard. "Fellini was fun last week."

I looked at him, feeling myself calm down. I wanted to talk to Matéo about this new killing, but not at a river with a bunch of other people. "Yeah, it was. They're having an Iron Man double feature next Sunday. Let me know if you're around."

"Will do." He turned to face me, and it was odd, because here we were, almost lying on my bed, facing each other. It was kind of like being with Jennifer, until he leaned over and kissed me. I'd thought he was leaning over to whisper or something; we'd firmly established the only-friends thing. My pulse quickened even as I pulled away from him, eyes wide.

"What are you doing?" I asked.

"It has occurred to me," he said cheerfully, "that we can be friends . . . with benefits."

My eyebrows rose up into my hairline.

"You're not seeing anyone. I'm not seeing anyone. We like each other but don't want an actual relationship," he went on. "We're over eighteen. Why shouldn't we do the wild thing? I mean the regular wild thing, not the *grrr* wild thing." He made one hand into a claw and swiped gently at the air.

I was speechless, my few pathetic, failed dates having in no way prepared me for this situation.

"You're beautiful. A strong, beautiful girl. A haguara. We could have exciting times together—in any form." He quirked one eyebrow suggestively, a smile on his handsome face.

An image of two jaguars racing through the woods flashed into my mind. Then the gold jaguar caught the black one . . .

Alex leaned in again, and I drew back quickly in true terrified-virgin style.

"Ah, no," I said clumsily. "It's really better if we're just friends."

"Look, I'm okay simply being a placeholder until you meet someone more suitable. That would be fine." He propped his head on his hand, grinning: the most reasonable of men.

I bet. I was so in over my head. My mom would have known how to handle this gracefully. What would she have done? I pictured her smiling, confident face.

"No, I don't think so; it's not a good idea; thanks anyway" was the best I could come up with.

Aly appeared in my doorway. "You coming, sweetie? We're going to pick up Popeyes chicken on the way." She saw my face and her eyes narrowed. "What's going on here?"

"Nothing," said Alex smoothly, sitting up. "Just trying to convince Vivi . . . to come with us."

Aly looked at him suspiciously.

"I wish I could go," I said, trying for sincerity. "But I have to work." I knew Aly would want to know about what Jennifer had told me, but something in me wanted to talk to my cousin first.

"Call in sick," Aly said.

"You're going to the river?" I asked, deflecting her. "It's November."

"It's seventy-eight degrees," Alex said drily. "But it's nice that it gets dark early."

Less chance of being seen.

"Wish I could," I said again.

"Some other time," Aly said. "Come on, Alex, quit bugging her."

Alex winked and made the *call me* hand signal. I rolled my eyes at him and he laughed, then headed across the hall to knock on Suzanne and James's door. "Get a move on! Ten minutes! Also, we need your car!"

After that first time, I had never been to the river again, though everyone else went every couple of weeks. Sometimes Matéo looked at me like he thought I was being a sissy, but what could I say? Even if I wanted to be fully haguari, which I didn't, there was still the nakedness issue: Everyone shucked their clothes first so they wouldn't get lost or torn. I mean, no thank you. I wanted to stay right here in my cocoon, not taking risks.

In fact, since the first time I successfully changed by myself and changed back, I hadn't done it again. Nothing upsetting had happened to force a change, and I'd stopped practicing. It was all getting a little too close, and I'd wanted to step back toward regular personness.

It had been relatively quiet recently, until this news item from Jennifer: There had been no weird attacks, no one showing up at my house in Sugar Beach. I was getting more settled here every day. Soon I would really have to decide if I was going to move here— if I was, I probably needed to sell my parents' house. That would be weird. Jennifer would be upset. Though I did think of Matéo's house as being a cocoon, I knew that every cocoon had to split eventually and let the adult emerge. My time was coming.

After everyone left for the river, the house was quiet and there was no faint, subtle pulse of energy that told me someone was near. No one was home except me. Glancing at the clock, I saw that Coco should be home any minute. I went back online and searched for the reporter who'd written the news report. His name was Nicholas Tareynton, and the paper listed his e-mail address.

With trembling fingers I sent him an e-mail:

Hello. I wanted to talk to you about the murder that happened in NY, outside of Woodstock, I wrote. *Please e-mail me. It's important. Viviana Neves.*

Shutting my computer, I knew I had to distract myself. Who knew when he would get back to me? If I didn't hear from him in the next couple of days, I would try calling the paper, I decided. I slid off my bed, went to the bathroom, and splashed water on my face.

What had Alex been thinking? He'd been thinking that I was a good shot for no-strings sex, I admitted wryly. And if I were experienced, as he assumed any eighteen-year-old probably was, it might not be a bad thing. But I wasn't, and there was no way my heart could handle anything like casual sex, even with an easygoing friend like Alex.

I pushed up one of my French windows and wandered out onto the balcony. Matéo had hired a tree service to trim back the branches of the magnolia—it would be hard for someone to jump from the tree to the porch again. The autumn sun shone on my skin, and I slanted my face toward it, closing my eyes. It was a beautiful day. I should go do something. Go somewhere. At least until someone else came home.

In the end I wound up driving to Audubon Park, which was uptown, right across Saint Charles Avenue from Tulane and Loyola Universities. There were running paths and benches and kids' playgrounds, and a small lagoon that had ducks and turtles in it. Enormous live oaks, still fully leaved, made pockets of shade. I parked on Saint Charles in front of the entrance and locked my car.

The main entrance had two big gateposts with manicured flower beds all around them. A three-tiered fountain marked the center of a large circle lined with tree-shaded benches. Two teenage girls wearing Rollerblades sat on a bench, laughing, and on the other side a woman held her toddler up to drink from a water fountain. A man jogged up, his border collie on a leash, and the dog jumped joyfully into the fountain, splashing and leaping and drinking while the man laughed at him.

Past the fountain was the paved road that cars had once been allowed to drive on but that was now blocked off and reserved for bikers and pedestrians. On such a beautiful day it was almost crowded, and I checked for bikes before heading out on it. Everything had gotten so confusing. On paper my life sounded simple: live at cousin's house, work at coffee shop. But in some ways I'd never felt this pulled in so many different directions, never felt so incapable of knowing what to do. I needed to figure out my life.

A quick walk in the park should take care of that, right?

Suddenly I felt overwhelmed and lost—I had left my life in Florida and settled here, but I was in limbo, waiting for some unknown shoe to drop. I was no closer to knowing who had killed my parents or Matéo's parents, no closer to understanding the weird situation with my mom and dad and Matéo's mom. I had no idea if I wanted to go to Seattle next fall or ever, or if I wanted to stay here. Being haguari automatically felt like being sentenced to be a freak, except I saw every single day that that wasn't true. For so long I'd felt I didn't fit in anywhere, but I did actually fit in well with my cousin and Aly and their friends. I fit in just fine—and that would be perfect if I wanted to change much more often.

I just didn't know a single damn thing about myself.

Hot tears came to my eyes. Without deciding to, I broke into a run, easily passing casual joggers, moms with strollers, little kids on bikes. In high school I'd longed to be on the cross-country team, but I'd felt I couldn't take the chance of suddenly being weird in a locker room or on a bus. Now I ran smoothly and almost silently on the pavement, feeling my lungs pumping, my heart beating only slightly faster. My hair streamed out in back of me because I hadn't thought ahead to put it in a ponytail. Or to put on shorts or a sports bra. I held my arms up in front of my chest, trying not to look too obvious.

This is what you call running away from your problems, I thought, and gave a small laugh even as tears spilled from my eyes and ran down my cheeks. My legs were pistons in my jeans and I pushed myself to run faster and harder until I was whipping by everyone, even grown-ups on bicycles. The little map at the front of the park had said the path was just about two miles long—I lapped it twice, until my face was burning, my lungs aching, and my legs felt like warm rubber. Clouds had moved in, and it was late afternoon, starting to get dark. The park's old-fashioned iron streetlamps came on. My shirt was stuck to my back with sweat and my hair hung in long, stringy strands. Gradually I slowed to a jog, then a walk, then stopped, hanging over from my waist feeling like I might faint. My hair dragged on the ground, my long hot jeans had rubbed my skin raw in places, and I wanted to throw up, then cry, then die. In that order.

"It's too much," I whispered, gasping. "It's too much. I can't do it."

It took me a few moments to notice the blurry hand parting the curtain of my hair and holding a water bottle under my chin. I stood up quickly, sweeping my hair back. My chest was heaving, sweat ran down my face, and I was still crying.

Rafael stood in front of me, holding the water bottle. "Drink this."

Wordlessly I took it and drank. The water was cool, and it felt amazing, making a lovely, soothing trail down my throat to my stomach. I wiped some of the condensation off the outside of the bottle and patted my forehead with it, then drank deeply again.

When I handed it back, it was almost empty.

"Thanks." I was panting less but felt itchy and hot and tingly all over. Maybe I should go lie down in the fountain like the border collie.

"You can run amazingly fast," said Rafael. He brushed his arm against his forehead, and I saw that he was a sweaty mess too, his hair wet and spiky, his tank undershirt stuck to him transparently, showing the dark hair on his chest, his sharply muscled chest and arms. He was just so beautiful and he would never be mine and it almost made me hate him.

I nodded.

"What were you running from?" he asked.

"Nothing. I was just running."

He shook his head. "No. When someone runs like that, they're trying to get away from something."

I wasn't going to talk to him about it. We got along at work because we didn't interact very much. For weeks I had tried to train myself to not find him attractive, but of course I still did, so I'd given myself permission to lust after him physically but not emotionally.

I was such a mess.

"What are you doing here?" I asked.

He nodded toward a shiny blue bicycle leaning against a bench. "Just riding around. I usually circle the park and go up by the river, then ride home. You want some more water?"

"No, that's okay. Thanks. I forgot to bring some."

Across the road from us, a determined toddler was insisting on pushing her own stroller while her parents walked behind her, helping her steer without her knowing. It was cute and I watched her, feeling Rafael's eyes focused on me.

"Do you want to get something to eat?"

That got my attention and I looked at him. "What?"

"Do you want to go get a po'boy at Domilise's?" he asked. "It's not far. Do you have your car?"

An image of us sitting close, eating and talking and laughing, me gazing at him with adoration, flashed painfully into my mind. Far off I heard the soft, low rumble of distant thunder. The soft smell of rain came to me, and I inhaled.

"Yeah, I have my car, but . . . that isn't a good idea," I said. "We have to work together." Totally the right call, like with Alex earlier, but it didn't feel like the right call. It felt sad and lonely.

Rafael frowned, but he had only himself to blame.

"Well, I'm going to go," I said, and turned to head to the front of the park. "Thanks for the water." As if on cue, a fat raindrop fell, splashing against my cheek. The next one landed on my head and seeped beneath my hair. Perfect. It was probably a mile back to my car. In the rain.

Rafael's voice stopped me. "Vivi, we—I want to—"

Blinking against the quickening raindrops, I turned to see him wearing the same tortured expression he'd had the night we'd kissed. He just looked . . . upset. Frustrated. Uncertain. The next moment, his face cleared and he closed the space between us. Looking determined, he held my shoulders and kissed me. Just like before, all my nerve endings lit up. I was getting kissed a lot today.

It should have been disgusting because we were both gross and sweaty, but instead it just felt very . . . primal. Like nothing could stop us. Like nothing else mattered. Soon we were pressed tightly together from knee to mouth, and if I could have, I would have crawled inside his skin to be closer still. I didn't know what drew me so strongly to him, but whatever it was ran darkly and powerfully through my veins. My hands slid up his hard, wet forearms, then to his muscled shoulders. His skin was warm and silken and he just felt . . . perfect. A perfect fit. My ideal. There was no one who would feel better than this.

It rained steadily and gently as night fell around us like a curtain. At some point Rafael pulled us deeper into the darkness beneath the patchy shelter of a thick-branched oak. I stumbled on a root and he caught me against him, mashing my chest against his, our hips hard against each other. Despite my relative lack of experience, I felt I knew what to do, what I wanted to do, and I did it. I held the back of his head with one hand, feeling the short, soft hair against his skull. Boldly I pushed my other hand beneath his damp shirt, feeling his skin, smooth and wet from rain. He shivered and made a sound against my mouth and I smiled.

I was strong, I was a haguara, and I leaned into him till his back was against the tree. Threading my other hand beneath his shirt made the wet fabric bunch up, and I ran my hands anywhere I wanted. Harder and harder I kissed him, and he kissed me back just as hard. Then his hands were under my shirt, smoothing across my skin. I shivered too because of the rain and my feelings and the cooling night air. His hands ran across my bra and with deft skill he unhooked it. That should have made me pause, should have made me consider what I was doing, what I had never done with any boy before. But all it did was stoke the fire, the desire inside me.

When his shockingly warm hand moved over the cool, wet skin of my breast, I gasped. He drew me to him more firmly, kissed me more deeply, and I was borne away on a swelling wave of emotion and excitement and sensations I'd never imagined. His fingers kneaded and stroked and explored more urgently, and I felt like I was going to ignite. When his hand dropped to the front of my jeans, I made a sound and pushed my hips against him—and then I realized what I was doing and pulled back.

He followed me, his hand moving expertly against the wet, heavy fabric, and most of me thought, *yes, yes,* and wanted him to keep going. But a small, insistent part of me was like, *Whoa, Vivi, what the hell?*

With difficulty I stopped kissing him, almost delirious with desire and shock, and pulled my hands away from his chest.

His hand stilled. His eyes, leaf green rimmed with gold, gazed at me steadily. He was breathing hard, his chest rising and falling quickly.

I didn't know what to say.

As he had done the first time we kissed, he dropped his forehead against mine, and we both panted into the rain-spattered darkness.

"Take me home," he said.

It took a second for my brain to process the words. Did he mean he wanted a ride? 'Cause he was on his bike and it was raining?

"Take me home to your bed. Or come home with me to mine."

Wide-eyed, I looked at him, saw the flush across his cheekbones, the intent on his face.

"We haven't even been on a date." That was the first, and embarrassingly inane, thing that popped into my head and right out my mouth. But I had gone eighteen years without anyone trying to sleep with me, and today I'd had two offers. Both without the benefit of love or a relationship or anything, really.

My words seemed to shock Rafael as much as his actions had shocked me.

"Oh . . . right."

It was satisfying to see that he seemed to be having as much trouble putting words together as I was. I had done that to him.

"I want you." He seemed almost mystified by that, as if he had said it without meaning to or against his will. His hand on my back, he pulled me firmly against his hips, as if to prove his words.

It was very dark here, but I could see the confusion on his face. He ran a hand through his wet hair, making it spiky, like a pelt. We were both sopping—the rain was still coming down.

"I . . . can't," I said, wishing I could come up with something casual and knowing. "Not like this."

"In a bed." Oh my gods, did he think it was just rain and mud and tree roots that were stopping me?

"No. I mean with a stranger. Who doesn't love me. Who I don't love."

The muscles in his jaw tightened, highlighted by the dim streetlamp ten yards away.

If he just turned and walked away, I would kill him. My teeth ached, and I remembered with horror that jaguars kill their prey by biting their skulls. *I didn't mean it!* I thought quickly. Was that muscle in my neck clenching? No. No, I couldn't feel it.

"I'm sorry," he said at last, while I was still scrambling to feel 100 percent human. "I didn't mean to . . . hurt you this way. Again."

"I didn't mean to ever let you."

We regarded each other warily.

"What are we doing?" he asked.

I shook my head. "Hell if I know." All of my energy was gone, my strength sapped by my run and then this emotional collision.

"I want to kiss you, be with you, all the time." He spoke fast. "Every day at work. When I'm home by myself. When I'm with other people. When I don't know where you are or what you're doing or who you're doing it with . . ." His voice trailed off, and the desperation on his face took me aback.

"But you don't want to go out, like normal people?" I was just too confused.

"No—it's—"

"Are you married?"

"No. Of course not. It's just . . . I don't know. And you . . ." He sounded so angry.

I shivered again, this time only with cold, and decided that this episode was over. "I'm going home now."

He drew in a shaky breath but didn't try to stop me. I sloshed through the wet grass and leaves till I reached the path again, then headed toward the front of the park. Not once did I look back.

CHAPTER TWENTY-ONE

COCO'S VAN WAS IN THE YARD WHEN I GOT HOME.
For once I wasn't afraid when I got out of my car and went to
the kitchen door. The mood I was in, I would have taken on any
attacker with one paw tied behind my back. In the empty kitchen
I grabbed some leftover Chinese food and nuked it, then ate as I
walked upstairs. Coco's light shone under her door, and I heard
Charlotte's soft laugh, so I didn't knock. In my small bathroom I
turned on the hot water, finished the Chinese food, then peeled
out of my wet clothes. Then I sat on the shower floor, trying not to
cry, while the hot water poured on my head and warmed me up.

Why was I so drawn to Rafael? Besides his incredible good looks,
patience, kindness, family loyalty, etc. Ugh. Again and again I thought
of the portrait he'd done of me, the one he'd never hung up in Ro's.
I'd wanted to ask about it—if he didn't want it, I did—but also
didn't want to let him know how much it had meant to me. There
was someone in the world who saw me that way. I had looked that
way to him, at least once. And was he a haguaro? The self-portrait

as jaguar seemed so obvious, as did my overwhelming lust for him. Why couldn't I tell? Did the fact that I couldn't tell mean he wasn't one? And if he was, could he tell that I was one too?

Long after I turned pruney, the hot water started to cool, so I got out, wrapping my wet hair in one towel and drying off with another. It was infuriating to be this confused. In Sugar Beach I'd wanted things to stay nebulous, tenuous. I'd discouraged my parents from having real talks with me. I'd kept my nature hidden from Jennifer. I'd never shared the true depth of my dismay over being haguari with my parents. Every day I'd dodged questions, given half answers, lived in the future, when I'd had the naïve idea that being in Seattle would make me not myself.

Now I anxiously wanted everything to be nailed down, definite. I wanted to know for sure whether Rafael was a haguaro or not. I wanted to decide once and for all if I was going home for Christmas, or at all. I had to decide what to tell Tia Juliana, because I was tired of living one more lie if I didn't have to. Six months ago all I'd wanted was to be self-determining. Now that I was nothing but self-determining, I realized that it often sucked.

In my room at the front of the house I rarely heard cars pulling into our backyard, but I felt the vibrations in the house when Matéo and the others came home. Quickly I turned off my reading light, pulled on my big T-shirt, and snuggled down in bed, pretending to be asleep. In reality I lay there, miserable and dry-eyed, for another three hours, reliving those incredible kisses with Rafael, my imagination running wild with everything else I had wanted to do to him. Looking up at my coral silk tester, I laughed wryly: I was eighteen years old, and someone had finally gotten to second base. Almost third base. Pushing my face deep in my pillow, I smothered my whimper. I'd really wanted him. Still wanted him. Really disliked him. Was really mad at him.

My dreams were horrible and I woke up bizarrely late with a headache and in an awful mood. I pulled on some shorts, headed downstairs, and found Matéo leaning into the fridge.

"You missed a great time at the river yesterday," he said, taking out the orange juice.

Automatically I fixed myself a bowl of coffee, then remembered I'd made croissants yesterday morning. There were still a few left and I grabbed one, then sat down at the kitchen table, trying to decide if I was ever going to go to work again.

"The weather was great, until it started raining," Matéo went on. "Did it rain here?"

"Yep," I said grimly.

Straightening, Matéo looked over at me. "What are you eating?"

"Croissant." I waved it at him. "There's more in the Tupperware thing on the counter."

Matéo pounced on the container and popped it open. "Did you make these?"

"Uh-huh. Listen, I need to talk to you." Morosely I drank more coffee and buttered another hunk of croissant. Adding butter to a croissant was like adding more chocolate chips to chocolate-chip cookie dough: You could conceivably overdo it, but you could go pretty far before that happened.

"What about?" he asked.

Outside, the November midafternoon shadows were already growing long. I hadn't slept this late in ages. The temperature had plummeted down to the midsixties, and between that and the autumn light, all I wanted to do was bake and make soup and sit in front of the fireplace in the front parlor, moping.

"Does our fireplace work?" I asked Matéo, stalling.

He nodded, chewing. "I need to clean it out so we can use it," he said, his voice muffled. "Cold front coming through—it's supposed to go down to like forty-five tonight."

"Ooh." We grinned at each other, two southerners who were used to scraping coziness together at the slightest excuse. Then I just jumped in and told him about the killing in New York, the missing heart, her name, Margaret McCauley, and the fact that I had e-mailed the reporter to try to get more information.

"Gods," Matéo said.

"Yeah. I want to know more about it. I tried a search on 'missing hearts' and all I got was a punk band in the eighties. The thing is, this person seems totally unrelated to us: Margaret McCauley. That's not someone in your dad's family, is it?"

Matéo shook his head. "Not that I've heard of. And, I mean, we don't even know if she was a haguara. Though it sounds really similar."

"I know. It could be some regular nutso killer," I said. "Not someone targeting haguari."

"Okay. Maybe I'll poke around on the Web, see if I can find anything else. Part of me hopes it's just a nut job, so that we don't feel so targeted, but part of me wants it to be a haguara killing, because then we could really be sure it isn't just about us, our family. It would mean all haguari. Which . . . actually, never mind. Both scenarios suck. The whole thing sucks. Gods." He shook his head, and we sat there for several minutes, each lost in our own dark thoughts. Finally, as if making himself reach for normalcy, he asked, "Got work today?"

"I think so." My shift started soon, and no one had called to say I didn't need to come in. What had happened with Rafael last night was yet another layer of uncertainty and pain, on top of everything else. It was smoldering inside me and I had no idea what to do. Jennifer was at class. Aly was at work. I wouldn't talk to Tia Juliana about this.

"So, Aly said that she thought Alex might be bothering you."

Alex's offer of being friends with benefits came back to me. My Gods, yesterday had been a weird, awful day.

"Oh, no. He was just goofing around. We're just friends."

"Okay, but you tell me if he gets ideas," Matéo said. "He's going to be my brother-in-law someday, and he's not evil or anything, but I've never seen a bigger tail chaser."

"Oh, very nice!" I said, and threw my crumpled napkin at him.

He held up both hands. "It's true. I hate to say it, but it's true."

"So all I am is a piece of tail?" After Rafael last night, that hit much too close, catching me off guard. Before I knew it, I had burst into tears.

Eyebrows raised, Matéo looked horrified, and he glanced around as if hoping to see Aly or some other female come to my aid. Then he grabbed a paper towel and pushed it into my hands before awkwardly patting my back.

"Vivi, I'm sorry—what did I say? You know you're not just—I swear, if Alex was playing you, I'll—"

"It wasn't Alex!" I blurted.

"What?"

The paper towel rasped the skin on my nose, but I didn't care. Matéo was my cousin and I'd grown to love him, but he was still a guy and I would much rather have talked to Aly or Jennifer. But he was right here, kind of the brother I'd never had, and it all came pouring out, to our mutual horror.

"It's my boss, Rafael!" I said, and then told Matéo all about him, from watching him at work, the portrait, our first kiss, how nice he was to everyone even if he didn't smile much, how gorgeous he was, how I thought about him all the time, how we'd avoided each other for the last couple of months, and then how last night I'd wanted to eat him alive. Almost literally.

To his credit, Matéo tried to rise to the occasion, listening, making soothing noises, getting me another paper towel, but I was sure he wished Aly had been there instead, and I did too.

"I don't get it," Matéo said when I'd finished. "Why can't you go out, like normal people?"

"That's what I asked!" I said, slamming my fist on the table. The glasses rattled, and Matéo jumped slightly. "I said that exact same thing! He doesn't have an answer! Just he can't, it's him, it's me, he doesn't know, blah blah blah!"

"Do you think he's just a player?"

"I don't think so. He said he never kisses anyone. He seemed as surprised as I was. Talia at work has never seen him date."

"And he's not married?"

"That's what I asked!" I practically shouted, and saw Matéo wince. "He says no."

"Hm," said Matéo. "So he's just an asshole. Do you want a beer? I'm getting one."

"I will never drink again," I reminded him, my stomach turning over at the thought. "But that's the thing—he doesn't seem like an asshole. He seems . . . tortured. Like he regrets it. Like he really wants to be with me and then remembers he can't. But he's not married. He's twenty-one. And I don't think he's terminally ill."

Matéo popped the top on his beer bottle and sat down, looking thoughtful.

"I've wondered if he's a haguaro," I went on. "But I can't tell. Wouldn't I be able to tell? I mean, he painted his own face onto a jaguar on his mural."

"What's his name again?" Matéo asked.

"Rafael Marquez."

"I don't know him," Matéo said. "Not that that means anything. I sure don't know every haguaro in New Orleans."

"Talia told me his parents live in Mexico," I said. "And his grandmother is French, I guess—Fontenot."

"Maybe he's a haguaro, but from a different clan? And he has to be with someone from his own clan? Our grandparents rejected my father because he was from a different clan."

"Yeah, I guess. Assuming he's haguaro."

"I can ask around, try to find out," said Mateo. "See if anyone knows any Fontenots or Marquezes."

"Part of me hopes he is, and most of me hopes he isn't," I said, sniffling again.

"Your mom never tried to fix you up?" Matéo asked. "You got off lucky."

Oh, my gosh—I remembered all the times my mom had in fact tried to set me up with her friends' sons. "No, she did. Geez."

Car tires crunched on the shells in our parking area, and I recognized the engine as being Aly's Camry. It pulled to a stop outside, and then we heard the car door slam and her footsteps approach the cement steps.

"She's home early," I said, glancing at the clock.

"Yeah. I got stuck with Aly back in high school," Matéo said, raising his voice as Aly's shadow covered the kitchen door. "Just because she's the only female my age from the right clan within five hundred miles!"

He had to be joking—his own parents were from different clans, so surely they would have been fine with his choice.

Aly's key clicked in the lock, and she opened the door, grinning. "Poor thing," she said. "Too bad you had no choice."

Matéo grinned back at her. She dropped her purse on the

table, kicked off her businesslike heels, and came to sit on Matéo's lap. He made space for her, his hands going around her hips to pull her closer. I loved their relationship. I wished I could have something like that. Which would mean being with a haguaro, right?

"After all," Aly cooed, stroking Matéo's face, the rough, auburn stubble on his unshaved cheeks. "I had several choices. There was Javier Olivado . . ."

Matéo quit smiling.

"Tomás Marián," she went on. "He adored me. Marc Barella—his father owned that boat-building company. Enric—"

"Okay, whatever," Matéo said.

"But I chose you," Aly said, pulling his face to hers and kissing him. He kissed her back, starting to smile again. "Even though you were half Irish. Because I love you."

They gazed into each other's eyes, and I was so jealous of what they had. And so happy because of what they had.

"And . . . you're saying I'm really lucky," Matéo said.

Aly got up and went to the fridge, pulling out the pitcher of iced tea. "Sugar, I'm saying you are incredibly lucky."

Matéo laughed. "You're right," he said, and they smiled at each other in a sexy, private way that was a little embarrassing.

Suddenly Aly looked at the wall clock. "Vivi—don't you have work? It's ten after five."

"Oh, crap!" I jumped up, grabbed my car keys, and slid my feet into my high-top sneakers. "Get her caught up on the saga," I instructed Matéo. "And the other thing too. We can all discuss later, over ice cream."

I was half an hour late to work—the first time I'd been late. When I pushed through the back door, breathless, I dumped my bag in the employees' room and raced up front, grabbing an apron on the way. A line of ten people had formed at the counter, and Talia was moving as fast as she could.

"I'm so sorry!" I told her, darting behind the counter. "I can help the next person in line, please!"

"I was getting worried," Talia said. "I can set my clock by you."

"I just wasn't paying attention." I was putting a microwaved scone on a plate when Rafael came behind the counter, carrying a bin of clean dishes. My heart gave a flutter inside my chest, feeling like a hummingbird's wings, and the look he gave me would have lit tinder.

"Thought you might not come in," he muttered, kneeling right by my legs to put dishes on the shelves beneath the counter. I stepped back and handed the customer her scone, then took another order.

While the blender was going, I said, "Sorry I'm late. Lost track of time." It was a relief to focus on pouring drinks, remembering recipes and procedures, cleaning equipment. Rafael didn't say anything more to me, and I ignored him, which was easy because he stayed in the back. Lately he'd been cleaning up the large, professional kitchen that no one used. I wondered if he was planning on selling all the equipment.

At nine o'clock Rafael came out again. "Everything okay?" he asked Talia.

"Sure," she said.

"Okay, I'm taking off." He stood there, not leaving, until I looked over at him. "Talk to you later," he said, seeming to mean only me.

I didn't respond, just asked the next person in line what she wanted. Finally, out of the corner of my eye I saw him leave and heard the back door shut behind him. Whatever.

An hour later the front room had calmed down and only eight tables were occupied out of thirty-two. Talia and I used the time to clean things, organize, take inventory of what we had up front, refill the napkin and silverware bins. Work like this was predictable, tidy, and satisfying.

I was sweeping around the counter area when the doorbell jingled and I looked up to see Matéo, Aly, Dana, and Alex coming in.

"Hey!" I said. "What are you doing here?"

"We just had dinner at Benito's," Aly said, "and decided to come see you for coffee and dessert."

"Yay," I said, putting the broom away. "This is the highlight of my day. Talia, this is my cousin, Matéo, and my friends Aly, Dana, and Alex."

"Pleased to meet you," Talia said, giving our sugar canisters a final swipe. "Boy, where did you get that red hair from?"

I grinned at Matéo. He'd heard my stories about Talia.

"My dad was Irish," he answered, smiling. "Are the cream-cheese brownies good?"

"Yeah, they're good," I said. I didn't say that a touch more cream cheese would be even better. Basically, I found fault with almost every baked item we had, thinking of what I would have done differently. "I have personally sampled our wares in order to provide the most accurate customer service possible."

"You're so conscientious," Matéo said, and I grinned.

"How's the pumpkin spice latte?" Dana asked.

"It's good," I said. "Very autumny. And the pumpkin bread is good too." *Though I would have used pecans instead of walnuts.*

"Bring it!" Dana said. "Carb me up!" Laughing, I started on her latte.

Matéo and Aly ordered cappuccinos while Alex was still pondering his choices.

"You guys go sit down," I told them. "I'll bring your stuff to you."

With Dana leading the way, they chose a table not far from the mural. They'd heard about it from me, and now I saw them examining it. I quickly filled two espresso portafilters and locked them in place, then poured cold milk into a small silver pitcher for the steam wand.

"Hey," I said to Alex. "Did you have fun at the river yesterday?" Had that been only yesterday?

Alex was examining his choices through the glass, but looked up and smiled. "I would have had more fun if you'd been there," he said, wiggling his eyebrows with fake flirtiness. It was so overdone that I laughed. His dark brown hair hadn't been cut in ages, and it curled down onto the collar of his purple button-down shirt. His black jeans had been ironed, and I bet he was wearing those narrow-toed Italian shoes he loved. What a peacock.

"I'm sure," I said to Alex. "Do you know what you want yet?" Moving the steam wand, I put it into the small pitcher of milk and turned it on.

"If I can't have you, then I guess a double espresso and a chocolate torte will have to do," he said, looking sad.

"Uh-huh," I said. "That's about as good as you're going to get."

Alex laughed and stepped back, and I shot him a grin. There wasn't any real weight behind his flirting, which was why it was fun. Talia finished wiping the glass shelves behind us, but I felt her glancing at me. I would have to explain Alex to her.

Behind me the espresso machine quit hissing and I quickly fixed two cappuccinos, frothing the milk and sprinkling cinnamon on top. I got Matéo's brownie, Aly's palmier, and Dana's pumpkin bread and brought it all over to their table.

"Thank you, ma'am," said Dana. "This looks perfect."

"Oh, Vivi, Téo told me about the missing heart in New York," Aly said sympathetically. "Have you heard back from the reporter?"

I shook my head. "I haven't checked since I've been here, but I don't think so. It's weird, isn't it? And I feel like, okay, it's happening in New York; that's far away. Can we relax? Then I feel awful."

Aly sighed. "I know what you mean. We can talk about it more later. But . . . is Rafael here?" she asked in a low voice.

"We wanted to give him a look-over, see if we could answer any questions for you." Like if he was haguaro.

"That's a brilliant idea, but he's already gone for the evening," I said regretfully. "But let's definitely try to get you in here sometime when he's here. That would be great."

Matéo, Aly, Dana, and Alex stayed for almost an hour. Every once in a while I glanced over to make sure they didn't need anything, and once or twice Alex winked or blew me a kiss, trying to rattle me. I just rolled my eyes.

Finally they got up to leave. Aly came to hug me and said, "See you at home soon, okay?"

"Okay," I said. "Thanks for coming in."

The place seemed quite empty without them, and I started the end-of-evening putting away and cleaning up.

"They seem nice," Talia said.

"They are really nice," I said. "Matéo's the cousin I live with. Aly's his girlfriend. Dana is another one of our roommates, and Alex is Aly's brother."

"He sure does seem sweet on you," said Talia, and I groaned inwardly. "Does he live with you too?"

"No, he doesn't. And he was just joking," I said quickly. "There's nothing between us."

By midnight the rest of the customers had left, and Talia locked the front door and turned off the outside lights to show we were closed. We finished cleaning up, putting chairs upside down on tables so we could mop, etc.

We were fast and efficient, and walked out to the parking lot by twelve thirty.

"Good night, honey," said Talia, her can of spray mace in her hand. "You drive careful, you hear?"

"You too, Talia. Night."

CHAPTER TWENTY-TWO

THANKSGIVING HAD BEEN THE ONE DAY MY
parents and I didn't argue. Maybe because it was a purely American
holiday not related in any way to our heritage. Maybe because
we all liked food. I don't know. But it was a day of truce for us,
watching the Macy's parade, cooking all day, stuffing ourselves that
evening, living on pie for days afterward.

This Thanksgiving Jennifer was staying in New York, and
other than the family book that I needed to search for, I didn't
really have a reason to go home. I was starting to want things from
my house—my baking supplies, warmer clothes, some favorite
DVDs—but so far nothing had been worth going back for. When
Coco had suggested having a big Thanksgiving here, I'd been
happy to agree.

Together Coco and I had planned the menu and assigned people
chores. Doing something besides mooning over Rafael was a welcome change. Consulting with Matéo, we'd agreed to ask Charlotte;
Tink's boyfriend, Peter; Alex; and a friend of Dana's, Michelle. Partly

for fun, and partly to have something totally occupying my time and imagination, I decided to get really ambitious with the cooking, and Coco had been totally into it.

Ro's was going to be closed on Thanksgiving Day, but I was forced to ask Rafael for Wednesday off. During a lull on Monday night I left Talia at the front counter and went down the hall to knock on the office door.

It opened immediately and Rafael was right there. The room was dark behind him.

"Do you have a minute?" I asked.

Nodding, he stepped backward and turned on the office light. That was when I saw he had his backpack over one shoulder and had obviously been about to leave. He started to close the door behind me, and I said, "That's okay—this isn't private."

Keeping his eyes on me, he shut the door and leaned against it.

"Really, I just wanted to check in," I said briskly. "Joey has agreed to switch shifts with me on Wednesday night. Talia has off too, and she's gotten Kathy to cover for her. So it would be Kathy and Joey. Is that okay?"

Of course it should be okay.

"Why do you want Wednesday off?" he asked.

"It's the day before Thanksgiving. We're having a bunch of people for dinner, and I need to cook."

I made myself meet his beautiful green eyes calmly and not turn away. As usual, he looked like he was having a hundred thoughts that he couldn't express.

"I didn't know you had a boyfriend" was what came out of his mouth.

"What?"

"Your boyfriend, Alex."

Oh, thank you, Talia. Because I need this.

"I don't have a boyfriend. Alex is my friend's brother."

"It sounds like he wants you." Rafael blinked, as if he hadn't meant to say that.

Anger ignited in me: at Alex, for his stupid flirting; at Talia, for gossiping; and at Rafael, for daring to even question me about this. "Yes," I said tightly. "I believe he does. No one wants to actually date me, but guys keep wanting to get in my pants."

In a split second his anger mirrored mine. "I want to date you," he snapped. "It's just—"

"Oh, my gods," I snapped back. "Here you go again with the 'I just,' 'you don't,' 'I can't,' 'it isn't' crap again! You're so full of it! I know what you want from me, and you can go screw yourself!"

His lips were pressed together; his eyes were dark and narrowed. Tension radiated from his lean, muscled body, the body I remembered all too well.

"You have no idea what I want from you," he said in a low, rough voice.

I crossed my arms and almost snorted. "Trust me, I got the picture. Do I have Wednesday off or not?"

Seconds passed as we stared angrily at each other. The really sad part was that I wanted to reach out and grab him again, like I had in the park. *I could push him down on the desk, and—*

"You're having people in for Thanksgiving?" he asked.

I blinked several times, trying to jump into the new conversation. "Yes."

"You're cooking for everyone?"

Jeezum. "Yes. My friend and I are cooking."

Silence. He was still leaning against the door. I was afraid to push past him, as if the slightest touch would make every defense I had crumble.

"That sounds fun," he said.

Whaat? "Yes, I think it will be," I said after a second. "What are you doing for Thanksgiving?" I had not meant to say that. Rafael and I were made for each other. Gods.

His surprise mirrored mine. "I'm going to my sister's, in New Hampshire."

The idea of Rafael having a sister was somehow shocking. He seemed like he'd been hatched from a spiky dragon egg or something.

"Is she at school there?" I couldn't help myself.

"No," he said. "She's a pediatrician. She has a couple of kids. And a husband. We go to her house because it's big and there's usually snow, which is still a novelty."

My mouth actually dropped open. Brooding, mysterious, angry Rafael was a little brother. His sister sounded totally normal. This was too fascinating.

"Who else goes?"

He took a breath and seemed like he was about to tell me it was none of my business, which of course it wasn't, but then he said, "My two other sisters who live in America. We usually go."

"You have two other sisters? Three sisters?"

A corner of Rafael's finely carved mouth turned up. "Actually, I have four sisters. My little sister lives with my parents in Mérida, Mexico."

"You have four sisters. Are you the only boy?"

"Yeah. My dad was so relieved. He's pretty traditional."

Had my dad been disappointed that I was a girl and they'd never had more kids? I would probably never know. Rafael had four sisters. I tried to imagine him younger, surrounded by girls, but it was impossible to come up with images.

"How come you're not going home for Thanksgiving?" he asked. "Are your parents coming to your cousin's?"

It had been only six months, and it still caught me off guard. It had been six months.

"Um . . . my parents . . . uh, died in an accident last May. I don't have any siblings," I said, getting the words out. "It was just me, so I came to stay with my cousin for a while."

"I'm sorry," Rafael said, frowning. "I'm really sorry. That's awful."

"Mm. Well, I'm glad I have Matéo, and Aly."

"Yeah. And you have to cook."

"Uh-huh. So it's okay if I take Wednesday off?" Just like that we were back to boss and employee, but I'd had a vision of him that was completely new, and I intended to savor it later.

"Yeah, of course," he said. "No problem."

"Okay." I looked at the door that he was still blocking and hoped he wouldn't do anything that would cause me to completely disgrace myself. Like if he made the slightest move toward me. That would be bad.

After a moment of hesitation he turned the doorknob and got out of the way. I went through before I had a chance to change my mind.

"This looks incredible," Tink said, and Peter nodded.

"Everyone find your name card," I instructed. Suzanne had gone Martha Stewart on us and made beautiful calligraphy name cards that she had cunningly stuck in slits in tiny lady apples. She'd also made the amazing centerpiece of pine cones, pomegranates, orange persimmons, and dark purple grapes.

Matéo had searched for and found his mother's best tablecloth. He'd also found crystal candlesticks and other holiday serving pieces in the big credenza in the dining room. I got the impression that last Thanksgiving they hadn't done anything—it had been the first one since his parents had died, and he wouldn't have felt very thankful. Gods knew, if I had been at home by myself, I'd have been doing nothing.

"Can we dig in?" Dana asked. Her friend Michelle was from Mississippi and seemed nice but very shy. I assumed she was a haguara, and I couldn't imagine the delicate, timid jaguar she would become.

"First, let's all sit down, join hands, and say what we're thankful for," Coco suggested. "Then we can make a line and load up our plates."

My seat was between Matéo and Peter, and Suzanne had written my whole first name, Viviana, on my card.

"Vivi, why don't you go first," Aly suggested, "because this was your idea?"

"Um, okay." Deciding to keep it short and simple, I said, "I'm thankful for family." The irony was not lost on me.

Next to me, Matéo squeezed my hand. He said, "I too am thankful for family, newfound and old. I'm thankful for friends. I'm thankful to be with the most amazing woman I've ever met." Across the table, Aly blew him a kiss.

Next was Charlotte. "I'm thankful for love, for food, and for friendship."

We went around the table like that: Coco, Tink, Michelle, James, Aly, Dana, Peter, Charlotte, Alex, and Suzanne each gave thanks.

Everything turned out better than I'd expected. Matéo had made special Thanksgiving spiced hard cider. I tried half a cup and it was delicious, but I stopped there. Coco and I had cooked. Tink's boyfriend, Peter, had made bourbon whipped cream for all my pies: sweet potato, pecan, and apple-raisin, two of each. The turkey that Coco had brined and roasted was perfect and beautiful.

As I looked around the table at people talking, laughing, and eating, I realized how truly thankful I was to be here. Last summer had been the worst summer of my life, and I was including all my future summers in that. But I had been offered a new home here; I had a new family in Matéo and Aly.

True, we still didn't know who had killed our parents. We didn't know who had attacked Tink. We hadn't gotten any more information about the person killed in New York. The reporter had never returned my e-mail, and when I'd finally called the *New York Times*, they'd told me that Nicholas Tareynton was away on assignment and they didn't know when he would be back, or if he was checking e-mail. So that seemed like a dead end—very frustrating. And we didn't know for sure what had happened to split Matéo's family from mine.

But in forming our own relationships, I had to admit, we'd made the answers a little less scary.

And I was thankful for that.

"It's Thanksgiving there, no?" My tia Juliana sounded very far away.

"Yes. I think I'm gonna die." I lay on my bed, feeling like a blood-filled tick and wishing I had made better choices in terms of desserts. And seconds. And thirds.

Tia Juliana laughed. "You feel like that every year."

"True."

"I'm glad you celebrated Thanksgiving with friends, darling," she said. "I was worried about what you would do today."

"Well, I thought about getting a Hungry-Man turkey dinner and eating it by myself in front of the TV," I said. "But then some friends were getting together, and I decided to force myself to go."

It was not fun lying to my only aunt, pretending I still lived in Sugar Beach. I felt even more guilty about being glad that she lived all the way in Brazil so it was less likely that she would discover my lies. Every once in a while Matéo and I talked about simply coming out and asking her, introducing her to Matéo and seeing what happened. So far we had been total chickens about it. But we really needed to do that. And soon.

Tia Juliana laughed. "You made the right decision."

"How are things there?" I asked, and for the next twenty minutes we talked about my young cousins, my tio Marc, the crazy weather there, her new manager at work. Until now, she'd always been my tia, my mother's sister, someone I loved but didn't really know that well. Now we had our own relationship, and I was thankful for that, too.

Around the beginning of December, the weather turned dank and wet. It wasn't super cold, only in the forties, but somehow the chill cut right through everything. Matéo's house, like most houses here and at home, wasn't very well insulated. The tall ceilings that handled hot summer air so effectively did just the opposite in cold weather: Any bit of heat immediately went above head height, leaving us all shivering. Sometimes the only way to feel warm was to sit under a hot shower or by the fire that was usually burning in the parlor fireplace.

Work, however, was comfortable physically, if not emotionally. For the most part, Rafael and I stayed out of each other's way—the closest I got to him was his signature on my paycheck. We didn't have any more personal talks, and though I'd spent hours thinking about his sisters, about what he would be like as a brother, outwardly I remained casual and a little standoffish.

The first week of December he brought in a tall, beautiful Christmas tree and set it up in a corner by the windows. Hayley went to the storeroom and dragged out several boxes of Christmas and Hanukkah decorations, and we all helped decorate. Rafael programmed holiday music into the sound system. It was chilly and rainy outside, and it felt unbearably cozy to be putting up Hanukkah streamers and dreidels. Kathy and Joey hung Christmas streamers and big ornaments from the ceiling. When the tree was decorated and covered with lights, all the customers clapped.

My parents had celebrated Christmas, but just the secular part—the decorations and presents and Christmas specials. We didn't go to church or talk about baby Jesus or anything. Apparently Matéo and everyone at our house did pretty much the same thing: Aly had decorated the altar where Tzechuro and Tzechura stood guard, but had also decorated the stairs and the front of the house with Christmas bows and lights and greenery. I loved the scent of the evergreen wreaths and garlands, but tried not to think about having Christmas with my parents. For the tree, Suzanne and James were heading to Texas for a brief camping trip, and they planned to stop at a cut-your-own Christmas tree farm on the way back.

"Get a big one," Aly said.

"At least ten feet," Coco agreed. "And when you get back, we'll have a tree-decorating party. Vivi will make cookies."

"Oh, can you make extras?" Aly asked me. "I'd love to bring homemade cookies in to the office."

"Make extras for me too," Tink asked. "I need to bring some to Peter's parents."

So I had been elected to make twenty gazillion cookies. It was going to be great—and a good distraction from this first Christmas without my parents.

That Thursday night work was slow, and I was looking forward to having the next two nights off for Cookie-Mania. I'd stocked up on supplies and planned to basically hole up in Matéo's kitchen, watch Jane Austen movies on the little kitchen TV, and bake, bake, bake. I was going to make some to bring in to Ro's also. Who knew, maybe Rafael would want me to make cookies for the shop. Maybe he would be bummed that he'd rejected me—twice—when he tasted my espresso meringues.

Maybe I was unbelievably pathetic. Wishing that a guy liked me for my cooking skills was going to set the feminist movement back about fifty years.

"Did Rafael come in today?" I asked Talia that day at work.

She shook her head. "Hayley said she didn't see him this morning."

So maybe he'd be in later. He usually made some sort of appearance, which gave me the satisfying opportunity to ignore him while he seethed quietly at me. Yep, a couple of cookies were going to clear all of that right up.

I was cleaning the display-case glass and thinking about how the scones I made at home were better than the scones we bought when the doorbell jingled. I turned to see old Mrs. Fontenot, dressed all in black as usual, her winter coat engulfing her tiny frame. A big shiny car was parked in front of Ro's, and a chauffeur in an actual uniform held the shop door open for her.

"Hi, Mrs. Fontenot," I said cheerfully as Talia slunk quietly toward the back. I made a mental note to say, "Bawk, bawk, bawk," when she got back.

"You! Girl!" the old woman said, waving her cane at me.

"Can I make you some coffee?" I headed behind the counter.

"Yes! Like you always do. Don't cut corners! Don't try to sneak that modern junk in there!"

"You know I don't do that to you," I said, getting to work as she pulled out a chair and sat down at a table, her feet barely touching the floor. I wondered if she had been taller when she was young, and had shrunk in old age. As I made the coffee in one of our little French presses, I thought that Mrs. Fontenot seemed anxious, kind of fidgety. I guess she always was, but there was an alert nervousness to her that was new.

She always liked our palmiers, so I put one on a plate, wishing again that we had a toaster oven instead of just a microwave. When her coffee was done I carried it all over to her table.

"Here you go. I got you a palmier, too."

The tiny old woman sniffed the coffee, inhaling deeply, then took a sip. Her whole body seemed to relax, and she drank more.

"You," she said, not looking at me.

"Yes?"

"Has my grandson been in today?"

"I don't think so. Not yet."

Mrs. Fontenot frowned fiercely and bit into the crisp palmier, unable to avoid a rain of sugary crumbs landing on her plate.

"If you see him, you tell him to come home." She seemed upset, not looking at me.

"Yes, of course, Mrs. Fontenot." I was surprised—had he not been home in a couple of days? When had I seen him last? Yesterday? Tuesday, maybe?

The old lady tipped the cup and drained the rest of her coffee, then stood, almost a foot shorter than me. "Thank you, *petite fille*," she muttered, and then walked stiffly to where her driver waited by the door.

Little girl? I thought, trying to remember my eighth-grade French.

"Come back soon," I told her. Her driver took her elbow gently and helped her get into her big black car. It was gusty outside, bits of leaves and paper skittering along the sidewalk. The other businesses on this block had also decorated for the holidays, and Mrs. Fontenot's shiny black car reflected red and green lights as it drove away.

I walked to our hallway and called, "You can come out now, you big chicken!"

Talia immediately poked her head out of the former kitchen. "She's gone?"

"Yes. I don't know why you don't like her. She's perfectly fine," I said innocently, aware that Mrs. Fontenot had pretty much made everyone who worked here cry at one time or another.

Talia rolled her eyes. "Good. I'm glad you think so. You can deal with her all by yourself, till kingdom come."

"She seemed odd," I said, replaying the visit in my mind. "She said she didn't know where Rafael was."

Talia shrugged. "He's probably off drawing or painting somewhere. Maybe someone hired him to do a mural or something."

Or maybe he had met someone. Someone who would take him home to her bed, like he had asked me to. "I guess. Well, he'll turn up."

When I got home that night a little after one, I was surprised to see lights on and people moving inside the house. Sometimes someone was awake when I got home, but more often people were either out, or at work like Matéo, or asleep.

"Vivi." Aly looked upset.

"What's going on?"

She shook her head. "We've all been so busy, but this afternoon I realized that Suzanne and James should have been back yesterday."

"Oh." Automatically I felt a little jolt of fear—the attacks had receded a lot in my mind but would never disappear. Trying to think clearly, I said, "They left, what, four days ago? Maybe they decided to stay for an extra day?"

"I think they would have called," Matéo said. "But it's probably nothing. Maybe their phones died. Maybe they just decided to stay an extra day."

"Yeah." Aly looked unconvinced. "I've been trying to call

them, and then I saw Suzanne's calendar here." She pointed to a small open notebook on the kitchen counter. "It looks like she has an important exam on Monday. It seems odd that she wouldn't already be back, getting ready for it. You know what she's like."

Overprepared and anal? Yes, I knew.

"That is weird. I don't think she would skip an exam, or skip preparing for it. So what are you thinking?" I was trying not to let my imagination run away—that wouldn't help anyone. In all likelihood they were fine. But after everything that had happened, it was concerning.

Aly glanced at her watch. "It's late. Maybe I misunderstood when they were planning to get back. Maybe Suzanne brought her books with her. I think I'll give them till tomorrow afternoon. But if we haven't heard from them by then, we need to do something." She said that last part to Matéo, and he nodded.

"Agreed. Let's get some sleep and come up with ideas tomorrow, if we have to."

"Okay." Aly still looked troubled, and I wondered if she'd be able to sleep. For myself, I was hoping that Suzanne was being thoughtless, rather than in danger.

Upstairs, my room felt cavernous and chilly. Matéo kept the heat at sixty-five degrees because it cost so much to heat such a big house. Cold air wafted around the not-modern window frames, and I pulled my curtains closed against the damp night. Maybe tomorrow I would go buy a space heater. Or maybe I would bribe

Matéo to crank up the heat. I was willing to pay for it.

Huddled in my bed, trying to get warm, I thought again about Suzanne and James. Surely they were okay—they'd probably just lost track of time. But deep down a shard of fear remained, and I prayed to the Tzechuri to protect my friends as I listened to the wind blowing the tree branches to and fro.

The next day I woke up feeling as if something important was about to happen. A minute later I remembered about Suzanne and James. Quickly I braided my hair, put on sweatpants, and went downstairs.

Matéo wasn't in his workroom, but I found two notes on the kitchen table:

Haven't heard anything. Went to work. Will check in with you this afternoon. A.

And:

Helping Charlotte move furniture. Back soon. M.

Which left me with nothing to do except wait. Worry was starting to overcome me—Suzanne and James weren't my favorites of all our roommates, but they were in the roommate family. I thought about Margaret McCauley, who had died up in New York. At least Suzanne and James were together.

This was pointless. I rolled up my sleeves, preheated the oven, and pulled out my Cookie Mania supplies. Every year of high school I'd made a ton of cookies for my teachers, our neighbors, people my parents worked with. I'd gotten it down to a production line. This year, making cookies was the last thing I'd thought I'd be doing, but it seemed right, and I found myself measuring out flour and sugar with a sense of . . . almost acceptance.

The long afternoon went by without hearing anything from Aly. Matéo was home by three, and after stealing some Mexican wedding cookies, he disappeared into his workshop. We were now both worried. There was no house phone—everyone had a cell phone—and each time Matéo's phone rang, we jumped. By the time we heard Aly's car pull onto the wet crushed shells, it was dark and chilly outside, a winter's night.

Inside, the kitchen was toasty warm and full of all of the best smells: vanilla, brown sugar, spices, butter, peppermint. Though I'd been on my feet all day and had burned my hand at one point, I felt about as together as I could, considering. The familiar actions of rotating cookie sheets in and out of the oven, of mixing and wash- ing bowls and reusing them, had helped me feel less out of control.

Now Aly came in the kitchen door, shutting it against a gust of air that threatened to push it open. "You haven't heard anything, have you?" were her first words.

"No. There's no reason I would," I said. "But I know Matéo hasn't. And I'm guessing you haven't."

"Nope." Aly dropped her purse on a chair and kicked off her work heels. "I called their parents this afternoon. They hadn't heard anything, didn't know Suzanne and James were late getting back. And I called the police. They say that I don't have a definitive due-back-by date, and there's no evidence of foul play."

"Damn it," I said. "So what now?"

"We have to go find them." Aly strode intently to the kitchen doorway. "Téo! Téo!"

"Hey, babe," he said, coming out of his workshop. "Nothing?"

"No. They aren't back and no one's heard from them. We need to go find them." Aly was no-nonsense, and it took Matéo only a few moments to process everything, including the look on Aly's face.

"Okay. Let's throw a few things in the car. We should bring some of their clothes."

"Thank you. Look, we'll be back probably tomorrow," Aly told me. "This might be for nothing, but I'm worried and really want to know for sure."

I had already washed the flour off my hands, and I turned off the TV and the oven before saying, "I'm going with you."

They both looked surprised. Aly hugged me. "Thank you, sweetie, but it's fine for you to stay here. Hold down the fort."

"Look, I don't know what I can do to help," I said honestly. "I don't know what your plan is or anything. But you guys—you're my cousins, my family, and you're upset about our friends. Of course I'm going with you."

Aly hugged me again, and Matéo smoothed his hand over my hair with a smile.

Coco came home while I was throwing water bottles into a bag. "What's going on?" she asked, and Aly quickly explained.

Coco was clearly not thrilled. "I can't go with you—I've got to help cater the Cavalitto wedding tonight and the breakfast tomorrow. But what if you guys don't come back?"

"Then you go to the cops," Matéo said, coming into the kitchen with a sleeping bag under his arm.

"Where's Tink?" Coco asked.

"At work. He had to go down to Plaquemines Parish this morning," Matéo said. "No clue when he'll be back."

"What about Dana?" Coco was frowning, her hands on her hips.

"Dana went to Amsterdam early this morning, remember?" said Aly. "A TKD exhibition."

"Tzechura help us," Coco muttered, running her hands through her short hair. "Okay, I can't stop you. But please be extra careful. If you guys get hurt, I'll kill you."

Aly hugged her. "Understood."

It was almost seven by the time we left, and a cold December rain had started falling. The chill went right through my sweater and jeans, and I was glad that the Camry's heater worked.

As Matéo headed west on I-10, I popped the top on a can of Barq's Root Beer and felt a little excited and a lot scared, like a kid going on an adventure that would end up forming my character much more than I wanted it to. I had even brought a pillow and a blanket, the way I had when I was little and my parents would take me on a road trip. "Do we know where they were planning to camp?"

"James mentioned the Sabine National Forest," Matéo said. "I've never been there, but I know it's in Texas, just west of the Louisiana border."

Aly was looking at the GPS on her phone. "It has three different campgrounds, and there's one road that goes up through the middle. We can start asking questions there, so head north at Orange City. We can eliminate the campgrounds one by one."

"I'm hoping that they're living it up at a Marriott and didn't think that we might be worried," I said. "I'd much rather be pissed than scared."

"Me too," said Aly, taking Matéo's hand.

What would it feel like to have someone to lean on, like Matéo and Aly had in each other? To know that you could count on someone? Just one more thing I hadn't appreciated about my parents, and now I wondered if I would ever find it with anyone in my life. Everything felt bleak and scary, and a small, ashamed part of me wished I were home again, making cookies.

We drove through the night and the rain, west across Louisiana and then north. Sometimes the rain was a fine mist that made the wipers squeak; sometimes we couldn't hear each other talking because of the drops hammering the car's roof and windows.

There was a lot of time to think—too much. Lying on the backseat, my knees bent so my long legs would fit, I looked up through the back window at the water sluicing down. We were on smaller country roads now, and there were no lights except the occasional gas station or restaurant or bait shop. The interior of the car was washed by a faint green glow from Matéo's radio, but the stations buzzed in and out as we got farther from New Orleans, and finally he turned it off.

One after another, thoughts, questions, concerns, and fears scrolled through my mind: What did I feel for Rafael, and what did he feel for me, if anything? Where were Suzanne and James? Who had killed my parents, and would I ever not miss them so much, or feel so much guilt? When was I going to break down and tell my tia Juliana where I was and that I knew about Donella? Or would I just go back home and pretend I'd been there the whole time?

And I did want to go to college, didn't I? I did want more in my life than working at a coffee shop, right? Why had I been able to be so aggressive with Rafael that night in the park? What had he done with my portrait? What was happening with my home in Sugar Beach? Mrs. Peachtree hadn't reported anything weird lately. Would I ever be able to live there again?

All these bits and snippets of thoughts and feelings whirled through my brain, kicked up by a storm of uncertainty. Seven months ago I'd been able to look ahead and see my future clearly defined by my step-by-step plan to live my life far away from my parents while not severing all contact forever. It had been mapped out: a very distant school, maybe junior year abroad, a job not in Florida . . .

Jennifer was my best friend, but she alone was having all the college experiences I'd expected to share. Her life seemed odd and foreign to me, and mine seemed boring and inexplicable to her.

Though she was still my best friend, I was keeping so much from her that I might as well have been a stranger. But I was growing closer to Aly every day—in some ways closer to her than to Matéo. She knew who I was, all of me. I didn't have to hide anything from her. I could tell her anything, and had. Even when I gave Jennifer edited versions of my life here, she'd never met Matéo or Aly or Rafael, so they didn't seem real to her. Just like her friends and her come-and-go girlfriends didn't seem quite real to me. Was this how we would drift apart forever? I had planned to leave my parents and keep them at arm's length. Now I was losing Jennifer. How come the only way I could be myself was to leave everyone I loved behind?

I didn't know. And I still had no clue as to who "myself" was.

Around eleven o'clock we found a drive-through and got fast food that I wolfed down and then regretted. I was tired of the darkness, tired of the rain, tired of myself, and wished I were home in my big bed with the silk half tester on top.

Around one in the morning there was a slight break in the rain, and a few minutes after that we reached the first campground. The small office was closed.

"We might as well get some sleep," Matéo said.

"Maybe we should just . . . go search," Aly said.

I'd looked on my phone's map: the Sabine National Forest was a big, irregular stretch of land and helped define that part of the border between Louisiana and Texas. The Toledo Bend Reservoir separated it from Louisiana, and there was really only one main road that cut through the forest's middle, south to north. All the campground entrances were off this one road, which should have made the search simpler. But it was the middle of the night and we were all beat.

"I know how anxious you are, sweetie," Matéo told her, rubbing her shoulder. "But I think it would be better if we slept until morning, then asked questions at the three campgrounds. This park is huge. If we could narrow down the area to cover, it would help."

"You're right," said Aly, her face drawn with fatigue and worry.

We ended up staying in Matéo's car, right by the campground office. I was okay with my pillow and blanket in the backseat by myself, while Matéo and Aly made do in sleeping bags with the front seats reclined. I didn't think I'd be able to sleep, expecting all my weighty concerns to press down on me as soon as I closed my eyes . . . but finally I dozed off, and when I opened my eyes it was morning and I was freezing. Uncoiling my too-long body, I stretched, feeling hungry and stiff and needing to go to the bathroom.

The campground office opened at eight and was staffed by one college student. She was very nice, and she hadn't seen Suzanne or James. Mostly what she did was verify hunting and fishing licenses—there were certain limited areas of the forest where hunting was allowed as a means of keeping the deer population down. She didn't remember seeing Suzanne's green Subaru. We got the same answers at the second campground, and Aly almost cried with frustration.

"Third time lucky," said Matéo, putting his car into gear.

The third and final campground entrance was only four miles away, but the road was narrow and twisty, and it took us a good twenty minutes to get there. It looked like few people ever made it this far in their quest for camping access. The road was unpaved but covered with crushed oyster shells like our parking spot at home. The sound of our tires on the shells was incredibly loud, and I peered through the windows, hoping that Suzanne and James would hear us and come running. Maybe they'd simply had car trouble and gotten stuck. Maybe they'd lost their phones.

Finally we reached the third campground office, which was smaller and less tidy than the first two. Inside, Aly showed the park ranger the pictures of Suzanne and James on her phone.

"Yeah, I'm pretty sure I saw them." The ranger was an older guy whose belly strained the buttons of his khaki shirt. A ten-point deer head was mounted on the wall behind his desk, and his radio was playing classic rock. This scene was eerily reminiscent of some weird movie from the seventies.

He frowned at the photos on Aly's phone. "Pretty girl; tall, dark guy. Yeah, I could swear they came through here, what, four days ago? Let me check." He opened a beat-up gray file cabinet and ruffled through his permits folder. "Yeah, here they are. Five days ago. This them?" He held out the copy of their camping permit, which Suzanne had signed.

"That's them!" Aly cried. "Have they come back?"

The supervisor shook his head. "I have no idea. This office isn't manned around the clock, and they wouldn't need to check in here anyway. They could easily have left when no one was around."

"Were they given a permit for a certain campsite?" Matéo asked.

"No, that's not how we do it. This is a free, 'rough camping' site, where they can pitch a tent anywhere as long as they don't leave any trash behind."

Matéo looked at him. "And the forest is how big?"

"About a hundred sixty thousand acres, give or take," the ranger said. "I'm sure they're fine—it hasn't been freezing on any night— but I could call in a search party if they've been missing for forty- eight hours."

Aly bit her lip, thinking. "We'll look first and let you know, okay?"

"Okay. I'll be here till five."

We drove several miles away from the camp office, looking for Suzanne's Subaru, but though we saw tire tracks, there was no way to tell what car they belonged to. Finally Matéo stopped at the very end of one of the distant parking areas. There were no other cars around. The rain had started up again, making it feel colder than fif- ty-two degrees. The forest was too thick to go off-road, and with all the rain the ground was so sodden that even if we tried we would make big, rutted tracks and probably get stuck.

In the front seat, Matéo and Aly looked at each other, seeming to communicate silently. I remembered Mami and Papi doing the same thing.

Aly turned to me. "So, we're going to search the forest for Suzanne and James."

"Okay." I took a deep breath. "Let's do it." Had we brought rain-coats? Flashlights?

"We can search the forest much faster and better in our other forms. Obviously."

It had occurred to me that this would probably be the case. Good thing I'd impulsively insisted on coming along. Well, Matéo and Aly were my family; James and Suzanne were my friends. Time to put on my big-girl . . . claws. I swallowed hard. Forcing myself to let go of years of prejudice and fear wasn't easy. But I could do it. I could decide to do it.

"That makes sense," I said bravely.

"Do you want to . . . wait here?" Aly asked.

"No. I want to help search. Just tell me what to do."

The looks of love and pride on their faces made me feel warm inside. Again I was reminded that I could have had those same looks from my own parents, if things had been different. If I had been different.

"Just change, and the hunt will come naturally," said Matéo, and a shiver went down my spine. "We brought some of their clothes so we can match the scent. We'll split up to cover as much ground as possible."

Memorizing their scents was easy: Suzanne wore Eau d'Hadrien by Annick Goutal, and James wore Polo by Ralph Lauren. They were preppy haguari. I was surprised their jaguar coats weren't plaid.

"Do you want to go first?" Aly asked. "We'll put our clothes in the trunk and leave it unlocked. You'll be able to retrace your steps and find the car again."

"When should I come back?" I asked.

"When we find them," Aly said grimly.

I got out of the car, squinting against the chilly, drizzling rain. Looking around carefully to make sure we were alone, I went to the blind spot toward the back of the car. They were family, but I wasn't used to public nakedness.

Quickly I stripped off my clothes so they wouldn't tear, and tossed them in the trunk. Immediately I was freezing, wet, and miserable. If this didn't work, I was going to be super embarrassed. Still, I closed my eyes and concentrated on finding that spot at the back of my neck. The animal muscle I had to grab and hold on to. The spot that Papi had rubbed my whole life.

Overhead, the long pine needles dripped rain steadily all around me. Drops hit my head and shoulders as it occurred to me that even if I managed to change, I might not manage to change back. I'd only done it once, after all.

Now I was shaking with cold, getting panicky that I wouldn't be able to pull this off. My head lifted, my nose catching the scent of wet pine, soaked earth, the gas of our car. And then . . . there it was, that strong place that felt like a handhold, felt like if I squeezed it, it would become stronger. Imagining my father's hand on me, I reached for it. Clenched it.

This time I was present enough to pay attention to the process. My limbs swelled painlessly, all my senses coming to life as if I'd been living in two dimensions and was now aware of a third. My jaws stretched and grew heavy with power. My tongue ran over sharp fangs two inches long that folded neatly into my mouth. Dropping to all fours, I rolled and stretched muscles that hadn't been used in too long a time. I felt alive and full of power and joy.

I open my eyes

I am more than Vivi. I am a haguara. I am Ha-Vivi.

People family Matéo Aly looking at me I go closer to them

I am not cold rain is running off my dense black fur

Aly rubs my head I purr she holds out cloth I smell lemons I smell spices I smell dark-haired girl I smell tall male elegance

Rub against them mark them as mine Aly scratches my head

"Beautiful girl. I'll see you soon." words are quiet

Want to be away in woods car smells bad like hot metal like burning oil

I glance back I see two jaguars we meet eyes I turn away

I head into the woods alone

Chapter Twenty-Three

FEAR SLIPS AWAY LIKE FOG MY FOOTFALLS ARE like fog too

Almost silent on the wet pine needles and leaves every so often I stop and rub my head against a tree it feels good it leaves my scent I will be able to find my trail

Wet pine smells different from wet sycamore smells different from wet cypress

There are no people the air is chilly it is raining

Rain runs down my nose I am not cold

I am running so happy it is easy to weave through the woods like a needle

Easy to leap over fallen trees with dirt-clotted root-balls six feet high

My lungs work so well my eyes are like crosshairs my muscles are tireless

And everywhere a steady stream of intoxicating exhilarating scents

They wake my brain my nerves they paint the world as I've never known it

I smell rabbit I see it between the roots of a live oak

I smell deer they are running to escape me

My nose tells me about woodchucks and beavers and foxes and bats and squirrels and chipmunks and so many birds and mice and moles and voles and rats they all smell different they all live in this forest I never knew that

Vivi was afraid of what Ha-Vivi would do when hungry I let that go it is stupid like cloth it is stupid

Clouds like bruises hide the sun I know the night is coming

I run I open my mouth to smell better I do not smell lemons or spices

I run until it is dark

In the darkness everything is outlined tiny sounds and thread scents and thinnest shadows make a picture so clear like it is burning in sunlight

It is time to wait

I head upwind I lie still on the wet ground

Rain drips on me my ears twitch at every sound

I separate the squeak of a mouse the rustling of leaves the shuffling of owl feathers the scritch of a squirrel's claws as it shifts in its nest high in the trees

There

My nostrils flare it is a deer a female

I track the landscape slowly my gaze locks on the small form it is cautious it is alert and wary it will not pick up my scent in time

My muscles coil my stomach is hollow I need energy here is dinner

I start to move

My paw breaks a twig the deer takes off it bounds eight feet it is panicked it zigzags through trees it turns sharply it knows this land

But I am a jaguar

Within twenty seconds I knock it to the ground I do not play with it I kill it instantly its skull is fine and delicate under my heavy jaws it does not suffer

I am exhilarated

I have smelled wolf and coyote I drag dinner up into a tree it is a little difficult my jaws ache

I eat it is delicious it is life and drink and full belly I am alive I am happy I can sleep

The sun is not up but will be soon it is raining heavier

My fur is wet I am chilly I do not eat I am not hungry I leave my kill in the tree

Turkey buzzards will eat it rats and mice will eat it ants will eat it there will be nothing left of my victory

Day is marked by a slightly brighter area in the sky there is no warmth on my shoulders

The world is dim and wet and cold I head toward the sun sometimes I trot

I do not smell lemons

The splotch in the sky moves I have been a jaguar for a long time it is still new

I am beautiful I am strong I am a hunter I lope through woods I cross streams that rush above their banks

It is still raining hard

I can go and go there is so much to see and smell and hear I do not smell other jaguars I do not smell lemons or spice

The covered sun arcs across the sky

Now night is coming I sense something new I sniff I turn I trot

My paws land solid and steady never sliding never slipping

There is a clearing there is a building there is short grass around it

I smell cars but there are no cars now

I am quiet in the trees I look at the house there are no sounds no lights there are dark windows and more dark windows by the ground why so low

The night is black I am black too I creep out of the woods

I don't like this building it smells like people it doesn't smell like lemons

I have forgotten why I am looking for lemons

I go on my belly on the wet grass I get close to the low window I look in I see nothing

I look again my eyes pick out something

I see them now

My muscles get tight like steel springs my lip curls above my teeth my eyes are slits

There are jaguars underground

Under this house there are cages there are jaguars in cages

There is water they are standing in it partway up their legs

They are pacing tightly in their cages

There are stairs there are no people

One cage has two jaguars they are angry they are afraid

There is one jaguar in a cage it is angry too

I can't smell them through the glass who are these jaguars are they haguari are they jaguars why has someone caught jaguars

Sudden lightning flashes like the sun I see the golden fur the wide-pupiled eyes

I shrink into the shadows and bound toward the woods

I need help

Matéo Aly help should I roar should I run fast pick up their scents find them

Stop

Stop be still think

The caged jaguars are they Matéo and Aly

I've never seen Ha-Aly I saw Ha-Matéo only close enough to bite

Were they in the cage I don't know I don't know

I sit down I do not know what to do why am I thinking about lemons

This forest is so big what should I do

I am strong I am fast I do not know what to do

I want to run away where is Vivi I want to run

I ran when Mami told me to

I shouldn't have run I shouldn't have left

I pace back and forth the sky is starless still raining

The water will rise the cats are in cages they will drown

I hear an engine I see lights shooting through the trees

It is getting closer

I hunker down but they could never see me I am so dark

Soon I see a car I smell the stink of exhaust but the rain dims
everything

The car parks in front it is quiet doors open a man a woman run
through the rain

I move closer to see

They go into the house they turn on lights the woman low-
ers shades

The down-low windows get bright

My heart beats quickly adrenaline whispers through my veins

I am strong and afraid I know I'm afraid

Slowly very very slowly I slink through the rain

I get close to the house I stay in the shadows I creep up to the
down-low window

The man comes down the stairs he splashes through the water

The water is rising it is higher the cats are trapped

They snarl at the man they bare their teeth

Outside in the rain I bare mine also

The man is furious he has a stick he hits the cage with the stick
there is an awful clang of metal

The man is shouting "Go on, turn!" He bangs the stick on the
cages again

The cats snarl

My fur rises in a line down my spine

I want to bite him take him down like a deer crush his skull

"You know you want to! You have to! The water's rising and your time is running out!"

One of the cats swipes at the man through the bars of the cage

The man gets angrier and hits the cage again and again

A growl rises in my throat and I quiet it

"I should leave you all here to drown! You're going to die in here!"

Think Ha-Vivi think with your smart brain

I see stairs I see the bars on the cages I could never bite through those

There are locks on the cages the man is wearing keys on his belt he is jingling as he hits the cages

I want to cry but these eyes can't I am so mad I can't fix this I am alone

The jaguars will die I am not strong enough

I run back to the woods I pace I need to think

I must do this those jaguars will die think Vivi think

An idea forms it is part Vivi part Ha-Vivi I have to be both for this plan

It might work it might save them

It will either save them or I will die too with them

I can't see any other way I have to try this

I have to be strong I have to be all of me together

I jump on the porch I am soundless I hear loud voices inside

My brain translates

"We can't move them! We'd have to drug them!" That is the woman she is mad "Then carry them up the stairs! How do you plan to do that, smart guy?"

"The water's rising fast!" That is the man he is mad at her he is mad at the jaguars he is mad "We could lose them now, before we've had a chance to use them. All of our work could be for nothing!"

"There's more where they came from. We need to get out of here now. The river is flooding its banks! This whole place could be under water in an hour! Get our stuff and let's go!" That is the woman

"Unless . . . unless we take their hearts now."

The man wants their hearts I feel dizzy I feel sick

Did he take my parents' hearts are these the ones

This has to be the one who killed my parents

I want to kill him

Think Vivi stick to the plan

I reach a paw up I press on the small button I hear a jarring buzz

The voices are quiet I back away coiled to spring I feel sick can jaguars throw up

Answer the door you murderers

I hear footsteps my heart pounds my stomach is churning

The man calls "Who is it?"

It is your karma calling

"Hello?"

Come on come on . . .

The lock clicks open I am waiting

My tail lashes back and forth my lips curl away from my fangs I take a deep breath

This is the plan wait wait

The woman cries "No!" but the door opens it is only a crack it is enough

I bellow a roar I spring I misjudge my spring I am so strong I hit the door too hard

The door snaps off its top hinge I smell fear I smell people I hate them

The woman is screaming I plow into the man he falls backward hard his head cracks against the floor he is surprised he goes limp his eyes roll back

My jaws open I want to crush his skull he is a murderer he killed my parents

I look up the woman is holding something

It is a gun she is aiming at my head

I see a flash I hear a sharp crack a white-hot pain stripes my cheek

I am much faster my claws are made of steel

I smack the gun from her I slice her arm deep she cries out

She is glaring at me she isn't scared she's furious she should be scared

Will she change into a jaguar

My eyes narrow a loud roar tears out of my throat

I step on the man's chest he grunts

"I don't know who you think you are—" The woman surprises
me by talking

I jump at her I ram her shoving my shoulder into her stomach

I knock her against the wall she gasps I roar in her face

She winces I raise a paw her blond hair flies her head snaps sideways she falls to her knees

I roar again

Now she is scared she gets to her feet she runs out of the house

She is dripping blood she is holding her arm her blood smells
like copper and salt

I follow her into the rain the cold raindrops feel good

Will she change now is she a haguara

The woman scrabbles at the car door she climbs in

I jump on the hood I have never been so mad I slash the canvas
of the Jeep

She shrieks and dodges me as I shred the roof

I want to smile a jaguar smile

I run back to the house the man is down he has not changed

There is a door I start down the steps it smells like water mold
metal old wood

Then I remember I need Vivi I need Vivi

Slowly I breathe I search for Vivi I remember Matéo rubbing
my forehead

I remember Mami kissing my forehead

Then I feel I don't know . . . a white flower

A tiny one

I focus on it it blooms it looks like me

Vivi is there and I am Vivi and we are Vivi

My bare skin was cold against the wooden floor, and I opened my eyes to find myself naked and human, the world oddly flat and precise. My cheek burned. I touched it and my fingers came away covered in blood. The bullet had grazed me but hadn't made an actual hole.

An old plaid shirt hung on a knob by the basement steps and I grabbed it and put it on. I felt shaky and disoriented—after two days of being a jaguar I needed to get my human self back in balance. Staggering slightly, I went back to the unconscious man, trying to stay out of sight of the woman in the car. I snatched the key ring off the guy's belt and then made my way back to the basement steps.

After two steps I turned to see if there was any way to lock the door from down here, but there wasn't. I took a moment to tie a bungee cord around the doorknob, looping it around a stair rail. It was the best I could do.

Holding tightly to the wooden railing I went down the steps, appalled to see that the water was lapping the first three steps.

The large cats were pacing, snarling, standing on their hind legs.

"Matéo? Aly?" I cried. "Or . . . Suzanne? James?" Gingerly I stepped into the black water, grimacing at how cold it was. It came up past my knees, and I waded clumsily over to the cages, praying there was no loose electrical wire that would electrocute all of us.

"Are you haguari?" I cried pointlessly, since they couldn't

answer. Fumbling with the key ring, I found keys that matched the padlocks. If these were real jaguars, then I was committing suicide. They wouldn't know I was saving them; they would just be pissed, and would probably kill me. But I couldn't let them die. I had to give them a fighting chance.

"Please don't attack me, please don't attack me," I muttered as I struggled to open the padlock. Finally I pulled the hasp free, and then the two big cats surged against the cage door, knocking it open and sending me sprawling in the frigid water.

"Yiyiyiyi!" I shrieked and got to my feet as fast as I could, sopping wet.

The jaguars were snarling, moving through the water. Overhead I suddenly heard loud footsteps and shouting voices. That way out was blocked.

"Quick! The transom window!" I yelled, pointing at it. I stood on a wooden box and pounded the lock open, managing to swing the narrow window outward. "Only a human can get through it! Please, please be haguari!"

To my relief, the jaguars began the bizarre contortions that preceded a change, a process I still found weird but no longer thought was horrific or repulsive.

"Oh, my gods," I breathed. "Matéo!" The smaller one was Aly. They stood trembling in the cold water, their human skin showing harsh scrapes and ugly bruises. "Go!" I yelled, pointing at the window. "Go, go, go!"

Grabbing Aly around her waist, Matéo practically shoved her

through the window. She scrambled through, not caring about new scrapes or splinters. Her feet disappeared, and then she leaned down, her face at the window.

"Hurry!" she cried.

"Vivi! You next!" Matéo said, holding out his hand. Someone was slamming against the door at the top of the stairs, and I knew the bungee cord wouldn't last more than a few seconds.

"What about this one?" I hurriedly started to unlock the padlock of the second cage even as the jaguar snarled and tried to climb the cage bars. "Is he haguari?"

"Yeah, I think! He was here when we got here! Come on, let's go!"

I unsnapped the padlock just as I heard the basement door splinter and bang open. The other cat smashed through his cage door, hitting me with it, and then splashed through the water toward the stairs.

"This way!" I yelled, even as Matéo grabbed my arm and dragged me to the window. "Change! Get out this way!" But the jaguar ignored me, not changing into a human, not coming to the window. Matéo shoved me through the narrow opening, and the last thing I saw was the cat bounding up the stairs just as the man and woman rushed down.

Aly helped pull me through the window, and once I was outside with just human skin and a thin shirt, the rain was shockingly cold. I dropped to my knees, then went flat, reaching my arm down to help Matéo. I heard the other jaguar roar, heard the gun fire again, saw the flash and smelled the acrid scent of gunpowder and hot metal.

"The other jaguar!" I yelled as Matéo gave a jump and pushed himself through the window.

"Leave him!" Matéo shouted. "You let him out; that's enough!" He grabbed my hand and Aly's and pulled us both toward the woods. "Run!"

Still I hesitated—and then I heard the woman scream, a third gunshot, the man shouting, and the horrible snarling roar of a cat in pain. Matéo pulled on my arm. Aly had let go and had reached the woods already.

As I watched, the other jaguar leaped out of the front door. Even in the night, in the rain, I saw the large, dark red stain marring his beautiful golden coat. He raced toward the woods in the opposite direction, not looking at us. Then Matéo yanked my arm, and I turned and ran as fast as I could.

CHAPTER TWENTY-FOUR

THE BLACK FOREST WELCOMES ME WELCOMES US
Without speaking we immediately become jaguars

We run fast and noiselessly through the inky slippery darkness

Matéo and Aly hadn't come this way

Leading the way I easily find the trees marked with my scent

I don't falter I lead them out of the woods

I am a girl jaguar scout

It took me a whole day to find the house but we run and run

We jump over creeks surging over their banks they are flooding

The ground is running with water the rain is coming down like sheets

The air is solid water we run through it we are sodden our fur sticks flat to our skin

We are cold we stop to drink from puddles from leaves dripping with rain

There is the edge of the woods there is the car the sun is not up yet

We wait in the shadows by the edge of the woods for minutes

Nothing to hear no alarming smells nothing moving

In the woods we change back I go first I am scared I won't be able to

But again I find Vivi she is waiting for me I go to her and we become one

We become her we are Vivi and we are right here

It was becoming easier and easier to change form, as everyone had promised me it would. It was no longer at all scary, though it was still odd. Weariness swept over me as I lay on the ground naked, wet, and cold. As a human, a new appreciation for everything that had happened filled my mind with shock and amazement, so I hardly even cared that I was naked, that Matéo and Aly were naked. As people, we felt our bruises and scrapes more; my cheek stung fiercely as if it had just happened. We practically crawled to the car. I slumped against the dirty tire as Matéo popped the trunk and threw some dry clothes at me. Putting on dry clothes when you're wet is hard, but I did what I could and then climbed into the backseat. A few moments later the front doors open and Matéo and Aly practically fall in.

"Jesus," Matéo said, sounding as wiped out as I felt.

"I'll drive," said Aly, also sounding wiped out but a little more awake.

"Thank gods," Matéo said, getting into the passenger seat. "Just get us the hell out of here." Rain began to fall harder. It was starting to feel like we should expect an ark to come along at any moment.

"Start up quickly and pop the gas," Matéo advised, "in case we've gotten mired down in the mud."

Aly nodded, looking drained and upset but still somehow together. She started the car, popped the gas pedal firmly, and we leaped ahead a couple of feet. Then she quickly put it into reverse, backed it up, and turned to head down the narrow shell road.

"Nicely done," Matéo said, reaching out a hand to touch her cheek. "That's why I want to marry you."

Aly managed a slight grin, then winced and touched a bruise on her face.

"Who were those people?" I asked after a few minutes.

"I don't kn—" Matéo began, but Aly interrupted him, saying, "What's that?"

Leaning forward, I saw a dark shape on the road in front of us.

"Some car," Matéo said. "Without its lights on. Campers, I guess."

"This is a narrow road. Someone's going to end up in a ditch," I said, and then watched in amazement as my life turned into a James Bond movie: "Oh my gods, that's the Jeep from last night! The top is all shredded! I did that!"

"Are you sure?" Aly cried, and then the car's bright headlights blazed on, almost blinding us. The man from last night leaned out the Jeep's open window with a shotgun.

"Crap!" Aly said. "What should I do?!"

"Should we change?" I cried. "Should we abandon the car? How do they even know our car?"

"They saw us!" Matéo said tensely.

The Jeep was racing straight toward us. On one side we had the thick woods; on the other side we had a four-foot ditch. They had a Jeep; we had a Camry.

There was a loud blast and simultaneous flash, and our windshield shattered, safety glass blowing inward as we all winced and ducked.

"Go off-road!" Matéo yelled as another blast slammed into our hood, digging ugly holes into the metal.

"How? Where?" Aly shouted.

The Jeep was closing in fast. We would definitely lose in a head-on collision. They were close enough now that I could see the woman's face, furious and pale, as she clenched their steering wheel. One of her arms was sloppily bandaged and was leaking blood. I had slashed her pretty hard.

"Crap," I muttered, feeling my fight-or-flight catch fire. The muscle at the back of my neck started to ache. They were less than twenty feet away when Aly suddenly yanked the steering wheel and we veered sharply toward the woods.

"What are you doing?" Matéo yelled as we crashed into a stripling, mowing it down. It whipped against our antenna and broke it off. A moment later the Jeep roared past us, and the man tried to find a clear shot through their open back. I heard their brakes squeal as the right side of our car crunched loudly into tree after tree, the horrible sound of scraping metal screaming into our ears.

Another loud blast exploded our back windshield, sending bits of glass into the back of my head and neck. Swearing, I dropped down toward the floor as Aly struggled with the steering wheel. Matéo reached over and helped her, and they managed to shove it to the left. Through our nonexistent back windshield I saw that the Jeep had stopped and was trying to turn around, slamming into reverse, grinding the gears.

We smashed through some underbrush and jumped back onto the road, and then Aly floored it, spitting crushed shells behind us. Rain and cold air blew in through our broken windshields. Matéo looked behind us as he tried to brush broken glass off the dashboard.

"What are they doing?" he asked.

"I think . . . I think they might be stuck!" I said, watching the Jeep. "They went backward too far, into the ditch."

"Are you sure?" Aly asked.

"If they are, it's just for a moment," I said, feeling the back of my head. My hand came away red with blood. "They must have four-wheel drive."

This road had been twisty, turny, and narrow when we'd come down it just two days ago. Now it was twisty, turny, narrow, rutted, and flooded out in places where creeks had jumped their banks. I wished we had a pickup truck, or something better for a back-road shoot-out than a Camry.

"Uh . . ." said Aly. Ahead of us was a twelve-foot stretch of stand-ing water. Maybe it was only an inch deep; maybe the road had entirely washed away and if we drove through it we'd end up stuck and a sitting target.

"They're coming!" I said, seeing that the Jeep had crawled out of the ditch and was barreling toward us again.

"Take a chance," Matéo said grimly.

We all held our breaths as Aly braced herself and hit the gas. Amazingly, the water was only a few inches deep, and we shot across, sending up a two-foot-high wake with our wheels. On the other side Aly peeled out, spewing water in back of us.

The Jeep didn't even slow down at the puddle. We prayed that we'd see a park ranger around the next bend, but there weren't any. The next ten minutes were unbelievably harrowing: The Jeep would gain on us, the man would shoot, and then we'd come up on a turn that our small car could handle at higher speeds. We'd gain a couple of seconds; then the Jeep would start to catch up again.

When we saw the small park office in the distance, I wanted to cry in relief.

But it was closed, windows dark, no cars parked out front. Aly slowed down, but when it was clear no one was there, she sped up again and raced out of the parking lot. The Jeep was right behind us, the man leaning out the side, aiming his shotgun.

Bam! Bullets ripped into the back of our car, and something hot glanced off my head.

"Ow!" I said.

"Are you shot?" Matéo yelled, peering over the seat at me.

"Stay down! I'm okay!"

"The road's just too wet and muddy!" Aly muttered. "I can't go too fast or we'll lose control."

"When does it become the paved road?" I asked from my place on the floor.

"I think right before we get to the second office."

"Hey," said Matéo. "Where are they?"

Springing up, I peered out the back window. There was no one behind us, no sign of the Jeep.

"Stop for a second so we can listen!" I said.

Aly slowed to a halt and turned off the engine as we scanned around us in every direction. "There weren't any turnoff roads," she said.

"I hear an engine," I said, closing my eyes to pinpoint it. "Over there." I pointed to the left.

"There was a field," Aly said.

"They're cutting us off!" Matéo realized. "They went off-road and will cut us off! It'll take us much longer! Start the car!"

Aly did and we tore off, sending mud arcing behind us.

Our only hope was to reach the second campground office before they did. I prayed that someone would be there.

Then . . . "Oh, no." Aly's eyes were wide.

The Jeep was heading right at us, cutting us off at a sharp angle. We could either try to stop and go backward, or try to go faster, which meant they would end up right in back of us again, shooting at us.

"Crap," I breathed.

"Huh," said Aly.

Matéo looked at her quickly. "What?"

"I wonder . . ."

The Jeep was almost on us. Then, with no warning, Aly yanked the steering wheel hard to the left. I cried out as our car went up on two wheels, threatening to roll over as we angled sharply through a turn. Then the wheels landed hard, rattling my teeth and bruising my spine, and we seemed to go airborne for long, odd seconds as Aly forced the Camry right over the ditch. We landed with a horrible, jarring shock on the other side, and once she gunned the gas again, we were back on the road in half a minute.

"I don't know what just happened," Matéo muttered, rubbing the top of his head, which had hit the car roof.

I craned to look through the missing back windshield and saw the Jeep mimicking our move from the other side, trying to follow us exactly how Aly had done. "They're still on us!" I cried.

But Aly's maneuver didn't translate to a Jeep's shape or height. They went up on two wheels but couldn't right themselves, and instead of leveling out and jumping over the ditch, they plowed sideways and headfirst into the other side.

"Oh yeah!" I said. "That will slow them down!"

Aly grinned at me in the rearview mirror, and Matéo slapped me a high five from the front seat.

"You are a goddess—" he started to tell Aly, but his words were drowned out by a startlingly loud boom! I'd been watching the Jeep to see if they could pull themselves out of the ditch, so I saw it suddenly explode, a fireball fifteen feet wide poufing up from the crumpled metal. In seconds the interior was aflame.

"Stop!" I said, smacking my hand on Aly's seat. But she'd already slowed the car, and now we all turned and watched the Jeep with our eyes wide.

"Oh, my gods," I murmured. "Do we . . . do we go back? Maybe they survived?"

"We don't go back," Matéo said solemnly. "They can't have survived that."

Moments before, I'd been lit up with hatred and rage against the couple in the Jeep; only last night I'd wanted to kill them myself. Now, knowing they were dead, had probably died in the crash if not the explosion, made the heightened unreality fade, and they became two humans that I'd just seen die. It was awful.

Finally Aly started our car again, and we drove at a cautious speed until we rounded the next bend. I wanted to cry with relief as we saw the second campground office, and suddenly the road was paved and smooth. Gratefully we left the noisy, bumpy shell road. Best of all, there were lights on at the campground and cars parked out front.

Aly pulled up close to the office and parked. We knew what we must look like: our car shot up, both windshields broken, all of us bruised and bloody. We had to tell them about the Jeep; they would have to send EMS and a fire truck out there.

"What in the world can we say?" Aly said.

I couldn't even begin to come up with anything.

CHAPTER TWENTY-FIVE

WE TOLD THE COPS JUST ABOUT EVERYTHING.
Everything except for the jaguar parts. We were looking for our
friends Suzanne and James when two crazy people kidnapped
Matéo and Aly. There was a house in the woods, though we couldn't
say exactly where. The people had chased us and shot at our car, and
it had wrecked behind us and burst into flame. We didn't mention
the jaguar we'd seen, running out into the night, blood darkening
its side. I hoped it had survived and was safe somewhere.

The cops dispatched the fire department to find the Jeep, and
they reported that the fire was out, the gas tank had exploded,
and that two bodies had been found inside the car. When he
heard that, Matéo frowned at the odd coincidence with his own
parents' deaths. Though a lot of details checked out—the police
found the house, the basement, everything—there were clearly
holes in our story, like the obvious signs of a wild animal attack.
Perhaps a bear, they speculated, judging from the front door and
various claw marks.

We didn't see any bear, sir.

We formally registered Suzanne and James as missing, and the police said they would search the area with dogs, starting at daylight. When the police were done with us, it was almost nine o'clock at night. Aly called Coco and let her know we were safe. She was so relieved, but upset we hadn't found Suzanne and James.

"Are you going to stay and help search?" I heard her ask Aly.

"I don't think so," Aly said slowly. "The only way we can help is as haguari, and that's out, since the place will be swarming with dogs and search teams. This has shown me that we need more than the three of us. The cops can mobilize a big effort. Maybe we should have gone to them in the first place."

"We had no idea if they'd just gotten lost," I pointed out. "Now it's definitely more clear that they're missing."

"Okay," said Coco. "I'm glad it's in the hands of the police now. I'm sure they'll find them soon."

"I hope so," said Aly. "I can't stand leaving without them, without any answers." She was silent for a few moments, as if weighing other options. Finally she shook her head. "We covered a lot of ground—I never caught the faintest scent. I don't think we can do much else. If the cops don't turn up anything in the next week, then maybe we need to call everyone we know and really do a massive search."

"Okay. I'm in. Now, how are you getting home?" Coco asked. "Do you need someone to come get you?"

It was easier to get a rental car.

It was a long drive back. Sometime after midnight we stopped for food. I was hollowed out with hunger and fell on my burger like a wolf. In midbite I remembered the deer, my first and only kill, and how satisfying and delicious it had seemed. Now the thought was incredibly gross, and though I tried, I couldn't develop even the slightest hint of wanting to eat raw deer.

After we ate, I drove the last three hours while Matéo slept in the backseat and Aly slept in the front passenger seat. As I was heading up the on-ramp of I-10 that would take us home, she stirred and sat up, her hair all clumped on one side.

"Hey," I said. "You holding together?"

She nodded, looking exhausted and pale. "Just barely." She reached out and put her hand on my shoulder. "You came for us."

"Of course. You're my family." I didn't mention how terrified I had been, how badly I'd wanted to run away and pretend I didn't know what was happening. It was amazing that I had overcome those fears and forced myself to step up.

"You changed back and forth quickly," she said. "So it seems easier now?"

I nodded, keeping my eyes on the road. "A bit. No, it's definitely easier. And I was super relieved that I could change back. But I still have to think about it and focus on it."

"It will get easier." She stared out her window at the night, no doubt remembering what yesterday's night had been like.

Matéo groaned and I saw him in the rearview mirror, sitting up and brushing his dark red hair out of his face. "Hey, is that

Veterans Avenue? We're almost home!" For a moment he looked happy; then his smile faded. "We didn't find Suzanne or James. But those cages had obviously held other cats before—other haguari." His face was grim.

"We found names scratched in the cement floor," Aly told me softly.

"Oh, gods. Did you know any of them?" I asked.

She shook her head. "But that couple—they must have been the people killing haguari, taking their hearts." She sounded close to tears.

"I heard the man say something like that," I told them, and repeated the couple's argument.

"They were probably the people who killed my parents," Matéo said. "And yours."

Gripping the steering wheel so tightly my knuckles turned white, I nodded. "That occurred to me. I wanted to just kill them. But are we a hundred percent certain? There was that weird death up in New York—was that them? We need to know more. I wish we could have trapped them somehow, made them talk."

"Me too. At the time I wanted to get as far away from them as possible," Aly said. "Now we'll never be able to talk to them."

I remembered the Jeep's interior, glowing with flame, and nodded soberly.

"There's got to be a bigger picture here," said Matéo.

"A bigger picture like what?" I asked, looking at him in the rearview mirror.

"That couple was collecting haguari for their hearts. That other jaguar wasn't a member of our family, you know?" said Matéo. "He was just some haguari. It looks like what we talked about—it's not just about my parents, not just about your parents; it's not about our family. It's about haguari. That couple is collecting our race. They are killing members of our race. And I think it's on a much bigger scale than we realized."

"Why? Why would they do that?"

"Maybe they hate us," Aly said. "Maybe they think we're monsters and freaks and want us all dead."

Her words were a slap in the face. Six months ago I had felt the same way. I had spent years of my life hating what I was, thinking I was a horrible aberration. I'd been furious with my parents for making me what I was. I'd wanted to punish them, to get as far away from them as possible.

I felt quite differently now. Not a 100 percent embracing of the lifestyle, but I'd come to feel acceptance where I had felt revulsion. I saw truth where before had been confusion and pain. When I was a jaguar and I caught sight of myself in a stream, I thought I was beautiful, and I thought I looked like me.

"What if that couple had other haguari caged somewhere else?" Aly asked, looking at Matéo. "With the people dead, no one will know to go rescue them."

"We can't help what we don't know," said Matéo. "We just have to do the best we can. But I don't think those people were killing haguari just because they hated us," said Matéo. "They were collecting hearts—like as trophies, or for some other crazy reason."

My brain was racing. "We've got to figure out if there was a bigger plan. We've got to stop it somehow. Worse—what if that couple was working for someone else?"

"They didn't seem all that organized," Matéo went on. "But what if they were like middlemen?"

They might not have even been the ones who killed my parents. There could be others who were doing the same thing as that couple.

I slammed my hands on the steering wheel. "Goddamn it!" Angry tears rolled down my cheeks. I snuffled and brushed my sleeve across my nose. "Goddamn it."

"We're almost home," said Matéo. "Here in New Orleans we can be real detectives. We're going to find out what the hell is going on, and how we can stop the whole thing."

"We can't stop till we know," said Aly.

The rain had drizzled itself out, and the clouds were rapidly clearing from the dark sky. I felt like we'd been gone a week. I was sad that we hadn't found Suzanne and James. They might be dead. I thought about everything Matéo and Aly had said, and realized that my life had acquired a purpose when I wasn't looking.

I wasn't moving back to Sugar Beach. I wasn't going to Seattle. I was going to stay here in New Orleans, and I was going to devote myself to figuring out who was killing my kind. And I was going to stop them.

"Hey, *prima*?"

"Yeah?"

"Thanks for risking your life to save ours." Matéo smiled at me and brushed his hand against my hair.

"You're welcome," I said, and felt better.

Turning onto Esplanade Avenue felt like coming home, coming back to safety and acceptance. All I wanted to do was cry in the shower for a while, put a Band-Aid on my cheek, and collapse in my bed for a long, long time.

"What's that?" Aly said, pointing. I'd been so focused on aiming Matéo's car between the brick pillars of the driveway that I hadn't even noticed the large, wet lump on our kitchen steps.

"Is it a person?" I asked, just as the headlights shone on dark hair. As I parked the car, the person sat up, rubbing her hands over her face.

"It's almost four in the morning," Matéo said. "And it's been raining. Who is that? What's she doing?"

When I looked closer, my mouth dropped open; then I jumped out of the car and ran to the steps. The girl looked at me without smiling, and in the dim light from the kitchen I took in how much weight she had lost, how unhappy she looked, and the fact that she had a huge duffel bag on the steps beside her.

"Babe," I said, holding out my arms to hug her.

"What happened to your face?" Jennifer asked, getting up stiffly, and then I was holding her, feeling her dampness and thinness. She rested her head on my shoulder. "Columbia sucked," she said, her voice muffled. "I've run away."